JAKE

JAKE

Tom McBride

gatekeeper press™
Columbus, Ohio

JAKE

Published by Gatekeeper Press
2167 Stringtown Rd, Suite 109
Columbus, OH 43123-2989
www.GatekeeperPress.com

Photography by Corinne Elaine

Library of Congress Control Number: 2021948350

ISBN (paperback): 9781662918575

Contents

The Get

I begin this account of the life changing adventures of a cast of characters who, as a group, with no common connections but for a few individuals, would not engage in any sort of mutual endeavors unless very unique circumstances brought them together. My name is Gus and I am, for the most part, a lifestyle writer for a Chicago based Newspaper. According to my editor I need a project so she has put me in touch with one of the principles in this story. I have been commissioned to write this narrative and bring forth the scenes, the characters and the realities as assembled from the memories of those involved.

This year the world experienced several notable events that illustrate the impact of this one year. The Rock and Roll Hall of Fame inducted its first members. The first meeting of what is known as the Internet Engineering Task Force, who knows what that will turn out to be. The disaster of the Chernobyl Reactor, in The Soviet Union, was discovered by satellite, having been denied until the discovery.The Prime Minister of Sweden, Olaf Palme, was assassinated and the Space Shuttle Challenger exploded just after lift off from The Kennedy Space Center in Florida, killing all aboard. The adventure that I am to tell you about, as in the past and so too in the future, will not be in the news although the implications reach across the boundaries of societies and the lives of individuals.

The story begins on a typical late fall day in Chicago, Illinoi, in the year 1986. The day's essence quietly enters the resting awareness of Rand's sleeping mind as he slowly awakens to a new morning. Without opening his eyes he reaches for Lana next to him to find she is not there. She is gone. It has been almost three weeks now. Rand reaches for her each morning and smells the perfume of her hair that still clings to her pillow.

They have been together since July of 1985. He is a hometown boy, still living in the same city where he had grown up. She an immigrant from a land she never revealed to him. She had fled from there for reasons not fully explained. Rand knows that she is older than him but he is still guessing at late forties, so maybe five years older. She never wanted to talk about her past except to say she would have to return there someday.

Now fully awakened with thoughts of her stirring his mind, he begins to stretch and raise his head to look outside for a glimpse of this Friday morning. This Friday, for him, has been greatly anticipated. This Friday will be the last workday before his much needed vacation, the first in many years.

The sky is very gray and close to the ground as most fall days when the rains settle in for days at a time. The first cool temperatures have arrived and the sun sets much earlier now. There are distant flashes of lightning and an almost continual rumble of thunder both far off and at times near.

Rand finally gets out of the bed and walks to the large window of his second floor bedroom. Looking down at the sidewalk he can see umbrellas passing each other as his neighbors hurry to join their busy day. He stretches again and turns to begin his own ritual of preparation for encountering the world outside.

By now his thoughts of Lana are, once again, submerged beneath his thinking mind and his rush to complete this day's tasks. After today he can finally escape his lifestyle that has been focused on getting ahead, making a living and securing his retirement. The box has entrapped his soul for far too long. Rand often contemplates the wonders of happiness and contentment. He questions peace as the absence of evil and success as somehow cloaked in hardship. Well, such questions still await the time needed to think them through. That time is still waiting for Rand to make it happen. At forty-three he thinks he is definitely getting a late start on such things. This day, when finished, will be the beginning.

The air outside seems fresher than the day before as Rand steps back from the curb to avoid the splashing cars while trying to hail a cab. Getting to the office and closing the loop of loose ends is all that matters today. There is a 6:10 p.m. flight with his name on it and he will be on it regardless of any distraction or event short of his own loss of life. Now inside a taxi, half soaked from the twenty minutes it took to get one to stop, Rand begins to seriously consider that one possibility after thirty seconds of the cabbie's driving. He is either drunk or insane. When Rand tries to talk to him the only response is muttering which Rand cannot understand. Somehow Rand arrives at his office building by way of a route he has never traveled. To Rand's mind it is a sort of exclamation mark to his decision to escape the torrents of critical second guessing by unqualified individuals that his life has been.

As Rand maneuvers through a series of phone calls and short meetings he can sense the rising energy level of his psyche preparing for the escape he will make. The anticipation is building within his emotions for the long overdue fulfillment of the promises he has made to himself over the years. As his final wrap up meeting begins Rand checks his watch. "3:30" he whispers to himself, "make it short" he says to the others. Everyone nods agreement. They all know Rand needs to leave.

As the meeting adjourns everyone exits the room quickly, except for Rachel. While everyone returns to their respective work areas she approaches Rand as he gathers his notes and packs his brief case. He hasn't noticed her approach until she reaches across the corner of the table and touches his arm. Rand, slightly surprised, looks up and into Rachel's gorgeous hazel eyes. They smile at each other and then embrace as loving friends. Rand and Rachel have known each other for five years. They have had lunch together, drinks after work occasionally and long conversations about many topics. They have always had an internal, unexplainable connection but never a romantic relationship. Each has wondered privately why but just as some dreams are never spoken, some aspects of relationships are never developed. As the two embrace Rachel wishes Rand success on his adventure and Rand reminds Rachel, as he regularly does, to "be safe and save a smile for me." Rachel leaves the room and Rand refocuses on his moment of liberation. He checks his watch again, "crap, it is 4:30 and I should be gone" he whispers through his teeth.

Rand hurries to his office and puts his notes and brief case in the safe. He knows that if he brings anything from work with him it will nag at him until he pays attention to it. So he closes the safe door and gives the dial a spin. His phone begins to ring. He checks the number to see that his brother George is on the line so he answers.

"Hey there bro," Rand greets him. "How are you?"

"Just wonderful!" answers George, "How about you?"

Before Rand can answer George continues, "I know you are on your way out of town so I will be brief. Have you had any contact with Lana since she left?"

Rand is put on guard by the question. His answer slowly, "Uh....NO! Why do you ask?"

"Well," George responds, "I received an odd message on the recorder at home two days ago. The voice sounded like Lana but the caller did not give her name. And then today I received a second one from her phone number but the sender did not include a name." George continued, "I responded but there has not been a reply."

Rand did not need or want all of this to happen right now. He asks his brother the obvious question, "What was the content of the message?"

George did not answer. Rand could hear background noises and his brother breathing deeply then the click of a disconnection.

"George!" Rand yells into the phone. He then dials back to George's phone but there is no answer. He checks the time again and it is now almost 5:00. Rand realizes he will miss his flight if he does not leave immediately for the airport. As Rand walks to the elevator he knows that he cannot leave without knowing what happened to his brother. He waits through the elevator ride to the lobby and then calls his brother again. There is no answer.

Rand considers his options and reluctantly hails a taxi, a little unsure of his destination.Before the taxi arrives, the public phone he had used rings, it is George.

"George" Rand answers, "Are you o.k.?"

"Yea, yea" George responds, "I was setting down my tool bag while talking to you and, being clumsy as I am, I took a tumble. I'm o.k., just a couple of bruises."

"So," asks Rand, "what are the messages you received? What do you mean when you say it was not Lana but it was her phone?"

"Well," begins George, "Lana's number came up on the recorder but the message was not in English but it did sound like her voice. I don't know what language it was, possibly Russian or Arabic or, I don't know…"

"And the other?" pressed Rand.

"The message was in English," answered George, "but all it said was, ""I must return, I will not be back."" George paused, "that's all."

Rand continued to ask questions. "Do you still have the messages? Will you save them for me and not mention this to anyone else?"

"If that's what you want." George responds.

"O.K." answers Rand, "I'm on the way to the airport and I will be back in eight weeks. If something else comes through on this matter be sure to save it. I will get in touch with you after getting off the plane."

"You got it" George replies.

Rand is a bit dazed by all that is happening as he is most unprepared to deal with any type of crisis at this time. Rand is determined to get on his 6:10 flight. As he arrives at the airport terminal he checks the time again to see that he has but thirty minutes to get through security and to his gate.

"Well, it's a good day for a jog through the airport." Rand jokes to himself.

Everything goes smoothly through security however he hears his flight and gate announced over the intercom because the flight is ready to depart. Rand is the last to board five minutes before the scheduled departure. The flight attendant at the entrance of the plane motions for him to be seated immediately. Rand tries to lighten her mood, "Hey, five minutes is five minutes, right?"

"Right," she answers without a smile.

Rand brushes the incident aside and takes his seat by the window which is the location that he has preferred since his first flight as a kid. As he relaxes into his seat he begins his personal pre-flight routine. This time alone with his thoughts as the plane is being pushed back from the terminal gate always reminds Rand of the ritual that was part of his minimalist religious upbringing as a Roman Catholic that is called confession. Most everyone on the plane is quiet as the flight attendant goes through the safety instructions with a calm voice. As she finishes the plane begins moving forward to taxi to the runway as the cabin lights are dimmed and the anticipation of takeoff begins to seep into everyone's consciousness. At this time Rand will often pray to thank God for the blessings that ordinarily don't come to mind and to ask forgiveness for mistakes that too often go unnoticed on a daily basis. Rand wonders how many others that were on board were doing the same thing.

As he finishes his silent prayer he briefly experiences the realization of a complete dependence on the flight crew, the aircraft, the maintenance crew, the fuel manufacturer and so many others behind the scene who play such important, yet mundane, roles in each and every flight that occurs every minute of every day, in every part of the world. It is truly awesome what people can do in such a systematic way over time so that such events become routine. Rand begins to ponder the grand scale of the Earth, human endeavors and the tendency to believe we can do such things by the strength of our will alone and by the discovery of our own knowledge. The question that arises for Rand is, do some believe in God as a way of discrediting our collective human potential? Do we have to believe in a higher form of being, intelligence or power in order to reach beyond ourselves and achieve even greater goals?

Rand thinks to himself, "More concepts to explore now during this time away."

The rains continue to fall as the plane is now poised at the end of the runway for takeoff. The jet engines begin to whine with an increasing pitch as the power builds just before takeoff begins. Rand looks out at the wing, the powerful engines and the rains making reflective ripples on the runway surface just below him. The lights of the complex are a sea of blues and greens, flashing amber and some reds. With the heavy cloud cover and nightfall the plane's lights shine through the mist to give the only light, from the plane, for the pilots while on the ground.

Suddenly the brakes are released and the jet streaks down the runway with the vibration of the wheels lessening then stopping as the aircraft leaves the ground and surges upward at an angle and soon banks to the right as Rand's ears begin to feel the rising pressure. Looking out his window the clouds that envelope the plane are illuminated by the plane's lights and the mist presses against the windows. Rain droplets are crossing the glass in increasingly horizontal streams. The plane accelerates and climbs upwards through the cloud cover.

From his window he begins to see the top fringes of the clouds with the dark sky beyond. Suddenly the plane escapes the mist to be above the solid cloud cover and into the clear night sky. The left side of his view is framed by the immense cloud they have just passed through. The rising column of cloud thousands of feet tall with a crescent shape from the wide base billowing up into the anvil shaped top. In the center of his view a bright moon illuminates the face of the clouds. The surrounding black sky is densely speckled with stars.

Rand is always struck by the immensity of the Earth, its atmosphere and the space in which all exists. Even the plane which appears so large on the ground becomes a tiny life support ship that is so vulnerable even though the craft is very sophisticated and highly developed. Rand's trip will require many hours in flight. This first leg is the shortest taking him to New York which is a two hour flight.

As Rand settles into the routine of the flight and the attendants prepare to take orders for drinks his thoughts are of his brother.

"Would you like something to drink, sir?" asks the flight attendant.

Rand was slow to respond from his thoughts, "Ah, yes, a water for now, please."

She acknowledges his request with a smile. Rand returns to his thoughts and looks out at the carpet of clouds now far below them. George and Rand grew up as brothers that loved each other although they did fight at times because of petty disagreements and at times because of jealousy or envy. Each would always come to the defense of the other. Rand, being the older, was bigger than George and would have to rescue him from bullies and other altercations that George's attitude and uncontrollable tongue would get him into. George, in turn, did occasionally have to rescue his older brother from his stubbornness that caused him to make some dumb choices and do things that would get him in trouble with the authorities at school and once with the police. That was all long ago and their lives have taken much different paths since they each have been on their own.

George was married at a young age to his then girlfriend, who was even younger, when she became pregnant. The next few years were tough for George but by the time his marriage was over he had two sons, a whole lot of debt and very little direction in his life. During the same time period Rand had moved far from home to set his own course and explore parts of the country he found exciting.

Spending time in Florida, California, Wyoming and Texas Rand realized that his home town was the place where he wanted to live. He has never married because he never met a woman that was more than a playmate or lover. All of his relationships have been short term. He thought that might have changed when he met Lana. She is smart and strong. She is the most physically beautiful woman he has known. Like him she has stayed physically active as a runner, cyclist and outdoor adventurer. She is pretty, fit and not easily talked into anything. Rand was accustomed to having his way with the women he was attracted to in the past but Lana was different. Rand had to prove himself deserving of her affections and her agreement to any decision had to be earned through reason. She was not an emotionally driven woman as his experiences had taught him to expect.

Rand was devastated when she left so suddenly and without warning. In the back of his mind he hopes that, somehow, he will find her during this time off. He knows it is a long shot but he knows that hope can accomplish more than a perceived certainty can guarantee. The only part of this journey that is planned is the first country of destination and the date of his departure. His trip beginning on October tenth is scheduled to end on November twenty fourth. The year 1986 is going to wrap up as the beginning point of his life's grand adventure. This first leg is from Chicago to New York and then to Paris. The one hitch in his plan at this time is the call he must make to his brother when he arrives in New York. He needs to follow up on any new information about the mysterious messages.

Rand begins to mentally review what he knows of Lana's background then realizes that he doesn't know very much. He knows her from the day they met at the street café that is half a block from his office where he would often have lunch. He has absorbed every detail that she shared. Whenever their conversations would begin to explore their pasts Lana changed the subject. Rand didn't think much of it at the time but now it seems an oddity of their relationship. He surmised that she may be from an ethnicity or a family history which she may not care to embrace. There were also times when she would be unavailable for no given reason. Lana would be elusive even after she had moved into his townhouse. Since Rand was accustomed to short term relationships he did not press such issues because his sense of privacy allowed her whatever space she needed. As Rand gets older he realizes this tendency of his is a flaw.

"Maybe the next time will be different." He tells himself as the flight attendant makes her second round to take drink orders. Rand asks for a Rum and coke. Perhaps he can relax after a drink and take a nap before landing in New York.

"Thanks miss" Rand says as she sets the small plastic glass on his tray.

Rand first sips the drink and then downs the entire contents. He returns to gazing out the window as he slowly begins to relax. Becoming drowsy he pushes back his seat and falls asleep.

The Loop Always Closes

Lana puts down the list she has been working on now for more than a week. The ink pen drops from her hand to the table as she runs her fingers through her hair and lowers her head to cry again. Her thoughts of leaving the life that she has robustly pursued since immigrating to the United States as a youth are punishing to think through. The realization of the expectations this change represents in her life has been restricted to Lana's sub-conscience until now.

Lana's father had rather abruptly insisted she leave for the U.S. because of her home country's political and social uncertainty. She did not understand the gravity of the threats at the time. Her father's position in government compelled him to stay and fight the forces at work to overthrow the power structures that had guided the country since before the great world wars. They had isolated and severely curtailed the progress her parent's generation had made. Since being an only child without extended family anywhere near for as long as she can remember Lana has long been accustomed to traveling alone.

The practice of making a list before packing is useful to her for organizing her thoughts and her belongings and focusing on necessities before niceties. Possessions become just one or the other in times of peril. It is emotional logic and balance that is upset when uncontrollable forces seriously damage one's hopes and dreams intentionally.

Lana has loved Rand since very early in their relationship. His wit and dry sense of humor has animated their interaction, their affection and their plans for the near future. This emotional/relational list is too difficult for her to make. Lana uses activity to cover the weakness and anxiety. She struggles to convince herself that to return to her father's country for the integrity of her father's name, even though he has since passed away is an extreme expectation. She must settle the conflict in her own mind and heart before finalizing her decision and telling Rand. Thoughts and feelings with waves and valleys of emotion simultaneously occur behind her practiced composure. Lana continues to struggle with her thoughts until a feeling of dizziness causes her to further lower her head and rest on the table before her with each hand now grasping her hair in clumps as though she can pull such discomfort from her mind along with the hair.

Lana checks the time, 2:00 p.m., and begins to put away her notebook. She has to put her thoughts back together so she can gently greet Rand when he returns from his latest excursion to California and Oregon on business. Her days are quickly passing and Lana must bring her preparations to a close. Her date of return to her homeland is scheduled so she must put things in order now. Rand, fortunately, will be the last item on the list.

As is her custom, Lana makes a quick trip to the florist in the lobby, for something simple to change the focus of a grueling day. Upon leaving the elevator at lobby level she is bumped by an elderly man moving quickly past her. His gate is unbalanced as he waddles from side to side and leans forward at the waist, his overcoat open and swaying with his motion. She thinks that for him to move so quickly must be difficult.

He pushes past her and touches her side. Lana recognizes immediately the man's feeble attempt to reach her pocket. The area of the city they live in is normally a low crime area so that such an encounter at this lobby is rare. Out of habit from experiences when she was younger and less comfortable with her surroundings Lana would not carry anything of value in a way that could be picked. She did not pause but continued to the flower shop. As she reached for her cash from her safe pocket she found a small pamphlet partially placed in the same pocket. Lana withdrew the pamphlet along with the money and previewed the title of the writing as, 'To Catch a Bird'. She quickly files it as 'later' and back into her pocket as she pays the clerk and prepares to leave. She turns from the counter and looks into the eyes of the elderly gruff who bumped into her earlier but she sees the face of a much younger man of maybe thirty.

He quickly steps back, "excuse me", he says. "I apologize for being so clumsy."

"You are fine," Lana smiles, "it is I who pushed into you."

"May I introduce myself?" the man asks as he extends his hand. Lana offers a fist bump instead and he responds in kind. As he turns over his hand and rolls his fingers into a fist his ring draws Lana's attention immediately. The quality of the craftsmanship and materials matches the stone which Rand will soon receive from Lana. The stone's casing is intricately illustrated with a blending of silver and gold. The difference to note for Lana is the letter U that is engraved into the face of the stone. As their hands met the young man quickly drops to one knee, looks into Lana's eyes and says, "I am here to serve you. I will be your guide home." Then, as quickly, he rises and introduces himself, "my name is Baetus."

Lana's reaction is to look around self-consciously for anyone who might have witnessed her encounter with Baetus. She quickly recovers, nods her head as acknowledgment and introduces herself as Ann. She feels more comfortable giving an alias at this point in the encounter. Lana was hoping for some help with the transition and the many loose ends her sudden departure is sure to create. For now she will be Ann. 'What an unusual name', Lana thought, 'Baetus'. She realizes that may not be a real name either.

Lana has a vague memory of her mother telling her, "The loop always closes." Lana momentarily ponders the near future and then mentally grasps the hand of fate to trust something greater as a substitute for predictability and security. Lana suddenly misses Rand and their life together. She reassures herself mentally and emotionally that she has at least a rough plan for their eventual reunion.

The remainder of the day will push Lana to the edge of frustration. She stands in line after line to close her bank accounts, get her passport and wait at the clinic for the necessary precautionary exam for travel to the countries she may be in. Lana's constant focus on the goal she now has of returning to the homeland and fulfilling her destiny is what keeps her from throwing up her hands and giving in to the temptation to let it all go. She prefers to remain the Lana that is living a low profile life as millions of others are doing in this beautiful country. However she knows the time to move on has come.

Back at the apartment, Lana reviews her birth certificate and focuses on her emerging role and her return to an unknown fate. Her birth name which she has not heard since early childhood is now unusual to her. Lana will soon be known as Fripree once back in her home country. As she pronounced the name aloud Lana has the sudden remembrance of her nick name as, Free. She could remember her father saying to her, "You are free to think, free to see, free to speak and free you are to be!"

The image of her family crest begins to form in her mind. The crest is a combination of old but common symbols which represent the principles of life's dynamic for humans. When discerned with a lens of perception that is gained through a relationship with the guardian of our life force. Lana recognizes the emblem as preserved in the design of a broach which held together a small bundle which contained the gem Lana received from her mother. Such thoughts were engrained in her memory. The full emblem will be in her father's notebook that Lana has yet to hold again. The bank safety deposit box should contain the notebook and other resources she will need to complete the centering exercise before her transition that is soon to come.

Lana realizes again that she will soon have to talk to Rand. The anxiety of the looming separation begins to crush her mood and challenge her determination to forge ahead and complete this part of her life's journey. Her first reaction to such considerations is to disappear and leave only a note for Rand to find. Lana quickly suppresses the thought and steels her mind and her emotions in order to face the reality of her commitment to fulfill her legacy.

Lana retrieves the small box of items she recovered from the bank safety deposit box and begins to inventory the contents. Some of the items are unimportant. The notebook and the small bundle, with the broach still in place, are bound together and wrapped in a man's handkerchief. Her father's initials are monogramed in one corner of the handkerchief. Lana cradles the cloth and its contents as though exposure to the elements would disintegrate the items' structure. She pauses for a moment, her eyes closed, breath slow and controlled. Once relaxed, Lana sits on the floor with a small table in front of her. She gently places the items before her and then she grins with the remembrance of her father. The notebook cover is illustrated with the overall appearance of the crest without the intricate details to conceal obvious messaging and direct the viewer toward the general appearance of the complete crest. The details are drawn in the notebook. Lana rushes to open the notebook and understand its contents. The crest is fully illustrated with notes on the next page.

At the center of a hexagram are three concentric circles. Each circle has a small opening as a passageway. The rings can rotate for the openings to form a variety of configurations that illustrate an individual experiencing, remembering or projecting any number of initiatives, recoveries, empowerment or application of memories that produce an understanding leading to wisdom.

There is no power or privilege endowed by the gem or a projection through the gem but for gaining an understanding of the principles. When embraced they may apply to any person, tribe, race or ethnic origin of human that chooses the way freely.

A transformation of the image occurs when the crest is viewed through an octagon cut gem placed directly above it with a light reflected from below it to generate the angles through the gem. The projection can be viewed on an opaque, light colored surface held above the gem or onto a ceiling possibly.

The Identifier is the one person who can fulfill the first step of the process that will release the Royal Guardian's presence into reality. This person may not understand the counterintuitive mechanism of their role until events begin to push circumstances into his or her life's path. It will be important to isolate the person's thoughts and words as a preparation of his or her emotions to align with the event. When revelation and circumstances compels the Identifier to act, the conscious awareness of that person will be flooded with a divine presence working through the person's understanding.

Also within the pages of the notebook is information for Lana's use that was entered before she was born. The categories include vocabulary and spelling, proper language and slang of her native tongue. Lana finds a listing of the days of the week. A good place to start, she thinks, as she attempts a recitation of the listing. Lana pauses then reads the description of a new and ominous phenomenon of what is called the days of darkness each year. She reads that the days are not known until the violence begins.

Lana begins to have second thoughts as she is reminded of the philosophical dimension. She mentally forms questions that she asks of her own studies, friends and teachers. The intricacies of the crest will draw a student in to begin a path of enlightenment for an understanding that is extended by each accomplishment along the way. The principle mystery is influenced by the nature of one's expectation upon entering the pathway of the crest. Lana questions in a whisper, "Are we attempting to conjure an image to worship? Does this emanate from our sub-conscience, from our imagination, from our prayers?"

With a plaintiff look outward as she raises her hands above her head Lana speaks as though someone is there to hear, "A Royal Guardian? Does your separation from us exist because of anger? Or pride? Or fear? Come to us," Lana almost demands. "We are searching for you." Lana releases a long breath, pauses and silently asks, "Can you not walk among the people?"

Such questions flood Lana's cognitive mind as she tries to adjust her paradigm of thinking. As preparation for travel Lana locates a section of the notebook written by her father. His observations, notes to self, remedies for socio-political scenarios, etc. With this last night to prepare, Lana tries to focus on absorbing the information. She knows she has to be able to function when she arrives and will need the language and customs to be somewhat familiar. Having left her home in 1940 the area and the social environment is much different. The emphasis on her goals and responsibilities will be more manageable after arriving and living the day to day life she will step into.

Turning to a tabbed page of the notebook Lana finds a writing of her fathers that may have been a speech he was to give during the tumultuous days leading to the convulsions of social and political changes that were sweeping the region. The changes which compelled her father to have her evacuated as were many others. Lana reads the words aloud, quietly, as she envisions her father standing before a large crowd with strength, conviction and courage to address the peoples' fear with hope, ""I look in on my children each night as they sleep. I smile as I remember each at a younger age and I laugh to myself. I am thankful for the peace and safety they have experienced and grown up accepting as normal. Outside of their spheres of awareness the world continues to churn with the constant clashes of ideologies, expectations, needs and desires both good and evil.

As they near the age of involvement and responsibility I become concerned they are not yet ready to undertake and endure this world that is not fair, is not so peaceful and secure and not so forgiving. I must do my part to prepare them and become confident of their ability. I must do my part to provide a society, a nation and a world that is respectful of the life and liberty of an individual. To provide an atmosphere that is conducive to a pursuit of freedom, of happiness, of opportunity and justice for all.

We have enemies because of envy and hatred both from outside of this country and from within. Some are quite animated and outspoken. Some are secretive and subversive. There are citizens of this country who side with our enemies knowingly while thinking the outcome of their flawed ideology will be different than history has demonstrated because they are different. Others have unknowingly supported our enemies because they have put their trust in the leadership of their affiliations without discretion.

Some are saying that we cannot recover. This outlook is foreign and must always remain so. Our hearts' desire is to advance, discover, utilize and share with civility and freedom. Useful and valid leadership will foster and reinforce the history of accomplishment this nation has written and defended with our blood and our fortune. Our leadership's posture to the world should champion our successes! Instead what we are seeing rise in the political arena is vile and evil. Many people are being fooled by rhetoric that is two faced.

We will overcome the obstacles of external challenges much more successfully when the internal discourse of our citizenry is discerning and enthusiastic in support of individual liberty, an engaged freedom and a proactive debate. This begins with a building block level of communication that repairs the breaches and reinforces the defenses of our nation from all threats. I call on you to embrace the freedom to acknowledge and emulate the realization of success.""

As her father's words ring in her thoughts she finds herself shaking from a combination of fear and inspiration. Inspired to take the leap she has been inching toward and a fear of facing Rand with her decision. This is her final night with him. Lana knows that she will hurt him.

Knowing the day is at hand she assembles her luggage and the necessities for a flight with the flexibility to transition as circumstances change. Lana has attempted, several times, to formulate how she will explain her situation and her decisions. The words always become blurred in her mind as she hears herself speak the thoughts that seem rational as thoughts. She is reminded that the sound of a word can change the perception of intention almost completely.

With 1:00 a.m. rolling around Lana finishes her preparations and retires for the last night in this city, in this townhouse, in this bed. Her last thoughts before sleep are that this time tomorrow she will be leaving the arms of her only love in this world. She is accepting an unbalanced exchange that is holding her dreams just out of reach. "We will see about that!" is Lana's response to the thought. Her optimism is reassuring her determination to have her life with Rand back at some point. "Obligations first," her mother's memory reminds. "Desires fall in line, the body after the mind", was mom's mantra at bed time with a smile.

The rains have started early and a wet weekend with falling temperatures is the television's lament. Lana awakens and covers her head with the pillow. She steals a brief moment to clear her mind before rising to a cold room from the overnight change of weather. Rand's flight is due in at 9:30 a.m. with a day of rest the usual for him. Lana had planned to pick him up but the weather makes that idea impractical. A cabbie will get him home much quicker. She will use the time to complete the arrangements for the evening and the special gift she has prepared for him.

Lana rushes through the house without a covering, her toned, athletic body a complement to any surroundings. A pause in front of the bay window with the brightening, gray sky causes her reflection to appear as a spirit gracefully passing across the morning dawn. Rand has often told her that her beauty, as part of creation, reflects the kindness of the Creator. Lana's discretion prompts her to cover her form for all but Rand. Her thoughts of leaving him begin to overwhelm her and the smile fades. As expected, Rand calls, "I am on the ground." He announces, "How are you my sweet Lana?"

"Hey you," Lana responds. "I am so good and I long to see you," she adds. "Look for your name, a cabbie is there for you."

"Thanks so much! The weather is a bit surprising," Rand continues. "Are you in the office today?"

"I am off today and I will see you here very soon."

"I will call you when I am down stairs." He reminds her.

"Just come straight up. I have a few errands and I may miss your arrival." Lana is not good at subversion. She must transfer her things to Baetus for transport and customs processing.

"Soon then," Rand closes.

"Soon," Lana hangs up.

As arranged, Baetus is waiting for Lana in the lobby. She is able to carry everything to the elevator. As she reaches for the 'door close' button a man enters the elevator and pushes the button for the top floor. Lana cannot directly see the man's face but she thinks that he looks familiar. Dark glasses cover his eyes and gloves cover his hands. The suit and overcoat he is wearing are of high quality but his shoes are worn and appear outdated for the rest of his attire. As the elevator doors close the travel was up as the man has chosen. Lana does not need the added distraction and loss of time. Becoming slightly frustrated she stomps her foot and strikes the 'ground' floor button with a hard slap of her hand. The man did not react. He didn't move as she tried to stare him down but she couldn't see his eyes through the dark glasses.

"Sorry for your delay, are you in a hurry?" the man smiles as he speaks.

"No matter of yours!" is Lana's response. "I have better things to do than ride the elevator." She realizes her temper is flaring and takes a deep breath to relax.

"I will need only a few minutes of your time when we reach my floor and then…" the old man was interrupted.

"And then?" Lana questions. "I'll have nothing to do with you except to see you off this elevator at 'your floor'" Lana stiffens.

"And then you will be free to continue your journey," the man continues.

"Do I know you?" Lana asks. "I will do nothing but let you out and then never see you again!"

The man disengages from the encounter by stepping back to the rear wall and remaining silent. As the elevator rises Lana feels as though its' size has begun to compress and the light level dim. Lana realizes that her tension level is inducing tunnel vision that alters her perception. Her uncertainty grows as the elevator nears the top floors. Though the ascent is only a few minutes Lana is anxious to leave the confines of the elevator even if it is the top floor. Lana begins to consider the possible connection of her destination and destiny with this current situation. This could be abduction, an assassination, an enemy's harassment or possibly another guide/assistant? The elevator was now slowing to a stop at the 49th floor. The man said it was 'his floor'. In response her instincts evaluate the confinement, her vulnerability and method of escape if needed. Concluding the likely need for tactical maneuvers Lana discretely re-positions herself.

The man did not speak during the ascent. As the elevator doors open he motions, with his outstretched hand, toward the door for Lana to exit before him. Lana returns the gesture and he lowers his hand as he begins to exit the elevator.

"We must have this time together," he says. Removing the glasses he looks directly into Lana's eyes to capture her gaze and speaks with a strong, male voice of a much younger man even though he appears to be about her age. "I am here for two reasons." The man continues, "I do apologize for drawing you into what may very well be an intimidating situation for you."

Lana recognizes that she has experienced this phenomenon once before. "Are you Baetus?" Her imagination and curiosity engaged.

"No, we are very similar in many ways but I am not he." He pauses, looking squarely at her as he continues, "I am Yarjies."

Lana asks, "Your purpose here?"

Yarjies, "I am to accompany you and Baetus. He will leave us at the appropriate time as we journey into Europe."

"As simple as that sounds, I have some things to get done before I go anywhere. You are currently interfering with my time and you need to be going." Lana scolded him as inconsiderate. Her raw feelings and anxiety over leaving Rand is beginning to come through.

"I can accompany you now and we can talk during the commute?" Yarjies pleads his case with a softer voice.

"No, that will be too distracting. I will meet up with you and Baetus at 3:00 a.m. There is a 24 hour café on this block, Nick's I believe is the name. I will leave it up to you two to find it." Lana presses the elevator button and the waiting elevator doors open.

Yarjies reminds Lana, "Come prepared to begin your journey at that time. May I call you Fri...?"

"You may call me Ann," Lana interrupts. She will not be ready for anyone to use her proper name, Fripree, before arriving at her homeland. For now she is Lana or Ann. "I am also running behind." She concludes their conversation, "Three O'clock!" The elevator doors close and Lana selects the ground floor.

The doors open at the lobby and Lana spots Baetus in the foyer. While holding the elevator door open she calls his name. Baetus walks swiftly to her. "I just met Yarjies," Lana hisses.

"I assumed." Baetus shrugs and smiles. Now with Lana's bags under both arms Baetus leaves as quickly. Lana pulls her long, reddish blonde hair back from her face and ties it which fully highlights her daring, alluring look even when wearing shabby, lay around, baggy shorts and a tee shirt.

Baetus is healthy, strong and athletic. He is about 5' 6" tall with blondish brown, curly hair, deep black eyes with, as Lana's mom would probably say, an Irish nose and lips with teeth a little offset. A smile is always close by and his gaze is direct, looking past the words of a conversation for the person inside of the thoughts. He is always confident and energetic even though young and inexperienced. Lana is both amused and encouraged by the energy of his pace and approach to each minute. As Baetus is walking away Lana recognizes that his shoes are the same as Yarjies', brown wing tips, but newer and better cared for.

With but an hour now before Rand will be home Lana re-enters the elevator and selects her floor. She leans against the rear corner wall to rest as the elevator climbs upward. The door is beginning to close on her time with Rand and her experiences of normalcy that she has lived during this part of her life. As is her method of breaking a tense feeling she asks herself, "Will I now be given a pair of brown shoes?" A smile lightens her countenance as the elevator door opens.

As Lana walks the hallway to their home time begins to slow. She absorbs everything now as though her memories will be her only link to this time once she has left. Lana first takes in the 'little picture' as Rand would refer to the small details such as the floor tiles' pattern, the wall texture, the lighting and the sounds. Then, at the doorway, she turns to look back at the area and expands her vision and awareness. She takes in the 'big picture' as the elements combine and she emotionally joins the life of the area as a continuous element in space and time. Lana closes her eyes, breathes deeply and slowly to relax in the moment.

As the door key drops from her hand and hits the floor Lana is jolted back to the present. She opens the door quickly and enters. Now the time begins to move quickly as Lana pulls a vase from the counter, fills it with water from the kitchen faucet and lays the fresh flowers on the counter. Once arranged she places the beautiful array on the small table by the window in the breakfast area. The colors are enhanced by the backdrop of a gray sky and the spattering rain drops against the window to create a rhythm. She begins to tap her foot against the floor and her fingernails upon the counter. She transforms it into a jazzy tune that energizes her to complete preparations for the night.

Lana has already decided to avoid too much attention to details about the food. She has picked up prepared meals from their favorite shop that specializes in healthy, organic meals that avoid additives. The dishes are warmed and ready quickly so Lana can spend more time on the details of her announcement to Rand and the gift she has prepared for him. A special gift that he would not understand at first but she knew he would figure out her message before long.

As Lana finishes her preparations and places the food in a warmer to keep until time to serve she hears the front door opening. Rand is home, she assumes. Walking from the breakfast area to the living room Lana is startled to see Baetus and Yarjies at the opened doorway. Lana freezes in place and Baetus speaks, "Sorry to startle you, Miss Ann, but an emergency has forced us to intervene in the time table of our departure."

"How did you get in here?" Lana shouts, "I will call the police if you don't have a damn good answer!"

"You provided the key without knowing it." Baetus responds.

"You mean that you stole it?" Lana reaches for the phone to call the police.

"You must not." Warns Yarjies as he intercepts her reach and grasps her hand gently. "You must listen and follow our instructions." He continues.

"You are to be subordinate to me!" she insists, "I am close to losing all patience with you two."

With the door still open Lana hears footsteps along the tiled hallway. "Rand is almost here and he will deal with you."

As she speaks both Baetus and Yarjies signal for Lana to be silent and they both vanish without a trace. Lana gasps and then swallows deeply as they have literally disappeared. Though Lana has never witnessed such an event she has heard of it happening as a myth or illusion. She quickly composes herself and looks down the hallway to see Rand coming toward her. He appears tired, his shoulders slightly lowered, his briefcase pulling at his hand as though it has great weight. Perhaps it has been a bad or arduous day for him.

Lana smiles and greets him with a strong hug and a kiss. He is cold from the rainy conditions. They squeeze through the doorway together and Lana experiences a pang of love and compassion. She realizes the feeling as a result of knowing this night will be their last. Knowing that her ability to project the future is not reliable she is determined to see her plans through. Rand pulls away and goes to the fireplace to light the gas logs and warm the room. Rand then takes a few steps back to the large chair that he frequents along with Lana at times. Dropping into the chair with eyes closed Rand relaxes and begins to hear Lana's bare feet crossing the wood floor and the exotic song of her breath.

Opening his eyes Rand first sees the bright flames of the fire. As he expands his gaze the slightly shadowed, elegant, perfectly beautiful woman he enjoys and loves to be with in any circumstance is moving slightly. She sways to her own melody, as she can at any moment to instantly bring all of Rand's attention to her. He smiles as she hands him a glass of their favorite wine. The backdrop of the fire light creates an aura around Lana. Her hair has an enchanting glow and as she moves closer he opens his arms for her to be absorbed by him and the chair. Lana gently enters Rand's embrace and rests on his lap, curling her legs up to be completely within his control. Rand hugs her tightly and breathes deeply to take in her fragrance.

"I have missed you, Lana, and I have so longed for this time with you." Rand says softly.

"Don't you always miss me?" Lana asks.

"I do," Rand responds. "I always look forward to seeing you but this trip has been very consuming so, maybe I was not thinking of you as much until I arrived here."

"I have missed you too," Lana interrupts. "Something is different right now and I have been eager to see you also." As Lana begins to enter the uncomfortable explanation which must be given, she did not intend to blurt it out as she was close to doing. Rand put his hands on either side of her face and pulls her to his warm, eager lips for a passionate kiss. As their lips meet a knock on the door surprises them and they separate. Lana gets up first and goes to the door. As she opens the door the smell of burnt wood and pine brushes her face and she pulls back. Rand meets her at the doorway and opens the door fully to find no-one there.

"Do you smell that?" Lana asks Rand.

"I only smell your hair." Rand responds, standing behind her as he buries his face into her hair and kisses her neck.

"No seriously!" Lana pushes back. "It smells like a camp fire."

"A camp fire? Are you thinking that the Boy Scouts were at our door? Maybe it was Beelzebub!" Rand tries to relax the moment.

"Yea, that's it, Beelzebub." Lana has lost the moment. She realizes it must have been Baetus. "Or maybe his sidekick," Lana jokes back. "You know the one who does his dirty work." Lana tries to throw it back to Rand as a way of ending the sudden tension as she tries to understand why Baetus would do this. To return to normalcy Lana closes the door and turns to embrace Rand. He is very close behind her with a glass of wine in each hand. "What do you really think?" Rand asks.

"Your right, the Boy Scouts." Lana quips and smiles as the door closes. They embrace and kiss until Rand begins to spill the wine as they engage each other. The heat of the fireplace overpowers the room as Rand and Lana's bodies radiate their own passionate energy. Rand pulls away from Lana to turn off the fire and Lana begins removing her clothing. Rand turns back from the fireplace to the voluptuous, firm, engaged sexuality that engulfs him as Lana invites him to join her in the big chair. As he removes his clothing Lana positions herself to receive him fully. She moans slightly at the sight of Rand's nakedness as he approaches her with the energy, desire and heartiness that he always brings to their loving explorations of body and soul. Lana's level of fulfillment and pleasure will soon challenge her rationale for what is about to take precedence in her life and affect Rand's life as never before. Lana, though not accustomed to the practice, prays for the strength and courage she needs to complete each necessary step.

Rand's movement under her returns her awareness to the present. Knowing he will sleep easily now, Lana rises from the warmth of their bodies together. Rand moves to the bed and falls asleep. Lana must now begin the process of separation. Pulling her prepared back pack Lana leaves it by the front door. From her side bag Lana retrieves the jewel she will leave on her pillow for Rand to find. The change of timing for her departure prevents her from saying goodbye the way she had planned.

Returning to the front door Lana senses the door beginning to open as she reaches the handle. Slightly startled she pulls the door open by reflex and finds Baetus and Yarjies ready for the adventure of it all. Without looking back Lana leaves and gently closes the door behind her. The next seconds and minutes become a blur of walking quickly, entering the taxi and arriving at the airport. Once in motion the taxi accelerates quickly to merge with the city traffic and Lana loses her composure as she begins to cry.

Baetus, flustered by the show of emotions, tries to speak but cannot. Being pushed aside by Yarjies, Baetus distractedly looks out the side window. As Lana begins to calm slightly Yarjies slides over beside her and puts his hand on her shoulder. "You will be back here if you remain strong and courageous." The firmness of his touch and the kindness of his voice calm Lana to a peaceful state of reflection and control of her spirit.

"I hope you are right. I choose to believe you are right!" Lana begins to be energized. "I still have a knot in my stomach though."

Baetus responds now that the emotions are being controlled. "You very well are of the right character for this undertaking Miss Lana."

Yarjies becomes engaged quickly, "You know, Miss Lana, each part of this journey will have its own struggles. I would like to suggest we focus and accomplish each aspect individually and in order."

Lana kindly responds, "I am not ready for any multi-tiered, analytical report on our situation." She smiles at Yarjies as she attempts to burn a hole through him with her focused stare. "I do want to discuss strategy," Lana says calmly.

Baetus interjects, "'Keep it simple, stupi...., er silly is a good idea Miss Ann, how about we check our tickets and itinerary for any discrepancies."

Lana picks up on Baetus' deflection, "I believe we have the bag here with our documentation. Let's get ready to transition."

"Good word," Yarjies rejoins, "I am ready."

Their taxi becomes absorbed in the flow of motion and Lana's individual sense of existence quickly fades as she prepares to confront the challenges. The early morning sunrise finds the three boarding a flight to Frankfurt, Germany via London. Lana begins to learn that the diversion to London is necessary for a replenishment of funds for travel and to accommodate the first day of study and preparation with a trainer. Baetus will also leave their company during the London visit. Lana finds that she can speak easily with Yarjies but she gets more real information from Baetus.

"Baetus," Lana asks, "on what basis is such a trainer certified? How is the trainer selected and prepared for service? How have the 'facts' been edited?" Lana questions the off handed mention of the scheduling without her notification.

Baetus responds, "The facts are easily found once the question has been asked."

"At this point we are all following orders, including you, Miss Ann." Yarjies projects his authority with a calm command. "This entire grand event is to be the end to all wars for this people. This requires us, on a micro level, to remove the barriers and unite as human beings."

Baetus draws back and bows to one knee. Not in homage to Yarjies but in prayer and consideration of Yarjies statements. Baetus realizes Yarjies is becoming ascendant in his role now and soon he will be re-assigned later in this stage or at the conclusion of this attempt should it fail. Baetus rises and accepts a descendant role now in Yarjies' presence. The trainer will fill his slot. Baetus knows her from his Cadet class. Norsha is her given name. Baetus never learned if there was a first or last name. Norsha is not filling the position of a physical conditioning trainer because more emphasis is to be on language, culture, civic history, family history and fundamental positions.

Even so, Norsha's average frame conceals her exceptional strength. With solid muscle and body structure she slays her dragons with her eyes. Her mind, when expressed, directs the unfathomable into channels of control that invites a willing submission. She has arrived ahead of the others to prepare for introductions. By beginning her work from the first interaction Norsha takes command of a group quickly as a defensive move to disarm any major disagreement with maximum effect. Lana has a lot to learn during three days of structured, intense and extensive mental and emotional conditioning. Some aspects are accomplished metaphysically, some require simple memorization and some time, at a later date, will be devoted to physical endurance, weapons' training and emergency survival tactics.

Lana, feeling the closing of a phase, steps toward Baetus and places her hand on his shoulder as a show of solidarity and appreciation. Baetus returns the gesture, placing his hand on

Lana's shoulder. "Baetus, before you go I want to discuss strategy going forward with you and Yarjies. I value your perspective." Lana speaks softly to Baetus.

Baetus smiles and looks into Lana's eyes. "You have a kindness that cannot be taught. I am so thankful for the opportunity to contribute to your success."

Yarjies draws closer and answers Lana's question before asked, "We have some time right now, not later. Once your trainer is introduced we will lose contact with you for some time. You will be reoriented when we reunite. Let us convene our strategy session now."

Lana has second thoughts. "Upon arrival in London we will have a rest period, correct?"

Yarjies nods agreement. Lana continues, "We will grab a room at the airport hotel and use our time for strategy and review to this point of our journey."

Yarjies and Baetus silently agree with a nod.

Lana has a nervous smile as she concludes, "I suggest we try to sleep for the remainder of our flight. I am tired, shall I go first?"

"Yes mam, why certainly Miss Ann," Yarjies and Baetus reply half-heartedly.

At their destination for this leg of the flight, past the tumult of the airport and security, the three meet at the lobby of the hotel, as planned, to check a room. Yarjies requests two adjoining rooms. They each look at the other as though their conspiracy is underway although the reality is a good use of their time which the trainer should appreciate. Once in the rooms each refreshes themselves briefly and then exchange knocks before opening the common door. Though Lana was ready for a strong drink and some light food both Baetus and Yarjies rush into Lana's sitting area and attempt to begin with a forthright approach to the discussion Lana was asking for.

"Though I would prefer something stronger I will have a glass of wine. Will you each join me?" Lana invites, "We could use a refreshment and nutrition don't you think?"

Baetus stares at Lana as though she is becoming something foreign. "I think Miss Ann is a little nervous now," he whispers to Yarjies. "Are we being too serious?" Baetus, being young and inexperienced, is insecure with any deviations from the instructions.

"She is but wouldn't you be?" Yarjies defends Lana. "A release is what she is looking for. A lot of pressure is building as her time draws closer." Yarjies advises Baetus, "She is a controlling person and I know a brief pause like this will help. We will begin in a very short time, Baetus."

As Lana has her second sip of the warm, red wine she snaps to a sudden awareness of the time. The brief quiet time now broken, Lana places the glass on the table next to the sofa and invites her two companions to join her. Each takes a seat nearby.

Yarjies begins, "We should begin if you hope to gain from our experiences and our knowledge."

"As always, Yarjies, you are quick and to the point!" Lana responds.

Baetus, visibly agitated, begins to speak excitedly, "Our people are experiencing changes that are driven by outside influences. Our struggles, within our communities and our regional society have always been contained and resolution determined locally. I, being of a younger generation than Yarjies and yourself, am in agreement with the effort to eradicate the creatures, these Rochukas. They have terrorized us for the years of my lifetime. I have been taught and believe that their existence is not of a natural origin. They are from a human seed that has been completely possessed and infused with demonic paradigms as a result of their treachery. They can only be stopped by annihilation!"

Baetus catches himself and is momentarily embarrassed. "Excuse me for being so forward with my thoughts."

Cross Road of Worlds

Rand's flight from New York to Paris is scheduled for an 8:30 a.m. departure. After arriving and settling into his room for the night he checks the time, "10:30, not too late to call George." Rand says out loud. "Let's call room service first." He again says to himself aloud. Rand's call to George is not answered until the third attempt. George answers with a lot of background noise making it difficult to hear what he is saying. Rand did understand that George is at work because he is on call and in the manager's office, close to a machine that is running. He could hear George say, "hold on," followed by a disconnection. As Rand sat on the edge of the bed the phone rang, it was George.

"Can you hear me?" George asks.

"You are clear now," Rand replies.

"Sorry about that, I am outside the kitchen now. Are you in New York?" George asks.

"Yea, I'm here until morning", answers Rand. "Any more news or contact from our mystery person?"

"No," responds George, "but I think the police should be told about this. What if we let this go and Lana can be helped or even rescued by letting the police know!" George exclaims.

Rand tries to calm him, "I don't think we should over react. There must be a reasonable explanation. Perhaps someone called the wrong number and there is no connection what so ever."

George responds, "But shouldn't we let the police make that determination? I have enough on my hands without getting caught up in one of your affairs."

"Hey Bro," Rand shouts, "You are getting carried away now! I think we should put this whole thing behind us. I really don't think this is anything more than either a prank call or someone got the wrong number. Besides, has Lana ever contacted you before like this?"

"Well no," admits George, "and I don't know how she could. I have never given her my contact information as far as I can recall."

"Okay. Then let's drop it," concludes Rand. "I am leaving the country in the morning and I will have limited contact with everyone until I return in November. You call me if there is an emergency. Otherwise I will call you when I am back home, okay?"

"Ok Rand," George agrees. "I love you and I hope you find what you are looking for on this trip."

Rand knows that he should seriously consider his brother's suggestion to notify someone. George is very good at anticipating actions and consequences by exercising his level two thinking which he uses to counter ideology or peer pressure that can control one's thinking.

He will take the next step before choosing a course of action or aligning with a decision. Rand recalls George's explanation as a consideration of possible outcomes and alternate consequences that can occur by thinking through a scenario to all possible conclusions. This type of thinking allows a person to be truly open minded by considering all points and then making judgments that lead to the best choice and not simply accepting all views in order to be accepted.

The reality for Rand is that his brother is probably right but the thought of changing his plans and rescheduling his flight makes him cringe. Rand does not allow himself to have many weak moments. His stubbornness serves him well when his emotions begin to blur his focus. Rand slowly picks up the phone and calls his brother's home number. There is no answer so he leaves a message: George, you are right. Please wait until tomorrow, after my flight has left, to notify the police. If I am not contacted by anyone by the time I leave Paris…, Rand stops the message. He realizes that the recording creates a history that he may not want his brother associated with. He will call again to speak to George. After all, he hasn't done anything wrong. "Besides," he says to himself, "she is the one who left without any explanation and who hasn't been heard from since!" Rand can't believe his mind is being squeezed like this. A check of the time, now midnight, is too late to call George tonight. Rand will call him in the morning from the airport. That way he will not have to manipulate his brother.

Rand arrives at the airport two hours before his flight. He wants to have enough time to talk to George and work out any disagreements so that George will be comfortable with the situation. Rand gets to his gate with an hour before boarding. He first calls his home number to check for any messages and finds a message from Lana's number. Rand listens to the message with a nervousness that is unusual for him to experience. Excited by the opportunity to speak to Lana he is quickly disappointed by the man's voice that begins to address him.

"This is for Randal Wayne." the man begins.

The caller continues, "I am calling on behalf of your friend that you know as Lana." The man's voice was measured, almost monotone as though he was a police officer or a professional mediator of some sort. "She asked that I call to tell you she is well. She has returned to her homeland for the good of our people. She regrets she cannot speak to you directly at this time.

She will contact you at this number as soon as she is free to do so." The man concludes and disconnects the call.

Rand is stunned and slow to react as he tries to absorb what has just happened. After several minutes of gazing out the large airport window Rand blinks and returns from his imagination to hear the first call for the boarding of his flight. He quickly calls George, "Hey, George, I actually heard from Lana and she is okay." Rand lies to protect his brother. "Great," responds George, "I was worried about both of you. Well, no harm done then. Are you still in New York?"

"I am about to board the plane now. I'll talk to you when I get back." Rand continues, "So, if nothing changes I'll be back in about eight weeks."

"Okay bro have a good time. I want to hear all about it when you get back and any news about Lana." George concludes, "Bye now."

"Later bro!" Rand hangs up and places a call to Rachel before getting in line to board his flight to Paris.

"Hello, Rand" Rachel answers. "I hoped you would call. How are you?"

"Hi, Rachel, I just want to talk to you before my plane leaves. I have only a few minutes." Rand relaxes at the sound of her voice. Rachel always balances Rand's emotions whenever he comes to her for encouragement. With the calming sound of her voice, even when she has disagreed with him, Rachel's body language and her way of cutting through to the heart of a matter with grace and kindness has always been reassuring to him. Rand continues, "One day and I miss your smile, your wit, you. Anyway, keep a lid on things while I'm gone, as I know you will."

"Everything will be just fine. Eight weeks is a long time for you to be away." Rachel reassures him, "be safe and come back to all of us on time, okay?"

"Will do" Rand replies, "Take care and 'save a smile for me'", they said together and laugh as each disconnects from the call.

Although Paris is a wonderful tourist destination Rand considers Paris to be a starting point only. After spending two days there his plan is to spend time in the rural parts of Europe. This trip is all about a change of pace, a change of perspective and an opportunity to realign his core self to discover contentment. To become centered for the remainder of his life so that more will be remembered about him than the surface elements of his life. Rand has known for years that the core of his being has been neglected because of his lifestyle choices and the shallowness of most people's expectations of him. Rand wants more of himself. He wants to live life as a meaningful quest producing lasting results that are judged to be good in light of the eternal truths, whatever they are.

Growing up he did not find such meaning from religion or social values. Rand realizes he may not have taken the time or exerted the energy to realize those eternal truths but now is the time if it is not too late. Rand's memories drift to the evening, weeks earlier, when he and Lana dined alone at home and he humbly offered a toast to their relationship.

The surprise, confusion and hurt that Rand is coping with now strain his memory of Lana. He briefly relives the morning when, upon waking, he found the gift box she left for him on her pillow. The ruby is a very valuable and highly sought after stone that he understands to be a part of her family's crest. Rand has kept the stone close ever since and has it with him now. The letter A is engraved on the face of the large, rectangular stone. As Rand picks up the phone to call room service he thinks of the stone and of Lana.

"May I help you?" is the greeting from room service.

"I would like some bread, cheese and a bottle of Merlot, please." Rand requests in English.

"Any particular name?" is the response in English.

"Nothing particular just a good house wine," Rand answers and hangs up.

As some of the pieces of information and memories of events begin to connect for him Rand has a spark of interest in solving the mystery that is becoming unavoidable. "Would this now be the reason for his trip?" he wondered aloud to himself. "Or is this all becoming a distraction to keep me from my personal goals?"

Rand speaks to the empty room, "Damn!"

Room service is at his door now knocking lightly. Rand greets the young lady as she enters with a tray of bread and cheeses and a bottle of wine which she places on the table by the bed. As she turns to face Rand she asks, with perfect English, "Will that be all, Sir?"

"Yes, thank you." Rand replies as he gives her a generous tip.

"Anything else?" she asks a second time.

With his senses alerted by her second question Rand responds, "Let us share what you have brought to me," Rand injecting a double meaning that the young lady has already suggested. Rand is a little surprised by her forwardness. She introduces herself as Kim.

"Kim is not a very French name." Rand responds.

"I am Canadian," Kim answers. "I have lived and worked in Europe for about four years now."

Rand pours two glasses of wine. As he offers one to Kim he asks, "Tell me more."

"Well, mine is not an unusual story." she begins, "I wasn't ready to go to university so I decided to travel and to pay my expenses by working as I am now. I grew up speaking French and English. I try to pick hotels or resorts that cater to English speaking guests so the work has not been difficult to find."

"So, what has been the best part of your travels?' Rand questions.

"I think that meeting good people like you has been a big part of it," she responds with a look straight into his eyes that captures him.

"How do you know that I am good?" Rand continues.

"Well, I hope to find out very soon," Kim replies as she takes a step closer to Rand and touches her glass to his. Rand smiles at her and leans forward to kiss her. Kim pulls back as a tease, then reaches out, clasps the back of Rand's neck and pulls him close. They kiss fully and then part slowly to each look into the other's eyes. With Rand completely absorbed by her full lips and entrancing eyes, she begins to unbutton his shirt. . Kim knows this is the beginning of a full night of pleasure which each will receive and give to the other. She lay on top of Rand and matches his form, placing her arms, legs and torso over his. The two lay motionless for several minutes. Rand begins to move under her so Kim rolls off to one side of him on the bed.

Rand raises his head to look into Kim's beautiful, young face as she smiles and looks back at him. Rand, being past forty, has the appearance and physique of a much younger man. He reaches out and curls his arm around her waist and pulls her to him. They embrace and kiss deeply as Rand begins to return Kim's gift of pleasure with all of the skill his experiences have taught him.

The early morning sun finds them intertwined as they have been for the entire night. A cool breeze enters from an open window and sweeps across the room. Kim becomes chilled and her movement wakes Rand. He covers her and himself with the sheet and they rest until mid-morning. The day's heat fills the room and the brightness of the day through the glass causes both to awaken. Rand and Kim embrace momentarily before getting up to dress. Rand offers the shower to Kim. "Thanks, but I will go to my place. I have to be at work by 1:00 today." Kim answers.

"I will be leaving early tomorrow morning and not returning. Will I see you tonight?" Rand asks.

"Probably not," was Kim's only response as she left the room. Rand pauses for a moment to recall the night before and then continues as though it was any other day. The night before was now history and the new day has just begun. Rand reminds himself that this is the shallowness of expectations that he wants to change within himself. He is hungry for relationships that require more of him and offer more to him. After showering Rand wipes the condensation from the mirror and, seeing himself, reflects on the night before. The lust that passes for love in today's world contrasted with the power of love that brings a man and a woman together through the union of their bodies being more than a physical act. This too Rand wants to change in his own life. He thought he was on the right track with Lana. He has pretty much concluded that was probably history now too.

As planned, Rand brought enough clothing and other necessities for a three to four day stretch because that was what he could fit into a back pack to be carried when walking or cycling. Over the months before this excursion Rand assembled a tentative route that could be changed as necessary to allow for closeness to the country, its people, its history and its legends. Now, with a level of mystery about her, Lana has entangled his mind and emotions with her love of his ideas and his desire for a lasting, true commitment. Her sudden departure has, until now, occupied most of Rand's thoughts.

A change of focus is now becoming the force behind his planning. His thoughts have returned to his desire to be absorbed by the intimacy of life with others who will value him for his soul more than his smile. The first leg of his adventure begins at the cycle shop nearest to the hotel. With travel by bicycle so much more common in Europe than in America Rand's walk is very short. After discussing his general plans to ride possibly as much as 30 kilometers a day with the shop attendant and the possibility of putting the bike on a train when the transition is called for he bought the recommended bike. Next the shop owner suggested the proper accessories for carrying water, spare parts, tools and a unique topographical city map that would keep him from becoming completely disoriented, if he could understand it. Once the bike was fitted and he was dressed with seasonal clothing Rand stepped out of the shop. As he swung his right leg over the bike to begin his trek he pauses to take in the sounds and the whirl of activity taking place around him.

Rand has the momentary sense of standing still in time as the active, pulsing city breathes and vibrates at its own high speed pace. The moment of his adventure's beginning springs to life as he pushes down on the right foot pedal, rolls away from the bike shop and into the expanse. The path beginning on a small section of cobble stoned street led him to his first decision, 'which way do I turn at the corner?' He recalls from the map to go right and ride along the Notre Dame complex and across the bridge ahead to the Isle Saint Louis. Rand soon finds a bike lane along the Seine River near the lower bank that leads him southeastward. He finds the traffic to be a distraction and the map a bit confusing. He would have to make do until he could reach the outer city area where he plans to slow his pace and begin to take rest breaks.

With Rand's general direction being south from the city the big picture quickly refocuses on his immediate attempt to navigate a rather narrow bike path that descends along the river bank near the water line that is several feet below street level. The grade is gradual but the distance allows Rand to coast at a speed that pushes him briskly through the morning air. As it brushes his hair and across his face memories of his childhood excursions of cross country biking with friends brought a smile. Rand enjoys the feeling as he reaches the base of the decline and the bike's rear wheel slips slightly on the path as it levels out. Thirty minutes into his journey and the excitement is enlightening his day. Now about one hundred yards along the river he finds the first bench and a water faucet. A brief stop to make the first contact with his new beginning brought out the water bottle and the map.

Together the air, the river, the land, the sun combine as a symphony within the city's life. It is the symphony that Rand now hears with an inner ear that is becoming more aligned to his heart and the intrigue of discovery that he seeks. Drawing his awareness back to the bench where he sits and his surroundings Rand, again, swings his right leg over the bike and rides into the day watchful for the next moment of discovery.

Following signs and landmarks in a city to which this is ones first visit to avoid being lost altogether can become quite tedious. With a series of maneuvers and reviews of the map Rand navigates along the Seine and out of Paris to the Bastille. By mid-day Rand has passed through Montgeron and is preparing to enter the Forest of Senart. Though he was getting hungry a quick drink of water was enough to refresh him for now. While pausing for the water break Rand overhears a mention of the "Faisanderie" on the other side, about a thirty minute ride through the forest.

Before the two kilometer sprint Rand realizes that a key to his head long immersion into an unknown, foreign culture and its values will be to keep his head above the bike by keeping the bike under him and on both wheels. He anticipates the slopes of the trails across the forest correctly as being punctuated with tree roots crossing at various angles which would challenge every rider to pay attention. 'Too much work', becomes Rand's thought as he arrives at the much anticipated rest. He considers a shift in approach to his travels by transitioning to the train and a more distant destination.

The past few occasions when Rand has traveled within France he has relied on English speaking contacts because the language was difficult for him. While in high school he was required to learn French and this requirement struck Rand's natural tendency toward rebellion in just the right way, or wrong way for his teacher and parents. A negative bias developed which he realizes is now affecting him at a very basic level. The thought returned, 'this is too much work'.

Having lived in Germany as an adolescent and having learned the language both as a student and as an adolescent while playing soccer and cavorting with German friends, the language would be much easier to navigate. A rush of memories, so long ago hidden in a quiet corner of his experiences, captures his thinking for a brief, nostalgic replay. A daydream of no importance springs to life as he reaches the area to rest.

Rand begins to feel old as the stories of his past play through his mind. His sense of time rushing into his consciousness induces a flutter then a blink of his eyes as he looks up from the leaf strewn, uncut grass in the yard where he lay, gazing into the cloudless sky. Across from the outdoor cooking pit, near the edge of the forest at Faisanderie, Rand begins to see his journey's purpose unfold. At the nearest train depot Rand intends to store the bicycle, travel by train and set his destination for Heidelberg, Germany.

He regularly thinks of the years growing up as the middle child of a career soldier and a loving mother who kept the household together and functioning through the regular relocations. There have always been gaps in Rand's memory that left him with a sense of disconnection from his place and purpose beyond the everyday routines. Without realizing the moment Rand steps from his normally well-organized mode of functioning into the unrestricted day before him. The next steps are away from his planned itinerary and into his future. At a nearby shop for tourists Rand asks the clerk for the location of a nearby bike shop. Since Rand was traveling a popular cyclists' route he found a repair and sales vendor a couple of blocks away. The small shop, on the corner of a busy thoroughfare and a small side street momentarily takes on a surreal hue and focuses Rand's subconscious vision to enable him to see the spot upon which the shop stands as a crossroad of worlds and dimensions that is a metaphysical indicator that is momentarily visible to him alone.

Rand's thoughts snap back to his cognitive mind and the vision is gone. He is now entering a realm of exploration for which he has no explanation or indication of scope and duration. A true adventure that may lead him beyond the veil we all recognize as life. With excitement and wonder returning to Rand's conscious awareness a new energy for the day now empowers him as when he was much younger, energetic and driven.

As Rand approaches the cycle shop from across the street a young man drives up, stops quickly and gets out with an adolescent boy and rushes to the shop door. They appear anxious or angry as the pair quickly enters the shop. When Rand reaches the store front he can hear an argument from inside between the two and the clerk.

"You assured me the order would be in no later than today!" the young man was demanding as he nervously pointed at the clerk.

"I know, I know," replies the clerk. The boy was looking out the shops large front window, studying Rand as he approaches. The child runs from the window and tugs at the arm of the young man who is now shaking his head in disappointment. The young man looks at the boy and then turns to the window to see Rand parking his bike in front of the shop. As Rand smiles the boy, holding the man's hand, begins to jump up and down as though they have found a lost treasure. Both smiling, they open the door for Rand to enter the shop. A small sign on the door lets Rand know that the clerk speaks English.

"Good morning, Sir", was the clerk's greeting.

"How did you know that I would speak English?" was Rand's reply.

"I play this game with myself," the clerk jokes. "I speak English first to every second customer to set a relaxed tone and a conversation starter. Maybe a little weird but, that's me."

Rand congratulates the clerk, "Very good! "I need some help and I hope we can strike a deal that will benefit each of us." Rand continues.

The young man interrupts, "Excuse me, sir. I would like to ask you about your ride there."

"And you speak English also?" Rand asks with bewilderment.

The clerk responds, "This location is a common stop along a very popular cyclists' route, especially for tourists and semi-devoted riders. It seems English is most common these days."

"I thought I was getting away when I traveled to Paris and now here." Rand thought out loud.

Anxious, the young man introduces himself as "'Ryan Osborne' who has some time between appointments for a couple of days which has created this break to ride and explore while in Europe for possibly the only time this year." Looking for a particular style of bicycle to ride and having booked ahead, Ryan is very disappointed that the shop did not receive his bike as ordered. As I was informed, my bike is identical to the one ordered. With the peppering from the young boy adding pressure to the situation Rand asks the father, "How may I help?"

"Your bicycle, sir, is identical to my order with this shop and I am asking seriously that you please consider selling to me or trading with the clerk here for a suitable replacement so that this bike of yours will be available." This the young man proposes while cutting his glance to the clerk who is nodding his head in agreement.

"Amazing how things happen, sometimes!" Rand almost shouts. "I am stopping in to explore such an opportunity. My travel plans must change and I wish to transfer to travel by train from this area. I will thankfully sell to you, sir."

Ryan and the clerk quickly agree and shake hands. The clerk returns to his counter to print an invoice and write a check to reimburse Rand. Ryan and the boy approach Rand to thank him as well. Rand spends the next thirty minutes learning the details of their plans which Ryan and family are scheduled to begin this day. Rand and the young man are thankful that everyone has a ride for the cycling routes they have chosen in South France. Rand congratulates the father for the good timing, thanks the clerk and leaves the shop to catch the commuter that passes along the main street.

The train arrives at the tiny pedestrian platform and the doors of each car slide open quickly with hurried pedestrians striding from the cars. Rand as quickly switches gears, as it were, grabs his small bag and enters the next phase of his journey by entering the boarding car and locating his seat which he finds occupied by a child. Seated next to him was a young woman that, hopefully Rand thought, was the child's sister. As a response from his new, non-self-serving kindness Rand remains standing for the first portion of his trip to his unknown destination. He reminds himself that one of his goals is to experience the people and places for their own essence and worth. "Time to blend" Rand chuckles to himself.

At the first stop the young woman and child exited. Rand but a brief look into her eyes and he sees hunger. Not a physical or emotional hunger or even psychological hunger but a much deeper, possibly a spiritual hunger. Haunting, Rand thinks, possibly mourning of a kind. Thoughts of her piercing look compel him to leave the train to find them. Having never put his bag down, he has everything in hand and is quickly on the platform. A hurried survey of the area identifies no one familiar. Crossing the platform to the cabbie station Rand describes the boy and woman in hopes of someone recognizing the two. Rand receives the oddest looks from all gathered as the dispatcher spoke up, "Her kind don't use our services. They cannot enter a segregated area, facility or retail establishment unless state certified with a printed permit. Her people don't come here unless times are really bad in their territories. Usually famine or serious injury brings them out to seek materials or seed for food. These creatures that some consider people will not take food normally if they can get seed to grow it themselves."

His imagination and curiosity now thrown into the mix Rand interrupts to ask, "What do you mean by 'consider', some 'consider' people?" Are they not human beings? I am not following your meaning. "

Rand begins to learn that there is a people group that exhibit some characteristics or traits of humans. The social structure they live with and the legalized retribution that can be administered by anyone with a grudge is a form of chaos that is bizarre. She lives within a managed, perpetual cycle of kill or be killed taking place behind the scenes of everyday life that exhibits normalcy.

Rand follows up, "So, this tribe or group or society you are describing has always existed in this geographic area?" Rand now becoming a bit agitated, "EXPLAIN, PLEASE!" The growing number of layers to the intrigue and confusion are beginning to numb Rand's sense of reason. This peoples' prolonged isolationism has insulated their culture, as it exists, but it has also diminished their capacity to learn and understand. Routine of thought, action and social expectation has dulled their thinking to a mentality of slavery to an ideology.

Local legend is that this group was originally made up of survivors from the wars' internment camps. The isolationism has been by choice as a conditioned response to their captivity. They have survived by becoming feral humanoids. There were approximately twenty to thirty adults and a small number of children. The current population of their area near the Black Forest of southern Germany has grown and split into two factions. The younger generation seeks normalized life while the older generation's leadership is comprised of former enemy collaborators who continue the pursuit of rituals that produced the days of darkness. No outreach or intervention has been attempted by the government or society in general.

Since the wars' end more than forty years earlier a self-imposed indoctrination of decline has been promoted through their schools and has shackled this current adult generation with a susceptibility to deception. Rand shakes his head slightly as he remembers, almost as a parable, the truism that, 'a government that is capable of providing everything that you need is a government that is also capable of taking everything you have'.In this case a peoples' hope, motivation, desire to succeed and the will to pursue a higher level of existence are lost. This now is likely the last stage of the elder group's existence unless there is a fundamental change in their hearts, their minds and their souls. The young are hungry for life but the Rochukas continue to obstruct the separation that is inevitable.

Rand stops in his tracks literally and draws back, mentally frozen for a moment in thought. Then, as quickly, as the train begins to pull away from the terminal he turns again, catches the first opened door's hand rail and swings onto the car's step as the train's speed increases. He is still uncertain of his choice as he sits on the top step and stares down at the gravel bed and tufts of grass passing under him as a blur. Rand is becoming entranced by the sight and the sounds of the wind, the motion of the car and the steel wheels on the steel track. The sense of a lumbering, powerful beast that is useful as long as it is controlled. His daydream is interrupted when the ticket checker places a hand on his shoulder to warn him with a shout over the sounds that he must move into the safety of the train car and his seat, "ticket please," is the request.

As a result of his conversation with the cabbie stand dispatcher Rand realizes that he is just beginning to learn the common knowledge of the locals about a bizarre paradigm of self-imposed isolation knowingly allowed while the larger population of the region is vibrant. Rand changes his mind again and decides to get off the train at the next stop. He will make arrangements for a return to this area to explore the region and possibly find these lost people as well as the young woman he encountered on the train. She appeared normal and healthy for the brief time he was near her. His impression of her searching and longing eyes has ignited a desire to discover what is hidden. After checking his ticket and the schedule Rand finds that the next possible stop is more than an hour away. After a visit to the club car for juice and water he returns to his seat to relax and gather his thoughts.

The front page of a newspaper he picked up while in the club car featured a photo of an explosion. The first paragraph describes an act of revenge that is the type of common activity in the region of the forest since the internal conflict has been elevated within the hidden society. Evidence of a growing rebellion by those who intend to challenge the control of the leadership they have been raised under. The ones that have left and returned are educating the young about the freedom and liberty enjoyed by the peoples of the areas of light. The realization only fuels the growing restlessness of those struggling to exist under the repressive leadership and chaotic social norms of personal justice or revenge as a means of equality. A natural desire for self-determination is also fueling the movement of the younger class to push against the restrictions and find ways to join the surrounding population through assimilation.

The more Rand focuses on the local public sentiment of the competing groups and their struggle for dominance the more his interest shifts away from his personal goal of finding the young woman and child. His adventure is beginning to take on meaning outside of his self. Having a point of focus outside of his self is loosening the stress he has carried for years

Island of Light

After but a few minutes of thinking and reading Rand begins to fall asleep. With the second head bob he pushes his seat back and closes his eyes. His mind drifts into a dream.

Rachel, with Rand's hand in hers, takes one half of a step back from the bed he is laying on as though dead and begins to place his hand on the bed as a final act. He suddenly finds himself looking up into her eyes from his body on the bed. As Rachel releases his hand and withdraws her touch he attempts to react in some way that will get her attention but he cannot. At this critical instant of the dream he returns to consciousness and returns to his awareness in his seat on the train. Rand senses that his body reacted with a jerky movement. As he blinks and rubs his face with both hands he peeks to see if anyone near him noticed his movements. No one was staring at him so Rand assumes he has gone unnoticed. He pushes back in the seat as his self-analysis kicks in. He easily recognizes the correlation between his dream and the dynamic changes in his life during the short time on this mission. Perhaps his subconscious is beginning to grapple with a loss of the familiar and the reorientation of his personal focus away from the base elements of the animal needs that have defined Rand's lifestyle until now.

Looking out the window at the darkening sky he realizes it is later than he thought. A check of his watch shows that he must have been asleep for over two hours. Consequently he slept through the stop at which he had planned to disembark and the stop at the border. Now as a complete stranger in what is becoming a strange experience in an unfamiliar country Rand begins to circle the wagons mentally. He locates his map and looks for the next distance marker along the railway. His rough calculation is that he is now in Germany, traveling North East. In the distance, to the West, Rand can see a river. "That must be the Rhine River" he says to himself. The next stop will be the town of Offenberg. Rand locates his ticket and his passport because there will be some explaining for him to do when he tries to leave the train in a different country and location that is not on his ticket.

It is odd that the ticket check would not be a reason to have been awakened at the border crossing terminal. Rand was accustomed to travel and negotiating changes, misunderstandings and travel arrangements. A flash of some American cash and a calm approach to return to his planned destination should be achievable in time for the first return scheduled. Once at the terminal Rand easily exits his car with his bags in hand. A walking patrolman, as is customary in such public locations, walks directly up to Rand and speaks slightly broken English. "Officer Gierden, may I assist you?"

Rand was a little surprised and asks, "How did you know to speak English to me?"

"I have been at this for a long time. I know an American when I see one." The officer shot back with a smile.

"What does an 'American' look like?" Rand asked with a smile.

"That conversation will have to be for another time." replied the officer as hisdemeanor shifted to one of official business with no small talk, "Passport please."

"Yes Sir," Rand politely answers, "my passport." Handing the document to the officer he quickly considers the possibility that he will need to accompany the officer to a police station and resolve the issues.

Officer Gierden conducts himself as a seasoned, to the point, veteran street officer, asking, "What is your destination?"

"I do not have a specific destination, as such." Rand offers.

"Explain," the officer continues.

"I am a tourist on vacation. I actually intended to disembark before entering your country but I was sleeping and I was not alerted by the attendants of the stop either before or at the border."

With his hand out he calmly asks, "Your ticket, please."

"Yes Sir, my ticket." Rand senses a tension beginning to emanate from the officer.

Officer Gierden was now standing immediately in front of Rand and the closeness was a little intimidating. He could smell the officer's after shave and the scent of tobacco smoke on his jacket and even his breath.

"Excuse me sir I will be glad to answer your questions." Rand replies as he takes a slow, half step back from the officer.

"Yes you will," snaps the officer. "We must go to my office."

Rand isn't sure what the next move will be. The officer suddenly became agitated and for no reason that Rand could detect.

"I have a car about a half block away from here. You will not have to wear these cuffs as long as you follow my directions." Officer Gierden flashes the cuffs that are attached to his belt.

"I have no intention of disobeying or disrespecting you in any way." Rand responds as he steps to the side of officer Gierden and the two begin to walk away from the train. The platform is about three feet above ground level to match the train car entries with a short step up or down. As the two cross the platform the street and sidewalks become visible. The stairway down from the platform was very wide so that both Rand and the officer could descend side by side. Officer Gierden pointed at the dark Volvo parked to the left of them and instructs Rand, "This is my car over here, take a seat in the back please."

"Yes Sir." Rand responds as he enters the sedan and closes the door. Officer Gierden activates the door locks and walks back to the platform leaving Rand to wait without any explanation.

"Oh boy," Rand says aloud, exhaling heavily and leaning back in the seat. "Now what have I gotten myself into?" he thought. After about twenty minutes Officer Gierden re-emerges from the platform ticket office and walks briskly to the car. Opening the door and getting in the car quickly the officer is clearly agitated.

"I cannot finish with you right now. There is an incident at the border crossing that I must respond to immediately. You will remain in my custody until we return here."

"If there is not a problem with my papers," Rand begins.

"I do not have any time but to simply release you right here on the street with no clearance for you to leave the country. You can head back West to France but you will be stopped at the border and detained."

Rand begins thinking of alternatives as he would in a business situation. "Where are you going?" Rand asks.

"The border area, we have persistent local demonstrations and conflicts with a criminal element that crosses the border illegally," Officer Gierden becomes strict in his statements.

"Have you flagged my passport so that I will be detained? Just out of curiosity, of course."

"What are you asking?"

"I am trying to help you with scenarios to work through as a way of seeing an opportunity to release me to cross the border to France, or Switzerland or wherever you are traveling to?"

"You are going to be a complication for me because I cannot confine you during my activities but, for now you are under my control, uh, in my custody." Officer Gierden stares at Rand with the rear view mirror as he drives at an increasing rate of acceleration. The two gaze at each other and Rand nods in agreement.

Officer Gierden continues to speed along the finely maintained roadway with better control of the vehicle. After about thirty minutes the officer looks again to Rand from the mirror and begins to speak over the rattles of the old patrol car. "I am going to release you before we get close to my destination. I cannot have you slowing me down and I cannot take you into this region safely."

"Am I to be let out of the car on the side of the road?" Rand asks.

"That is what I am saying, yes!" Officer Gierden responds with an intense expression and his face begins to flush with anger. "I am sure, as an American, you are resourceful and can find your way."

Rand shouts back, "I have no idea where I am!"

Officer Gierden, "I will be taking you to the Willstatt area. The bus can get you to Restatt where you can make connections via the train."

"Have you ever flagged a ride before?"

"Well, when I was younger and adventurous I would hitch hike, as we would call it, around the area where I lived," Rand recalled

"This is not America. Most who would offer you a ride here will be kind to you."

"What about the troublemakers you are going to deal with? Are they not in this area?"

"I will drop you in a safe place. There is a bus stop along the way. You can probably pay the driver to let you on until the first station or to Rastatt, as I have already told you, where you can make travel arrangements as you like."

"Wonderful!" Rand sarcastically answers.

"You need to show some respect or I will drop you right here!" commands the officer.

The two men fall silent. The only sound was the road noise of the passing trees, the wind whistling in from a partially opened front, passenger side window and the tires' echoing the coarseness of the pavement. In an attempt to engage in a conversation and possibly improve his situation, Rand asks, "Just out of curiosity, what ethnic groups or diversities are violating your borders?"

Officer Gierden, still in a combative mood, shouts back, "Does it matter? It is a long and complicated story! I have neither the time nor the desire to reprise it for you."

As the crest of a hill slides under the fast moving car the new vista has a backdrop of light and the shadows of pedestrians that form kaleidoscopic silhouettes on the hill sides. Suddenly there is a momentary brilliance, the concussion of an explosion and the sound of structures disintegrating. Rand can only stare into the enveloping dark of the night that followed. With his vision focusing on the point of detonation the deep red and orange colors form curtains for his eyes. After looking away and massaging his closed eyes Rand thinks for a moment and realizes his mission is now seriously diverted and he has momentarily lost control of the situation. His fate has never been challenged, in his mind, ever. To be dropped into the middle of nowhere, in a foreign country? Rand recites to his self the all too familiar litany of problems he has allowed to develop then breaks the silence, "Officer Gierden, how close are we to the conflict?"

"Five or six kilometers possibly," He responds, slightly shocked by the explosion. Then more business like he adds, "You will be dropped soon for a bus connection as we discussed earlier."

Rand, "How likely am I to cross paths with these groups, these invaders?"

Officer Gierden, "If you follow the quickest route out of here, from bus to train and travel southeast, you will be fine. You will soon be sitting at a cafe with a large stein of beer!"

Rand, "So, this is a localized issue with these skirmishes?"

Officer Gierden, "Skirmishes? The level of engagement has escalated with that explosion we witnessed. That occurred in the area where at least two security forces' armories are located. The insurgents are becoming bolder in their attempts."

Rand, "I saw that for sure! So, south or southeast which will put me back in Switzerland."

Officer Gierden, "Be assured if you do not follow this route and stay on the train you will suffer the consequences on your own. This area is not for adventurers right now."

As the next crest is breached a lit bus stop station quickly approaches. Officer Gierden roughly applies the brakes and only the poor braking system prevents a sliding, screeching stop at the station. A single, overhead light, a small bus sign and an area to stand is Rand's little island of light, for now.

Officer Gierden, "Okay sir go South or Southeast."

Rand reaches over to the seat beside him and picks up his back pack and small bag as the dust washes over the car from the sliding stop. Looking the officer in the eyes, Rand gives a sincere nod and tries to speak honestly with the man.

"Thank you for your help, your understanding and this effort to get me out of here."

Officer Gierden, "You are welcome, go home."

Rand exits the car and as he begins to close the door the officer floors the accelerator and speeds away, the car almost brushing against Rand. Now he is alone with the single light bulb to mark civilization and highlight his form. He is the specimen to be examined by the cold fingers of the night air as it slowly envelops him. Rand pulls a light jacket from his back pack and shakes it open with a pop of the fabric. The pop echoes, so Rand first thinks, but it is then followed by several more pops in rapid succession. Rand quickly realizes the sounds are distant gun shots such as a semi-automatic weapon.

"Well, so much for the DISTANT skirmishes." Rand speaks into the night. "I hope a bus comes along soon!" he continues. As though his thought was heard and answered, a set of headlights become visible from the distant hill top. "Thank you!" His last words to the darkness, he hopes. The sleek but well-traveled bus makes a soft stop with the blustery puffs of brake pressure relief and the squealing of large brakes. Doors at the middle of the bus align with the staging area and open abruptly to a brightly lit entry. Either side of the small receiving area is a much different environment of low light and an almost humming, muffled sound of people talking.

The assumption, by the driver, is that Rand has a ticket. Rand is not going to raise any questions before arriving at a safe location on the border, likely Rastatt. He turns to his right so as to be seated close to the driver and to have an open road view of the trip. Rand realizes that, at home, with a trip on the agenda he would travel armed and be more secure in his activities. Here a permit to carry a concealed weapon is not permitted. Officer Gierden referred to this factor as a contributor to the increase of conflict and crime. His point being the conflict has developed as subversives become illegally armed by criminals. They become aggressive against the society as a whole while the criminals, who will always be armed regardless of the law, know that 'the one with the gun' has advantage over unarmed subjects.

"What are you thinking?" asks the young man seated to his left with heavily accented English.

"Why are you asking?" Rand responds while attempting to see the young man's face. Rand squints slightly to see a twenty something with deep brown, almost black eyes looking back from the dim light of his seating compartment area.

"Your gaze is downward, your brow is rather furrowed and your hands are tense." The young man explains. "I am asking if I can be of help."

Rand responds with a soft smile, "I am considering elements of my travel and perhaps some changes in itinerary not anticipated. Nothing earth shattering."

The young man again questions him, "Ever been to this area before?"

"No, no." Rand relaxes slightly. "I am on holiday and I am not tied to a schedule so I am flexible in my travels."

"Be careful where you go," whispers the young man. "Oh, forgive me I would like to introduce myself. Claus von Beus is my common name among men. Will you be taking the train from Rastatt?"

Rand queries, "What do you mean, 'among men'? Who else is here? Do you have another name?"

"I hope you don't learn," cautions Claus. "Days of darkness will come again."

Rand becomes concerned as the once distant popping of a weapon's fire is suddenly a loud crack just outside of the cruising bus. Claus explains, "We are nearing a terminal checkpoint and these amateurs will withdraw to avoid the police and light militia there."

"Amateurs?" questions Rand, "Amateurs with weapons?"

"Yes, amateurs of war that are planning and playing to be ready if called." Claus responds, his posture erect in his seat, slightly jostling the passenger in front of him as he attempts to salute.

"Are you a part of this turmoil?" asks Rand.

"I am a part of the solution." Claus shoots back. "I was born here and I will defend my country, my land and my people. These beasts will not increase!" The young man, now impassioned, is almost shouting over the noises of the bus and the people begin reacting to his statements.

Rand, now standing as well, quiets Claus and convinces him to be silent for a few minutes. The young man continues with a calmer voice, "We have been challenged in the past. It is our response, then as now, that shapes our future. We must reclaim the principles, ideals, hope, determination and rule of law for this nation to champion. We must reclaim this nation at the ballot box and in the public discourse of our citizens. We must rely on the truth of our unity to overcome threats to our nation both external and internal."

Rand interrupts, "You sound like an American."

Claus smiles slightly, "Some of us have learned from our defeat in the great wars." Claus continues, "Liberty requires vigilance to protect the freedom we each have to pursue happiness in this life. We must stand on the truth. If not we will crush the foundation of our hope. Looking in the mirror you will see an individual that is a part of a family, a group, a state and a nation. The one you see in the mirror is the difference maker. As a rule the character of a nation has been a reflection of the character of the people."

"Sorry to have to interrupt this conversation, Claus, but I must tend to my immediate travel arrangements. I have been told to go toward the Swiss border. Is the disruption and fighting occurring there?" Rand asks with increasing uncertainty.

"We are confined to the great forest which is south east of here." Claus responds. "You should go east to Stuttgart, then South to Switzerland."

The bus arrives as a train is pulling away from the terminal. The bus doors pop open and the night air, with a mixture of burnt coal and steam, hot brakes and cigarette smoke quickly blend with the cool, recirculated air of the bus. Rand steps from the bus with Claus at his side. "I must see the steward about my boarding pass." Rand informs the young Claus and pushes past him roughly as a show of his uncertainty about him. Rand thinks to himself, 'Is this Claus a rebel, an idealistic anarchist or a dedicated citizen?' Rand mentally continues, 'he is not armed and is fairly well dressed. He carries a bundle of fliers to possibly be distributed or transferred to someone else'. As Rand completes his transaction at the terminal checkpoint Claus taps him on the shoulder.

"So long and good luck to you," offers the young man. "Sorry for any misunderstanding, be safe and remember to avoid stopping in the forest."

Pulling a map from his bag, Rand selects a route to Zurich, Switzerland that does not enter the Black Forest but travels from Rastatt to Karlsruhe where he can decide to stay in Germany or continue on to Switzerland. Boarding the train Rand finds a comfortable window seat. After pushing his bags under the seat in front of his Rand sits and reclines the seat to rest and, hopefully, have an uneventful trip to his next destination. As the train begins to move Rand's thoughts begin to examine the recent events and the state of the shadow group of creatures, or people, as they once were. How could this situation have come about and been sustained without any intervention?

In his reading Rand has learned about the group's separation from the outside world for years by an authoritarian government that finally collapsed from corruption and degeneracy. Those left in the dust of the aftermath were hungry for freedom and opportunity. Much of the population was uneducated and poor. The new ruling class realized that a massive undertaking of educating a middle aged and older population would not be as advantageous as beginning with the young and pouring resources into the future.

This left many to survive outside of the socio-political institutions which gave rise to a barbaric class and a struggling minority that were at the mercy of both groups fight to control the area. Mob violence and vigilantes would challenge each other in every region of this fertile and potentially prosperous land. The violence so gruesome and vindictive yet the surrounding countries would not intervene nor even venture into the region beyond the fringes.

A barrier of fear and superstition keeps this swirling vortex of an abstract existence pulsating with a life force that causes strangers to withdraw and envelopes the one called to enter in. Such a one's fate valued for a hidden quality known only to the benevolent king who's throne is inaccessible to all but those selected through an empowerment both unearned and undeserved.

Recalling some of his research findings as part of a university level Comparative Religions course Rand reflects on a principle found in Judaism and Christianity. The term used was redemption. From the most ancient writings of Hebrew scripture the concept of redemption applied not only to freeing people but also to freeing animals and property from captivity. The Christian application refers to a personal and, possibly, a universal freedom from the bondage of self-centeredness through the selfless act of a perfect substitute. Rand senses his body relaxing as the slight movement and vibration of the train's cruising speed levels and he closes his eyes. The question of 'why' remains with his mind.

"Excuse me, sir." Rand is awakened, "Excuse me, sir," an attendant asks, "May I see your ticket?"

"Certainly," Rand responds politely. "What is our current location?"

"We have less than one hour to Karlsruhe." The attendant replies. "Have your passport?" she requests.

"Here you go," Rand becomes slightly nervous, remembering his encounter with Officer Gierden. "So, it will be daylight when we arrive?"

"Just will be, arriving at 5:30 and sunrise at 5:50."The attendant answers. "Here is your ticket and passport, enjoy your trip."

"Thanks, I…" the attendant is gone before Rand could finish the sentence. He looks back to watch her walk away. With time to waste Rand opens his map to absorb what he can visually about the terrain, transportation routes and distances. Rand realizes that he has chosen a route that does go near the Black Forest. He knows now that he will stay in Germany to experience the area as he had originally planned. From Karlsruhe he will go to Heidelberg. Rand's thoughts return to the phenomenon of this isolated group of survivors that have been abandoned long ago and yet have continued to attempt interaction with the surrounding population.

"How can I help?" the returning attendant asks.

"Not at all," Rand replies. "I will rest until we stop."

"Very well." Responds the attendant as she leaves. Rand returns to his thoughts and his questions about rescue and compassion as it has not been applied to this group of people. It cannot be said that they have been forgotten. Their regular contact with those around the area prevents others from forgetting them unless intentional. Perhaps in the beginning years they were forgotten as everyone surviving the Great War were engaged in restoring their own lives. Rand concludes there must be aspects of these issues that he is not aware of which would bring clarity to his understanding.

Again he returns, in thought, to his ethics classes when at University. One element contributing to such abuses and indifference is that of compartmentalization of one's life. This practice of separating aspects of a person's life so that what one believes personally in the privacy of home and what one espouses or practices publicly can be very different. Similarly, one's personal religious beliefs, for example, can be left at the door as one enters into public life. How else can a person, again for example, consider them self a peaceful and loving religious adherent and then accept speech and behavior that demeans, imprisons and murders innocent people? Similarly, how, in one's own mind, can the thoughts of compassion for an injured or endangered animal exist with the willingness to murder an innocent, defenseless child?

Rand emerges from his intense thoughts when the train shutters slightly as it slows to begin entry to the station at Badwaldheim. Rand's attention is on the sunrise that is about to explode with brilliant colors across the landscape.

Moving Northeast from the French-German border near Rastatt, Karlsruhe is the first metropolitan German city for Rand to visit even if only for a short time at the station. After buying his ticket to Heidelberg Rand chooses to remain on board and make his exercise an excursion to the club car. With many of the passengers leaving the train quickly and local people boarding Rand must be nimble to navigate the narrow aisle of the train. Reaching the club car during a short off time for the staff, during stops, Rand chooses a seat near the wait station so as to get easy service.

As the doors open a waiter returning from a smoke break notices Rand and asks, "Do you need something immediately? We are on break for another five minutes. Would you like something to drink?"

Rand, "Coffee is good for now."

Waiter, "Coffee it is, right away." And the waiter disappears through the forward door. Rand recalls the sound from the wheels on the rails and the rushing wind that creates an electricity of motion with such strength to move large coaches filled with people and possessions with speed and the exciting motion of a machine to transport into the next minute, into the next day. Rand senses the soul of a place by taking the moment to stop, listen, and smell the life within which he moves.

The city, regardless of name or location, does draw him back to everything he is trying to separate from during this time. The boarding alarm sounds and the doors of each car begin to close. Rand returns mentally from his brief excursion into contemplation to get his bearings and ask the waiter for a good German beer. The first taste brings to mind that his seat is not reserved and his bags are, hopefully, still there. Leaving a tip on the table Rand rushes to the second car back from the club car and to the seat to find it occupied. The isle seat across from his is available so Rand takes the seat and tries to peer over and see his bags. All was still in place so Rand turns to the young man seated in the window seat to introduce himself.

"Excuse me Sir my bags are there under the seat in front of yours. I was sitting there before this stop at Karlsrue. Hey, we have met before!"

"Claus, and yes I remember you. I am expecting someone to join me but I was not expecting you."

Rand, "Well, I doubt it is me. I have no plans to meet anyone unless, possibly, a woman. But she would have to be much prettier than you." Smiling, Rand hoped Claus is in a better mood than when he had first encountered him.

Rand, "May I?" pointing to his bags under the seat.

Claus, "Oh, sure," As he pulls the two bags from the floor and hands them to Rand. Rand pushes the second bag under the seat and looks across the aisle to find another young man watching him. Sitting up, Rand begins to extend his hand across the aisle as a greeting and the young man responds, "Good day, Sir, my name is Baetus. I am the 'someone' that Claus there is looking for."

Rand, "Would you like to sit here then?"

Baetus, "No, no you must be tired of moving those bags. Besides, I need to rest for a short time. Thanks, anyway."

Baetus is fatigued because he has just returned from a complicated assignment and rather than getting the time off he was expecting he, instead, is now reassigned to the field for what he was told will be an escort assignment.

Rand has already settled on Speyer as his destination from Heidelberg for entering a locale and immersing himself in the culture. After a brief stop in Karlsruhe the next stop will put him in Heidelberg early enough to reach Speyer before sunset. The remainder of this leg of his travels should be uneventful as the day winds down and everyone is beginning to settle in for the late afternoon travel.

Mirror Turns

Lana restarts the conversation, "Let me begin by telling you my memories. I will then also be asking for your thoughts. I am thankful for your help. This time with you and Yarjies is crucial to me. Everything is moving quickly and I am behind the timeline of preparation."

Yarjies speaks up, "We cannot know what has been planned by your trainer but we can help you know what we know."

"Thank you, Yarjies." Lana acknowledges his experience and addresses both, "I want your precise knowledge to be shared so I can have confidence in our success."

Yarjies acknowledges Lana's confidence with a nod and continues, "Though you and I are of the same generation we obviously have had different experiences. I, unlike you, was not able to escape the tragedies. I understand that you did not leave by choice. One result of your absence, though, is that you do not know, first hand, what was risked nor what was lost or gained, correct?"

"Yes, I have little bits and pieces of information and I was put out of harm's way by my father," Lana acknowledges. "I know that my father did what he thought was right and that he gave everything, including his life, trying to preserve our people."

Yarjies humbly responds, "Your Father was one of many brave leaders that did not abandon the fight for life."

"Okay," Lana agrees, "I need so much to learn from you each and to re-align my thinking with the realities of the past and the situation now." As each check the time they realize that they have but a few hours before they must get back on schedule and meet Lana's trainer.

Lana begins, "I love our people and I am thankful for the beauty of our forests, our mountains, our fresh, clean water. I spent so much of my time as a child away from the activities of my father and I did not ask many questions of my mother except for permission to go into the fields and the forest to play and explore. I often thought of myself as an elf or some invisible creature that could dance with the squirrels and fly with the birds." Lana realizes that she is off subject for this discussion and pauses. "I know I have much to learn about the realities of everyday life as you each have lived it over these past twenty years. I have only memories as a young girl that was protected, for the most part. It was in the last year of my life at home from the time I was eight that the outside world and the conflicts of that time began to penetrate my conscious mind and to affect my life dramatically." Lana pauses again and looks into the eyes of both Yarjies and Baetus.

"I have a role to fulfill as a part of my family heritage. I will soon join the fight you are both a part of. My role, in my mind, does not elevate me above you or anyone else. I hope to be successful so that I can then return to being a member of the social order we, together, have fought for and secured for our people." Lana offers a reassuring smile to both men before she continues.

"Even though I always loved going into the forest I also loved going to school. I was enrolled in our local school and I enjoyed science most of all. Mister Zimmerman was good at painting a mental picture for me when we studied the Earth and the weather. The forces that move around us are so powerful and yet

Yarjies adds, "Knowing the truth opens the way to freedom. I must add, though, that the way will present challenges that require the shedding of blood to accomplish the freedom of liberty."

Baetus pumps his fist in the air and shouts, "Liberty!"

Lana quickly reaches for Baetus' hand and pulls it down as she reminds all to quiet down. The three look at each other and smile silently. Lana warns, "We must have this unity to succeed but we must, for the present time, control our outward expressions. I know it is tough. We are each like a boiling pot that must release the pressure. Liberty is an ultimate goal which we will discuss more as the time draws near. To have liberty we must have the freedom to exercise it and we must have the means to defend both."

"Let us now focus on a more difficult and complicated aspect of the phenomenon we are engulfed by."

Yarjies, "I may be most experienced with the metaphysical or spiritual condition through which our social and personal existence has been perverted. There is a dimensional fracture that has emerged to threaten all of life as created."

Lana, "Please speak to us from your heart and knowledge of this."

Yarjies, "When I was called to service the training and the underlying principles were not as well understood as for Baetus' training in the practices by which we can disappear at times and our ability to change our level of functionality. The principles are based on the same methods that brought about the evil and the destruction of the Great War and its aftermath in our region. The question of, 'Why our region?' has never been answered. We are responsible for our region and the focus has always been on our region. I have no doubt that other areas of the world must be under the same influences and engaged in the same struggles."

Lana, "Please explain further?"

Baetus again loses control of his emotions and raises his voice to a shout, "The Creatures! The creatures are the soldiers of this evil! We must destroy the core of their existence and be free to live!"

Lana becomes exasperated with Baetus' lack of control and points her finger at him as she scolds, "You must control yourself! I will not continue to have you threaten our low profile and our efforts by drawing attention with your outbursts!"

Baetus immediately bows his head and becomes silent. "Forgive me," His only response.

Lana, "Yarjies, please continue. Our time is running out here."

Yarjies, "I will condense as much as possible. What I will try to explain may be difficult to understand. As with all wars there is an aggressor and a prey. In this case the aggressor is a historically dominant people who sought superiority on every level. When challenged or pressured to limit the aggression they would explode into a phase of rebellion that targeted the opposition with a destructive, personal fury that only death will vanquish.

The beginning pulse of the last Great War first occurred in the heart of one person. Perhaps God looked away from His creation for a moment and this one heart sought the darkness of evil and rejected all else. A split of this one point in the universe, of beings allowed the fullness of evil to enter and begin an alliance to elevate the supremacy of one man above all others."

Lana, "I am not fully following your explanation, Yarjies. Can one man become so powerful, so empty and driven to destroy?"

Yarjies, "It takes a man who's pride and arrogance, driven and inflamed by his perceptions of mistreatment by others to become the servant of his desires and a tool of the evil he invites by giving over his heart and mind completely. His choice possibly breached the universe and all of creation in that moment.

Eventually it would require the hand of God, working through the rest of mankind, to break the power that this one person absorbed and projected into the whole of civilization."

Lana, "There have always been tyrants in the world. That is nothing new. Somewhere people are being mistreated by a ruler or a group with a sense of superiority."

Yarjies, "I am not a historian and I do not have information beyond what I have been living. I see one of the peculiarities here is that within the people groups there is an ethnicity that preys on itself. The evil was borne by a member of this sect, or ethnicity, and his targeted prey was, ultimately, his own people. Through this pressure and turmoil, the threat to life and sanity, there were those who actually became a part of the enforcement of the destruction by participating in the evil so as to stay alive."

Lana, "Since this enemy was defeated how is it that this phenomenon of the beasts, the Rochukas, is related?"

Yarjies, "The Rochukas are the leaders such as this one and other nations, the philosophers and to a lesser degree the collaborators that make up a short list that has developed through time. As I have learned I have accepted the history without a clear understanding. I have chosen to trust the information as given. I can tell you what I have been through but I cannot convince you of the facts. I can only hope that you will accept what I am saying and trust me. The reality that you will soon confront may be more brutal than I can impart as a student trying to explain what I am still learning about these traitors and the origins of the beasts."

Baetus, "The reality is that we must never give up and we can only win if we fight!"

Lana gives Baetus a stern look that changes to a soft smile as she recognizes the sincerity and truth of his comment.

Yarjies continues, "All that occurred then and all that is taking place now is the outward, visible expression of spiritual activities which are the unfolding, over time, of the ultimate battle that has raged since before time began. When you recognize events from this perspective the dimensional interaction becomes clearer. This understanding does not diminish the reality, the struggle, the horror of what is taking place.

Our region has become a battle ground that shifts alternately between physical and spiritual. As a mirror that turns, when you are before the mirror you see yourself and your surroundings. When the mirror is turned away from you it becomes a window into another dimension and you are faced with a struggle that, at times, escapes or transcends barriers and washes into the other reality, be it ours or another."

Lana, sensing that Baetus has a need to express his perspective, before becoming too excited, asks, "Baetus please tell me what you see as the purpose of what we are doing. Be as brief as possible because we haven't much time."

Baetus closes his eyes before speaking to collect his emotions. "I realize the events we have witnessed and been a part of are outward expressions of metaphysical or spiritual activities. However, we live in a physical world that contains our life experiences. Our lives are what we have now, today and each day, to exist within. Within that life, as individuals, we do have certain freedoms, natural rights as humans and a responsibility for how we conduct ourselves privately and publicly. I embrace the hope we are born with, to live a life of liberty, with respect and honor. I must do my part to bring this hope to fruition."

"In this present age that means I must personally cooperate with others to be engaged in our struggle to restore the practicality of a fundamental society based on our traditional principles of personal liberty and responsibly protect our people, our ways, our freedom."

Lana, "Do you have family or other close relationships that you are providing for?"

Baetus, "I have only my dearest friend who is my special companion. Her name is Megan. She is unique and she is as deeply involved in this struggle as I. Even though she is not native to this region she has been here since she was an infant. She and I are about two years apart in age.She will be by my side on the day we bring about the defeat of our enemies."

Lana chooses to indulge Baetus by asking, "Please tell me more about Megan."

Baetus, "Though she was excluded from the training I received in the transformational arts she functions very well with the techniques naturally. She can out run me, out maneuver me and out think me. Her thinking is always two phases ahead of mine. She also gains an advantage naturally. Her appearance is captivating and when she is presented with an occasion to offer her beauty by shedding the camouflage of the field she is often the center of attention.

She is small of stature as I am. Her skin is the color of copper with a hint of gold when the light shifts at some angles. Her eyes are a dark blue and her hair is a chestnut brown."

Baetus pauses momentarily before concluding, "Please permit me one minute more. We each have family, friends and a future, hopefully, that we, as individuals and a society, will have control of. I am not speaking of a libertine approach so that there are no boundaries but within the rule of law we will have the liberty of life and the opportunity for success.

I don't think that anyone engaged in this struggle with us will want to replace the beasts we are fighting now with the beast of a centralized, national government that has many heads and many tentacles that touch every part of our existence. We must be united in our efforts, united in our morality and determined in our cause."

Lana, "Well said, Baetus, and may our peoples be united by such sincerity of purpose and understanding of the goals!"

Yarjies nods his head in agreement and adds, "I know that our time is very short. I ask you, Miss Ann, for a brief explanation of your role, as you understand it. You are going into this chaos from a much different existence as you have experienced the past twenty years."

"Briefly," Lana pauses and smiles. "Briefly hasn't worked to well for this trio so far. I don't have a solid or clear understanding as yet. This time together with yourself and Baetus has given me a background I did not have. I know there is an anticipation of the "Identifier" being revealed and all the event signifies for the future. That is one area I am not very knowledgeable of. I am expecting the trainer to focus on this aspect. I have not placed much importance on religion,spiritual or metaphysical philosophies during my adult life. I have vague remembrances of my Father's teachings except for one saying that has always stayed with me as a baseline truth. He would always end our discussions with, 'God is God and I am not. I do well to remember that HE has not forgotten.'

The elements you speak of, Yarjies, such as the reflective, interactive region of consciousness and the dimension of demonic and benevolent entities have been more of a subject of movies I watched rather than subjects for study or belief to this point, for me. I have much to learn, quickly."

Yarjies stands to conclude the discussion, "Our time together is now closed. Baetus will be leaving us to re-join his companions as they prepare for the next phase and to Megan who will be joining them as well." Baetus, at the mention of Megan, smiles and offers his handshake to Yarjies, "thank you."

Lana stands and also offers a hand shake to each, "Our goals are honorable and our cause just. We will meet again, Baetus, in due time."

In response Baetus places his hand on Lana's shoulder, as when they were first together and offers a respectful, affectionate touchstone for Lana to have a connection with her commitment if she falters along the way. "You must first find your center. You have a destiny not of your choosing. Remember the freedom of the forest you loved when you were young. Its return is in your hands."

Lana, with the same tone, answers, "I will," as she places her hand over his, they pause, Lana repeats, "I will." As Lana presses Baetus's hand he vanishes into transition. Yarjies, who has been waiting to proceed, smiles knowingly at Lana and nods his head. Lana steps toward Yarjies and wraps her arm around his neck. The two, with belongings in hand, leave the room walking in step and laughing away the fear of tomorrow.

After a routine check out Lana and Yarjies walk to the bus stop just outside the hotel and review of the posted bus schedule. They drop their bags and then drop themselves onto the couch. Lana realizes how tired she is and she recognizes that her goal of strategizing during their layover became more of a time to get to know each other. Yarjies was tired as well. As the two wait silently Lana's thoughts turn to her anticipated time with her trainer and her role in this struggle that she is being thrust into. She isn't as confident as those around her. She begins, again, to second guess her abilities. Her life as an adult has been rather carefree and of no exceptional importance or critical to others except for her relationship with Rand which was also fairly loose, with a low level of demands. To become an object of others' expectations is unsettling and a bit foreign to Lana's thinking.

Lana recognizes her senses becoming heightened to the emotional struggle that she has not experienced since she was young and her escape from home was induced. She is startled by Yarjies' tapping her arm, "The bus is here." Yarjies alerts her.

The two rise quickly, grab their bags and hurry to the bus. They arrive at the bus as the doors are closing. Yarjies motions to the driver who is slow to respond. The bus begins to roll slightly before the doors fling open. As they walk to available seating the bus pulls away.

After being jostled about the isle by the movement of the bus Lana finally secures a seat and slides over to the window so Yarjies can sit beside her. Lana's thoughts return to her youth and Baetus's comments before leaving them. She recalls a subject that she had struggled with as an adolescent. Lana's awareness transfers from within the bus to the kaleidoscope of scenes that animate her view of daily life occurring at the sidewalk level in the London suburb of Twickenham, at that moment. Lana thinks of her mother who epitomized the reality that life can be so fascinating when viewed and experienced with a sense of humor and a freedom to be engaged. Lana's dad was usually away for long periods of time and her mother was her primary adult figure growing up. Though both parents were religious her mother was observant and engaged in Lana's religious education. Primarily that meant getting her to church, to catechism and enrolling her in the parochial school. Her father was of a different faith but worked to blend the two as much as possible for Lana.

The specific concept that Lana could not quite grasp as a child was the makeup, presence or location of the soul and the effect of sin upon the soul. Her mother attempted to explain the elements of her questions after seeking advice from the priest.

The process alone of having to ask a priest what one is to believe rather than to independently discover the truths of scripture, assuming scripture was the source of the beliefs, was frustrating and invasive to Lana.

The bus slows quickly as traffic slows to a crawl because of an accident tying up traffic on such a heavily traveled street. Lana turns to Yarjies, "I suppose it will be understandable if we are a bit late because of this traffic?"

Yarjies, "Being late will not be a good thing. Let me check something," as he opens his bag. "I have the address and a local map. Let me check our location."

Lana, "Can I help?"

"One minute," Yarjies slowly responds. "Yes, we are but two blocks from our destination. We can walk it in twenty minutes, are you for it?"

Lana, "Let's go, it's time to move."

Each picked up their bags. Yarjies pushes open the rear, side doors and they jump to the street. Yarjies can see the driver, in the side mirror, cussing because the doors were opened. Yarjies pushes the doors closed and nods to the driver in the mirror. The bus idles forward ten feet as the two move to the sidewalk and continue north.

Turning East at the first corner they will have to cover two blocks before turning again to the North to reach the entrance of the building at 9393A where they will be looking for suite 412. Their arrival is on the correct day but still later than planned. As they reach the midway point of their hurried walk two police cars and an ambulance pass them with the emergency lights on but no sirens. As Lana and Yarjies reach the end of the block to turn north the smell of smoke grabs their attention. As they make the turn they find the police and other first responders at the entrance of a building with dark, thick plumes of smoke rolling from the first floor window near the far northern corner of the building. They immediately slow their pace and simultaneously recognize the building address as their destination. Both stop in place and look at each other with alarm.

Yarjies begins running toward the scene and Alana pauses before walking slowly in the same direction. She is stunned by the view of the scene and she is unsure about what to do. Lana stops again and decides to wait for a signal from Yarjies.

As Yarjies nears the barrier, already established by the police, the firemen that have stormed the building were able to clear an obstruction from the doorway with an axe. No-one was leaving the building. Without being familiar with the area Lana couldn't determine if the offices would normally be occupied or if anyone inside is injured or dead. To Lana it appears that Yarjies is arguing with the officer that is manning the barricade. As the badly damaged door of the entrance is forced from the remaining hinge the thud of heavy wood against the entry floor gets everyone's attention. Yarjies looks up to see paramedics carrying a stretcher from the building with a covered body. With one hand of the victim visible Yarjies recognizes the markings on the jacket sleeve cuff. It is a transitional government issued uniform and the small insignia was that of a rank the trainer, Norsha, would have with the Training Corps.

As Lana draws near she can hear Yarjies pleading with the officer to allow him to identify the person under the shroud. Upon the officers final refusal Yarjies turns away to be surprised by Lana's presence. His shoulders fall and his head remains lowered as though a mortal blow has been struck.

Lana grasps both of Yarjies' shoulders but he refuses to look at her squarely. "I will be held responsible for this," Yarjies whispers. Lana senses his growing weakness and embraces him with a calming, reassuring hug. Though she is stunned as well Lana does not have a personal connection to those lost as does Yarjies.

The police and fire personnel begin removing more victims from the damaged suites. Yarjies regains his composure and steps away from Lana's protective embrace. "As you have said, Miss Ann, it's time to move."

Together, Lana and Yarjies begin walking in a direction opposite the stranded cars and away from the scene. "Two blocks west then north will get us out of this crisis area and we can regroup before sundown. Once outside of London", Yarjies determines from his map. "There are provisions available for alternate scheduling tactics. I have means to replenish our currency and make local contact for lodging and provisions as needed," Yarjies continues, somewhat nervously.

Lana captures Yarjies' glance and offers reassurance. "I trust you. I am relying on your judgment and your guidance during this time in our journey. We will find a down time soon and we will be able to review and strategize our adjustments."

Yarjies agrees, "Adjustments indeed."

The two weave their way through the stopped cars at each intersection and listen for remarks that would indicate the nature of the situation that they encountered. Suddenly the sound and vibration of an explosion rocks everyone. This, combined with the event at Norsha's location, leads Lana to think multiple attacks are occurring with coordination. There have been local incidents such as bombings and fire fights with insurgent colonial separatists in London. To expect the same may be occurring here, combined with the possible loss of Norsha, the chain of command and planning may have been broken.

Yarjies and Lana are presenting an air of calm and confidence that is forming a fragile covering for their disorientation, anger and fear. Each knows that the other is struggling and that, together, they will move ahead one day at a time. Their primary goals will be to survive, identify the enemy and cross the channel for entrance into Norway. The three days planned with Norsha will now be their time frame for completing the final leg of their travels.

Catching a taxi after reaching an unaffected street, about ten blocks away, the first destination is the area of Westcliffe – On –

Sea. A safe house has been reserved for alternate scenarios so that they can be flexible. The Atlantis Guest House will accommodate them for two days only. More exposure would complicate security and the strategy of blending in for this the most challenging leg of Alana's travels. The commute is about 45 minutes.

As the cabbie weaves through traffic, speeding them to their next stop, while singing along with his radio Lana tunes out the noise and begins to realize the uncertainty and seriousness of her situation. All of the planning and travel to this point has been such an adventure for her that she has been living each moment without any real calculations of the dangerous nature of her role in the unfolding scheme. The risks of life and health are now becoming clear. She now is beginning to see herself as a stranger in a country, a city and a situation that she has very little control over. Her companion, Yarjies, is her only connection to reality now. She does trust him and she is getting to know him but the isolation is beginning to increase her fear. Lana turns to him, "Yarjies, I am nervous and a bit fearful about our predicament."

Yarjies recognizes her emotional vulnerability and returns the supportive embrace she had most recently given to him when he needed it. "Miss Ann, I do understand. We are now entering a critical stage of this operation. The loss of Norsha, as is appears, may not be as obvious as we think."

Lana, "Now you are confusing me. What are you trying to say? Don't invent something just to make me feel better!"

Yarjies reinforces his embrace then releases Lana. "I am not inventing anything. Let me explain."

Lana, now leaning back in her seat, "Okay, please explain."

Yarjies first tests the cabbie's attention by saying something in a clear voice for him to hear and finds that the cabbie is too distracted by his singing to pay attention to them.

Yarjies, "One of the methods used by our field personnel is to infiltrate and attach to outside groups that are operating in localities that are close to our areas of activity. They are similarly engaged in tactical maneuvers that we can use to travel and to communicate by manipulating their resources. This way, if any of our operatives are captured or even killed while participating as a part of the host group then our missions are not compromised. While our people are engaged with these host groups they can peel off as needed to complete their assignments for us. Do you follow what I am saying?"

Lana, "Do these host groups, as you call them, know this?"

Yarjies, "No, they are completely unaware. If these groups knew we would become their adversary. Our people are, to them, just another member of their group, fighting for their cause. The double nature of our involvement has never been exposed. This tactic has been one result of the development of our ability to transition. We..." Yarjies notices the driver looking at him with the rear view mirror and that he is no longer singing but he is listening. Yarjies clears his throat and looks back at Lana. "We must continue this discussion after arriving at our destination."

Lana notices the change and nods in agreement.

Yarjies, "Hey cabbie, we will get out at the next corner."

Cabbie, "Well, mate, you never did give a destination anyway." He pulls quickly over to the curb and checks the meter.

Yarjies, "Here is more than enough," handing the cabbie a sum he did not check. Yarjies is now a bit nervous and anxious to be rid of the cabbie.

Lana, "What are we doing?"

Yarjies, "I am hailing another cabbie did not say anything to give us away but it is better to be cautious. We will be at the Guest House very soon."

Lana, "I am becoming insecure as it is, I don't need to be second guessing my trust in you, Yarjies."

Yarjies is surprised, "You have no reason to miss-trust me, Miss Ann, I am being cautious because I know our enemy well enough to be suspicious of every circumstance right now. You must trust me, you must be courageous and we must be flexible."

Lana, "I understand. I do trust you. I am just a bit shaken by this day's events." The two hug as a taxi stops in front of them.

"Westcliffe-on-Sea, please." Yarjies uses a foreign accent to avoid possible detection.

Lana, "Let's not become paranoid now." She smiles as she tries to rib Yarjies.

Yarjies, "I thought it was pretty good," referring to his accent. "We will be there in fifteen minutes."

Now driving along the inland shore of the River Thames the view, though blurred by the misty air, becomes more tranquil for Lana. The scent of sea air begins to invade their taxi and Lana breathes deeply. While Yarjies studies his map and takes notes Lana relaxes and is reminded of days in America, spent on the shores of the Great Lakes at different locations each summer.

Yarjies quickly folds his map and alerts the cabbie to drop them at the next corner. This time, without the accent and it is the cabbie that gives him an uncertain look.

"Here you go, mate." The cabbie announces as he stops and checks the meter. Yarjies hands him the fee and they slide out on the street side with bags in hand.

Yarjies, "We have about a quarter mile to walk but I think it better to throw off any clues that have been generated by my mistakes today."

Lana, "I understand, once again, 'it is time to move'." They both laugh and begin their hike. With the terrain of the coast in this area being rocky, hilly and steep the streets are terraced to reduce the angle of ascent. The quarter mile to the Atlantis Guest House is up hill at varying angles between 20 and 30 degrees. Soon both Lana and Yarjies are breathing with a bit of difficulty and beginning to sweat. Lana stops to remove her jacket and Yarjies doesn't notice until he is almost thirty yards away.

While Lana struggles to pull the jacket over her shoulders Yarjies quickly returns to be by her side when she has removed the jacket. Lana, not realizing Yarjies' maneuvers is surprised that he is still breathing hard. "You okay Yarjies? I thought you would be in much better shape than I."

Yarjies, "Oh, working out in a gym doesn't quite duplicate real life activity, especially if adrenalin is heightened by stress or fear."

Lana, "You're afraid?"

Yarjies, "No, no, just giving you an example." Yarjies, all the while, thinking of the risk Lana is taking and her lack of awareness of her value as a captured prize for the opposition. "We have a bit of a hike still to come, Miss Ann, we should get there as quickly as possible to avoid a prolonged exposure to the risk of encountering our adversaries."

Lana, "I have much to acclimate to. I am so very thankful for you, Yarjies."

Yarjies motions for Lana to lead so she begins to trudge the hill before them. Yarjies looks over his street side shoulder and follows Lana. Once at the corner nearest the Guest House they stop for a breather, water and a brief few minutes of strategizing for their entry.

Lana, "How can this be set up so quickly? You have not communicated with anyone since arriving in London."

Yarjies, "Since the incident that took Norsha out of the equation a series of pre-planned messaging procedures were activated. This scenario is the first alternative."

Lana, "Are we being tracked?"

Yarjies, "We have our destination and our route is general but we have flexibility when we need it."

Lana, "I just want to drop this bag and rest."

Yarjies, "Well, here we are, thirty feet away!"

Walking to the entrance, Lana takes in the large Victorian building of white brick. It was once a home that has been restored to become The Atlantis. With a mixture of families and traveling business people accustomed to staying here, the inter-mingling environment is a natural camouflage for Lana and Yarjies.

Their accommodations are a corner location that provides an excellent view towards the River Thames from the second level with easy access from the lobby by stairway. They are near enough to the mouth of the river's expansion into the channel to easily find a local charter to cross into Holland when the time comes. First, rest, as the evening quietly begins.

Superior/Inferior

Once inside the room they find that the accommodations are excellent. Two beds with a night stand between them with large, plush, feather down pillows and top cover. There is also a fireplace and sitting area with a small refrigerator. The ceiling is very high with metal tile work that has an intricate design. Windows are on two sides to give plenty of light. It will be dark soon and both tired travelers are ready to shower, change clothes and have a good meal without any drama or interference. Yarjies defers to Lana who goes for the shower first.

Yarjies prepares the fireplace for the night as he listens to Lana, 'Miss Ann', humming as she showers then brushes her hair. Yarjies looks back from the fireplace to see Lana returning from the bathroom wrapped in a towel only which is modest enough for him. Yarjies is enticed by her beautiful, toned, muscular legs and he is thankful to see most of them.

Lana, "Would you like the shower now?"

Yarjies, "Thank you. I will enjoy every drop of it."

Lana, "Good then. Dinner after you are ready. Do you like wine? I am ready for at least one glass of wine and I hope you will join me."

Yarjies, "Excellent idea."

The two have, through their experiences, moved away from the superior/inferior interaction as Yarjies has begun to relax and Lana has begun to assimilate with her role and also relax in her relationship with Yarjies. They are becoming fellow combatants for their cause and for the heritage they intend to rescue.

As Yarjies closes the bathroom door Lana drops her towel and begins to dress. The night's cold, damp air will require warm dress for dinner. Once ready, Lana waits by the windows across the room, for Yarjies to finish. He emerges wearing shorts, sandals and a sweater.

Lana, "You are going to be cold."

Yarjies pauses, "Are we outside tonight? Maybe long pants then." He returns to the bathroom to change. Pushing the door to close, a small opening remains to reveal a thin slice of his physique while changing but it was enough to prick Lana's need as a claw to the flesh. Closing the blinds and crossing the room, Lana offers a light, mocking applause to Yarjies for his change of clothes as they meet at the door. Lana entertains the thought that this dinner, for this night, may be a grand adventure. First night in country, unfamiliar area, menu, hours of recreation, people who speak English poorly for an American's ear.

Food from the hotel kitchen is only full faire with too much delay for customs' sake, being a demonstration for the visitors. Though it is rather cool outside many patrons are on the patio with drinks and hearty food. Steak, lamb, lobster-real food! Lana is thinking, "Yarjies, let's visit the food court and really eat well."

Yarjies, "I like your tastes."

Walking across the courtyard becomes a maze for lack of a walkway. It is more like a grassy yard with many pieces of 'yard art' that have become local tradition. Yarjies is intrigued by some pieces but other elements of the night are more important. Once through the courtyard and across the street the night air changes to one of fresh air mingling with passing traffic and the humid, still air between passes of vehicles. A natural breeze clears the air once the street is crossed.

The food court is a once abandoned lot that is now subleased to vendors using mobile food service vehicles. A plaza results with the vendors on the perimeter so that every visitor has access to every vendor. The concept has not been widespread but it is popular where it has been tried.

Lana, "So, we buy our food here, re-cross the street, then grab a table in the courtyard and order our drink from there?"

Yarjies, "I think you've got it."

Now in the center of the courtyard the two laugh at each other as they turn to be back to back. They start slowly turning in a circle so each can see all of the choices. Playing like kids for a moment, both seeking an outlet for the tension that has built inside each of them, as the rotation is completed and they turn to face one another. Each points in the direction of their first food choice. Since their choices do not align each goes to their chosen vendors and meets again at the center of the courtyard with containers of their selections.

Yarjies, "I am so hungry. I could sit right on the ground here and devour this."

Lana, "Come on, caveman, we need a table and that wine."

The two return to the Guest House courtyard and take a table at the edge of the lit area. A server arrives just as they sit down. "May I help you?" the young man asks.

Lana, "We would like a Spanish Merlot and some water please."

Yarjies adds, "Bread and butter also, please."

Both relax for a moment, breathing in the cool air and allowing the feeling of calm to wash over. Lana looks over at Yarjies who has his legs extended, his head back and eyes closed. "Do you believe we are here, considering the events of the day?"

Yarjies, "Either of us alone would not have made it. I believe we have helped each other and we have both learned more about each other and ourselves by experiencing these events together."

Lana, "I know but that is all too technical. I am just so out of my normal element and I guess I am surprised by my own resilience. I know that you have been my security."

Yarjies, "I am more accustomed to getting through days like this one. My time in the field has hardened me somewhat and I have learned to rely on my network to succeed."

The server returns with their requests, sets the table and opens the wine for each to sample. As the server leaves Lana and Yarjies look at each other then they each give an exaggerated glance at their food. Each opens their containers of steamy and certainly delicious foods. Lana begins with a fork and soon is using her fingers. The meats are cut into bite sized chunks. She has medium-rare beef sirloin, medium-well lamb with roasted garlic cloves and onions. For Yarjies lobster in butter with a ground chuck burger on bread. He begins holding the burger in one hand and popping the lobster chunks into his mouth with his other hand.

The area of the courtyard becomes crowded as everyone's attention is drawn to the grassy area where the yard art stands. A couple of local musicians are offering an impromptu performance. Because of their seating Lana and Yarjies are now front row, stage right.

Yarjies pours each a fresh glass of wine and raises his glass to toast. Lana joins him as they both stand. The musicians are two guys a bit on the rowdy side, perhaps out of place for the atmosphere but the crowd sang along. Yarjies raises his glass to join in and Lana copies his move. The added activity and closeness of the people pushes Lana and Yarjies to back away to the perimeter. They are comfortable with being on the quiet side of the celebration.

Yarjies, "I am ready to go from here."

Lana, "A slow walk back will be nice. The day has been a flurry for me. I need to disconnect for my body and for my emotions."

Yarjies, "You want to disconnect? You will be better served by a reconnect with your body through your emotions."

Lana, "That is accomplished how?"

Yarjies, "It is accomplished through pleasure and release."

Lana, "I am not good at casual."

Yarjies, "I am not casual about pleasure."

Lana, "Are you inviting me to…"

Yarjies "Allow me to pleasure and please you, to release you by satisfying you."

Lana, "I know you are a confident man and I am in need of what you are offering but this may be a mistake considering our situation."

Yarjies, "For this night I am truly your servant. Tomorrow I will be your companion in service to our cause, your safety and the future of our people."

Lana, "Come here." As they face each other she puts her arms around his neck and moves closer to him but only slightly touching his body. Lana whispers into his ear, "I have the longing as you do." She kisses his neck and moves closer, into his arms. "This will be questionable to others. We will have to be very discrete and forgiving after this night because this will be misunderstood."

Yarjies, "I have a little game I have used before to test such insecurities. We will return to our room and play this game. The result will be the right solution."

Lana, "A game? I have played some risqué games that can lead to temporary arrangements for the hour or the night but I don't know which game you are playing now."

Yarjies, "No, this is more of a test that I learned from a dear friend who was my love for a short time during my early years of field training. This is too many details and we are losing the night to 'discussion'."

Lana, "We shall finish our wine and then play the test or the game or something!" Lana thinks to herself that this is inappropriate and that tomorrow will shine a new light on the unintended circumstances. The warmth of the wine, the celebration of the courtyard and the delicious, satisfying food, together bring a sense of normalcy that has been missing since leaving Rand and her life there. Yarjies has similar thoughts, reflected in his past, as the two climb the stairs to the second floor. Neither says more about their reservations.

Yarjies places the key into the door's lock and turns the key. Lana pushes the door open slowly as though opening a mystery package. Lana then pushes Yarjies into the room first, laughing as the combination of wine and warmth inside the room increases her sense of euphoria and relaxation in the moment.

Yarjies responds, "Hey, I'm going! Are you ready for the test?"

Lana, "Yes sir." Her response as she removes her jacket.

The door closes behind them to leave them in a pitch black room. Lana stumbles to the side of her bed, falls onto it and crawls across to the night stand and fumbles for the lamp switch. The light level is low but Lana can see Yarjies still standing at the entry and waiting to know which way to go. Lana, standing by the night stand between the two beds, motions for Yarjies to come near.

Lana, "Now what is this game or test?"

Yarjies places his glass on the small stand and moves in front of Lana. There is barely room for them to stand apart with a bed behind each. Their attention was on one another and the room faded from their focus on the moment. They didn't notice the slight movement of another person sitting on the floor, under the window.

Yarjies, "Okay, now here is the test. While remaining here before one another, with the light turned off, we will each, at the same time, undress fully without touching each other in any way. Then you will get into your bed and I will get into mine. We will both remain motionless and quiet for ten minutes. Now, here is the test; at the end of the ten minutes we will each call out the others name. If there is a response then the night's play time begins. But, if there is no response then the one speaking will consider the test completed and will go to sleep. Does that sound innocent enough?"

Lana, "Innocent enough I suppose and cruel as well. Two adults, ready to indulge one another, first they strip then separate, cover and wait? Ever cheat on this test?"

Yarjies, "I am offering you every opportunity." As they undress their bodies do touch because of the closeness. Yarjies begins to struggle with his self-control.

Lana slides into her bed and covers up. "Let the game or test begin. It will be a good time to warm up." Looking to her left, Yarjies has just laid down to cover up as well. Lana's only view was a side profile of his leg and upper thigh. With the dim light from the shuttered windows she did catch a glimpse of his arousal.

Sinking into the soft bed and feeling the fabric of her covering stimulate her stomach, the surface of her legs and shoulders, her excitement begins to rise. The ceiling's pattern becomes a black and white kaleidoscope of patterns and angles as an effect of the low light angle from the windows.

Ten minutes pass with no-one saying anything. Fifteen minutes pass before the sound of Yarjies lightly snoring can be heard by the hidden stranger in the room.

Elaborate Diversion

The young scout has arrived to help Lana and Yarjies with any gaps left by Norsha's loss and to facilitate their transition into Norway, en route through Rotterdam to Cologne, Germany before going south.

This field scout has a unique set of talents for operating undetected, day or night, regardless of the population level during an operation and is almost unstoppable by kinetic means. Yarjies knows her from years in the field together. She has been described as sleek and slippery, cunning and agile, fast and strong, smart and enticing. She is classified as a chameleo-distra technically with a personal classification as a woman to be mother. Lana will soon have a new friend and an early start to her morning. Yarjies will gain a welcome face to pull him back from the edge of indulgence.

The six a.m. whistle of the commuter train passing by the open shutters awakens Lana to the sound of movement on the floor. Rising up slightly and noticing nothing Lana drops her head onto the pillow and slowly emerges from her sleep. Once again feeling the caressing of her body by the bed covers Lana enjoys her body as she remembers the night before, the game-test and Yarjies' readiness.

Lana again senses a movement in the room and sits up to survey the area. The morning air is cold and the fire is yet to be lit. Further visual scanning of the room stops at the north side window. Lana is frozen by the image of a young woman emerging from the wall, under the window. Exhaling forcefully through her vocal cords her immediate response is, "Yarjies!"

Yarjies rises up quickly and looks to Lana who is pointing with her arm straight out and her breasts slightly covered. He forces himself to look away to the window. Now fully before them, Yarjies recognizes the scout. "I know her," Yarjies calms Lana. "I know her well. She is with us."

The scout sits on the foot of Lana's bed and smiles, "I am sorry for startling you, Miss Ann, I tend to relax too much when off of my schedule and my camouflage sometimes shows, although this time is official. You know, 'on the clock'."

Yarjies, "This one is a jokester, Miss Ann, but you will soon love her. She is another one of our young people who has lived this fabrication of a society and is committed to the restoration of traditional values, moral absolutes and the promise of opportunity."

Lana covers up and then wraps herself in the bed sheet while under the top cover by rolling across the bed. "I will go and dress now and you," pointing at the scout, who's name she does not know, "you may want to join me so that Yarjies can do the same."

Scout, "I will step out for ten minutes. Just here in the hallway." She exits and closes the door. Lana retreats to the bathroom to dress. Yarjies is left alone in the room to dress and be presentable before the two women return. He reverts back to his shorts, socks, sandals and shirt with a sweater.

Lana emerges in shorts as well, "What is this scout's name?"

Yarjies "Let me introduce her when she returns."

A knock at the door brings Yarjies to open the door and have the scout to stay outside of the room until invited by Lana as a formality.

Scout, "Thanks to you both for receiving me so early. I have been waiting all night but I knew you both had a long day so I didn't want to interrupt anything."

Lana, from across the room, "So, you were in the room when we returned from dinner? Then I guess you know me much more than I know you. Yarjies, If you know our guest please introduce us."

Yarjies, uncomfortable in the situation, first speaks to Lana privately, "Miss Ann, you and I were at the edge of our path after losing Norsha and we pushed the envelope last night. I ask your indulgence to restart now and introduce the next phase in our transition to becoming warriors and shepherds. Too much has been risked. Many have sacrificed in blood and fortune. My selfishness must not be acceptable. The enemy seeks our defeat with vigor. A greater purpose is the cause of your life. I am yours."

With Lana's invitation Megan steps over the threshold to acknowledge Lana's authority by offering her extended, open, hands with a slight bow at the waist and a nod of her head.

I am here Fripree, at your service. Forgive me for my casual treatment of our first encounter. I am loyal and trustworthy. I am Megan."

Lana, "So, you are Megan. You are Baetus's companion?"

Megan, "Yes, Miss Ann. I was redirected here to assume responsibility for your entry into the network through which you will reach your destination. You have two days here. Yarjies will remain with you, I will leave you now and I will return the evening of the second day for our final review of objectives upon leaving this location. I have preparatory assignments that will keep me busy until then. I am available as needed."

As Megan turns to leave Lana observes her movements and sees her skin color change as the room's lighting angle and level varies. Lana is intrigued by the effect and makes a mental note to question Yarjies about the process and the application. She now understands the 'chameleo' portion of Megan's classification but she questions the meaning of the 'distra' portion and adds it to her list to cover with Yarjies.

Lana, "Very well then we will see you soon."

Yarjies, "Megan, be safe out there. We will see you at dinner tomorrow evening."

With the clock at 7:30 a.m. on this Saturday, the sun pushing through the scattered clouds and the air clear, both Lana and Yarjies agree to breakfast in the Guest House Café, on the small patio, in the sunshine.

Lana, "Does your little test normally have a different result than last night?"

Yarjies, "Actually no, last night was the first time I have used such an approach."

Lana, "Explain please."

Yarjies, "I could sense the two of us developing a sexual tension that will challenge our roles and our commitment. I had the thought of such a game at that moment and I proposed it to you as I thought of it."

Lana, "So, this was an elaborate diversion?"

Yarjies, "I was not sure of the outcome. I was not sure of either of our reaction the next day. I should have just said something. I should have alerted you."

Lana, "You are too cunning at times but this one may have preserved our ability to continue working together. Thank you for that even though I may have to kick your ass at least once to return the pain of my loss."

Yarjies, "Loss? You have loss?"

Lana, "It is okay, that tease of undressing was exciting to me and the ten minutes of waiting was a time of expectation that had me ready. I had me ready. So, the tension you were recognizing has been intensified. I will resolve my needs, as I sometimes must, by myself now."

Yarjies, "An unintended consequence I could not anticipate. Please forgive me. I have become adept at separating my life into boxes or categories. I know it is not consistent or honest but I am compartmentalized. Our one opportunity was, most likely, last night. As Megan would say, 'We are now', or after breakfast will be, 'on the clock'."

Lana, "We have a lot to go over…after breakfast. Waiter? Coffee? Juice?"

After breakfast Yarjies first takes a few minutes to have a closer look at the yard art displayed in the courtyard. Lana returns to the room for another shower and to prepare for the day. She expects this day to be tense, enlightening and challenging. She has continued to have thoughts of Baetus's last words and knows that she needs to find that center or conviction or destiny or that faith that will direct her and guide her through the gauntlet before her. The generation of her birth is the latest manifestation of the human will to triumph over evil that is manifest in the form of an ideology of mastery, of dominance and of control. To be a part of bringing a people back to those days before the tragedies to a life she knew only as a youngster.

Lana whispers to herself the thought, "Don't you have to find something before you can share it?" She laughs a little, "I must be lost or nuts."

The room has a convenient sitting area before the small fireplace which is opposite the windows. The light from the windows creates shadows on the wall before Lana. There is a small couch and a chair with big, padded arms and a deep seat that she will curl into with a pen and notepad. She often writes down ideas, thoughts that are abstract or serious, phone numbers and memorable dates. So, with Lana expecting a lot of information with details she will not immediately remember she has armed herself with her 'Memory Kit', as she calls it, and falls into the security of the chair. Yarjies will sprawl on the couch just fine, she thinks.

As Lana settles and waits for Yarjies her thoughts return to Baetus which leads to her memory of her mother. A return to this level of evaluation and thinking adds an emotional level of experience that may be tipping the balance for Lana. This two day immersion may become a nightmare. Lana reminds herself of her mother and the reliance on the priest for information that was not readily available. Lana has always strived to maintain self-control and self-determination. She knows that she can't relax and she must confront spiritual, physical, mental and emotional challenges. Some will be incidental and unintended. Others will be intentional, malicious, evil and destructive. The key is to have discernment and understanding, combined with clarity of experience that will produce a value of truth possibly leading to wisdom.

Lana is anxious to get through this aspect of the planning. Since the loss of Norsha Lana has become more engaged emotionally and committed to intentionally fill a role even if quite different from the expectations. She knows that, often, the person at the right hand of a leader will wield more power and control through his or her influence to facilitate and anticipate the leadership's needs. She is reminded of her father's notebook. She has not opened it since leaving Chicago. As she begins digging in her bags for the notebook Yarjies returns with a knock as he opens the door.

Yarjies, "I lost track of time. Some of the art work in the courtyard is fairly interesting. Some of the intricacies are familiar but I cannot place them exactly. Anyway, it is quite interesting."

Lana continues disassembling one bag for the book at the bottom and not responding because of the effort to find the notebook.

Yarjies, "Are you stuck in there?"

Lana, "No, no, just trying to remove something. Did I miss anything?"

Yarjies, "You may like to have a look at the art downstairs. It is pretty interesting."

Lana, "I will later in the day. What I would like to do, as soon as you are ready, is to begin to review and assemble an outline of our goals and a timeline for our activities."

Yarjies, "I am not a certified trainer, as Norsha, but I can give you most of the information as she would. I think that the overall view that I can clarify for you will be enough understanding for you to be grounded and prepared to step forward into your responsibilities. Megan will also be helpful when she returns."

Lana, "I cannot absorb everything so I will be taking notes. Also, I have my father's notebook which has been my only connection to our people and our history. There are sections that I have not spent any time with because, at first reading, I did not understand the subjects. Hopefully you will be able to clarify the context for me."

Yarjies, "I will do my best. If you are comfortable there, as you appear to be, I will take the couch here and we will go until we need a break. As much as we will need to talk about issues, I know you will need time to reflect and contemplate some of the subject matter. We will attend to those points along the way as you become aware of them."

Lana, "Let's get started."

Yarjies, "Give me just one minute, please," as he rushes to the bathroom, "to much coffee this morning."

Lana sits back in the large chair as she closes her eyes to focus her awareness and attention on the room, the sounds from activities outside and her own breathing rate. As she exhales slowly and feels the sense of calm extend through her body and the lengths of her arms Lana hesitates momentarily before breathing in slowly as a way of absorbing her awareness, her energy, her edge, her courage and all that she feels of a spiritual presence and understanding.

Lana's connection to her remembrance of spiritual or metaphysical principles has not been advanced by her studies since her adolescent years. At age fifteen she no longer recognized the relevance and interconnectivity of the spiritual realm or the adherent religious rituals and regimens. Lana completes her exercise as Yarjies returns to the couch where he takes a relaxed, sprawling position as though he is about to fall asleep.

Yarjies, "Let us begin with a big picture perspective. Then we will discuss as many small picture elements as necessary for your understanding."

Lana, "Good strategy, Yarjies, I agree."

Yarjies, "The base line goal is to establish and renew our regional security, integrity and self-reliance. There will be many gradual steps that will be necessary which must inter-connect to accomplish our overall goals on a personal, philosophic and cultural basis. This will mean combating both our obvious enemies and the subversive elements living among us and even within each of us."

Lana, "Briefly, on that point of 'among us and even within us', this is one of those small picture elements for further discussion."

Yarjies, "Okay, noted, but for now a little background. Others have been gathered and working together as the leadership group for us with the exception of you, Miss Ann, through no fault of your own. Your location was not known until archives were discovered hidden at the church rectory. When examined for links to this generation your whereabouts was pursued. We are now in the gap and it is our duty to remember, strengthen and promote the advancement of our people. The past is our anchor and our foundation. The present is our contribution to the building of the civilization our forbearers established. To establish individual initiatives through a freedom of opportunity that is tempered with moral absolutes.

You, Miss Ann, are becoming a Warrior Shepherd. You are one of four. You have the natural assets and the trained skills of your everyday life that will be sharpened and enhanced to the degree you allow."

Lana, "You have given me a slight sense of relief. To know I am part of a group and a team, which is excellent. I am accustomed to working as a contributor rather than a leader. Sorry if that surprises you."

Yarjies, "I pretty much have figured that out and I know you will excel once the blinders, so to speak, and barriers have been removed."

Lana, "That being said, then, I want to focus on my portion of the leadership first and briefly then move quickly to the warrior part."

Yarjies, "Okay, why?"

Lana, "It doesn't matter what my role is if I don't get there. I am ready for one on one action, not so much the slinking and hiding in plain sight. I know that it has been necessary until now. I am ready to 'transition' as you put it, of course, with a different meaning technically."

Lana's verbal jab wasn't missed by Yarjies. "Enough with the personal or I will be kicking your ass, most respectfully, of course." Yarjies gives back and then nods slightly as they both smile.

Lana, "I was raised near the area that is north of our traditional region. Where are the other three members of the leadership group from?"

Yarjies, "You grew up close to the town of Pforzheim. As you might expect, the three are each from one of the other zones. We have a lot of open terrain, as you must remember, with very dense forest and very rough, extreme changes in elevation. The villages form a unique grid and platform to plan and operate from. You will remember as soon as you are within the area again."

Lana, "The forest I will never forget. I was a part of it when I was growing up. So, why me? I have been out of the country for more than thirty years. I am an American for all practical purposes."

Yarjies, "That is a large measure of your value. It is your experience, your education, your sense of liberty and freedom that we are trying to renew here. You can speak to the reality of the principles that give common sense reasoning to the questions we have only been able to answer from our technical understanding. We have not had the experience of living it."

Lana, "That is a bit vague but I will begin to process other aspects that we cover through that lens. Nuts and bolts concerns now, we have to get from here to Rotterdam,"

Yarjies, "That is one of the assignments that Megan is taking care of since she has local contacts to work with."

Lana, "I want to delve into the metaphysical/spiritual elements and what I need to understand to be on the same page, so to speak, with everyone else within my role. Again, to review, I was raised as a Christian simply because my mother was Christian. I did not understand what we believed. My father had become a bit of a rebel in this arena and he had begun reading and researching the scriptures for answers, for guidance and understanding. He was of the faith shared by our ancestors. To do so in those days was to think outside the box. He had only begun to teach me what he had come to understand when the fighting erupted and we were separated."

Yarjies, "What do you remember most? You mentioned before that you have not been religiously observant or involved for your adult years. What are your positions today?"

Lana, "I am not connected in any way. I don't have a great desire to be involved in a religion. I side with my dad. I need more information for reflection."

Yarjies, "We have some time for these subjects because these issues are fundamental to your personal foundation."

Lana, "I referred to my mother earlier. She gave me this explanation of what the soul is and how my soul is affected by my decisions. Keep in mind that I was eight or nine at the time and she was trying to explain a curious concept to a child.

I understood, of course, my body and that a part of my body is my brain or mind. It is soul or spirit, unseen but present, that I did not understand. Her description was that my soul is similar to an invisible, special shirt that I liked more than any other. I cannot take it off but I can make it look bad, get it dirty or even ruin it. I can affect it with the presence of sin in my life because each time I sin I put a stain on or a tear in the shirt.

The only way to remove the stains or mend the tears is to ask forgiveness and to make different choices. The consequence of refusing to seek forgiveness by admitting guilt and changing will be a separation from God while in this state and when I die if I remain in this state."

Yarjies, "That is a unique description of the soul and sin's effect. I have heard variations that are similar. I really believe that children should have access to the same information as adults. I see how you would be skeptical and confused about the subject. What have you done with the information since then?"

Lana, "Actually during my early twenties I found myself growing anxious about life's meanings, personal goals and my purpose in creation. I had read a lot about alternative religious beliefs. I was beginning to explore."

Yarjies, "Did you resolve any discrepancies?"

Lana, "I did resolve many. I did resolve the questions of soul and sin. The references and notes of my father's notebook became the framework of my study and influenced my conclusions. I need to spend some time before leaving the safety of this place renewing my understanding of his writings."

Yarjies, "I would be interested in your resolution of soul and any references that I can check."

Lana holds out the notebook for Yarjies to see the emblem on the cover. Yarjies is surprised by the emblem and comments, "Miss Ann, something is familiar in some of the yard art outside." Pointing he continues, "This part, the three concentric circles with the offset gaps or doorways in each, is in one of the pieces."

Lana, "I have seen a lot of art, both ancient and contemporary with concentric circles. It is a common design form."

Yarjies, "I understand but I think this style is unique. I don't know what it represents in either this emblem or the artwork."

Lana, "You have actually pinpointed the emblem's representation of the principle I was just discussing, within the context of a bigger understanding of human nature."

Yarjies, "You are knocking on my door, so to speak, with such discussions."

Lana, "We are getting off track again. This is no longer about me saving the universe. I feel it is important to first dissect the zeitgeist of our people. In this dynamic I am responding to my technical sense of a people and a place I have not experienced since childhood."

Yarjies, "You are in that area of exploration and understanding now. You said earlier that you first have to discover something before you can share it."

Lana, "Yes."

Yarjies, "Whenever you pursue solutions by finding the path that begins with you the answers will be there. Seek clarity and truth will appear."

Lana, "You are correct. How about lunch first?" smiling.

Yarjies, "We can walk down to the café and I will show you the art I mentioned. If you need more time away from this – okay, but we do have limited time, so please keep that in mind."

Lana, "I am okay with getting something for the room and eating here. I do not want to waste time. I haven't spare time to give. I do appreciate your consideration."

Yarjies, off of the couch quickly, reaches for Lana's hand to extract her from the chair, "here we go now!"

Concentric Circles

Lana begins while chewing the first bite of her sandwich, "If you want references they are in the notes. I will speak of what I know from my father's writings more than from personal understanding. I am working on it." Teasingly Lana adds, with a mischievous grin, "Sounds familiar Yarjies?"

Yarjies, "Now the humor comes out. You're getting nervous? Huh?"

Lana, "Quite so" as she loses the smile. "These are old subjects from long ago."

Yarjies, "I will see you through, Miss Ann. I will see you through."

Lana, having finished most of her meal, brushes her hands together and sits back into the large chair. "Humans are made up of body, soul and spirit. The references do vary slightly in terms but with the same root word meaning. Most of this is rudimentary but not obvious unless the language of origin is understood."

Yarjies, "Okay?"

Lana, "So, now, the body is the physical creature experienced through the five senses of sight, touch, smell, taste and hearing. The spirit is the one part of us that is created in God's likeness. That leaves the soul. The soul consists of three elements; the mind, the will and the emotions. Are you following me?"

Yarjies, "Yes but I am the one needing to take notes. You are giving me a lot to review and explore."

Lana, "Okay, the next consideration is the inter-connectivity of the three elements of the soul with the three spheres of each creature that is human based on the presence of all three components."

Yarjies, "Are you leading to your resolution of soul?"

Lana, "This subject can blossom."

Yarjies, "We can stay with the big picture-little picture approach."

Lana, "Well then, big picture, we are human and we are made up of body, soul and spirit. Little pictures abound. How long have such subjects divided the minds and hearts of individuals, groups and nations? How much pain has been inflicted because of ignorance and the manipulation of truth to gain power?"

Yarjies, "Let us go back to the individual."

Lana, "The three concentric circles represent the human. The outer is the body, the middle is the soul and the inner most is the spirit. The assembly of the three rings is positioned within the center of a hexagram with each side representing one of the gateways for interacting with the outside world of creation.

Those gateways are listed in the notebook as; reality, imagination, reason, logic, faith and intuition or discernment. Each side has a portal. The three concentric spheres are moveable and will rotate as the individual determines either consciously or instinctually. Are you still with me, Yarjies?"

Yarjies, "I am there. Of course, these symbols represent what is working within each of us and around each of us whether we are aware or not."

Lana, "That is correct. Those who do understand are able to manipulate these elements to affect their own contentment, circumstances, other individuals and to a certain extent, the risks and rewards. Those who do not understand or are unaware of these elements are being manipulated and controlled without any flags being raised. One reason morality or an honorable character is necessary for liberty and freedom to succeed is because these dynamics can swing to either extreme and destroy any opportunity for the success of good."

Yarjies, "What, then, is the connecting path from spirit to body?"

Lana, "Well, this area of thought can be more open to interpretation. Often this point offers religion the opportunity to manipulate doctrine by establishing a dogma that may alter, pervert, embellish or sanctify a principle so as to establish an authority."

Yarjies, "You really struggle with authority."

Lana, "I struggle only with inept, immature, arrogant authority that thinks it only needs to stomp its foot to get what it wants."

Yarjies, "Your very words are highlighting our need for the leadership that is being assembled with your arrival as the last piece. You see, this is what you bring. You speak inspiration from your experience. No planning, just naturally from within you."

Lana, "Okay but this is an understanding of what operates in the background, so to speak. How these principles are interacting through individuals as a society on the governing authority is our challenge to focus on. Let us transition now to the rest of the team. That is, you and Megan, right now."

Yarjies, "Why do you say, 'right now'?"

Lana, "I want to be optimistic but reality has been knocking us around lately."

Yarjies, "I understand. We do face every possibility of changes being made but, hopefully, they will be constructive. So, what are you saying you need?"

Lana, "First, I think we should bring Megan back as soon as she is available and include her in our strategies."

Yarjies, "She will join us as soon as her assignments are completed."

Lana, "What about you, Yarjies, do you have a close companion?"

Yarjies does no respond immediately. He pivots on the couch and puts his feet up on the opposite end of the couch so that he now faces Lana. "I did but I don't."

Lana, "This is not a good subject for you?"

Yarjies, "Briefly, there was someone. Her name is Amber. She was not a bit involved in our struggle or controversies. The fight we are engaged in was never near her door, so to speak. Well, not until the days of darkness devoured her. We met on a free night at a popular brew-house. Random seating, as this place is known for, put us together at a table when the show was about to start."

Lana, "What kind of a show is it?"

Yarjies, "Well, there will usually be a solo musician or comedian or magician on stage. The real entertainment though is the patrons entering the venue. You see, the entrance to the club is a hall way that leads to the back of the stage so that everyone becomes a part of the act as they enter. Some are fools waiting to be discovered and some are terrified by the experience. It is quite hilarious and frightening at the same time. The experience is very unique."

Lana, "So, you two separated mutually?"

Yarjies, "No, she was murdered by the Rochukas during the days of darkness not long ago."

Lana, "That is twice now that you have used this term, 'days of darkness'. What do you mean?"

Yarjies, "Part of our struggle over the years has been to control the 'days of darkness' which occur somewhat randomly.

We should go into this subject later in our timeline. Let us complete the individual level first."

Lana, "Megan, her skin, her ability to change and her classification."

Yarjies, "May we take a break? It looks like it will rain again. The clouds and mist are back. I want to be outside for a few minutes before it is so dreary. There are times when I need to literally touch the earth, a tree, something of nature. There have been times when just running my fingers through the grass has a calming effect. I struggle with the loss of Amber. The brutality and horror she experienced was more than anyone should experience."

Lana, "I am sorry for bringing up sorrowful thoughts."

Yarjies, "I think of her daily as it is. Her memory fuels my desire to see our adversaries defeated and destroyed."

Lana, "We will succeed, God willing, very soon."

Yarjies, "Megan's classification is Chameleo-distra. She is one of only ten individuals, advanced field scouts, who have the ability, as a chameleon does, to change her colors and blend with her surroundings. This is accomplished by application of a coating on her skin, similar to a lotion that has several color pigments combined in a cellular level micro-crystalline polymer base structure that absorbs and reflects light to affect the pigments which interact with the properties of her skin. Megan can also manipulate the effect by using her emotional control to mimic stress or excitement and other such psychological tactics to change her color. The compound remains active until it is removed. Once removed the compound is similar to old paint that loses its useful properties. It dries out very quickly to be discarded as a powder.

The distra represents her ability to distract or re-direct the attention of others in a subtle way during an event or other interactions as she may determine."

Lana, "Was this compound developed by our people?"

Yarjies, "It was not developed as much as it was discovered. About ten years ago a container of a similar substance was found in the possession of a beast that had been trapped during a raid on an encampment of the creatures during the 'days of darkness' several years ago. We are not sure if their use was for the same purpose or if the effect on their putrid skin was the same. Again the effect was discovered during analysis when a small quantity was put on a volunteer so the process could be observed. Through trial and error it was found that not everyone can use the substance effectively or learn to manipulate the effects as Megan and the others can."

Lana, "Let us take that break now." She rushes to the bathroom, refreshes and returns, ready to go outside. Yarjies had moved to the window to check the weather, Lana assumed, then stopped quietly. Yarjies was crying silently. Lana recognized the shudder of his shoulders and the tension in his neck. She now understood the depth of his desire and commitment to not only the cause but to the retribution due for the taking of his one, true, exotic, fulfilling joy in life. Lana walked quietly to him and put her arm around his neck, "I am here."

Yarjies turns to her and they hug tightly. Yarjies, "Forgive me. I loved her."

Lana, "Her soul can live through you because of your knowledge of her and your experiences with her. If she is in your heart, she is in this life."

Yarjies takes a deep breath and releases from Lana. "Okay, how about that break."

With the day beginning to pass and the evening of their last night before entering the network very close Lana begins to feel the pressure to double down on her efforts and to move along with their improvised timeline. First, though, Yarjies needs time to recover his focus.

The two walked together slowly through the courtyard and into the midst of the yard art. Lana, "For what it's worth, I also have lost someone for this cause. Not to death but by separation. It is likely forever, so I do empathize with your feelings."

Yarjies, "Thank you for your understanding and strength."

Lana, "Please show me the art piece with the design you were describing. You know, we will both need courage and strength in the days ahead. I have learned and changed through our experiences. I have leaned on you a lot and I want you to know that you can lean on me as well."

Yarjies, "I am excited about tomorrow's change of pace and our entry into the final leg of our trip into Europe. We will, within two days, be at our destination and be in preparation for our first assault... or assignment."

Lana gives him a shove to the side with her shoulder, "Soon it will be 'time to move'!"

With dusk now upon them the tour of the art comes to an end. Yarjies, "Let us grab some dinner while we are here and then head for the room to eat and make the most of our remaining time."

Lana, "We will be making the 'most of our time' while 'on the clock'." Alana makes the quote signs with her fingers.

Yarjies, "Yea... that's what I meant." They both laugh and walk to the food vendors' plaza which now has a sign by the street as a marque listing the vendors for passing foot traffic and those on the roadway. As they pass a large tree on the side of the street Megan walks from the tree where she was concealed while waiting to join them. Her colors fluctuate slightly as she approaches them.

Lana, "Hello stranger, it is good to see you again."

Yarjies, "Hi Megan. Hey, are you alright?" Yarjies notices her irregularity of appearance and knows that she is struggling.

Megan, "I may be tired. I have been feeling good until just now while waiting by the tree."

Yarjies, "How long have you been covered?"

Megan, "Not that long. I don't think I am having a rejection but my emotions are spent after this trip to make our arrangements."

Yarjies, "Did something out of the ordinary take place? Were you in contact with any of the forbidables?"

Lana, whispers quietly to herself, "Forbidables?"

Megan, "I am clean as far as I know."

Lana, "We will help you to the room so you can gather yourself."

Megan, "Thank you Miss Ann."

Yarjies, "Miss Ann, if you will help Megan to the room I will go to the drugstore for the supplies that we will need for her cleansing."

Lana, "I may have what we need in my bag, what is it?"

Yarjies, "We will need uncontaminated isopropyl alcohol that is at least 85% pure, Mediterranean oregano oil and apple cider vinegar."

Lana, "See you back here soon."

Megan, "I have not been exposed."

Lana, "Let us get out of the public view, then we will solve the problems."

Lana goes ahead of Megan to open doors and check for any guests that may accidentally cross their path. As she looks back at Megan she sees Megan's color fluctuate as she moves slowly. Lana returns to Megan's side as she begins to climb the stairs to the room. "Let me help you," Lana insists, "a team takes care of one another and we are a team."

Once in the room Megan drops onto the small couch and begins to perspire profusely. Lana's reaction is to check her vital signs. She notes that Megan is conscious and aware but confused and anxious to get up and move around.

"Recline with your back flat on the floor with your feet higher than your heart," Lana commands. Megan responds to each instruction without hesitation. Suddenly she returns to her common cognitive state of mind as before.

Yarjies returns from the store, goes straight to the bath and begins filling the tub with cool water. Returning then to the sitting area he asks Lana to re-evaluate Megan's status and be prepared to perform the cleansing needed when he asks. Agitated, Lana asks, "What is your evaluation, Yarjies? Am I at risk by doing this?" Lana pulls Yarjies away from Megan's hearing, "I think you should explain what needs to be done. I have no problem doing what is necessary, as long as I understand the situation and as long as I am not played for a fool. Though I value my calling and my apparent sanction I do also value my life."

Yarjies, "Now I must question your commitment!"

What neither Lana, Yarjies nor Megan have understood is that their current situation, the harshness and the confusion are the effects of an attack by their adversary at a much higher, spiritual level than they are operational in. Through subconscious correlation the cycle is fear, freight, terror.

Megan, "We know that this is our struggle and this is our fate."

Yarjies, "For your sake," pointing to the half-filled tub, "Megan, this is your struggle and this is your fate! Get in now!"

As Megan enters the bathroom Yarjies withdraws, closes the door and signals for Lana to wait for him at the window. "You need to Just rest in the water Megan."

Yarjies walks toward Lana and recognizes that she appears to be afraid of him. Her eyes widen and she attempts to step away but bumps into the wall behind her.

Yarjies, "Miss Ann, though you cannot see anyone else here with us I know, from experience, that we are being attacked. It is a spiritual, sub-conscious level of attack. Are you listening to me?"

Lana, covering her face with her hands, "Your image has changed and your appearance is frightening to me."

Yarjies, "It is an illusion. Trust me and open your eyes. I have not changed." The soothing nature of his voice calms Lana so she lowers her hands to see the man she knows.

Lana, "I have never experienced something so bizarre. Is Megan alright?"

Yarjies, "She is fine. She has experienced such attacks. It is her assignments which take her into areas of extreme spiritual turmoil and warfare. There are times when the entities follow her and cause this type of upheaval and conflict. Calm has returned now. What I need for you to do is to help Megan. The removal of the coloring compound is usually a simple procedure of washing. There are occasions when either the formula has been exposed before use or something environmental has affected the quality. Our researchers do not have a precise answer for this. When this type of adverse reaction occurs a more involved process is required. I am asking you to do this because of the gender difference in this case."

Lana, "If you will tell me what to do and I will get it done."

After a detailed explanation and review of the procedure Lana starts for the bathroom. Yarjies begins looking out the windows as though he is expecting someone. From the courtyard below a flash of reflected light catches his attention. The courier has arrived with their essentials of currencies, passports and transportation tickets. Yarjies has but a couple of minutes to make the exchange. He grabs his jacket and walks to the bathroom door he knocks, "Everything going well in there?"

Megan, "Yes, I will be ready soon."

Lana, "Okay, we are okay."

Yarjies, "I need to step out for a few minutes. I will return quickly." The door closes behind him as he walks briskly to the courtyard. Now, with the skies beginning to darken, the misty, wet air now dripping with condensation on cool surfaces everything is wet. The cold is penetrating. The only pedestrians are patrons of the Guest House crossing the courtyard or dining at the café. Yarjies' contact has moved inside to the café to blend as much as possible. Yarjies stops before entering to remove his cap and jacket and shake off the cold. Walking past the desk Yarjies seats himself and lays his jacket on the chair to his right with the courier across from him.

The waiter begins to ask, "May I …"

Yarjies raises his hand slightly, "Tea please."

The courier slips the envelope under his cap on the chair. The tea arrives quickly. Yarjies hands the waiter more than enough, "Thanks so much."

The courier, without speaking, gets up as the waiter leaves, bows slightly at the waist and then leaves. Yarjies has but a few sips of his drink before returning to Lana and Megan. Lana opens the door for Yarjies. Megan is resting in the big chair. Yarjies places the envelope in his bag and walks to the sitting area, inviting Lana to join him on the couch. "It is time for us to begin a discussion of our next phase which will be the stretch run and the most dangerous part of our travels to get to our center of planning and operations."

Megan, "What I am beginning to see as I travel and especially on my way here is an intensifying of activity. There are more skirmishes along the French border and there is a lot of chatter within our communications networks. Our local friends that have been sympathetic are beginning to distance themselves to avoid a direct involvement in any conflict that could cause the government forces to be activated."

Lana, "I need to know what our immediate strategy is for completing this journey. When we arrive will we know what to do next?"

Yarjies, "If I may, Megan, did you have an opportunity to see Baetus before coming here?"

Megan, "Only briefly because we were both in network at the time. You know how impersonal that can be."

Yarjies, "Well, hopefully, we will all be working more closely together soon."

Lana, "What is meant by 'in network'?"

Megan, "The network is our system of logistics and management of resources which are primarily people. Once you enter the network you become the responsibility of handlers who control the decision making. They manage the transfer points, the other tangible resources such as money, travel vouchers or tickets, housing and personal supplies such as food, clothing and hygiene products. You become part of a network that is behind the scenes and in control of the scene as it pertains to resources. In this case, the three of us, are the resources."

Lana "Sounds very restrictive and controlling. Are we limited to the 'in network' system?"

Yarjies, "The network is very efficient and reliable. We have been under the umbrella since the day before you and I met."

Lana, "Such a machine like system can be suffocating."

Megan, "You won't realize the need until a crisis occurs and then afterward, when you look back you will recognize the advantage of such a network."

Yarjies "Let me run through the schedule that we are now set to follow. We will travel from this area to Rotterdam by charter boat as part of a group. From Rotterdam we travel by train to Cologne, Germany before stopping for the night. We will depart Cologne early in the morning and arrive in Speyer, Germany where we will be housed until you, Miss Ann, are to be received by the group you are to join and Megan is reassigned. I will remain available to you during a short transition period."

Lana, "What do you mean by short?"

Yarjies, "That will be dependent on your rate of assimilation."

Lana, "I want the three of us to talk on a personal level without reverting to slogans or talking points that are political. For example, I would like to understand how our people, who have always been a minority within the minority classes, can never just live our lives among other groups in peace. We attract hate from others without deserving it. We even turn on one another when our enemies have us cornered."

Yarjies, "We are not the only ones to put self-preservation before other commitments."

Lana, "I understand but I am focused on OUR group. Our people have such a history of both hardship and blessing. The hardships are usually self-induced. The adversary we face now is from our own source, even our own seed!"

Megan, "I think we must first defeat our enemy of today before we can set a cornerstone for tomorrow."

Lana, "It is the gap between those two steps that is critical. If a vacuum or void in time is allowed to take hold we will not survive the chaos with any strength left to set that cornerstone."

Yarjies, "I am fully committed to the annihilation of the Rochukas. More than our physical survival is at stake. A healing and a renewal of our spiritual relationship with God must be a goal if we are to succeed."

Lana, "I ask again, why this struggle? The war is long over. Can we not start over and rebuild as so many have? Tell me your answer, Yarjies and yours Megan?"

Yarjies, "Since this geographic area is the place of the breach it is to be the trans-dimensional battle ground. We all want to go home and live in peace. First we must defeat the enemy to allow the healing of the tear in our existence."

Megan, "We carry the battle for ourselves directly and for humanity as our ultimate goal of victory over the Rochukas and the evil from which they are produced."

Lana, "Where is God? Can He not walk among us? Where is His hand at work in all of this?"

Yarjies, "He provides the guidance which we must discern and understand. He provides the strength and endurance when we need it."

Megan, "He causes every beat of our hearts. He gives each of us every breath that we take."

Lana, "My perspective? It was a human that invited the evil and it will be humans that end the horror of this evil. Each person must choose a side and accept the consequences of their choice because each of us has a free will."

Yarjies, "You are beginning to question yourself again. I know you are moving from the peaceful and somewhat relaxed lifestyle of a great city in America to a high stakes leadership role with people you don't really know. This may seem like, to you, a rural feud that is only locally significant."

Lana, "I am nervous and scared, plain enough?"

Yarjies, "You have performed beautifully to this point. I have every confidence you will be prepared, able and proficient at the tasks you engage. I trust you, Miss Ann." Yarjies reaches over and puts his arm around Lana's neck to pull her close and whispers to her, "Be strong and courageous."

Megan repeats aloud, "Be strong and courageous."

Lana, "Okay, okay, I will suck it up and ask for help when I need it."

Yarjies, "One area that I know the trainer was to brief you on was local terrain, boundaries, strategic locations and historic background, which you may not need. Even though it is getting late I think we should spend some time, before sleeping, discussing these topics based on my and Megan's knowledge.

Any maps or topographical information will be available when we reach our destination."

Lana, "Why are we operating from the Speyer/Heidelberg area?"

Yarjies, "I think it is because leadership thought it wise to have some distance between the operations center and the conflict zones."

Megan, "Only your group and the support staff are in Speyer. Couriers are our primary mode of communication with the field."

Lana, "I know these are ancient towns and the people, our ancestors, have been here more than a thousand years. That is our heart. That being said, where is our brain? There are resources available that we may be able to use. Do you know what I am talking about?"

Megan, "You are referring to the portable radio? We don't have a grid here. We are still occupied by the Allied Military that can monitor such communications. We may not be on the cutting edge of technology but our system works well for us."

Yarjies, "It is now past midnight. Let us review some of these topics."

Lana, "Okay, you take the lead, Yarjies. I will ask any questions that come up."

Yarjies, "To begin, each of us grew up in different locals of our ancestral region which is the area encompassing the Black Forest. I was born in a small village near Herrenberg which is south of Stuttgart, on the eastern boundary. Megan was born in Offenburg, on the western boundary, which was home to many of our people until the wars when they became the victims of repression and, eventually, deportation to the containment areas. The ancient history of this greater area includes the first demands for individual rights and democratic government in the history of Germany. Having been declared a Free Imperial City of The Holy Roman Empire in the early thirteenth century the area was a target of Napoleon who destroyed the city. Offenburg, being very close to the border with France, was subjected to their cruelty in the seventeenth century.

Miss Ann, you are from Pforzheim? This is, I think, to become our center of operations soon. The city and the area have been conditioned by wars past and rebuilt more than once. It being at the northern edge of our state, as it is called now, allows access to the conflict zones by river, road and trail. The trails are of special use by our couriers who travel by foot and by bicycles that have been reworked to handle the terrain. The convergence of the three rivers, Enz, Nagold and Wurm and the valley in which the town was built gives it the name of 'The Three Valleys Town', in English."

Lana, "This now is what I remember. As part of the forest our back yard opened into a lifetime of discovery and adventure among the large rocks, structures of sandstone and the trees that were life systems for so many creatures. The soft floor of leaves, needles from the conifers and moss all mixed with the native hardwoods which, to me as a child, were huge pillars holding up the clouds and standing as guards against the wind. I have missed it all for years. In this sense I am so thankful to return."

Yarjies, "Do you recall our discussions not long ago about the tactic of shadowing groups for our purposes?"

Lana, "Yes I do but not clearly."

Yarjies, "This is a change of subject but I will need to share information as it comes to mind. I will have to decide if it is relevant or not, okay?"

Lana, "And where is this going?"

Yarjies, "My thinking now is of the different areas of operations that are currently being engaged. I remember a report in the last two or three weeks about aggressive activities along and across the French border, in the Rheinau stretch of the river frontages. I wanted to explain that this may actually be a case of these other groups, such as The New Red Army, and their offshoots of anarchist groups clashing with the police and local law enforcement."

Lana, "And the connection is?"

Yarjies, "The clashes, at this particular time, complicate our activities because the law enforcement response in this geographical area and that the number of personnel they commit increases so that our ability to move around and engage our adversaries is restricted."

Lana, "So, the local government and the occupiers are not our adversaries?"

Megan, "No! The Rochukas is our enemy!" Lana sees flashes of Baetus in Megan's reaction.

Lana, "I am finally beginning to understand that our activities are more of a guerilla style strategy that must remain underground as much as possible. Is that correct?"

Yarjies, "That is correct. We are the current day Warriors of Ortenaukreis! We do not seek confrontation with the peoples of the cities, their authorities or the press. The thinking is that if we can remain in the background and contain the conflict within the remote areas of this interactive zone then the whole phenomenon can be masked. The results of our victory will be seen as the outcome of other initiatives by other individuals or groups. In the end the breach is closed and healed, our people's needs are met and society's balance is restored."

Lana, "Okay, I am ready to leave the philosophical focus and get into the struggle and get my hands dirty as the saying goes. It is time to make things happen so we can all move on with our lives and send the enemy running into the darkness."

Yarjies, "Are you saying, 'it's time to move!'?"

Lana, "Yes Sir! Megan, stand up here with us. Let us raise our hands and join together. Come here, Yarjies and Megan." The three stand close together, facing each other and each with their right hands joined overhead to form a point. Now repeat after me, 'For life, for truth, for liberty'! The three chant together loudly, "For life! For truth! For liberty!" As they separate and step away Yarjies checks the time, "Hey, everyone, it is now after one o'clock in the morning and we will need to be up by five a.m. to be on time for our connection with the travel group which embarks at six thirty a.m. I have already taken care of check out here so that all we have to do is dress and go in the morning. A shuttle van will pick us up here at five thirty."

Lana, while looking at Yarjies and smiling, "Okay no games tonight. Tomorrow we move!"

Megan, "I am ready to move!"

Lana, "Megan, would you like to sleep here rather than the couch?"

Megan, "Thanks but I will be fine on the couch. It is just my size."

Yarjies, "Okay, everyone, see you in a few hours."

With the lights out everyone is asleep quickly after a very active day. The cold, wet air will soon have them very awake and missing the warmth of their beds. Too soon the alarm sounds but no-one jumps up ready to go. Megan is the first up. She checks her skin tone and coloring for any lingering damage. She is pleased to find none. At the foot of each bed Megan lifts the covers and throws them back to uncover both Yarjies' and Lana's feet.

Beginning with Yarjies Megan lightly touches the souls of his feet to stimulate a response. Yarjies jerks his feet away from the stimulation and sits up, "alright, alright!" Before Megan can reach Lana's feet Yarjies' complaints wake her as she turns to her side momentarily before raising up to uncover and get out of the bed. "We're running behind already?"

Megan, "We have just run out of time to rest. We need to be out the door in twenty minutes."

The three, having gathered their bags, meet at the door with Yarjies muttering to himself. Lana jabs his side, "To early for you princess?"

Yarjies forces a smile, "You are the princess and I am the frog you will eventually have to kiss and make better."

Megan, "I think we all need to get out of here before we miss our ride."

As they make their way across the courtyard the sound of a car passing is the only indication of other activity. Once through the gate and onto the sidewalk in front of The Guest House their wait is very short as the taxi van pulls up to the curb. Only seats for the three of them are available. The other passengers, part of a group they have been merged with, are older tourists. They are welcoming as the side doors are opened for boarding. Everyone greets them in English with varying accents.

Megan offers a generalized greeting, "Hello, everyone, are you ready for the day?"

They have joined a group of tourists who are on their way to Holland. The group has agreed to take on new members as a way of sharing the transportation expense. This is what they were told by the tour guide. The tour guide is a member of the network. They each begin to blend into the group by beginning conversations with their new traveling companions. From Southend-on-Sea they pass Clacton-on-Sea and travel up the coast to Harwich for their trip, almost due East, across the North Sea to Rotterdam, following the 'Hook of Holland' route then the inland waterway into Rotterdam and eventually travelling from Rotterdam Southeast to Cologne, Germany.

First, the ride to the Port of Harwich which is a thirty to forty minute trip through business sectors, residential areas and commercial farm land northward along the coast from the Guest

House. The early morning air is cold and damp. As they near the Harwich port the sunrise begins to lighten the dark night sky as a light rain begins to fall.

Once out of the crowded van everyone stretches to loosen up then gather their personal belongings. Lana inhales a deep breath of the salty sea air blowing inland from the North Sea. The Harwich International Port complex is a commercial facility that serves cruise ships, commercial freight vessels and smaller, private water craft.

As everyone walks across the large parking area to enter the passenger terminal a shuttle pulls alongside the group and some of the elderly go aboard rather than walk. Lana, Megan, Yarjies and a couple of the group decide to walk. The air is heavy with moisture and the wind is gusting. One of the ladies walking with them has her baseball style cap blown from her head by the wind. As it skips across the parking lot the lady decides to just let it go and waves it good bye with a laugh. Megan runs after the cap but it eludes her attempts and with another strong gust of wind it is whisked into the water of a small ditch that drains to the waterway. At this she stops the chase and raises her hands in surrender. She shouts back against the wind to the group, "sorry!" and trots back to join them to enter the terminal.

As they walk up the steps of the rail road track cross over they can see the top decks of the large cruise ship that is moored at the docks. The day is predicted to be clear but the early morning visibility is still limited. The activity around the dock is minimal. As they walk into the terminal building they are passed by two street people being escorted from the waiting area by police officers. A pungent odor washes over them from the street people's clothing. The police officers are trying to keep them at arm's length as they push them out the doors and into the walkway.

Lana is relieved to find out their passage is aboard the cruise ship. She had visions of a rough, scary crossing in a small craft that would skip across the tops of large waves to escape being devoured by the huge, rolling, cold North Sea swells. Megan touches Lana's arm to snap her back to the present. "Are you ready to board Miss Ann?" Megan asks with an encouraging smile.

"Ready as I can be, Megan, let's move." Lana responds with a sudden rush of excitement.

Yarjies, ahead of them at the gate, motions for them to catch up. As they walk up behind him the Steward hands the tickets back to Yarjies, "Please board and enjoy your time with us."

The other members of the group gather to review their itinerary. Lana, Yarjies and Megan walk to the aft deck for a quick discussion of their immediate plans.

Yarjies, "Okay, this should be a simple, non-eventful, short sail to Rotterdam. The sea should not be very rough and the mist will clear as we enter open waters. I don't know what you ladies may prefer but I always like to be on a top deck, nearer the bar so I can avoid any smell of the ship and absorb the fresh air of the sea."

Megan, "I am comfortable with that. And you, Miss Ann?"

Lana, "I will do better inside. I like the wind in my face for about five minutes and then it becomes uncomfortable. You two can stay up top and I will go to the club room on the main deck."

Megan, "Are you alright?"

Lana, "I am fine. I am not much of a sailor."

Yarjies, "You prefer the mountains and the forest?"

Lana, "Yes, I will scale a rock face and sleep suspended on the side of a mountain and I am comfortable in the branches of the mighty trees, that's me."

Megan, "Why don't you like the sea?"

Lana, "My trip from Europe to America when I was young still un-nerves me a little when I think about it."

Megan, "Want to tell me about it?"

Lana, "Sure, but let's sit inside.

Megan, "Sure, Yarjies, I will catch up with you."

Lana continues, "You must realize now that I was a kid and unfamiliar with the ocean, okay? The first couple of days the weather was beautiful and the sea was relatively calm. There were a lot of children on board and we had activities to keep our interest within the ship. The only outside activity that I participated in was table tennis which was on the third deck, port side. To play the table tennis in this environment was comical because the wind was always blowing and the ship would roll slightly. As we played, if one of us hit the ball as the ship rolled it was impossible to anticipate where to intercept the ball for a return. We lost several over the side. Eventually we were told there were no more so we had to call it a day."

Megan, "So you were in trouble?"

Lana, "Yea, with the other kids. There just weren't any more."

Megan, "Not the best idea-table tennis on a ship in the open ocean I suppose."

Lana, "There was also a small movie theater on a lower deck that played cartoons and movies almost every hour. I spent a lot of time there. I didn't ever feel sick until the third day. The weather changed with the winds becoming stronger and the sea much rougher. The ship began to roll and pitch with more force and the distractions of the activities began to fade in effectiveness.

For the first time, during dinner, my plate slid from in front of me as I ate. It was funny to try to catch a piece of meat as my plate moved. The dining hall which is usually filled with the sounds of people talking and the motions of the servers among the tables was noticeably quiet as many began to consider the situation.

After dinner we were asked to return to our cabins and to remain there.

As I became quiet I began to focus on the sounds of the ship's structure groaning and creaking with the stress of the flexing materials. The sound of distant bells, growing louder as I listened, confused me until I recognized the chimes of the porter in the passageway."

Megan, "The porter was walking the passageway with the ship moving so much?"

Lana, "Yes and this is one memory that causes me to laugh each time I remember it."

Megan, "Why is it so funny?"

Lana, "Once I recognized the sounds of the chimes I pulled open the cabin door to look down the hall and saw the first indication of how much the ship was rolling side to side. I had to brace myself with my left hand against the wall with my right hand holding the door. The view down the hall gave the appearance of the whole structure rotating maybe thirty degrees with the floor almost becoming a wall and a wall becoming the floor. Then everything rolled to the opposite side. With all of the motion the porter, obviously very experienced, is traversing the length of the hallway with complete coordination to the movement. Whatever was under his feet, whether it be wall or floor, his path appeared to be straight and he never missed a note on the chimes!" Lana laughs, "I will never forget it!"

Megan, "With so much fun and excitement what is it that scares you about the trip and now the sea?"

Lana, "Well, in the morning, with the storm still raging we had to get to the dining room if we wanted to eat. As I walked past a door that opened onto the main deck I looked out the window and saw only water. I couldn't believe it. I stopped to open the door for a better look. As I slid the door open just a little I could then see only sky. I was real confused but I was being called to join the others that had walked on without me."

Megan, "Did you ever get a good look outside?"

Lana, "Well, after the meal, we were returning to our cabin. As I approached the same door I began to slow my pace so that others would go on past me."

Megan, "Being a bit sneaky were you?"

Lana, "Yea, my imagination and curiosity were taking control. I just had to figure out what was happening!"

Megan, "Were you scared at this point?"

Lana, "No, I was just driven to know what was happening. The mystery was growing for me. I approached the door and as I began to open it a crew member startled me by suddenly appearing beside me. He took my hand from the door and picked me up by my shoulders, you know, gently of course and set me down again out of the door way.

""Remain out of the way!" he commanded me as he opened the door and began to step out."

Megan, "With the weather so bad why would he be going outside?"

Lana, "This is where it gets scary. The door remained open with the wind and rain coming in. I looked out to see another man, possibly a passenger, clinging to the railing and looking very afraid. The crewman also held onto different pieces and took short, searching steps because the force of the wind might blow either of the men overboard."

Megan, "I can see how you would become frightened."

Lana, "I held onto the door frame just to keep my balance. I watched the two men struggle to return to the opened door. Then the background became the center of my attention."

Megan "Sounds like an intense time."

Lana, "The ship we were on was not a small craft at all. It was a commercial transport ship. However, the size and power of the waves in the open sea were so much greater. Whenever we were at the crest of a wave a person would have to look over the side rail and down to see the water and when at the trough of a wave one would have to look up to see the crest of the wave. This view, combined with the rain, the wind and two men clinging to anything within reach to survive was just so consuming for my inexperienced mind that I was frozen with fear and shock."

Megan, "Did the men make it inside?"

Lana, slightly dazed by the remembrance of the trauma that day, answered after a pause, "Yes they made it back in okay and I was soaked from standing at the doorway."

Megan, "You know, we as humans, can become so consumed with projections of self-worth and importance. We often forget, I think, how small we each are within this grand creation."

Lana, "You are right."

Megan, "Each of us is important. We do have a purpose, I mean, each has a unique role to play but our tunnel vision can limit our ability to see the big picture."

Lana, "That is very true. Myself, in that moment, as a child aboard a manmade vessel bobbing like a cork in the midst of an expansive, powerful, chaotic, churning ocean that could possibly swallow the entire group of us and we would never be found or heard from again! Amazing, isn't it? When I have remembrances of that experience I am drawn to a principle that is illustrated by the account given in the scriptures of Adam and Eve being enticed by Lucifer."

Megan, "Now that is a leap, from bobbing like a cork to being enticed by Lucifer?"

Lana, "Yea, well I could explain that a little better. Although Lucifer spoke to Eve, Adam could also hear the conversation. There was a connection between a human and an angel. The human was powerless if the angel had chosen to destroy them. Yet the angel chose the whisper of a lie to convince the humans that they could be as God. At that moment the point of focus was set on the pride of man. It has been the thorn in our collective side ever since. As I go back in thought to the little girl on a ship with other humans, bobbing like a cork at the mercy of a powerful force of nature I was not thinking of myself as a god. I was trying to decide if I could become a fish!"

Megan begins to laugh as Lana pauses with eyes opened wide and then joins in the ridiculousness of the thought.

Megan, "How long did the storm last?"

Lana, "I think it was three or four days. After it subsided we learned that we had passed through a portion of a hurricane. The rest of the trip was calm and uneventful by comparison."

Megan, "I can understand why you would be uncomfortable with sea travel. You are so amazing and funny Miss Ann. I enjoy your stories and your company. However, I think I will check on Yarjies and see if he has been staying out of trouble."

Lana, "Okay, I may join you soon. I want to wait until we are away from land to see how rough it is before I try to come topside."

As Megan left the club room area and started up the stairs to the upper decks Lana moved to a lounge chair close to an open window. Though she doesn't care for the wind to be in her face she does love the sounds of the water and wind mixing with the movement of the ship. She stretches out and begins to relax in the peaceful atmosphere, falling asleep.

Yarjies had found a nice, sunny part of the recreation deck to pause and survey the area for any activities, especially taking note of any interesting young women there. Unfortunately this trip's passengers seem to be older and the women were with husbands or boyfriends. Yarjies thinks to himself, "Man, our planners can do better than this! One of the risks of letting circumstances control planning!" He laughs to himself, knowing the joke is on him. Having fun these days is a kind coincidence at best, a fleeting tease, for the most part.

As Yarjies gets up to go in search of a drink he turns to see Megan walking toward him. She is swaying with the movement of the deck and occasionally losing her balance a bit so that her steps are jerky. "Hey there beautiful!" he shouts.

Megan stops, jokingly turns around as though to see whom he may be talking to, then turns again and points to herself with a questioning look. "Are you talking to me? Are we the only ones on board or something?" She continues to verbally jab at him.

Yarjies, "Yea, but you are beautiful. I am momentarily suspending the seriousness of our assignments but there is no-one to play with." He smiles as she steps to his side and he puts his arm gently around her shoulders. "Will you join me for a drink?" he asks.

"Actually", Megan responds, "I would like a large beer and some snacks."

Yarjies, "Alright, then, let's see what we can find. There has to be a crew mate here soon." Spotting a uniformed young man he calls him to come over. "Excuse me, sir, may we have a menu?"

The young man begins walking toward them but then stops. Yarjies sees the startled look on the crewman's face and instinctively pushes Megan to the side, away from him as he dives to the ground in the opposite direction, rolls to his back and removes a handgun from his waistband. Sitting up in a defensive firing position and looking back Yarjies sees the back and shoulders of two men retreating down the stairs at the end of the deck they were on.

Once pushed, Megan reacted appropriately by rolling away and seeking cover because she was not armed. Her instincts triggered her camouflage and she immediately blended with the table, chairs and wall that was behind her position. As soon as the threat was diminished they both realized Lana was not present. The two simultaneously rushed for the stairway and almost collided as they looked down to the club deck.

Megan moved to the side of the deck and began to slowly descend the service stairway. With the ship now clearing the jetties and entering the open waters a strong wave struck the windward, port bow of the ship and jarred the entire vessel slightly. Megan is slammed against the bulkhead but is able to maintain her footing. Yarjies was dislodged from the stairway and slid down the last couple of steps to the deck below.Remaining in a crouched position he quickly surveys the area to find no one there, including Lana. Thinking aloud, Yarjies comments, "What kind of a mess are we in now?"

Lana steps from the shadows at the far end of the club room and responds. "Yarjies? Are we okay?" Is Megan okay? I don't know what happened, exactly. I had a weird dream, I think."

Yarjies could hear movement nearby but could not see anyone. He quickly glanced to see Megan standing still which told him there must be a transitional there, with them. Using his wide angle, peripheral vision, which he had developed as a hunter, Yarjies began to detect a presence near the bar that was across the room from Lana. As Yarjies trained his focus on the darkness and began walking in that direction a figure emerged from the background. The form was large but moving with agility. Then Yarjies caught a glimpse of an insignia on the shoulder area of the individual.

"Norsha, is it you?" Yarjies asks with surprise. "So, you did escape the attack!" He briskly walks to her and embraces her, although his arms barely wrap around her shoulders. Norsha is forty years old, a morph with the psychological, emotional, sensory and intuitive attributes of a female and the physical strength, stamina and muscular build of a male.

Lana, "Who is this?"

Norsha, "I am here for your service. I am pleased to see that the network has kept us all on track to be together at this crucial time."

Lana, "Aren't you the trainer I was to meet in London? I, we, thought you were dead!"

Norsha responds coldly, "Well, if I am, no one informed me. I was able to avoid the plot to stop us and here I am."

Lana responds, "Welcome." Although she suspects there is a lot of detail missing.

As the ship turns into the wind a spray showers over the bow and washes the deck slightly. The reunited group goes to the dining room for lunch. The trip to Rotterdam is about two hours with good weather conditions so the four will have little time for training.

Yarjies, "As we eat we should focus on this next stage and discuss the logistics of our next couple of days."

Megan, "Let's eat first. I am very hungry and I do not want to become weak again."

Norsha, "Are you struggling, Megan?"

"I am fine," Megan responds quickly. "I just don't want to create any weak points as we ramp up for the next stage."

"Good thinking," Norsha answers, putting one hand on Megan's shoulder. Let's have a seat here. They rushed through an uneventful lunch because of the limited time.

Lana, "I know that once we arrive in Speyer I may be overwhelmed by my role but I am ready to get there. Since losing our time with you earlier Megan has been invested in providing what she can to supplement what we thought we had lost."

Norsha first turns to Megan, "Thank you Megan, I have every confidence in you to fill in for me if needed. Well done, faithful one." Norsha turns quickly to face Lana and steps forward to be very close and face to face with her. "You will succeed and I am here to make sure if it. Your insecurity will be changed before we arrive in Speyer and you will be ready."Norsha places a hand on each of Lana's shoulders and moves even closer so that their noses are almost touching and says with a firm, calm voice, "Your purpose, established before your birth, will be honored with strength and courage. Your ability to succeed is the responsibility of your soul and the vision of our cause. Another will secure the final victory but you must set the final work in motion by identifying the one to restrain."

Lana, "My role is The Identifier?" She immediately absorbs the spirit of Norsha's words and enters a transformational state as she is indwelled by a spiritual force of empowerment that is raising her psychological awareness, her sensory alertness, her cognitive capacity and her physical endurance.

A sense of an out of body awareness gives Lana a euphoric lightness of separation from the present surroundings. Norsha recognizes Lana's heightened sensitivity and adjusts her tone of speech to one that is more casual so as to return Lana to the presence of her surroundings.

Norsha, "Lana, you are a bit over the normal threshold of sensory awareness that is needed right now. This tells me that you are ready for the preparations I am here to see you through."

Lana, "I am ready. I will follow your directions. Let's move!"

With Norsha leading, her small entourage leaves the dining room for the cabins. They have adjoining cabins on the first deck, near the center of the vessel. Everyone enters together and Lana, led by Norsha, passes through the group and enters the second cabin with the door closing behind them and the lock clicking into place.

With Lana and Norsha alone the mood immediately becomes still and focused. The energy of the room is one of peace and calm. Lana begins to sit on the couch but Norsha takes her hand and lifts her up to stand. Norsha moves two straight backed chairs with slightly padded seats to the center of the room and facing each other, about a foot apart.

Lana joins her and the two sit to face each other. Norsha begins, "Lana I will briefly identify our adversaries and give you enough background to familiarize you with the challenges we face because of the nature of our goals."

Lana, "Thank you, Norsha; I do need this time to learn and understand."

Norsha, "During the time of great conflicts, when you were sent from your home, there was an evil at work that few could comprehend beyond the barbarism almost everyone was exposed to. It is difficult to imagine the depravity that people were reduced to for the hope of survival. There is no excuse for what some did but it is understandable in an abstract way."

Lana, "I am not sure what you mean."

Norsha, "I can easily say, from here, that I would not give in or become an animal for my own selfish sake. The anguish of all who had to make such decisions had to be rising as horrific screams to the heavens."

Lana, "I am becoming uneasy as I picture your descriptions."

Norsha, "The adversary we face, in many ways, is a potential that we all poses. Let me tell you about someone, as an example, who entered this gauntlet of survival by the most extreme measures. I have never met this man but I trust the accounts I have heard from others that were very close to him before this time. His name is Menachem. At the time of the compression our people were being consolidated into groups at separate locations. Families were being separated and individuals were becoming isolated. Many died from injury, starvation and neglect.

The elites were not able to maintain their control of the multitudes because of the accelerating events of the wars, the rising resistance of our people and our efforts to escape."

Lana, "I am sorry, Norsha, you are being too vague and I don't understand the context. This is during the great wars, right? You are speaking of the genocide against our tribes, correct?"

Norsha, "Yes! I am not complaining about some school yard bullies! Why do you think we are here?" Norsha realizes that she is beginning to lose her composure. "Miss Ann, I am sorry. I have spent my life getting to this point and I occasionally lose my temper. Please forgive me."

Lana, "Forget about it, I am the one being slow and maybe too cautious. Please go on."

Norsha, "The bottom line is that some of our own people were coerced into collaborating with our enemies of that time and did fully engage in the dehumanizing control and degradation that was everyday existence within the containment centers."

Lana, "How is that possible?"

Norsha, "The account of Menachem's ordeal, which began where he lived early on, will answer your question. He was given the nick name of, 'the knocker'. He began a practice, when the home invasions by police started, to learn of the families targeted on a given day and he would run the streets sometime during the night or early morning, before the raids, and he would knock on the front doors with a unique rhythm that became the signal to evacuate or prepare for the unannounced kick at the door and the rough treatment by the police which always led to an arrest and internment. Some would attempt to hide within their homes or buildings nearby. Some escaped but most were captured. Everyone dreaded the knocker's rap but everyone also knew it would be the only warning to expect."

Lana, "Sounds like he was trying to help people. What is wrong with that?"

Norsha, "Nothing was wrong until he was caught during one of his nights on the street."

Lana, "I know where this is going."

Norsha, "During interrogation Menachem revealed his sources of information. The interrogator thought the knocker could be useful and methods were used to extract his allegiance to the enemy. Everyone believes that his own well-being was not Menachem's justification. The release of his mother and father was his assurance from the police. Menachem did not realize at the time that he would give more than his own life for an empty promise but he would sacrifice many other lives as well."

Lana, "Oh, God."

Norsha, "If only God had been present!"

Lana, "I didn't mean it that way."

Norsha, "I did. I struggle with the whole idea of such war and brutality somehow being a part of God's will."

Lana, "Is this where we are going now?"

Norsha, "No, I want to tell you more of Menachem, the Knocker's reality in that time and his descent into the tortured hell of extermination. It is relevant.Being from one of the affected tribes the Knocker was placed in one of the camps with the others because he was born as one of them. He lived among them because he was one of them. He was a young member of the community before the war. Nothing appeared out of the ordinary. He was one more lost soul. He may have been tortured in his heart more than most even though his physical life was to be spared."

Lana, "I would think a psychic separation would have to take place, even insanity, for him to function."

Norsha, "When I have finished you will understand."

The Knocker

Menachem awoke abruptly, cold and shivering with only a thin, tattered sheet covering him as he lay on the wooden floor of the police station jail. He has been without food for two days while waiting to learn his fate for being involved with the resistance by directly affecting the lives of some by giving them a chance to escape.

"Get up you little rat!" is the command of the jailer, "Stand up, now!"

Moving slowly and with difficulty from the pain of the last interrogation an hour earlier the 'knocker' rose from the floor. Looking up and into the cold eyes of the jailer the 'knocker' turned his face away slightly for fear of the blow that he knew was coming to batter his will again.

The jailer immediately back hands him to the face and the 'knocker' flinches in pain. "I have told you to stand straight up before me. You must do as you are told!"

Menachem turns to face the jailer squarely and stands as erect as he possibly can without folding over in pain. "Yes sir?"

"My superior, Commandant Viesser, will be in momentarily so you must be respectful and compliant. Do you understand?" The jailer threatens.

Menachem's very dry sense of humor keeps him going and keeps him engaged although the engagement usually means more derision and pain. He thinks he is better off knowing that his mind is still working.

"Wonderful", the 'knocker' responds. "I have the honor of meeting another fine gentleman this day!" With a wicked smile that is short lived as he is pushed against the wall with force by the frustrated jailer. "Shut up before I rip that filthy tongue from your throat." The jailer's speech slurred with hatred as his saliva is sprayed from his lips by the force of his rage.

The jailer slowly composes himself as he realizes that the scene would be quite unacceptable if witnessed by the Commandant who will be arriving unannounced. Menachem breathes quietly as the jailer steps away to leave the room. He twists the door knob, jerks the door open and looks back over his shoulder at the 'knocker'. With a low, strained voice he makes a parting threat, "I will have my way and you will see the wisdom of joining me." The jailer walks from the room, closes the door with a slam and turns the key roughly.

Menachem looks up at the ceiling as though he expects to see an angel, a god or something that offers hope. Peeling paint and mold are his answer, his vision. Speaking aloud as to that angel or god Menachem's voice echoes in the empty room. "If I am a part of the tribe that is supposed to be of Your 'chosen people', then how can I believe this fate is the better of life's offers? Is this God actually cruel and cold and so hideous, so blood thirsty? The ones with the power seem to believe it this way. Are the teachings of love and compassion really the delusion? Could I actually be a servant of the evil I presume to be against?"

Menachem looks again to the ceiling and raises his hands high to plead but he realizes his hope is in vain. "God or no God I am left with this choice to survive by submitting to my captors' demands. Do I participate in this evil or do I die one second at a time as the torture is applied by my tormentors. There is only evil here." His hands, still raised, begin to move in rhythmic patterns as he dances and begins to sing his jig. It is a dance that will become routine over time.

He lowers his hands as he hears the footsteps of someone approaching from the hallway. The door's lock is rattled before the door is pushed open. A soldier enters and turns to face the Commandant as he enters the room. Menachem turns to face the commandant and his body language relaxes slightly but he soon learns that was a mistake. A quick snap of the Commandant's fingers brings a sharp salute from the soldier who walks to Menachem and shoves him against the back wall with force. He is then spun around, his shirt roughly removed and then he is slammed against the wall again. Blood begins to trickle from his nose as his face is pressed against the wall.

"I am not here to ask questions." The Commandant states coldly, "I am here to tell you what will be, without any question of my authority, or doubt about my willingness to end your life at the first hesitation from you." He signals for the procedure to begin.

With his head and chest pressed against the wall by the soldier a second soldier enters the room with a type of harness. The leather straps form a belt around Menachem's waist and a connected strap crosses over his left shoulder and connects to the belt at the front and back. This positioned a cuff at the spine and between his shoulder blades. Menachem's right hand and arm is turned and folded back as when one is being subdued. His hand was secured by the cuff so that his right hand was now restricted at this position in the middle of his back and his shoulder, elbow and chest would have to stretch to accommodate the contortion. Once secured, the soldiers stepped back, one on either side of Menachem as he turned from the wall to face the Commandant.

"Who is directing you?" asks the Commandant. "Who has been providing you information?"

Menachem calmly responds, "No one. I am the only one responsible for my plan of action."

The Commandant, "To carry out your plan you would have to know ours. Such information is not readily available."

Menachem, "I have the discernment to sense when people are plotting or planning activities that are deceptive. I don't know why this is possible but whenever I have acted on my impressions the consequences have confirmed my suspicions."

Commandant, "My intention is to spare you and allow you to have a role that is going to be essential for saving your family and the future of your people. In exchange you will be one of my informants now."

Menachem sneers and nervously laughs under his breath, "I am so special and so stupid?"

Menachem, "What I do is not so grand or honorable. I know a setup when I hear one!" He begins to struggle within the harness and feels the flesh of his wrist tear.

Commandant, "You are the type of little rat I need and I know you are capable. I will construct your environment and you will find the place of darkness in your soul to carry out your task. I have confidence in your ability to isolate and I know what I can bring out of an animal such as you."

Menachem lowers his gaze and stares at the floor as the sounds and motion in the room fade into a numbness of his senses. The Commandant, knowing his point is made, turns away from the prisoner and leaves the room. The soldiers follow and close the door with a creek of the hinges and a latch of the lock. The lights turn off. Menachem remains in his tortured position with nothing but his mind, conscience, emotions and the weakness of his will to resist any longer.

The next twenty four hours would find him in such a state. As his knees weaken Menachem slides down the rough wall, crawls to the corner and collapses with his chest and head against the wall and his left shoulder pressed into the corner for stability.

A third day begins without food and little water. The pain will keep him awake though dazed and unable to think clearly. Menachem attempts to complete one last gauntlet of rationalization for his condition and circumstance. To try and make any sense, to give him any way out, other than to do what the Commandant will demand. Unable to complete such thoughts Menachem finds his memory of running through a field and into the forest, as a boy.

His true sanctuary, as a child, where he could imagine anything and where he could become anything that his imagination would conjure. He may be a snake, a buck deer, a bumble bee, a snail, a hunter or whatever adventure his impulses would reveal. For Menachem the forest, hills, streams and creatures were his solitude, his courage and his strength. God could be found in the forest. Menachem could be found in the forest.

As he snapped back into reality Menachem drew in a long, deep breath. With an overwhelming awareness of his presence, his condition and the situation, a torrent of fear and agony cut through his emotions to compress his mind and force a sound from his constricted throat as that of a threatened bear or lion about to attack. The scream consumed his energy and he fell again against the wall.

Metaphysical Journey

Norsha, "The 'knocker' was one of a group of men that were coerced into collaboration because of the sadistic joy of the enemy at having their victims responsible for manipulating the emotions of their own people as they were led to their deaths in various ways. This method of indirect control allowed the soldiers a sense of deniability and it was very effective the longer it was practiced."

Lana, "How is this relevant to our situation now?"

Norsha, "Though others in the same situation were coerced there have been a small number of individuals over time who chose the evil of turning on their own people. There will likely be others to emerge in the future as well."

Lana, "Who might you be referring to?"

Norsha, "A partial list would include individuals who intentionally chose to betray their own as leaders of nations and philosophers of Socialist Utopias which always degenerate until falling into a chasm of destruction. The movements as a whole are simply different forms of Communism. The names can be found in any World History textbook compiled after 1950. A more ancient example was before their time as Herod, a 'king' under Rome, during ancient Roman times. Thinking of the future there will likely be survivors of the wars who have fled as children before the conflicts began. They will have grown up with a seed of domination having been planted in their psyche.

Once they grow up they will do their part, likely behind the scenes because they are cowards, to harvest the fruit of their destiny as well."

Lana, "Does it matter?"

Norsha, "You asked but it only matters in the context of the consequences. To abandon one's heritage in order to gain advantage, to reject the history by denying one's ancestry or with the expectation of gaining control is a false hope and a betrayal of one's self."

Lana, "I understand the paradox. I did not understand the situation in those terms."

Norsha, "The beasts that we hunt and we are hunted by during the days of darkness are the core of the evil leadership and philosophers who inspired the evil intent. Also the ones who gave over their heart to evil and those who relished in the torment they inflicted." Norsha takes a deep breath, "The psychic separation you referred to earlier became more of a psycho-spiritual, metabolic and neurologic transformation that perverted their soul and body. Their visual appearance is a result of the debasing that turned each into a beast seeking blood and the flesh of humans that is, sometimes, to be consumed at the culmination of a prolonged copulation."

Lana, "But you mentioned offspring earlier."

Norsha, "The days of darkness occur at the end of their copulation period. Some of the creatures, for unknown reasons, leave their nests prematurely and attempt to interact with the population of humans. Some have theorized that this time, for them, of heightened arousal and hormonal fluctuation may affect their minds and induce an arcing of the gateway between the past and the present which causes the unusual, unexplainable behavior. Regardless the rejection by anyone they pursue will likely result in death."

Lana, "Do we destroy them because we don't understand them?"

Norsha, "We destroy them because we understand that they are attempting to destroy us! Their origin is deceit, betrayal and death! There will be no sympathy or understanding for them!" Norsha becomes enraged by Lana's softness.

Lana recoils, "Stop! I am asking now so that I can respond appropriately with understanding rather than to react inappropriately."

Norsha turns from Lana and allows her hands to drop to her sides, her head bowed as she breathes slowly. Turning again to face Lana, "I apologize for my outburst. We are on the edge of the sword. Let us continue."

Lana, "I understand a primary goal is to close this gateway and atone for this perversion of creation that was spawned by the evil of our collective past by association with the one's you have mentioned but the key word here is p-a-s-t." I recognize, once again, the need to rid ourselves of the beasts and the days of darkness must end. I do not want to stop one form of evil by engaging in another act that can have unintended consequences of the same sort. Do you understand my concern?"

Norsha, "I can 'understand' but I do not consider such issues. I am here to complete a series of tasks in support of an effort to validate our place as a people in this life. I am doing what I have been trained to do without question."

Lana, "Everyone is doing what they are told but who is directing our actions?"

Norsha, "Now it is you who is straying from our goal. I will not participate."

Lana, "Oh, what happened to 'yes, Miss Ann, I am here to equip and support you, Lana'?"

Norsha, "The leadership has been passed down from the heroes of the earlier conflicts, such as your father, when our existence was threatened."Norsha's resentment at being doubted and questioned was beginning to suppress her confidence in Lana and she was beginning to question her strength.

Lana, "If I were to be captured would I be of value to the enemy?"

Norsha, "Yes, of great value. Without you and the successful execution of your role we will fail. The entire purpose will fail."

Lana, "Couldn't someone else do what I am doing?"

Norsha, "It is not so simple. There are priorities related to tradition and lineage. There was a supreme decision by our guiding spiritual advocate that dominates our personal decisions because of a higher authority whose ways are perfect and whose purposes are much greater than our existence."

Lana, "Sounds like you are talking about God or some spiritual hierarchy that is the 'controlling authority'."

Norsha, "I cannot explain what I do not understand. I lack the sensitivity, the discernment to understand such things. You obviously can or you would not be the one to have the role that you do."

Lana, "Now I see that we are straying from our duty. Give me the basics and touch me as you must whether physically, mentally, emotionally, even spiritually."

Norsha, "Before I do you should understand that I will leave you alone in this room at times and you are to remain here until I return."

Lana, "Okay?"

Norsha removes one of the two chairs and has Lana sit in the one remaining at the center of the room. "I will now place my hands on you, my left hand on your left shoulder and my right hand on the top of your head as I stand behind you. You will hear my voice and feel my touch but you will not see me. I want you to have your eyes opened or closed as you feel comfortable doing."

Lana, "Am I going to be hurt?"

Norsha, "No, you may be startled and you may become disoriented emotionally but nothing physical will harm you. Your experience will be within your mind and spirit as a melding of two powerful controlling forces of your humanity to form your purpose. You will become intuitive and less dependent on your sense of caution. I will be here to protect you as your awareness and your consciousness will be separated from your body for a short time."

Lana approaches Norsha and stands facing her with the chair between them as a temporary, symbolic barrier. She looks deep into Norsha's eyes for an indication of deceit or fear. Lana becomes calm and assured by her sense of trust and confidence coming from Norsha.

Lana smiles briefly then turns around to sit on the wooden, straight backed chair. Lana's breathing becomes calm and her heartbeat resting as she reclines on the chair. The room begins to have the feel of static anticipation as though the atmosphere is primed for a reaction to movement of the air by sound as soft as a whisper. Lana's sense of anticipation suddenly accelerates as Norsha steps closer from behind the chair and places her hands just above Lana's left shoulder and the top of her head.

Norsha, before placing her hands on Lana, begins a chant of low tones and at a low volume. Lana chooses to close her eyes and as she does she becomes immediately enveloped by the sounds and the intensity of the moment.

Norsha stops the chant but Lana's awareness remains completely engulfed by the affects as she begins the metaphysical journey within her being. Norsha remains standing behind Lana and as she removes her hands Lana remains outwardly quiet and calmly seated. Norsha knows of the transformational journey that is now unfolding within Lana and that the calm exterior will remain as the convulsive shifts within Lana's being will course through her transformation.

Lana recognizes the sounds of the chant beginning to fade as though she is moving farther from the source. Though her eyes are closed Lana senses motion as though she were on a train, passing through a very dark tunnel, designed to confuse the senses with motion in total darkness. Lana remembers a time, as an adolescent, in Chicago with friends when she experimented with drugs frequently. This one night she, with friends, had taken LSD. She was walking through an abandoned house without any lighting to experience the night, the people, the place without any restrictions and a desire for adventure. The night ended when a guy jumped from the building because of hallucinations that had overpowered his ability to control his actions. As he lay bleeding and dying the group danced and hugged and laughed as though he was okay or was faking his condition.

Lana recoils now from the memories and her body reacts slightly as her back stiffens against the chair. Norsha sees the movement as an indication the journey has begun. She remains standing behind Lana.

Lana opens her eyes, whether actually or only mentally she does not know. The scene before her is of the forest she knew so well as a young child. Near the edge of the forest but within the tree line Lana, as a young girl, is looking back across the tall grasses of the field that separates her from her home. She can see her path of dislocated and flattened grass from the back yard fence gate, still open, to where she now stood. The day was sunny with small, puffy clouds quickly crossing a light blue sky as the wind moved in gusts and the tall grasses danced with the wind.

Lana stood with her back pressed against a large tree and her feet reinforced against the roots. This was one of her pillars of strength and security as a youngster. Lana began to hear again the last syllable of Norsha's chant increase in volume and reverberation as though coming from the forest and being carried by the wind with increasing strength. Lana felt the great tree she was against begin to vibrate with the sound as though it had a voice and was joining a chorus of energy focused on and driven by the chanted syllable, Yod.

As the intensity increased Lana began to see her home shudder against the wind and the vibration of sound. As the fence and building began to tear apart Lana again reacted in her body by quivering slightly in the chair. Norsha continued to observe and loosened slightly the placement of her hands on Lana's shoulder and head.

Norsha recalls her time through this process and she knows the random chaos and the peaceful moments between convulsive shifts in memory and realization will culminate at some point for Lana. The calm confidence and courage she will emerge with cannot be gained any other way and, when tested, will not fail.

Lana begins to scream as her memories, represented by the childhood home, disappear over the horizon of her experience that is taking place in her mind and soul. She feels the same vibrations of the tree within herself and her spirit beginning to shudder as though she is being opened up physically to release the essence of her being from within. During this violent stage Lana begins to physically, knowingly open her eyes to find relief, to get help, to see someone or something she recognizes as normal.

Norsha again increases the pressure with the placement of her hands for Lana to recognize and she begins to sing a child's lullaby that Lana immediately responds to by calming her physical reactions and releasing the troubling visions from her imagination. She mentally returns to the darkness of the first experience.

This process of transformation will continue until Lana reaches a point of exhaustion which Norsha will recognize. She knows there remains one phase for Lana to complete that will produce the enlightenment needed to fulfill her role. First a short time of rest and nourishment is needed for Lana. One hour has passed which is longer than usual but time is a factor only for the overall schedule. This process must be completed or nothing else matters on the 'schedule'.

Norsha removes her hands from touching Lana and raises her arms as though reaching out, over her head and looks up. A calming chant returns the environment of the room to its natural state. Again the last syllable is prolonged but with a low, calm, soft feel. A spiritual breeze washes through the room and across Lana's mind and emotions. Norsha closes her eyes as she lowers her arms and Lana moves slightly, then opens her eyes and turns her head to locate Norsha.

"Are you here?" Lana asks.

"Right here." Norsha responds as she steps from behind Lana and walks around to face her. The two embrace and Lana hugs Norsha with all her strength. They stand together for a prolonged time, silent and tightly embraced yet calm. Lana then releases Norsha and they separate.

Lana, "Can I get something to eat and drink? I feel like I have been on a very long hike but I know I haven't taken a step."

Norsha, "We will have a short time of rest and nourishment now. You will need your strength."

Lana, "I may need a psychiatrist or a priest or a wise person of some sort. I kind of just relived or reviewed many aspects of my life but in a very disjointed, chaotic, alarming sequence. I have the sense that there is a particular emphasis that guides this experience and a point of crisis is looming. Do you know what I am saying?"

Norsha, "I am that one to help you through this. In general I do know what your concerns are but specifically I do not. Each of us making this transition experiences a crisis of belief at some point. The goal is to strip away our fantasy, our good intention, our dishonesty, our doubt. Belief in something or someone can be cozy and easy until we must act on our beliefs. This point of action is your destination."

Lana, "I first need a little food and rest."

Norsha, "Of course, we have thirty minutes."

The Whisperer

The knocker's battered, weak, lonely mind falters as the memories, once again, become his escape from the abuse as he runs into the forest of a young boy. He has a friend there that he has never met and never spoken to because of his fear of revealing his presence. He doesn't want to stop her from coming there because he may disrupt her carefree presence there. From his background observations and distant emotional interactions of his imagination by watching her as she plays in the forest he knows they are good friends.

Often she will run to the forest from across the fields to her place within the protection of the trees. There she role plays and explores among the large rock formations and sometimes relax and sing.

Menachem was often tempted to introduce himself but he did not want to break up the peace and tranquility of her time there. He was so lonely because of his self-imposed isolation. He did not think of himself as good enough or interesting enough or even attractive enough to expect others to accept him much less like him or embrace him. From a distance he can imagine anything, accomplish anything, be whatever or whomever he wants to be. This was his peace and tranquility that he cannot upset and will not threaten by reaching out to someone. He is a perfectionist of a kind, a self-determined and self-centered martyr.

His memory of one particular day he recalls with both joy and regret. This was a day of boldness and courage on his part. He knew his friend would be in the forest because she is there every Saturday running the rabbit trails through the trees and wading in the shallow waters of the small lake.

Today he is going to cross her path and today he will say her name for the first time because today he will introduce himself and reveal for the first time his presence in the forest. Menachem wakes up before sunrise, having slept on top of the rock that he thought of as his fortress. The elevation gave him a vantage point from which he could see to the edge of the trees and the portion of the fields that extended from the tree line outward to the 'outer world' as he called the rest of creation.

While waiting for enough light to maneuver through the rocks to the forest floor Menachem sits on the edge of a large boulder with his feet hanging over and his hands on either side, resting on the rock. He did not know how or why people prayed or could reach out to something or someone that could not be seen or touched. He does have a vivid imagination and he embraces moments like this to express his inner yearnings through sounds that can be considered singing or chanting. As he would chant he then would listen for a response and he allowed his senses to become hyper-aware of his surroundings.

Sitting comfortably, his back straight, his gaze upwards to the remaining stars that were visible through the forest canopy, Menachem becomes enmeshed in this time of 'gathering' as he calls it. He allows the syllables of sounds that he has not been taught to naturally emerge. Near silence follows as the wind, brushing the high tree leafs, provides a rustling background sound accentuated by the piercing, strong insertion of a Blue Jay's call. Menachem repeats the sounds and pauses to listen. He actually hears either a response or a faint echo of his chant. Menachem feels a chill rush up his back. He has never experienced a response, never. Again he repeats the sounds and listens.

With complete silence now he is sure there was no response. Was his hearing deceiving him? "I knew there was nothing else out there anyway," his comment. With daylight now bright enough for him to find his way Menachem moves downward through the rocks swiftly and then he leaps the last ten feet to land at the path's edge. The path is mostly red clay, dry and dusty with occasional areas of exposed rock surfaces. Dense undergrowth borders the common path and the crossover trails are recognizable by him alone because of his familiarity and frequent use of the paths to run to and from the 'outer world'.

Menachem nears the area that the girl usually occupies and pauses to expand his field of view to check for any activity or sounds. There are none except the rustling of the grasses in the field as she nears the tree line to enter the forest.

Lana pauses at the tree line where the area transitions from the bright sunlight to the cool, lower light level of the forest canopy. As her eyesight adjusts Lana picks up a movement in the shadows beyond the cleared area she usually goes to. Thinking it is an animal she makes nothing of it, for the moment.

Menachem, thinking he has been seen, freezes in place. He begins to review, mentally, his plan and its significance. As quickly he stops his thoughts which usually lead to his withdrawal. "No!" He says audibly, under his breath to himself, "no, I will!"

Menachem remains behind a tree to observe the girl's movements. He watches as she enters the cleared, orderly area and proceeds to walk along the outer edge of the area, forming a circle. She completes the outer ring and then, from the ring she continues in a spiral inward to the center of the area and then sits on the ground at the center point.

With her legs extended in front of her and her hands at her sides, resting on the ground, she begins a melody of syllables similar to Menachem's series of sounds he used earlier.

Menachem became relaxed and peaceful immediately as he heard the melody. It was the same he had heard as a response to him that early morning. He became frightened and excited simultaneously as he strained to hear the chant clearly. He is sure of it now, the same peaceful and inviting sequence as the response that morning.

A sharp, searing pain rips the 'knocker' from his interlude of hope. What remaining hair he had was wrapped in the grasp of the jailer who was attempting to lift him from the floor. "Get up you piece of shit!" The jailer slurs at him.

Menachem screams with pain, surprise and fear. The 'knocker' is again in the grasp of his tormenter. "I am getting up! I am sorry, please let me get up!"

Unable to do more than pull the hair from Menachem's head the jailer looks with disappointment, at the few strands he has. "Get up now and stand before me!" The jailer again shouts.

Now on his feet and leaning slightly into the same corner as before he brushes the front of his tattered shirt as though it was his uniform and stands with his arms straight at each side with his palms against his legs. Menachem attempts to portray a soldier ready for inspection. Again his sense of humor the only humanity he can grasp at such times. A very wry smile from one corner of his mouth enrages the jailer who snaps the 'knockers' head to one side with the force of a strike with the back of his clinched hand. "You keep it up and you will not survive this little game." The jailer speaks lowly with his mouth close to Menachem's ear as though someone else might hear. "I will have you my way."

As the jailer backs away Menachem can hear the footsteps of someone approaching in the hallway. The door swings open and two soldiers enter the room followed by the Commandant. The soldiers make one sharp turn to their left and face the 'knocker'. The Commandant enters and turns as well. The three move forward before the soldiers stop and the Commandant moves toward Menachem and the jailer. The jailer continues to retreat and allow the Commandant full access to the prisoner.

"Alone, alive and ready?" The Commandant asks. This is your only opportunity to accept this role, to be spared and to provide for your family. This has been explained to you?

Menachem responds softly, "Yes Sir."

The Commandant continues, "Let me make everything clear. Your mother and father's survival is dependent on you and your survival is dependent on my approval of you. You have your stealth, your cunning and your craftiness. That is all. Your role is that of a go between, a representative and a confidant to those in your influence within this situation. There will be very little rest and even less understanding. Be yourself, be a spy, a savior. Whatever you need to be to keep me satisfied, you must be. Do you understand?"

Menachem, "I do."

Commandant, "Tomorrow we will see."

Even though everyone has left the room Menachem feels claustrophobic as though he is in a crowd. He is alone with only his thoughts and feelings but he has not the will to consider either. He is weak and numb from the starkness of his choices and the confusion about his role and his purpose except to see his family safe, together and free.

The long night is turbulent and wicked. A separation of thought and intentions occurs in order to allow his working, cognitive mind to develop a method and a routine to work within as a sense of normalcy. Menachem is beginning to formally compartmentalize his psyche. After all, he is expected to carry on as though everything is normal when among the people and to then be the informant that is working with the enemy of this same people, his people?

Menachem senses that his conscience and any morals he has left are being confined to an increasingly smaller portion of his awareness and his soul, as it were, now living in the corner of the attic in a large house. The void is being filled with cold as steel determinations about what he must do as both the savior and the executioner. Evil is growing in his heart and the gravest of treachery is consuming his will to survive.

Talking aloud to his self, "Tomorrow I am no longer The Knocker. I will become The Whisperer. I will be cunning and shrewd, discerning and discrete for the purposes to which I am assigned. Though God will condemn me I will be proud of saving my family."

Two Men Approaching

Lana and Norsha return to the cabin after their short break. The coast of Norway is now less than one hour away.

"Okay, Miss Ann, we are down to the wire now. Though this may seem like a cookie cutter approach with a program of steps it is not. We are being as flexible as possible." Norsha begins.

Lana, "I see your point. I know our time is confined but the transition must be completed. Should we wait until we are on land to begin this last phase?"

Norsha, "That would be too much wasted time. Once we transfer to our land group events and timing will likely accelerate. We will use the time remaining now to complete this phase."

Once seated again in the chair at the center of the room Lana relaxes as Norsha initiates the final stage. Lana feels compelled as her spirit yearns to join Norsha's chant. As Norsha continues Lana begins to separate from the activity as her awareness assumes a third position. She begins observing herself and Norsha from several locations at once. The effect is similar to looking through a multi-faceted prism or viewing the design of a kaleidoscope.

As her perception begins to withdraw further so that she sees more of a wider view a movement across the scene begins as a ripple would appear on the surface of a pond when something is dropped into the water. Lana's memory is sparked and a verse written by her father to capture a brief moment they spent together becomes her focus.

The memory of a rainy day when Lana was four or five she and her father were standing near a shelter after a rain shower. Though her dad was talking with another man she was standing near him. Her attention was fixed on a small puddle of water into which water drops from the tin roof above them were falling. The puddle of rain water was clear and Lana could see the many pebbles that covered the ground where the water gathered. As she leaned over to look into the water she could see a reflection of the clouds and the sky and her face. For Lana, at that moment, her young mind was captured and her understanding was teased by the ripples that each drop produced, entrancing her for a time. Her focus sharpened and Lana chose a group of pebbles that she then collected a hand full of. The remembrance of her father's prose calmly returned her to the current reality.

Cold, clear pool
Formed by angels near
Rippled dance of wonder
Reflecting innocence pure
A child sees your face
Your presence as the air
Exciting, inspiring, clear
Thunder startles thought
Pebbles firmly grasped
Adventure grand is life.

"Adventure with purpose," Lana's thought continues. Norsha can feel Lana's relaxed posture beginning to change. Her muscles reaction to the subconscious impulses of her experiences allows Norsha to relax her touch and step back slightly to avoid any contact that could disorient Lana or break her focus.

Being fully engaged in her psycho-spiritual journey, Lana turns her gaze to her right to see her father walking toward her. He was too far away for her to see his face clearly but she recognizes his movements and is certain it is him. Behind him there appears to be another person also walking toward her. From her point of view, looking south, the setting sun is to the right so that the shadows are to the left and are covering the path to two men are following and the field that is between the forest edge and her home is striped by the trees long shadows. The scene is perplexing for Lana and she becomes anxious to understand its meaning.

As Lana contemplates the two men approaching her, the person in front who she has assumed is her father, suddenly turns to his right and begins to walk into the field, toward the house. The figure that is following turns to his left and begins to enter the tree line of the forest.

Lana's body reacts with the shaking of her shoulders and a slight stiffening of her neck as though she were crying. Norsha releases her touch completely to allow Lana free movement. She circles around to observe Lana from the front and sees tears running down her face. Norsha recognizes the crisis is developing and Lana's psyche must push through this conflict to reach her understanding, her resolution, her commitment for self so that she can transcend self and serve the purpose of her great work.

Lana watches her father continue toward the house. Also, she sees that the second person is now waiting within the tree line, obscured by the lowering light level and the undergrowth of the forest. Lana's sense of choice is very strongly pushing her to see who this second person is.

Walking slowly along the field's edge Lana does not have any fear of this possible encounter but her senses are guiding her to move cautiously. As she nears a bend in the path and a place close enough for her to see the person, he retreats further into the trees, walking away from her to avoid contact.

Lana stops with the thought that she may be walking into a trap. Following her counter-intuitive impulse Lana begins to slowly run toward the forest entry point of the stranger. Looking into the shadows Lana sees no-one. Her awareness, within her dream like state, questions whether or not she is in a dream. At this point her mind returns to consciousness and Lana opens her eyes.

"I saw someone." Lana speaks softly to Norsha. "My impulse was to run to him. As I did he hid his presence from me."

Norsha, "Did you recognize him?"

Lana, "No…... not recognize but I feel as though I know him."

Norsha, "Did you see him well enough to recognize him again?"

Lana, "I cannot picture his features now so, I don't know. I was so strongly compelled to go to him."

Norsha, "Are you sure it was a man?"

Lana, "Oh, yea, a man. He has a dark beard, a golden brown complexion and powerful eyes."

Norsha, "I thought you couldn't recall features."

Lana, "Well, I could not see him clearly. It was getting dark and he was never close." Both Lana and Norsha smile at each other with the understanding between them that attraction is not all visual.

Norsha, "You are pressing too much. You must engage the experience and enter fully. The doubt or fear of new experiences must be released. When you return to the point of decision again about this person I encourage you to push yourself and break through the barriers of your feelings and habits. Push the point and discover the purpose, the meaning of your experience."

Lana, "I will not return to you without completing this." Lana takes her place in the chair and immediately enters into a calm state with her eyes closed. Now within her altered state, at the forest edge, looking into the darkness of the trees' shadows she finds no-one there. Lana begins to hear the faint melody of Norsha's chant though it is not Norsha's voice.

Lana realizes the choice she must make. She must either pursue the ways and the path of her father which, for her purpose now, may be regressive. The other choice is to pursue the unknown but inevitable mystery of the man that is concealed within the forest. In a new way the forest becomes a place of adventure, unexplored risk and depths of surprises for her to become familiar with by following the trails leading to her fulfillment. Lana recognizes that her childhood experiences within the forest had trained her for this time in her life.

Her true choice must be to pursue the mystery, the future, her purpose. She now turns toward the forest and begins a life changing journey.

Though Lana, as a child, was very familiar with the portion of the forest that she was entering, she quickly found herself in new surroundings. The path was no longer well marked from use. The trees and rock formations ahead are none she has encountered before. One huge rock that is in front of her forms a peak that the hill leads to. A roughly outlined, stone stairway leads to the rock by circling up the hill on the left side as Lana faces the formation. The twilight sky behind the rock forms an image that seems to dance or vibrate with the contrast of darkness on the rock formation face and the forest growth with the brighter sky that has a light glow from the lower angle of the sun at twilight. Lana stands silent to hear the wind moving through the high branches and leaves of the tallest trees. She takes a deep breath and closes her eyes for a long moment to be engulfed by the tranquility.

Lana is then startled by the sound of footsteps very close to her. She opens her eyes to see the man she has pursued standing very close and looking into her eyes. Though she is momentarily uneasy with his closeness, calm pours over her and she relaxes immediately.

"I don't like being surprised." Lana speaks slowly and softly, "I thought I was alone." She knew that she would usually react quite differently to such forwardness, especially by a man she does not know, but not this time.

"Oh, you are not looking for me? I have waited for you to come near. I know that you have reason to be here." The stranger spoke calmly with a smile as though he knows more than he should.

Lana, "I am here but I am not sure what I will find."

"Let me answer your questions. First, my name is Yeshi."

Yes, I Will!

Menachem is awakened by the sound of the door being opened. An unfamiliar rattle can be heard as a guard approaches the room. Entering, he is carrying a tray of food for Menachem. The guard lowers slightly and drops the tray onto the floor with a metallic bang against the wood. No food has been given to Menachem while imprisoned that was more than a bowl of something unidentifiable. The tray has a collection of vegetables and some bread which will be a feast. Menachem has to wonder if the food is poisoned or if it is to be removed at the last instant as a tease. To keep it from being taken he immediately begins eating with both hands shoving the food into his mouth. Once he has consumed the food he knows he is going to be sick because his body will reject the rich, boiled vegetables. It has been at least a year since he has eaten such food and it has been days since eating at all.

After vomiting most of the food onto the floor Menachem is given a mop and bucket to clean up the mess and a pair of pants and a shirt to change into afterward. The clothes, he realizes, likely were taken from another prisoner either before he died or just after, before the stench would be too great. Menachem, at this point, didn't care. To have clothes that covered his body that will provide some protection from the cold will be a great change in his circumstances.

He begins to think, "What might I gain from my new position?" Of course he will never make such a statement aloud but his mind is changing and his survival is becoming more important than doing the 'right' thing. "Whatever that means", he thinks to himself. "The next 'thing' might just be the one thing I will not otherwise do", the personal mental conversation continues. "Will I lie? Yes I will. Will I steal? Yes I will. Will I injure someone I know? Yes I will. Will I betray someone I love? Will I? Will I kill? Will I?" Menachem stops his thoughts and looks at his hands. First the palm's, lined and scarred with the dirt of life ground into the pores. Then the backs of his hands, rough with veins protruding in patterns that seem chaotic. His fingers slightly curled from abuse and the damage of manual labor with jagged finger nails, some very short from his nervously gnawing on them.

Again the internal questions, "Will these hands do what must be done? Can they squeeze the life from someone or be the tools of someone's rage against a group of people? Will the mind that controls them become insane, self-absorbed, wicked and cruel?" Menachem begins to quiver as he answers himself, "Yes they may, yes I might, yes, I will, do anything to save my family!" The rationalization will console him for now he tells himself. "Anyone here will do the same if given the opportunity." Menachem reiterates to himself, "I will." He releases a slow breath of exhaustion.

Standing silently and looking away from his hands, upward into the emptiness of his spirit, his eyes closed as a force of dark thoughts begins pressing his conscience to abandon all sense of restriction and forsake all boundaries. Menachem feels the rhythm of a drum beat from within that moves his body and the celebratory jig of a flute that he begins to hum as he dances around the room. Smiling, he releases a giggle of mischief that grows into a laugh of wicked intimacy. Clapping his hands above his head Menachem dances and sings until he collapses. The dance has become a celebration of determination realized, even in failure, as each day teaches. Falling to the floor he knows that a transformation has taken place which has left him cold, cruel, arrogant and obedient to the evil he has given himself over to. Should he somehow escape this place he will be a beast more than a man.

With the return of the guards Menachem is jolted back to consciousness and a reminder of his place as he is kicked in the back. "Get up!" The guards command, "You have five minutes to clean up this mess. Get up now!"

Menachem crawls to the vomit on the floor and begins to scoop up the mess with his hands. The guards watch and one begins to antagonize him, "Looks like a fine meal you had there. Have another taste of it why don't you?" The guard has bent over Menachem, reaches down and pushes Menachem's hands toward his face. To avoid a beating Menachem consumes the handful of his own vomit while looking up at the guard when he swallows.

The other guard responds, "There you go, another fine meal for our guest." The two laugh. Menachem uses the bucket of water to wash the remaining mess on the floor into an opening between the planks of the flooring then stands to dry mop the stained area. The guard, "Now put on your clothes so we can go."

Menachem simply pulls the clothes over what little he has on, buttons the shirt and steps toward the guards who are at the door. He has not been outside of the small building for over a month and he isn't sure what to expect. The guard opens the door and motions for Menachem to walk ahead and out of the room first. Turning left to walk the hallway toward the front desk was a challenge for him. He begins to think but he knows that to think will be to embrace his greatest adversary – himself. The second door is opened as he approaches the outside world. The glaringly bright daylight causes Menachem to raise his hand and shield his eyes. A momentary headache causes him to see spots until his eyes adjusted.

Before him, as he looks down from the doorway, three concrete steps leading to a barren courtyard. Looking past the guards he can see a row of buildings that appear to be barracks, possibly for soldiers with a pathway from the center courtyard to the closest end of each building, left and right and between the buildings to the far ends of the barracks. Just beyond the buildings, two side paths, one right and one left, each leading through an attended gate in the tall, barbed wire crowned fencing that surrounds an area on either side, containing the prisoners' areas.

Menachem does not move for fear of doing the wrong thing. He takes a deep breath that produces a long sigh that causes the two guards to knowingly smile at each other. As they turn to him one shouts, "Okay, little shit, it is time. You have your instructions, now it is up to you to work for the release of your family."

Menachem, "Instructions? I have no instructions. What am I to do?"

Second guard, "Survive, assimilate, find someone to recruit as your replacement and know the answer to any question about the population here that the Commandant asks. These are your people, but remember you are not one of them."

Menachem, "This is impossible. Just shoot me now and it is done."

Guard, "Really?" As he shoulders his rifle and aims above Menachem's head and continues, "Am I to go to hell with you? No, I will not. I will be here to see to it that you make the trip after your work is done." Smiling, the guard fires the rifle shot over Menachem's head. The bullet passes close enough for Menachem to hear the sizzle of the bullet passing. He flinches and responds, "I have my instructions!"

Menachem's gaze remains on the pathway as he walks away from the guards toward the gate. The white gravel of the pathway stops at the gate. The freshness of the sunlight and the air seems to also stop at the gate, now open enough to allow him in. Stepping across that threshold is like stepping from a paradise into a black and white still frame by frame movement. As he looks up the environment transitions to a slow pace of movement as everything around him stands still by comparison to his movement. He feels as though he is being enveloped by an atmosphere that is painful, grinding, near lifeless, wickedly draining the strength from every plant, animal, insect and even the air within its sphere.

Menachem turns back to see the guards watching him shrink under the pressure of each step he takes. He knows that he needs the vision of hope he will return, even to them, outside of hell. What lay ahead for him now is impossible for his deteriorating sense of conviction to grasp.

The fire of anger and hatred begins to infuse Menachem with a rage that numbs his conscience and compels him to act and not think rationally. He will be the 'whisperer' by mingling with the others, learning their names, their backgrounds, their fears, their schemes. He will speak in a hushed manner and identify those who are listening as those who are still thinking.

Walking into a group of men who are standing together closely to conceal their conversation Menachem intentionally bumps into one man to draw the attention of the group.

This Epic Trail

"Yeshi?" Lana questions, "An interesting name and when you say, 'for you', are you known by another name by others?"

Yeshi responds, "Yes, I have been known by a few variations of my name over time but I am the same always."

Lana, "I know that I may have the responsibility of identifying the Stroy that is the evil manipulating the beasts we are to confront. The Royal Guardian will lead us once we subdue our enemies and will enable the establishment of peace."

Yeshi, "And how will you know that one when the encounter takes place?"

Lana, "That is my dilemma."

Yeshi, "Is it possible that you are being misled and that the battles were fought long ago?"

Lana, "I know that there were catastrophic events during the great wars and the outcome was peace, according to our interpretation, that has lasted until this present time for many."

Yeshi interrupts, "True, although I was referring to a time long before these recent wars."

Lana, "Then I may not know what you are referencing. I know that many of our people have rejected the idea of a just God or the desire for a relationship with a God that would inflict such suffering on them. I recognize that there has to be more to know and understand before coming to such a conclusion but I was not there."

Yeshi, "I tell you it is true that there is much misunderstanding and that man's tendency to be self-centered affects such choices and the consequences whether intended or not."

Lana, "I trust what my father told me when I was very young and I have chosen to trust those who now seek to correct the mistakes of the past."

Yeshi, "I am of your people. Your ability and your choice to trust will be vital to your success."

Lana, "In what way?"

Yeshi, "You will not recognize the one you seek by outward appearances. Your willingness to trust coupled with the discernment you have, as a gift, will lead you and you will have a confirmation as you recognize the one."

Lana, "How do you know these things?"

Yeshi, "Over the years I have been with others who were given this task but failed. I was not allowed to prevent or correct their failures. It is a matter of free will and the potential for failure that must be allowed. You, also, may fail. Your understanding and discerning trust will be the difference."

Suddenly the ground, the trees, Lana and Yeshi all begin shaking. Lana feels something pushing on her shoulder. As she turns to look her consciousness begins to change and she realizes that her meditation is being interrupted. Lana's mind returns to her immediate reality. She opens her eyes and also hears with increasing volume Norsha repeating, "Miss Lana, return now-we are approaching the coast. Our time has run out."

Lana, "I am with you. I am, uh," as she rises from the chair slightly disoriented, "here. Where are we?"

Norsha, "Rotterdam. Soon we will be at the port."

Lana, "Will we be disembarking here?"

Norsha, "Yes, Miss Ann, we will be traveling by train for the remainder of our trip into Germany."

As Lana begins the motions of moving about and preparing to disembark her thoughts are grappling with the vagueness of her brief conversation with Yeshi. Lana reminds herself that she is not on some quest for recognition or to gain credit for doing something heroic. She has a purpose to fulfill as everyone does. It is becoming obvious to her that the question to answer is not what but how.

With everyone now together with their bags and preparing to leave the room and the ship for this last leg of their travels into the next chapter of their collective legacy Lana sees everyone looking at one another as though they will never be together again.

Lana, "Hey, everyone look alive now. We have come a long way and we have much to be thankful for." As she stands with both arms out Lana invites all, "Come, let us form a circle and have this moment together to be calm, to pray, to focus and to know each other's presence."

The group forms a circle with arms around one another's neck in silence. Yarjies breaks the silence with a prayer. "Almighty, be mighty for our days are in your hands. Guide our thoughts, reveal what is not and equip us to walk this epic trail to your heart." Each person raises their head and looks into one another's eyes. As the group separates the ship touches the pier slightly. The shudder of the deck has everyone grabbing their belongings and leaving the room. The silence quickly vanishes as the fresh air rushing from the open deck and through the corridor invigorates everyone.

Yarjies takes the lead position of the assembled group and Megan the rear, sweep position. Both are armed and prepared to protect the group. Since the skirmish with the two assailants on board Megan has been attentive to the details of security. Consequently there have not been any complications but this leg of their journey will be the most challenging because it will put them at the most vulnerable level of exposure. The crowds and close contact with other travelers will lessen their ability to isolate Lana and protect her. The cabins are adjoining but the nature of travel by rail is more open and interactive. Megan is in her element when challenged. Her determination will prove valuable when everyone is unaware of her presence during her activities behind the scenes to support normalcy without interruption.

Yarjies signals Megan and the group. Following his lead, they begin to move toward the exit point of the ship. Lana continues to ponder her thoughts about Yeshi. He left so much unsaid, she thought, and she needs to understand clearly what he intended. She dislikes being left with so much room to fill in the meaning herself. Lana realizes, in the moment, that this tactic was used by the priest her mother relied on for answers although she rarely received real, substantive answers at all. Lana sees this as a way to later imply a misunderstanding in order to control the situation and always put the questioner on the defensive. Kind of like providing a guideline when a rule is in question.

Moving with the group, Lana walks from the dock area to the terminal. She ponders the sudden interruption of her session with Norsha and the subsequent acceleration of activity and now, with a transition of their journey, as though her time with Norsha was little more than a distraction. Lana determined to confront Norsha about the sudden abandonment of her preparations after emphasizing their importance. Without a completion of the experience an element of confusion is beginning to creep into Lana's vision of her purpose and her goals.

Moving through the terminal is routine and everyone in the group wants to move through the baggage check and be free of the crowd. The destination now is Spayer, Germany.

Walking from the terminal to the boarding platform Lana catches up to Norsha who is walking briskly to separate from the others. Grabbing Norsha by the arm Lana pulls her back and shouts up at her, "Why such a hurry? I did not complete the preparations that were deemed so important and I won't understand without asking evidently."

Norsha stops and looks down at Lana. Taking a breath before answering she speaks firmly, "Miss Ann, sometimes circumstances become controlling and sometimes we must question what we do not understand."

Lana responds angrily, "Out here in the middle of a public place like this is not the place to have this conversation!" while pointing at Norsha. The others in the group begin to look at each other as the scene and the situation becomes tense.

Norsha leans close to Lana to speak to her quietly, "Miss Ann, as soon as possible, once on board the train you and I will separate from the group and have this conversation."

Lana calmly answers, "I know we have a schedule and I know you are doing your best. I feel like I am being led around like a child sometimes. I am reacting maybe as a child, because I don't know enough about what is coming next to be able to respond appropriately."

Norsha, "Don't give up. All will work out. Be aware that we are moving into a time that will require more thinking and less feeling."

Once everyone is settled on board the train Megan prepares to leave the group and return to her standard role as an advance scout in the field of operations. This time has been a re-assignment that has become a learning experience. This will help her understanding of the background that she is preparing for. Also, she likely will cross paths with Baetus soon which is her hope and she will be re-united with her friends and companions Pilo and Kania. Megan is always prepared for every assignment and she is equally prepared for the fun, the risk, the challenge and the release of pent up energy that flows from her time with friends when away from the crush of responsibility when on assignment.

Irrational Thoughts

Rand arrives at his destination to find that he is not in Heidelberg. He goes to the ticket office to find out what has happened. The ticket for Heidelberg should have been for route #313. Rand's ticket is for route #331 which is through Pforzheim, going to Bad Wildbad which is nowhere near Heidelberg. Rand has unknowingly placed himself on the northern boundary of the Rochukas. It is late in the afternoon of a sunny, warm day that glows as the sun begins to set. The few clouds above seem to absorb the crimson red rays of the sun as though to hold them until morning when they will be released to reignite its flame and illuminate the next day. The tops of the clouds are a darkening blue as the sky above them has begun to blacken with the coming night.

Rand hurries through the train terminal so that he can get to the bungalow that he was able to rent early enough to shower and change because he wants to relax from the long trip as soon as possible to have his energy level restored by morning. So, the plan is for an early bed time and a start on the new day when he awakens, without an alarm.

The next morning Rand awakens later than he hoped and he seems a little fuzzy from the night before. He remembers having one drink with dinner and that isn't usually enough to give him this effect the next day. As he reaches for his glasses on the night stand by the bed he has a flash of memory about something he had observed, kind of out of the corner of his eye, the night before. At the time he attributed it to fatigue. He didn't dwell on it then but obviously his sub-conscience retained the image that his eye only partially and quickly captured.

Continuing to be somewhat groggy, his mind cannot assemble a clear recognition of the images so he mentally shoves it aside and begins to get out of bed. He makes his way across the dark room to open the tightly closed window coverings. The coverings are heavy shades made of wood strips that fit together tightly and completely block out all light. As he begins to tug on the adjusting cord at one end he hears the grinding of metal as though the apparatus is broken and the shades are not going to open. So, with a little impatience Rand jerks hard on the cord and the whole covering comes crashing down on top of him, knocking him to the floor.

There he sits, straightening his glasses on his face and trying to remove the wood slats from his shoulders and legs. "What a way to start the day." Rand thinks, "Haven't been here twenty four hours and I have already made a mess. I guess I am where I need to be although I don't know how I messed up this bad. I will make it work out somehow. " After remaining on the floor for a few minutes collecting himself and getting his bearings he throws the remaining pieces of broken wood against the wall under the window and stands up. "Now," he says to himself, "let's try this again!" With the window shade in a heap on the floor the room is brighter and the Moon is full. Rand's eyes widen slowly, in disbelief, as he looks out to see a night sky when it should be morning.

"The Moon is still bright?" He gasps, "Where is the Sun?" Once again he is talking to the room. He checks the clock quickly, looks at his watch to verify the time and calculates the time changes to realize that he should be seeing the Moon because he has slept but a couple of hours and the local time is 3:30 a.m.

Turning on the small television set in the room he switches channels, looking for local news. The guide identifies channel 2 as a regional news channel. Switching to the channel Rand catches the last part of a reporter standing before a rail line with the wreckage of a commuter train.

Reporter, "Once again we have reports of fatalities and injuries but no numbers. The local witnesses have steadfastly insisted that they heard an explosion as the midsection of the passenger cars began to derail. When questioned about the possibility of sabotage, the local officials would only say that they have no conclusions at this time. Reporting from just north of Speyer, this is Claus von Beus, back to the station."

Rand looks away to the window then turns and walks slowly back across the room to a chair that is at the foot of the bed. He falls onto the chair as though exhausted and stares at the floor. After a few minutes he realizes that he must motivate himself to find out more. He had just met the reporter, Claus, on the train before arriving in Heidelberg. The other young man, Baetus, whom Claus was expecting on the train, had mentioned the two were traveling on to Speyer from Heidelberg. What a coincidence the same reporter is traveling to the location of such an incident and now is reporting on the event. Could he have anticipated or had prior knowledge of what was happening? Rand had already questioned his impressions of Claus, whether he was a patriot or an anarchist rather than a journalist. The young Baetus raised the same questions in Rand's mind. Rand spends but a few minutes with such thoughts. More pressing concerns push them out of his mind.

He locates the telephone on the lamp stand at the head of the bed. Dialing zero for the receptionist he waits anxiously for someone to answer. He had spoken with the receptionist when he arrived the night before. Her name is Amber, a petite, young woman with an equally petite sounding voice. The person answering his call is a female, he thinks, but a different voice. The gruffness of the voice sounds artificial. At this point in time it doesn't really matter. Rand just wants to calm his mind and stop the flood of irrational thoughts that are overwhelming him.

The answers to his questions are short and terse. He first asks, "What is the time?"

"Get a grip!" the answer.

Rand, "Is there a doctor available?"

"See for yourself," the reply.

Just as the phone on the other end is being hung up, Rand can hear a snickering laugh in the background. Rand decides that something very strange is going on. Possibly robbers or vandals are holding the receptionist hostage and ransacking the offices when he happens to call. All kinds of absurdities cross his mind. None the less, he decides to go to the office and see for himself.

He quickly puts on his shoes and a shirt but leaves his flannel pajama pants on without thinking and heads for the office, stopping just before the door locks behind him and grabs his key from the jacket pocket that is hanging nearby. As he steps down the single step onto the small concrete patio he hears the door click shut behind him. He reaches back without looking to assure himself the door is locked. As he rattles the door handle his gaze becomes fixed on an image that is only partially visible from his vantage. His patio is enclosed on either side by Honeysuckle and Morning Glory vines. The front, facing east, is open to a small street which isn't much larger than a bike path. Across the street is another bungalow like his and a large yard with no fencing. Behind the yard a field of tall grass which is bordered by the forest beyond.

The image holding his attention is what appears to be, from a distance, a person possibly standing on something and leaning back against the wall. With arms outstretched and facing his view through the front window of what would be the main room. The figure did not move. Rand senses that this is the same image that had caught his mind's eye subconsciously.

Rand becomes uneasy with the thought that he may have never reached his planned destination and that he has ended up in some alternative reality or unknown dimension by some quirk of physics. Through all of his musings about the figure across the street and where he might actually be he has forgotten why he has left his bungalow in the first place. The sudden jolt of remembrance brings him back to his anticipation of rescuing the receptionist. He decides to resolve one crisis at a time and will go to the office first.

Cautiously he walks from the shaded protection of his patio onto the street then quickly to the complex offices where he should find the receptionist. To get there his path led him around several buildings. The complex was sectioned into areas of buildings similar to apartments. After weaving his way past them he finally comes to a small playground which is at one end of the office building. Rand decides to cut through the sandy playground in order to get to the side of the building as quickly as possible. His judgment at this point is to be as inconspicuous as possible. He is expecting to find the receptionist held and possibly mistreated by her captors. He is beginning to have trouble differentiating between reality and possible hallucination.

As he looks around the corner of the smooth brick building he can see light coming from the front office. There is no sign of movement from this vantage so Rand begins to slide along the wall, approaching the lit window. As he reaches the edge of the window he hears a muffled scream. Rand begins to step away from the building at an angle that will allow him to see into the room. Just as he takes the first step the office door is flung open with a force that slams it against the adjacent brick wall. The door is solid and the handle chips away a piece of brick which lands near Rand's foot.

Before he can retreat against the wall a human figure emerges from the open doorway. The person is tall, possibly six foot, eight inches or more, with a muscular build. It is a man with a round, shaved head and recessed eyes with thin but defined brows. His mouth hangs open in a relaxed, almost disjointed way. His breathing is vibrating in his throat. The man is struggling to walk because he is dragging something heavy behind him. Rand has not yet seen any sign of the receptionist and no other sounds are coming from the office. Suddenly the large man lurches forward as though he was being shoved from behind. Now, whatever he is dragging is becoming visible. Rand can see that he is pulling a bundle across the ground from the office walkway and that the bundle has movement from within.

Rand realizes with a pang of fear that he is now plainly visible even though it is dark and he is against the brick wall. There are no bushes or structures or trees behind which he can hide. He can do nothing but squat down where he is and hope that he will go unnoticed.

He looks back at the open doorway to see another figure filling the area of the office door. It is a smaller person that is completely covered in some sort of a body stocking that covers even the head. This person is carrying a bag or satchel such as a tool bag of canvas and leather. The bag appears lumpy and the small, thin person leans slightly to balance the load. As he walks the contents clink as the bag is jostled by the movement of the small man's limping gate.

The two figures make their way across the lawn in front of the office building to a small growth of trees. There is one tree that is straight, with branches growing from either side of the trunk, giving the tree a balanced, geometric shape. The squirming bundle is deposited at the base of the tree. The large person bends over to begin untying the bindings and the second person begins to open his bag which is next to the bundle. Rand realizes that he is becoming both intrigued and horrified to the point of becoming oblivious to his vulnerability. If either of his subjects looked his way he will be easily discovered. It is obvious that their interest is at the tree.

Whatever or whoever is inside the bundle is beginning to struggle against the cords that bind it as the large man becomes excited by the activity. Rand can hear the man's breathing become heavy and rapid. As the cords are loosened the other person is beginning to remove articles from the tool bag. The moon's light is very bright and reflects off of one of the articles pulled from the bag. The article is about twelve inches long and either chromed or polished silver. It is difficult for Rand to distinguish exactly what the instrument is but he thinks it is a spike as is used on the railroad ties to hold the rail in place. As it is held overhead it sparkles and shines brightly in the moon light.

The smaller person that is holding it begins to stare at the object as though entranced by its reflection of the light. The creature begins to get excited and raises its other hand as though praying to the sky. It's face still obscured Rand cannot determine if it is a man, a woman, a human or a creature of some other sort.

The creature begins to nervously dance in place as the contents of the bundle is pulled from its constraints. The large man, or beast, has grasped the figure by the shoulders to lift it up as he shouts at the one dancing, "Finish Menach!" Rand gasps as he recognizes the figure to be Amber, the receptionist. He can see that she has been battered. She is trembling yet silent from the trauma of her experiences. She looks around, her head jerking in every direction for some sign of deliverance. She begins to shake violently and opens her mouth to scream but no sound escapes as she is thrust against the tree. Her head now limp and her chin against her chest.

Rand wants to both rush upon the situation and to run in the opposite direction just as fast as he can. It is unbelievable to him that this is occurring in an open area.

Who are these beings? Are they a fiendish duet of escaped mad men or worse, animals on the hunt? Has no one really seen the abduction and now likely murder of this young woman, except himself? Rand did not know what to do. He begins to think as quickly as he can of a way to escape the scene so that he can get help. As he surveys his surroundings on a broader scale he notices that there are others watching as he is. He can see the silhouette of a woman in a window on the third floor of an apartment building with a clear view of the entire area. She appears to be resting her elbows on the window sill, one hand raised with a cigarette that she is slowly enjoying as she watches the drama unfold on the ground. Rand has the sense that she is not alarmed or excited but is rather amused or even indifferent about the receptionist's plight.

Rand looks back to his left, across the office building yard to see a couple walking their pet on the pathway that surrounds the area. The path will lead them just behind the same small stand of trees. They too act unconcerned with what is happening as though it is routine. Rand thinks, "What madness is this?" He checks his watch simply because he needs a momentary distraction.

About two hours have passed since leaving his bungalow. It should be getting light soon, if it matters, in his current nightmarish reality. Rand gathers as much fortitude as he possesses and begins to move away from his position. He has been squatting for so long that his legs ache and he can hardly walk. His first steps are slow and difficult. He wants to disrupt the sacrifice taking place however, that much courage is not his. Bewildered he looks over his shoulder as he walks along the length of the building, back toward the playground. Once around the corner he stops because he cannot just leave. He becomes the audience of the bizarre and wicked as he watches.

The small creature stops his demonic jig for a moment as he reaches into the bag again and pulls out a large mallet. He immediately begins to dance again with both hands swirling above his head. The large creature has been holding the fragile woman against the tree with his left hand pressed against her chest. A gaping smile is now across his face. The dance is drawing to a crescendo as both participants begin to howl. Rand strains to see clearly from his distant, more secure vantage point. The large creature grabs his victim by each arm at the forearm and holds them, one across the other, up against the branch overhead. As he kneels to position the sacrifice his cohort in cruelty dances his way around the tree in a ceremonial way and then he roughly places the spike against the woman's twitching, pale wrists. A terrified voice finally escapes from the tightened throat of the helpless victim. A shriek of pure terror escapes as the hammer is drawn back and suspended momentarily before it is driven forward to impale its sentence of torture and death through flesh and muscle and bone.

With the first strike of the mallet blood begins to flow and each desperate breath, each heartbeat of the victim covers the two with her blood which is a delight to the older, more ceremonial and more emotional animal. With another strike a shriek of death over powers her senses.

Rand can no longer bear the shrieks of the dying receptionist and the howling of her executioners. He loses all control of his mind, his reflexes and his body. All he can do is run away, blindly thrashing at the air, delirious and lost. He runs until he trips over a hedge and lands face first in the dirt trail leading to the small road which passes in front of his bungalow. He lay there in a quickly forming puddle of sweat and drool as he pants and sobs.

As his self-awareness returns Rand slowly lifts his head. His bodily fluids have mixed with the dirt and tiny pebbles of the pathway to form a layer of mud that is now dried to one side of his face. Rand slowly gets to his feet and attempts to brush himself off as he trots rather disjointedly toward his bungalow. He opens his eyes and realizes that it was now early morning where he is. He digs in his pocket for the door key and thinks of nothing but getting inside the one bit of environment that he can rationalize as his temporary home.

Click, the door swings open and Rand peers inside. All seems to be as he left it. He takes one tentative step across the threshold and then another, allowing the door to close. Across the room the shade still lay in a pile under the window. Nothing else has been disturbed in any way that he can recognize. A shallow sigh of relief bubbles up from somewhere within him. For the moment he feels safe. His sanity is another topic for another time. His self-confidence is shattered because he has always done his best to be prepared for challenges. This experience, though, goes beyond the common understanding of the word 'challenges' for him.

Rand lay on his bed thinking about all that has taken place the last time he remembers being awake and hoping it may only be his imagination but he isn't sure of much right now. He turns on the television again for the news and hears the lead story of the broadcast as, "The third day of Darkness this month is a wash. Three are saved and three are lost." The news caster states the facts as a news caster always does, with minimal emotion and a smirk of discovery as though he or she is the first to make the statement.

Rand hesitantly calls the receptionist's number. A pleasant sounding young man answers with no hint of uneasiness or insecurity at all. Rand asks that a reservation be made for him on the next available flight back to Chicago. The receptionist takes his request professionally and ends the conversation with a promise to have someone stop by his room with the document for him to sign within the hour.

Within moments there is a knock at his door. Before he has time to get to his feet the door swings open and in marches a small entourage of five people. Leading the single file procession is a soldier carrying a staff emblem. He is followed first by a doctor, then a policeman, a priest and a rear guard soldier with a weapon that Rand does not recognize. The group files past Rand as he sits in his chair facing the door. They stop in the middle of the room, all turning to their left to face Rand. Each stands very erect and still as though they are performing a military drill formation. The visit is obviously not a social call.

Rand begins to get up from his chair and the rear guard, with the weapon, responds to Rand's movements as though Rand is a threat and approaches him. Rand freezes in his partially erect position as if any further movement by him will bring a swift reprisal from the guard.

The police officer in the center of the group instructs the guard to retreat and he advises Rand to be at ease and stand up. Rand stands but does not move. The only light in the room is from a table lamp in the far corner of the room which is behind the assembled group. With his 'guests' standing between him and the light it is difficult to see everyone's features clearly. Rand's view is more of their outlines and he can see their eyes.

The police officer takes one step forward and begins speaking to Rand in a monotone voice, "I must begin by apologizing for our lapse in security responsibilities. Somehow you were allowed to enter this region unescorted and your personal relations briefing was not conducted which would have prepared you for your stay here." The officer finally takes a breath and then continues. "All visitors are to be confined and entertained by a personal escort during our 'days of darkness.' This is our policy which was breached during your first day here and for which we are responsible. Again, our apologies for what has happened and the consequences you must now face as a result of your uncensored exposure to these most recent events."

Rand is waiting to see if the man will breathe again more than he is listening to every word spoken. However, he gets the point but does not understand the part about consequences for him. He doesn't know what bad karma has put him here in this situation but he is ready for it to end. Rand stares at the officer with no outward reaction. After his short monolog the officer steps back into line and stands at attention as before.

Rand is doing his best to remain composed but he can feel his inner man beginning to snicker. A sense of loneliness that he has never known before is also beginning to grip him. He finds himself staring into the space just behind the people before him as though he is expecting someone to save him from his predicament.

His normally optimistic outlook begins to fade as the doctor in the group takes his turn with Rand as though he is following a well-choreographed routine and is performing his part in four-four time. He checks Rand's pulse, his blood pressure, temperature, eyes, and ears. All done in fifteen minutes, neat, clean and he does not ask Rand to remove his shirt. "Well," Rand thinks, "two down and one to go."

The priest steps forward, waives his right hand to the rest of the entourage and the formation turns left, marches out of the room, through the front door and onto the road, leaving Rand and the priest alone in the bungalow. The priest's eyes are kind and soft in appearance. His movements are slow and deliberate. His smile is constant and he seems sincere. The priest has not spoken to him yet but Rand is beginning to feel somewhat more at ease but he is becoming weak physically to the point of collapse. He retreats to the chair which is just behind him and sits down. Having no experience with priests or preachers or philosophy studies as an adult Rand is not sure just what to expect from this guy. He has heard the usual stories about the hypocritical practitioners of many religions and the jokes usually heard in a bar. Rand has always believed in a higher power of some sort or a creator but he isn't sure of what the truth is. His parents didn't have an opinion either way.

The priest pulls up another chair and sits right in front of Rand, facing him with their knees almost touching. He looks directly at Rand as he begins to speak with a low, friendly voice. "Hello, Mister Wayne, or do you have another name that you wish to be called by?"

Rand, "Well, my friends call me Rand. So, I suppose you can call me Rand."

Priest, "Okay, Rand, I am Father Joe but you can call me Joe."

Rand replies, "Fine."

"Well Rand it looks like you have stumbled into quite a predicament without even trying. Don't worry I can get you out of this."

"Oh, really?" Rand asks with a smirk of resentment. "I have no idea who you people are. I have come here for a short visit only to find myself living out some nonsensical nightmare so far. I cannot even begin to explain what is going on and now you're going to help me out of a situation I didn't get myself into?" Rand finds himself shouting by the time he catches himself. The priest is unaffected by his agitation.

"I understand your anxiety." soothes the priest. "It must be very confusing for you but we must deal with the reality of your circumstances right now. Let's try to calm down, think clearly and find a solution."

"Okay", Rand concedes. "What can you do for me and how can I know that you can do what you say?"

The priest leans forward and whispers, "I cannot give you anything in writing to confirm what I am about to tell you. If you will do as I say you will be flying out of here tomorrow morning with no regrets." The priest then sits back in his chair and studies Rand's face as he waits for a response.

Rather than continue to look the man in the face Rand looks past him to the front door's window as his mind begins to evaluate all that he can allow in the brief moment that he now seizes for himself from the nervous silence. Hanging on his eternal optimism is the thinnest glimmer of hope. To his amazement he sees a small pair of eyes looking back at him from near the bottom of the right corner of the door's window pane. He can also make out the partial outline of a small face from the cheeks up and a small tuft of hair sneaking from under a cap. He thinks it must be a child. He tries to avoid acknowledging what he sees because he does not want to distract the priest.

Rand looks back into the face of the priest who has not detected his distraction. Rand, "Well, let's hear it. I can't agree to anything without first hearing some details."

The priest grins, reaches into his jacket pocket and removes a little notebook and ink pen. "Let's begin with some necessary information. First I will need to know what you do for a living."

Rand, "I am a business man."

"And how much do you make in a year?" is the next question.

"What are you getting at?"

The priest's practiced answer, "Patience my son. Do you have a religious affiliation?"

"No." Rand responds impatiently.

"Do you care about people so that you want to help them?" The priest continues.

"I suppose I do care about people and I can be really helpful if I know my aid is appreciated." Rand really hasn't thought about these things much in years. He is drawing more from his memories as a child and a young adult. His parents were always donating their money and used clothing to causes as a way of satisfying their conscience and self-imposed obligation to help others.

Rand does not consider his self to be cynical about helping the needy. He has never known anyone personally that has not been able to take care of themselves. Since no one has ever knocked on his door asking for help he has never given any. He can remember giving advice or a shoulder to lean on to a secretary at work or something impersonal like donating to a flower pool for someone who has suffered the loss of a loved one. Those instances were driven more by a hope of returned gratitude or preference in other ways.

Rand continues, "I personally don't see why just about anybody can't take care of themselves. I feel that there is always a way if a person will have the guts to just do whatever it takes to make it happen."

The priest replies, "That is an understandable outlook, Rand. However, if no one needs help the church will probably be out of business. We have a very developed organization that helps some although we cannot help everyone. We are powerless in some situations." The priest grinned. "That is why we are always looking for new sources of revenue. What we may lack in our ability to deal with all needs we make up with our ability to raise money for our programs." Again the priest smiles, "We are proud of our organizations, our recreational facilities and our large churches. They are designed to house the masses once every week for our services and to give the adolescents recreational alternatives during the week. We have been around for a long time and we plan to be here as long as people are walking this earth." Again the priest smiles and raises his eyebrows, being he is impressed with his persuasive appeal which he has developed through the years.

"Well, that all does sound impressive but what has any of this got to do with me?" Rand asks knowing full well a pitch must be coming his way.

The priest now sits up in his chair, his countenance and manner very business-like. "It all has to do with your desire to leave here." He begins to explain his conditions for providing help. "To receive our help in obtaining your release forms you will need to do the following. You must first become a member of the church and pledge a minimum of ten percent of your net earnings to the church. We will invoice you once a week. Attendance is not required however, late payments will be assessed a service charge. You must renounce any past religious organization affiliations. Of course, we do give you something for your money. We are, after all, a well-rounded church. We schedule social gatherings. We have a full sized gymnasium, a bowling alley and a theater within our facilities. Feel free to visit any time, if you should decide to stay." The priest realizes that he has slipped into his promotional sales pitch without cause. He adjusts his collar slightly and looks at Rand for a response.

Rand finds himself more intrigued by what he assumes is a child outside his door than he is concentrated on the conversation at hand. In an attempt to delay his decision Rand tells the priest firmly, "I must have time to think this through, at least the night."

The priest begins to protest then catches himself in mid breath and changes focus. "You can have the time you need but your delay may jeopardize the arrangements we have discussed. I do have someone I must answer to, you know." Feeling rejected the priest stands, adjusts his collar again and returns to where he was standing originally.

Rand doesn't remember the priest carrying anything in when he first arrived but he reaches down and picks up a satchel. It has a familiarity to it. As the priest walks to the door a clinking sound can be heard coming from the bag. The door closes slowly behind the priest as he makes his way to the side walk. Rand is again emotionally overwhelmed and lies down to clear his mind.

The Performance Club

Rand wakes up and checks his watch. It is three in the afternoon. It is partly cloudy and warm. He hopes for a normal day. After a long, hot shower Rand takes a look around his living quarters for the first time since arriving. Everything has happened so fast since his arrival that he is just now becoming acquainted with his surroundings in a normal way. He walks toward the front door for a look outside and he finds that he has a small kitchenette that he has not noticed before. There he finds a coffee pot and a small pouch of coffee, a cup and a sugar packet. After starting the coffee the brewing aroma quickly fills the room and gives Rand a sense of normalcy. Rand fills his cup and turns to the door's window to look out at the flowers on either side of the patio. Beautiful Heavenly Blue morning glories mixed with honeysuckle blossoms. He opens the door, to take in the aroma of the flowers and then plucks on honeysuckle to taste the sweetness of the nectar by gently removing the base of the flower and touching his tongue to the dripping, thick liquid. He enjoys the simple pleasure, as he remembers it from childhood, from a few select flowers.

With coffee in hand Rand checks his pocket for the door key then steps out. It appears to be a normal day. The bungalow across the street looks to be empty. He looks left toward the office complex and sees no one. He looks to the right and sees a young boy, maybe eight or nine, skipping along the sidewalk toward him. As he comes closer Rand recognizes him as the person who had been looking into his place from the door window as the priest spoke earlier in the day. The boy was skipping heartily with arms and legs moving freely and a smile on his cherub like face.

Rand wonders, "How can this innocence coexist within the hell he has experienced since his arrival in this bizarre place?" Rand grins and waives to the boy as he breaks from his skip into a run toward him. Right across the grass he comes running as hard as he can. He slows to a walk a few feet in front of Rand.

"Hi!" the boy says as he raises one hand in a quick wave. "Who are you?" he asks. "I saw you this morning. Are you in trouble?" The child is full of energy and he asks his questions in rapid fire succession. Rand answers as quickly, in fun, "Rand, I saw you too, no."

"Oh yes you are." The boy grins as he teases, "I know that whenever someone here has to talk to those guys its trouble."

"How do you know that?" Rand asks, thinking the boy is playing and not realizing how close he is to the truth. "Are you teasing me?"

"No," Replies the boy. "I was once in your position and I escaped."

Rand nervously gulps down his last bit of coffee thinking, "Here we go again. Weirdness times two!"

Rand asks, "Would you like to join me on the patio and talk about it?"

"Sure," replies the boy. "You look like you need a friend."

"You have that right." Rand answers.

"What I am about to tell you may sound very much off the wall but I suspect you are used to that by now." The boy begins to show a maturity well beyond his age. His physical appearance begins to fluctuate too as his face at times looks more like that of a man and would then return to the face of a boy. Rand is feeling light headed again.

"To start, my name is Michael. You see me as I project myself which I can do since my spiritual self-awareness has transcended adult concepts in order to accept the truths of life as they really are. Too fast?" Michael pauses.

Rand, "Is everything here abstract bull shit?" getting angry about the continual jumping from normal to weird.

Michael, "Let me just say I am older than I look. Now seriously, the three people you have just encountered are the projections of the three social aspects of every human. The police officer represents our need for guidelines in order to have a sense of precedence for our existence.

The doctor represents our innate ability and need to be helpful and supportive of one another as well as having a sense of being able to provide life where none may exist"

Rand becoming exasperated interrupts, "Alright, enough, I cannot absorb all of this. The priest, do you want to cover that one?"

.Michael continues without hesitation,"The priest is probably the most dangerous and the most pitied of the three. The potential of the priest is to be one of enlightenment, of healing and law with a divine sense of forgiveness and protection. In this priest you can see the potential has been adulterated to a level of greed, lust and unmatched hypocrisy. To toy with another person's mind, emotions, sense of spiritual morality and physical mortality as though, as a person, they were insignificant does not give another dominion. Are you with me so far?"

Rand, feeling slapped upside his head again, responds slowly. "On the surface I get the correlations but I think it is too late for a Social Studies class."

Michael, "Okay, I understand. I have already gotten my mind revved up with a little run. Let me finish the point and then we can rewind as you may need to."

Rand replies "Got it. I need some coffee."

Michael, "Those whom you encountered on the day of darkness as they claimed one of their victims because of her rejection of the creature's desires are the material personification of the corruption that spiritual degeneracy must produce.

I have learned these truths as you are learning them now. I was delivered here by no design of my own. You were likely guided here for a reason. Everyone born comes here, at least metaphorically, at some point in their lives. By here I am referring to the reflective, interactive regions of creation with invisible dimensions of spiritual, demonic and benevolent entities. There are other regions and other backdrops of the same level of principled conflicts through which the elemental truths are tested and affirmed. There are other events of history and future times through which these principles are enforced."

Rand again interrupts, "Are you saying this is all artificial?"

Michael, "This environment and the others as well, are designed with diverse terrain, climate and the amenities to accommodate anyone's particular experience which will lead them to a deciding point in their lives. There are some who insist their experience is psychological or emotional and not physical. What you are experiencing is unique to you. What I experienced was different but the same climax of conscience is reached.

There are seven days of light for anyone here to seek the truth and accept it. These seven days are always followed by days of darkness which are manifest here and in this geographic region. Both are a part of each cycle.

The cycle begins with a revelation of the potential cost of rejection, regardless of method, which was your experience today. Today is day one of seven for you. Our conversation is the first step for you toward making a decision. Will you seek the truth and embrace it?" Rand? Are you here?"

Rand's eyes close and the conscience behind them fades into a blank stare. He blinks his eyes slowly as the blood level in his brain returns to normal. He isn't sure what to say. He thinks for a moment and then looks into the eyes of the young fellow across from him and says, "I must know the truth before I can decide."

"You are correct!" Michael answers, "You're first day is about over. I suggest that you get a good night's sleep and be ready for what is to come tomorrow. We can work only when it is light. The darkness brings too much risk, too much danger."

Rand, "I don't know what to expect but I think you are probably correct. I hope to see you tomorrow. I sense that you will be able to help me if you are willing."

"That's why I am here." Michael answers, "You are a part of my great work."

The two agree to meet the next day without making any specific plans. Rand retreats inside to try and get some rest. He sits on the side of the bed, takes off his shoes and turns on the clock radio on the lamp stand and tries to find soothing, instrumental music. He picks up a station playing classical music. Its signal is weak but it is calming enough to his frazzled nerves that he let it play with static and all.

Rand lay across the bed as he listens to calm his mind. The experiment lasts about thirty minutes. He finds himself searching for a meaning in what he has been experiencing. Not just why but what higher purpose can this all serve? It is now early evening. Rand decides to dress and go out for dinner and some light entertainment. When the taxi arrives he hurries to the waiting auto and asks the cabbie to take him to a lively part of town.

"And what do you mean by lively?" asks the cabbie.

"Oh, nothing exotic," Rand replies, "I am interested in good food, possibly some good conversation. Are there any playhouses in town where I might get a meal?"

"About the only thing like that here might be 'The Performance Club' as it is called. I wouldn't call it lively for the most part but, again, that depends on your level of expectation," answers the cabbie.

"Why do you say that?" Rand presses.

"You can get a good cheese steak, a cold drink and entertainment of a sort which is usually a local poet wearing his heart on his sleeve or preaching about society's ills."

Rand jokes back, "Well, thanks for that critical review!"

The cabbie is not amused. "Anyway, that is it except for the usual strip with clubs and such nearby. This will give you a starting point." The cabbie smiles as he stops in front of the first night club on a street of lights and activity.

"Thanks, I will look for you later tonight for a return trip." Rand thanks thecabbie with a generous tip as well. He steps away from the curb as the cab pulls away. He looks across the street and sees mostly closed shops with an outside light on or a dim night light inside and very quiet.

As he turns to his left he looks down the street and sees his side very active with people walking along the sidewalk and people passing from multiple doorways to the cars that pause and then back. There are a lot of lights and sounds as is typical on any strip for active night people. There is a mixture of night clubs with comics, strip joints or 'gentlemen's clubs', restaurants and a movie house.

Rand isn't seeking so much activity but since he is on foot now he begins to walk up the street and check each doorway and marque as he passes. He walks slowly, absorbing the atmosphere, the smells, the laughter, the shouts, the sounds of a glass breaking. As he walks past one unlit entry way, with doors propped open, he sees two figures inside go by the door's opening. Each man had a hold of the others lapels with one going backward and the other pursuing him. From outside the walls Rand can hear the muffled sounds of the two slamming against a wall. Rand has the thought, "Not so many years ago that would be my kind of place but now...." Rand quickens his pace somewhat to clear the area as fast as he can without looking too obvious.

At the end of the block he stops to check the traffic. He slows his pace again and crosses the street. Three doors down on the next block Rand can see the sign for 'The Performance Pub'. The sign is unlit and made of wood with nails partially driven in along the curvature of the rough cursive spelling of the words. The atmosphere is quiet from outside of the closed door. Rand can hear a faint melody of jazz coming from inside the pub.

As he tugs on the door handle he notices that the door is made of roughly hewn wood that appears very heavy. Its hinges creak as it loosens its grip on the frame and slowly opens. Rand wonders if it was so sturdily built for keeping the unwanted out or the occupants in. Once he is finally on the other side of the door it closes with a thud. He finds himself in a narrow, dark hallway with a curtain at the far end, about twenty feet away. The light coming from the thin split at the center of the curtain is a dark blue, black light. He cannot see the floor as he walks toward the curtain.

The music and other sounds of the interior grow louder as he approaches the veiled entrance. Rand hesitates before entering the room as though he is about to penetrate a sacred place. Before he is ready the front door begins to creek open. The sounds of the street usher in two laughing voices. The man and woman are surprised when they see someone else in the passage way. Rand quickly separates the curtains with his left hand and walks into the room. He is on the stage which is a part of the entrance. He flushes with embarrassment, begins to turn back and then realizes the others that are behind him in the hallway are about to be waiting because of him again. He feels, for an instant, like a little kid who is caught between two bullies who are shoving him as they move closer together. His reaction is to turn to his left and hope to find a way out of the spot light.

As all of this is taking place at the back of the stage a middle aged man is at the front, center stage microphone reciting poetry. The audience is absorbing the entire scene as a combination of meaningful prose with a back drop of chaos. Rand stumbles off the stage with the light in his eyes as the couple that was behind him makes their entrance.

To his right he notices a couple seated at a tall table with stools. They are laughing and offering their applause to him for his comedic entrance as others look his way and are also clapping their hands. Obviously he has been the moment's entertainment. Rand shouts out, "Would anyone like to buy me a drink?" In response several people raise their hand to comply.

Fairgens

Having successfully navigated the gauntlet of acquisition within the 'light zone' a sigh of relief quietly escapes Pilo's quivering lips as she shivers with fear. Her bravery has always been just under the surface as a trait of her passive-aggressive approach. The release of fear always follows her return from the area everyone outside refers to as 'the light zone' because of the more modern, in reality current, infrastructure and lifestyle. The term is also a sarcastic term because of the lack of respect and moral decline of those living there.

Her understanding and that of her peers is that, if caught within a segregated area even death must be in silence to protect all who remain. The younger generation that she and Kania are a part of remains separated relationally and philosophically from the old origins of the Rochukas. Their hope is to survive by being a part of the resistance and placing one's trust in the coming of a solution through the one expected.

All went so smoothly this time through location and acquisition. Unfortunately, transport of the goods and supplies was targeted by the opposing security and stopped. Each excursion is meticulously planned and practiced because of the critical need of medicines, tools and materials that requires such intrusions. Failures are rare and must be accounted for. As the youngest generation of the isolated survivors their rejection of the elders puts them at a greater risk from both the native peoples of the area and the Rochukas. Foods are grown and meat hunted which is fortunate because of the training of the older survivors of the wars who formed the original group to preserve and, one day, restore their culture and freedom to live.

Pilo is often chosen for the most difficult targets because of her cross genetic makeup which gives her the human traits that normally are not evident in her ancestors or the present community makeup. She is five feet four inches tall, 115 pounds, very athletic and strong, with brown hair and very dark eyes. She is accepted without second thought. She is often pursued by the males when in her more human appearance as every woman is. The dignity and respect of the men in the 'light zone' is not familiar to Pilo. These same men, when in what they would call the 'wilderness', are much more intense and demanding.

The failure of this most recent excursion, for Pilo, will require an intrusive level of interrogation to both explain and justify every decision she made and the results. She was chosen because of her experiences with the many cross currents of peoples and authorities, both evil and good, that can complicate or facilitate their passage.

Even though the mission was not successful the encounter that Pilo had with a young man at her departure from the train to return her traveling companion to the family has continued to intrigue her. She is also compelled to understand the distorted reflection she saw of herself in his deep blue eyes. Rather than thinking of him as shallow and empty her sense is one of revelation and union. He was, in that brief moment, showing her that he knew of her somehow.

Pilo is beginning to think that, perhaps, she has been isolated too long. To have such thoughts or impressions is an indication of boredom or loneliness. When in her more natural environment and without emphasizing her human traits and appearance, her experiences with the males of her district have been threatening and debasing. Only a rough, crude level of physical raping is the normal practice of the male to satisfy their immediate desires. After ten minutes of brutal violation the female is discarded and left to live or die. The male returns to his duties as though he has just finished lunch and doesn't consider the condition of the flesh he has abused for enjoyment. "Well, maybe boredom can be tolerated." She muses, "I wonder what his name is."

It is because of the commonality of this kind of treatment that Pilo and most of the other females have attempted to form defensive groups in the past. The success of their attempts eventually fall short because of the limited resources as an equalizer to combat the differences in physical strength and the brute force of the aggressors.

With Pilo's generation has come the remembrance of the long hoped for Royal Guardian and the peace that is expected to be a part of the new revelation. The younger females, commonly known as fairgens, have formulated an approach to thwart the expectations of the younger males, commonly known as falpens. The strategy incorporates an offensive tactic of alert, confront and repel. This approach combined with the male's need for the essential supplies of food and the materials that are gained by the excursions into the segregated 'light zones' has been effective at curbing the assaults. The falpens cannot conduct the incursions into the 'light zones' because their appearance is obvious and out of place. No disguise has ever worked because their nature is quickly exposed. They have little awareness of their surroundings when in a relaxed environment and they are not able to transition to the state of acute awareness needed to conduct the incursions successfully. As Pilo would put it, "They are brutes that would be better served with a harness on their neck."

Pilo and her friend, Kania, are from Karlsruhe. Though they do not share the same recent ancestry as Lana, Yarjies, Baetus and the others, their fervor for the engagement with the beasts is a cause they have joined for purpose, adventure, challenge and a way to satisfy their quest for activities with extreme risk. The added benefit of the goal to end the torment of the Rochukas is the bonus worth offering their lives for. Their parents would have called their tendencies a 'death wish'. They call it life, a reason to breath and a reason to celebrate!

As this is the first free night since her return Pilo walks briskly the three blocks from her living complex to her favorite pub. Once there she leans against the thick, heavy, rough wooden door to push it open. Kania, a regular drinking buddy, rushes up and slams her hands against the door, a hand on either side of Pilo's head and pushes while exaggerating a grunt as they open the door and slightly trip into the long, dark hallway of the entrance.

Sounds of the street traffic passing by the doorway as the empty hallway invites them to add their voices, their laughter and their presence to the excitement heard from beyond the hallway's darkness. Each time Pilo visits she will search for the perfect spot inside of the entrance where the convergence of the two impulses of sound will vibrate in her ears.

"There you go", Kania kids as Pilo begins taking small side steps into the hallway, her hands out as though she cannot see. "There I go!" responds Pilo, "and here I am." Pilo closes her eyes as she stops moving. With Kania still near the door she hesitates before beginning to push the door closed, knowing it will slam when closed with no warning of the nearing thud against the frame. The surprise always jolts the occupants of the area inside, at the other end of the entry hallway. It is like a sound chamber that magnifies the sounds and it can be disorienting.

As the door slams Pilo's eyes pop open and she cuts her view to Kania's huge, silent smile. They both then howl and laugh as they embrace, both hopping up and down on their toes like little girls that have been excited by a sudden impulse. Pilo and Kania turn to walk into the club, arm in arm with the tap of their heals echoing slightly along the hallway until the laughter from inside the club overtakes them and pulls them through the curtain as though an unseen hand grasped them and left no other choice but to enter.

After the typical, stumbling entry and the harassment of those interrupted by the distraction, Pilo and Kania extend their middle finger into the piercing stage light to cast an obvious profile on the back stage curtain. Everyone erupts with cheers. The two quickly settle and order drinks. "I saw Baetus recently, just returned I think." Kania poses.

"I don't know how many more times I can get away with these incursions. I am pushing my luck, or should I say the Counsel is testing my odds." Pilo doesn't speak loudly but intensely. Her hand motions bump her glass, almost knocking it over.

Kania, "You are very good but you are right. You run the risk of becoming familiar to those you are mingling with. Too many trips too often and your security will be compromised. If you were to be captured on surveillance cameras and a profile started…."

"Exactly my concern," Pilo remains tense. "I will drop from circulation for a few days."

"Well then," Kania invites, "have a bit of this and we will see what comes next!"

"Prost!" Pilo toasts and consumes the shot of Uzo. "Whooo, Yea!"

Kania follows with a shot of her own. As she slightly drops the glass onto the table a new, noisy entrance is observed as a man, 'not a local', Kania observes, bursts through the back curtain of the stage.

"Is this going to be one of THOSE nights, Kania?" Pilo jokingly asks as a parent may say it.

The two look at each other as they each raise the shot glasses for a refill. "Let me see some money this time," shouts the bartender.

"I have cash", Pilo jumps in, "and here you are!" She shouts over the room of laughter as she hands several bills to the bar tender without counting.

"This guy on the stage, is he a tourist?" Pilo jabs at Kania, "We don't have tourists, do we?"

"We don't allow them!" Kania jokes, "He must be lost then." Pilo adds.

Rand is invited by the women to join them and after a few minutes the waiter approaches to ask his preference. "Well, if the ladies will allow, I will have this one-pointing to Pilo with a soft, red wine and this one-pointing to Kania with a double shot of Irish whiskey." With his back to the wall, Kania to his right and Pilo to his left he is quickly pressed against the wall by the two women. "Ok, sorry! I try too hard sometime to be funny! May I buy the drinks?"

The two release him at his suggestion and laugh at the look of uncertainty on his face. The waiter returns with their requests and hands the unopened bottle of wine to Rand along with a cork screw but no glass. Holding the bottle between his knees as he pulls on the cork screw with both hands the cork is freed. His trained nose can detect an unusual bouquet and a heaviness to the texture as it lay on his tongue. He takes as small a sip as he can from the turned up bottle. After a short pause Rand takes a full mouth full of the red elixir and swallows the warmth of a fire that sooths his raw nerves and frees his pent up emotions.

One more swallow and the flood gate opens within him to allow all of his doubts and disbeliefs and fears to flood his soul. Outwardly he looks calm and relaxed. Outwardly he acts reflective and inspirational. Then he begins to listen to Pilo and Kania talking about their day's activities. Their experiences become the fuel he needs to again see the adventure his travels began with. Rand begins to think that Pilo is the woman he had encountered on the train but he is not yet ready to ask.

Pilo, "I really enjoyed our ride today. The new designs for the bikes are going to make a tremendous difference on the trails. The suspension for the front will significantly reduce the pounding our shoulders get from the drops and the general topography we are navigating on the trails through the mountains, especially on the downhill sections. We will be better equipped to out run the bullets and the hounds. "

Kania, "I think the change in the sprocket ratios will also give us more uphill power and speed on the cross country sections. I can manage the technical part of riding but the added speed and cushion of the front fork suspension will be huge when we are being pursued."

Pilo, "Imagine this riding as a sport someday. Maybe we should work on that because this time of conflict has to end some-day."

Rand, "You ladies are riding bicycles down hills and cross-country on foot paths or trails? What kind of bikes are you talking about?"

Pilo, "We are 'wilderness outfitters and guides'." Pilo uses the terms to cover for their true activities as scouts and couriers for the opposition groups. "We are trying out some new bike designs that are being developed from some of the ideas that started during the wars. And, no, we are not really running from bullets. It is a saying we use to illustrate our quest for speed on the trails."

Rand, "That is very interesting. You know, as terrible as war is, there are developments born out of need that are adapted to a common civilian application. There is one such process that I am familiar with which was developed by the armies doing battle in the deserts of Africa."

Both Pilo and Kania give Rand a look and they both interrupt, "war stories?"

Rand, "No, just interesting, what happened during a war. Not now?"

Pilo, "Okay, go ahead. You look familiar by the way. We will stop you if we can' take it."

Rand, "The troops did not have the re-supply lines to keep them equipped with wearable goods such as tires for the vehicles. The troops would cut apart tires that were damaged but had useable tread, for example. Another tire carcass that had no tread left could be prepared with an adhesive applied to the roughed up surface of the old tread and the removed tread from another damaged tire wrapped around the carcass. The tire would then be secured with bands around the outer circumference so that the tread was compressed against the tire carcass. The whole tire would then be buried in the hot desert sands for twelve hours during which time the adhesive and the hot rubber of the tire and tread would bond. The result was a useable tire from pieces of other, otherwise worthless, tires.

Now that process with some significant improvements is in the public domain as a product that provides a method for what is called 'recapping' of tires for trucks and automobiles. Anyway, I am intrigued by your experiences."

Kania, "Not to change the subject, but to change the subject, how did you find yourself here geographically and here, here tonight?"

Rand, "I want to say, purely by accident. That would not be accurate because I am not sure why my time away from my usual routine has become entangled here and now. I had made friends on the train who suggested that I avoid this area and why. I have a tendency to do the opposite of what someone suggests when I get a glimpse of adventure or mystery. Actually you ladies have reminded me that I took this trip for the adventure of it. It's just that the specifics have been radically altered. This one young man, Baetus I think was his name, impressed me with his energy level and I had a sense of his good judgment. I guess I should have listened."

Kania, "Baetus? We know him!" Sometimes we harass him by calling him 'Sparkle'. He is smart, even more importantly wise, and he is funny. He is expected to be here soon, not here, here, but in the area in a couple of days." Kania also does not want to be too specific or forth coming about potentially sensitive information with someone she does not know.

Pilo gets Kania's attention visually and signals for her to change the subject. Pilo recognizes Rand as the man she crossed paths with on the train during her recent incursion into the light zone.

"Just an F Y I, for what it's worth, we have a friend who will be joining us here tonight so we may need to separate from you when she arrives. Nothing personal, we are enjoying your company. It is just that our friend has been away for weeks working with high stress factors that usually put her in a foul mood until we pump a few drinks into her. So, we don't want to expose you or any new friend to Megan when you might get the worst of impressions. We may see you later in the night or something. Does that make any sense?"

Rand, "Oh, well, okay, I get it. I will go ahead and move to another table now and see if I can get into the entertainment or whatever. Thanks for your hospitality and I hope all goes well with your friend."

Rand moves to an empty table closer to the stage and calls for the waiter to bring him another bottle of wine. He begins to listen to the new poet on stage. This time it is a lady of possibly fifty, dressed in a loose fitting, long, flowing cheese cloth looking, layered dress with a leather belt, sandals and crystal ear rings. He figures that she fancies herself some type of mystic or wise woman. Without paying real close attention Rand picks up a few verses that were meaningful and he could remember, hopefully, when the mist that has settled on his mind is cleared. The piece is titled, 'God Smiles'. What he remembers most are a few verses in the middle because they registered in his sub-conscience the same way that the bizarre images he had barely noticed upon arrival in this place have registered. He knows they both will come up again. Rand repeats what he can remember to himself,

"Believe that we are,
Nothing but ourselves,
Lost and stumbling,
Across the landscape of time,
Likened unto grapes,
Being crushed to become,
Someone else's wine,
Through stolen sight,
We too are blind …"

As he finishes the last line that he can remember he finds himself beginning to settle into a depressed frame of mind that is the result of all that he has been through up to this time on the trip. He is not correctly oriented to his goals. He remembers what the young boy, Michael, told him about having seven days to find the truth. He decides to leave the pub. Falling off of the high stool and onto his feet he looks around for an exit. He is slightly drunk now having the second bottle of wine to himself. Pilo and Kania had been joined by others that he assumes are Megan and Baetus. He thinks he recognizes the man as the Baetus he met but, "who knows," he thinks, "around here it could be every fourth male is named Baetus." He laughs to himself and gives up on being discreet about leaving. Assuming that he should leave by the same way he entered he heads for the stage. The last verse of a somber poem is just reaching his numbed mind as he crosses the stage to the applause of the crowd, "Written by the Sage, the Sorcerer, the meaning of time began. Born with a rage of hunger for what little is in our hands."

Rand raises his hand to push against the curtain as though it is a door. He falls through the curtain and onto the floor inside of the dark passageway. He can hear another roaring applause from the pub. Before he can get to his feet the young man, Baetus, pushes his way through the curtain and is there to help Rand up. "Hello Rand, I remember you from a few days ago on the train from Karlsruhe. It is so good to see you again. May I help you to your car or to get a cab?"

Rand, "No, I am okay.Good to see you again too. Perhaps we will cross paths again in town. Please return to your friends."

This last bit of self-inflicted embarrassment is, as the saying goes, 'the straw the broke the camel's back'. Rand thinks it is good that the passageway is dark and empty so that his tears can't be seen. He is not in the least prepared for what is happening to him nor does he understand why it is happening. He sits again on the floor, wiping away his tears, feeling his face flush and his shoulders begin to shake. He has never, ever cried over feelings of inadequacy or ineptitude. He has never had such feelings before. He has the realization that there is more to life and much greater considerations to be made than what to wear, where to live, who he will bed tonight. Consequently he is also beginning to question the need to pursue such questions. Life can be very simple when it is superficial.

Still upset, Rand gets to his feet, clears his eyes and heads for the door. He feels weak as he approaches the door. He places both hands on the handle and gives maximum effort as though he were moving a great weight. He hears a creak as the door begins to swing open. Immediately the night air surrounds him as he steps outside. The air is moist, cool and somewhat refreshing. All of the foot traffic is gone. There is an occasional passing car, distant giggles and deep voices carrying through the darkness.

It is now twelve thirty a.m. and Rand is alone on the sidewalk. He looks both ways for a taxi hoping to see the same cabbie waiting. There are none in sight. Rand begins walking in the direction that he thinks his bungalow might be. He really has no idea where he is. The night air combining with the exercise of walking begins to clear his head enough to allow him to begin rationalizing a solution to his present quandary of how to get home. He spies a telephone booth at the next corner and walks to it as he fishes in his pockets for change. As he reaches for the phone with his left hand he pulls some change from his right pocket and lifts his right hand to see what he has while placing the receiver between his left shoulder and left ear in order to free up his left hand. He finds a one half Mark and inserts it into the money receptacle, 'clink, clink' is the sound of the coin being accepted into the device. When the dial tone comes on Rand realizes that he has no idea what number to dial. He glances to his right and sees his cabbie from earlier in the evening setting across the street in his cab and waving to get his attention.

Rand hangs up the phone, collects his money and leaves the booth. He waves at the cabbie making a u turn in the intersection and pulls up in front of Rand on the corner. Rand opens the back door to get in but the cabbie says, "Hey, why don' you sit up front so we can talk as I drive."

"Sure", Rand replies, glad to see a friendly face. "I was just trying to call someone to pick me up and here you are!"

"Yea," grins the cabbie, "a good cabbie is like that, especially since we have so many visitors here. I try to remember each destination so that I won't lose anybody when these 'days of darkness' happen.

Rand, "I thought they occurred at regular intervals. Or, at least that is what I was told by an official briefing."

Cabbie, "That is the 'official' line. Actually they can happen at any time, in the twinkling of an eye, as the saying goes." The cabbie becomes very serious, "Have you made your decision yet?"

Visibly annoyed Rand responds, "Decision about what? I don't know what decision I have to make and why is it everybody's concern. Everyone keeps beating around the bush, as the saying goes, as though I am supposed to already know the question. I am very confused! I am a little drunk."

Okay, calm down", soothes the cabbie. "I will explain as best I can. First, though, let's get somewhere so that I can park the car and not be distracted by traffic, okay?"

"No!" snaps Rand, "I prefer to go to my bungalow and get some sleep. I have had enough for one day. If you want to talk then do it while you drive."

"Sure, sure," calms the driver as he eases into the lane and drives toward his destination. After a few minutes of silence he clears his throat and begins to softly speak from his heart. "If I may, sir, I would like to tell you a little about myself."

Rand, "Sure."

The cabbie continues, "When I was about fifteen a couple of friends and I made a pact to party ourselves into oblivion and be dead by the age of thirty three. We had already been drinking alcohol and running the neighborhood for a couple of years. As most teenagers, we felt pretty invincible and smarter than anyone else. Through the next few years, until graduation from high school, we carried out our plans to the hilt. Anyway, the process accelerated rather dramatically after high school and we began to include many different drugs, especially hallucinogens and other mind expanding formulas, as they were called, that were at times totally uncontrollable.

By the time I was twenty one I had serious liver damage and my mind was a frazzled ball of mush that couldn't connect two logical thoughts even if someone could give me a million dollars to do so. One of my friends almost died in a car accident. We went to visit him in the hospital and as we talked someone brought up our pact from not so many years before. We all shook our heads but didn't talk about it. I think we were each reconsidering our agreement and wanting to back out but no-one would talk about it."

"Hey where are we?" Rand demands, "I didn't know you were going to take the scenic route in the middle of the night!" Rand is agitated by the story and the cabbie's imposition on his liberty. "I don't care what stupid promises you weren't able to keep as a man years ago. Take me to my place."

"Uh, sorry sir, I thought you wanted to find some answers. I guess I am taking the long way around on both accounts. We are not very far from your bungalow so you will be there soon."

Rand leans his head back on the seat and closes his eyes. He feels the vibrations of the car on the road through his neck and against the back of his head. He begins to relax and listen to the car work to get him home. There is a faint squeak from one of the seat springs, the occasional metallic clinking of the keys against the steering column, muffled sounds of the rolling and pitching vehicle as it made its way down the narrow roadway which is offset with depressions in the ground on both sides of the roadway so that the car is never on a level path.

Rand almost drifts away into sleep until the metallic clinking of the keys resurrects an uncomfortable memory. He is brought back to his first night of darkness as he connects the sound of the keys to the similar sound of the bag carried by one of the two murderers who crucified the poor receptionist on a tree.

Rand jerks up straight in his seat as the taxi comes to a stop in front of his bungalow. Rand begins sweating profusely as he fumbles for the door handle. The cabbie, from his view, reflected by the mirror can see that Rand is upset as he turns and puts his right arm over the back of his seat and reaches for Rand's shoulder. He grabs Rand's shirt in an attempt to restrain him before he can get out of the car. "Wait!" shouts the cabbie, "what is wrong? Can I help?"

"No!" Rand shouts back, "I am just losing my mind and I need out of this cab, out of this insane town and out of this nightmare!"

"I can help." The cabbie says calmly, "I know what you are going through. I went through it myself."

Rand stops at the edge of the seat with his feet on the ground and his hands clasped to the opened door. He looks back at the cabbie and says, "You are the second person to tell me that but I don't even know what is going on myself, how can you help me?"

I know that you have been through a night of darkness, right? You have been interviewed by the public relations committee, right? Now you are down to a couple of days left after today and you don't know what to expect after that, right?"

"Okay, okay, sounds like you have been where I am presently." Concedes Rand, "I met this kid the other day who said he will help me too but I haven't seen him lately."

"That is probably Michael who lives in the neighborhood. How about if you go inside, get some sleep and I'll pick Michael up in the morning. We will come over and let you cook breakfast and then we will all sit down and work out this quandary of yours."

"Okay, sounds good, thanks a lot." Rand agrees. He is exhausted and wants only to sleep.

Black G. M. C.

Rand wakes up early feeling rested and relaxed. He has a sense of new beginnings for the time he has remaining. His first reaction is to look outside to see what the day looks like. It is overcast and a light rain is falling. Even though the weather is not grand for the first time since his arrival Rand is ready for a change of weather and a change of circumstance. He thinks that this day will be better as he remembers that his new friends are coming over for breakfast. He quickly refreshes himself and begins to see what kind of utensils and cookware is available in the small kitchenette. As he is rummaging through the under sink cabinet he hears a knock at the door. He looks up and back over his shoulder to see the faces of the kid, Michael, and the cabbie whose name he still doesn't know. They are both smiling with their faces pressed against the door window glass. Michael turns the latch and they both stumble in laughing.

"Well, you two seem to be having a good day so far." Rand smiles, "I am getting off to a good start too, so far."

Michael responds, "Great! We hope things are about to change for you. By the way, have you two been introduced yet?"

"No, not exactly," They answer simultaneously.

"Well let me have the honor then", Michael offers. "Rand this is Joseph" as he gestures toward the cabbie, "Joseph this is Rand." They politely shake hands and everyone smiles.

"I was starting to get organized in order to make breakfast as my part of the arrangement from last night. However I don't think I have the resources here to do it." Rand explains.

Joseph, "Can you make some coffee?"

Rand, "Let me check. I have coffee, a pot and some sugar. So, if there is water at the tap and electricity at the receptacle then I can manage that much," surmises Rand with a grin.

Michael, "That will work."

After a few minutes on the burner Joseph alerts the others, "The coffee is ready. Are you guys ready?"

"Yes sir!" shouts Michael.

"Uh, yea", Rand hesitates.

The group decides to sit around the table on the patio. Although it is rainy it is cool and relaxing outside. They file out and take their places around the small, round table. Rand instinctively sits closest to the door. He isn't completely at ease in this place or with his two guests. He still hasn't allowed himself to think about all that has taken place in his life since his arrival in such a peculiar place. He is hoping this little get together will shed some light in concrete ways and dispel his confusion. Rand doesn't think he is being given or been able to find any answers. Everyone is making suggestions but they are always open ended and not defining.

Joseph, "Well are we ready to begin?" Everyone nodded their heads in agreement. Joseph continues, "I don't know if you remember, Rand, but last night I was telling you about myself."

"Yea, I remember getting upset and cutting you off. I apologize for that."

Joseph continues, "I know you were a little drunk and a lot edgy so I didn't take it personally. I like you and I hope I can help you. If I may, I would like to finish what I was telling you last night."

Rand, "Please do."

"O.k., well, as my friends and I sat there in the hospital room in nervous silence a thought occurred to me. I did not want to die. I did not know exactly what I would do but I knew that I did not want to die. I wanted to live an exciting life that would be remembered and one that I could tell others about without any fear of rejection. I wanted to be exciting and excited. I wanted to be loved and loving. I wanted to have stories to tell my children, someday, that would teach them some life lesson from one of my own experiences. I really wanted to live and not to die at any age. So, I spoke up and said to my friends, "Hey guys I say we have got to give up our old ways or else we are not going to be anything but four piles of bones, inside four boxes, inside four holes in the ground with four odd shaped rocks to mark the spot! Everyone laughed as we looked at each other and agreed that the pact was broken."

Michael, "So, what did you do?"

Joseph, "We all shook hands and told each other, "May we each live long and happy lives.""

Rand, "So how did you end up being a cabbie?"

"That is another story in itself but you may find it interesting", continued Joseph. "Even though I had this mini revelation I still wasn't any wiser than I was before the revelation. I had always been aware of an empty place within my being. I could not be content no matter what was going on in my life.

I had been raised in a religious family but that wasn't filling the void. I thought that adventure and excitement would fill the emptiness. I decided to visit a friend in another city about eight or nine hundred miles away. I had bought this old panel van to fix up. It was a black G.M.C. with a ribbed metal floor in it and a few rust holes around the wheel wells. There was only one seat, a bench seat that was originally the back seat from a newer style van. The seat would normally be bolted to the floor but this one was not. I was in a hurry to explore the road and fuel the adventure of my soul. In other words, I thought I could get away with not bolting the seat down. It wouldn't be a problem unless I would have to stop real fast or if I took off to fast. The transmission was a manual three speed with a sticky clutch so the take offs could be an adventure. Since I was usually paying more attention to the radio dial or the tape player that ate my tapes or the pretty girl on the sidewalk the stops could be exciting too. The floor stayed shiny and I would have to check my chest for the bruised imprint of my steering wheel emblem, G.M.C. I found it there more than once. There was one safety feature that saved my life. The van would not go over fifty miles an hour, even downhill!" Everyone laughed at Joseph's rendition of a ride in his panel van.

Rand, "Oh, man that sounds so crazy, Joseph, are you making this up? How did an American vehicle become available to you here?"

Michael, "If he is he has got it down! I have heard this one before and he hasn't changed anything yet."

Joseph, "I am guessing the van was an old military vehicle."

They all laughed and everyone decided to go for another cup of coffee. Rand stood between the door and the kitchenette with his friends behind him making their coffee. He looks outside as he stirs his coffee and notices that he is feeling a little more lighthearted than when the day started. It is dreary outside but with the camaraderie and the normal, daily atmosphere present he can feel some perspective returning to his understanding. If there really was a higher purpose for his being here he feels confident that he will find it. He finds comfort in his new friends and their genuine friendship for him can help. Rand snaps out of his muse as Michael bumps into him intentionally to get his attention.

"Hey", sighs Rand, "I was almost home for a minute there."

"Yea, but where would that leave us?" shouts Joseph jokingly.

"Relax", comforts Michael with a smile, "You may get there before you know it."

Rand, "How about if we stay inside now. I think the rainy weather is getting to me. I get cold easily in this weather."

Everyone agrees so they move into the living room area which is a part of the large open room that makes up most of the bungalow except for the bathroom and the kitchenette. The living room area's main feature is the one large window on the back wall which gives a wonderful view of the countryside extending away from the building. First a sloping, grassy hill that leads to a valley with a mixture of trees and bushes, a rocky surface more so the farther down the slope until reaching steeply inclined hills that lead to the forested foothills of distant mountains.

Rand passes in front of the window to take in the view. He momentarily thinks about where he is and then just as quickly he pushes the thought out of his mind as he motions for his friends to take a seat. The room is dark because it is such a cloudy day so Joseph turns on the table lamp next to him at the end of the couch. Michael is seated at the other end of the couch with his feet dangling above the floor.

Rand begins, "I want you guys to know that I appreciate your friendship and I do enjoy your company. I want to tell you a little about myself too. Michael has heard some of my story already." Rand feels compelled to share. "I am not an idiot and I did not crawl out from under a rock yesterday. I have always tried to live a good, fair life. I know there is a part of me that is not fulfilled but I figure that is just the hunger of life that everyone has and that without it no-one will achieve anything. I have never known that there is anything more or anything greater than being successful in the world.

I feel that right now you guys are really trying to tell me that I have missed the mark and have come up short. Honestly, I resent it."

Both Joseph and Michael are stunned by Rand's statement. He has gone from wanting to share about himself to attacking them.

Rand continues, "So, Joseph, how did you get here? What happened between the wild trips in your panel van and your arrival here? I rolled in here on a train. I thought I was on vacation and now here I am in this place. Why are you still here? Will I never be able to leave? Is this some kind of hell?" Rand is becoming overtly frustrated that their conversations are always about everything but what he wants to know. Everyone seems to be trying to answer his questions but never do.

Joseph tries to return the atmosphere to the friendly discussion they were all comfortable with because he senses Rand's frustration. "Well, it can be hell I guess. However, it really depends on how you handle it. If I may, to finish my story and get to your question I will explain how I got here.

On one of my excursions a little later in life I was leaving the hill country and headed for the flat lands. To get there I had to pass through the river country or the land of the hot springs. I chose the river country because I was a little more familiar with parts of that region. The one particular area that I had to pass through was a slightly odd place. The people all sounded alike when they spoke and looked somewhat alike too."

Rand checks his watch to find that it is now one thirty. "With that, whatever that is, let's get some lunch. Aren't you guy's hungry? It is one thirty so let's pick this up again later this afternoon." Everyone agrees to meet back at Rand's at four to continue their discussion.

Fripree

Baetus transferred to the route through Heidelberg to Speyer. Claus is, unwittingly, Baetus's cover. Baetus has been represented to him as a security professional that Claus had requested from his employer because of the dangerous nature of the area he was temporarily assigned to. The clashes between local law enforcement and various subversive groups with his focus being a reasoned expectation of heightened conflict levels in the areas just outside of Speyer.

Baetus's current assignment may intertwine with the local events in that the group he is responsible for may be targets of any developing hostilities and also for him to be in range, socially, with his second charge of security for the reporter. This area becoming involved in conflicts with radical groups signals an expansion of the area in play. Baetus needs to avoid any direct conflict dynamics while being in proximity and possibly interfering with other's goals in order to accomplish his. The challenge is to be in place before all of the pieces begin to move.

Once off the train Baetus sheds Claus and picks up a motorcycle that is in storage near the train station. Passenger trains normally have cargo cars as a part of the overall makeup. Stops made along the route are for passenger transfers and also cargo loading and unloading. Baetus anticipates the stop will be at the dock in Schifferstadt which is before Speyer on the line.

Baetus's intention is to board the train during the brief stop to verify Lana's security and inform the group of the changes taking place which will directly impact their scheduling and destinations. To get there Baetus will have to negotiate the town of Speyer's traffic, pedestrians and any attention from law enforcement while ignoring every traffic control to quickly exit the town. He had no more than thirty five minutes to complete a forty minute trip and then board the train undetected.

When Baetus finds himself in such situations he wonders to himself, "Why can't I vanish or blend like Megan does?" Such thoughts always cause Baetus to dwell on Megan and wonder where she is and how she is. He does look forward to seeing her without distractions after this assignment. Leaving the warehouse district on the trail bike Baetus has a few questionable corners to negotiate. The wet cobblestone streets in the old town are not kind to speed and agility. A good suspension helps but a little skill will be helpful as well. Baetus is on a motorcycle like this only once or twice a year.

He makes his way out of down town, going north to connect with highway sixty one going west to the rail yard. The incoming train whistle is sounding as the train is slowing when Baetus arrives. He parks the bike and quickly mingles with the small group of handlers for the cargo being transferred. Baetus enters the rail car as a laborer to remove cargo to be transferred then passes through the car and jumps from the other side. He walks forward briskly to the first passenger car and climbs the ladder. "So far, so good." He thinks, "Now if this door will be unlocked?" He says under his breath. It is unlocked so he enters as though he is a passenger returning from a smoke break. No-one asked.

Baetus reaches the far end of the car without seeing any of his party. As he begins to pass to the next car the departing train lurches forward. He has only to find the correct cabin and get everyone prepared for, hopefully, nothing. Travel time to Speyer should be no more than twenty minutes. Baetus enters the next car and sees a man entering from the opposite end armed with a shotgun and wearing a protective vest. Baetus gambles that he has enough time and turns back through the door before a spray of buckshot or a led slug finds him. "Being small and quick are assets in some situations." He chuckles to himself. The round from the shotgun whizzes past him after punching a fist sized hole through the solid door.

Baetus is not armed so he leaves the car, dropping to the gravel rail bed and running the length of the car then jumps aboard, leaving the threat to catch him again. "It is time to move." Baetus checks himself mentally in preparation for the threat level anticipated when locating and extracting the small group without confrontation. Baetus is reminded that pivoting operations will pressure every relationship within the approved protocols. Everyone put in the position feels it just as Baetus does now, he being the pivot in this maneuver.

Boarding the second car he sees Norsha standing partially in the doorway and partially in the passageway of the car. She looks toward Baetus and lets out a shout, "There he is! I wasn't expecting you. Why are you here?"

Baetus, "The word has come down to change our location for field operations management and begin to re-orient our strategies for logistical support. We need to get off of this train and re-route to Pforzheim."

Norsha "Got it," as she steps into the cabin and asks everyone for their attention. "Okay everybody we have some changes to address and we will have to disembark and be re-routed. I need for everyone to be certain you have your materials and belongings. We do not want to leave anything behind. Be prepared to move quickly and follow directions without question.

Baetus leaves their company to relocate the armed man he first encountered and to assess the threat as either direct with Lana as the target or collateral with his group being in the wrong place at the wrong time. He finds the man at the rear of the train, four cars from the group. He is standing guard as to prevent anyone from boarding.

Baetus decides to leave well enough alone and move ahead of the group's car then work his way back to them while evaluating the situation. He can hear shouting from possibly the locomotive area or the security car which is close to the locomotive and before the passenger cars in the lineup. Baetus surmises that getting his group on the ground and away from the train immediately will give them the greatest opportunity to escape. He returns to the group to find that Norsha has everyone ready to move.

Baetus, "Everyone, we will be leaving the train and traveling on foot. Once we are away from this immediate area we will stop to give everyone a breather and better evaluate our approach."

Lana, "Do we have a source of water? I have maybe a quart."

Norsha, "We are sending an alarm so that by the time we make the stop Baetus was just mentioning we will have a better idea of how we must proceed. Most importantly we must clear this area as quickly as we can. It is time to move."

Baetus takes the lead with Norsha at the center of the group that is moving in a single file formation with Megan as the rear guard. They each drop down onto the gravel bed and step into the tall, waist high, grass of the field leading away from the rail yard. Once away from the small complex and out of the lighting the group pauses to make sure everyone is keeping up. They are about two hundred yards from the rail yard and can see the train in the lighting. Although shouting can be heard all of the activity is taking place on the platform side and away from their view.

The important point for them is that they are away from the threat.

Yarjies, "Everyone okay? We will be able to navigate our way to Speyer quickly by dividing into two groups. This will also allow us to use public transportation and to mix again with other pedestrians. While waiting here we must keep our voices low and avoid using any form of lighting. We will need to wait here until the activity at the train has ended. Everyone is welcome to join this conversation. Baetus, will you lead it off?"

Baetus, "Speyer is our short term destination. Our operations center is being relocated to Pforzheim. Our immediate goal now is to get to Speyer safely. We will have Norsha, Alana and Megan travel together while Yarjies and I will follow. We will meet again at the train terminal. We have transportation waiting there. Anyone have questions?"

Lana, "Why are the changes?"

Baetus, "We are entering a phase of compression with our network of patriots applying pressure to the engagement zone in order to contain events within the boundaries already in place."

Megan, "In other words, Miss Lana, we are moving everyone to the conflict zone to prepare for an offensive that will be the beginning of the end of this endeavor."

Norsha, "Lana, this now is the beginning of your purpose, your role. You will no longer be known by any other name than your given name of Fripree. You must not use or answer to any other name."

With a big smile Megan announces, "Fripree is your perfect name. You are free and you will set others free." Everyone smiles with excitement and agreement. They each place their left hand on the shoulder of the one to their left, saying together with lowered voices, "Fripree".

Yarjies, "This core group assembled here will remain together throughout the campaign. We are each responsible for ourselves and one another."

The rail yard lighting goes off except for the emergency lighting of the office and the parking area gate. All activity has moved away from the rail yard as a van leaves the parking area.

Baetus, "Now we will need to return to the dock area and then exit through the parking area to gain transportation. Once we get to the exit point of the gate we will separate into our traveling groups. Let us move as quickly and as quietly as possible. Is everyone ready?" Everyone quietly nods their head, yes.

The group moves stealthily through the field to the loading dock. With everyone eager to move away from the area they jog across the parking area and climb over the light weight security gate. Norsha, Fripree and Megan separate from the two men and briskly walk toward a pay phone booth a block down the street. They disappear into the darkness that separates the low level lighting of the street lights. Baetus and Yarjies continue watching until the three reappear in the next street lights hazy glow. Both men now feel their energy level rise and their optimism become more grounded.

Yarjies, "Baetus, again I am reminded that the one constant in life is change."

Baetus, "I agree and the better one is at negotiating change with flexibility and a bit of humility the more successful one will be."

Yarjies sees that the women have reached the phone booth. "Okay, Baetus, after the women hail a cab we will do the same. Sound good?"

Baetus, "We do have an alternative."

Yarjies, "Such as?"

Baetus, "I traveled here from Speyer on a small motorcycle. I left it nearby. It should still be there. We should both be able to fit on it. The back seat may not be very comfortable but we don't have far to go."

Yarjies, "Let's get to it quickly so that we don't get too far behind."

After a two block sprint to the storage facility Baetus goes inside to retrieve the bike while Yarjies hangs onto the fencing, trying to breathe. Baetus returns with the bike and activates the gate to open. Yarjies is no longer holding onto the fencing but he is still breathing deeply to recover.

Yarjies, "Man, I thought I was in pretty good shape but I guess I am not so fit. I am glad to find out now and not when someone intent on doing harm is chasing me."

Baetus, "Oh, you are okay for an older guy. We all have some conditioning to do."

Yarjies, "Yeah, older guy, you say. Come here and I will show you a thing or two."

Baetus, "Come here? You can't catch me?" Baetus is enjoying the rare opportunity to interact with someone of Yarjies' stature in such a playful way. Yarjies is one, if not the primary of three, Discree of our leadership.

As Baetus rolls the small motorcycle past the gate Yarjies walks to him and gives the seating a worried look. There is only a pad that is four inches wide and ten inches long for a passenger to sit on. It is going to be uncomfortable for one of them.

Baetus, "Do you have any experience with these?"

Yarjies, "Yeah, watching other people ride them."

Baetus, "Well then you will be the passenger. Do you think you can fit on?"

Yarjies, "I will fit. I may lose my balls doing this. You will need to find a good line to follow on those cobblestones."

With Baetus being smaller he is able to move up and sit partially on the fuel tank and still reach the shifter with his foot. Yarjies is having trouble compressing his legs enough for his feet to be secure on the pegs. Getting through the first gear shift went better than expected. Baetus's slightly long hair is becoming annoying to Yarjies by being blown into his face. They both quickly realize that it gets much cooler after sundown at forty miles an hour and especially for Baetus in the front.

Having arrived at the Speyer station the women are watching as the motorcycle quietly rolls into the parking area apparently out of fuel and coasting. Baetus brings the bike to a stop but neither one moves immediately. Yarjies has to move before Baetus can get off. Baetus has to thaw out before he can get off of the bike. With both feet on the ground Yarjies lifts himself off the seat and groans slightly. It is obvious that he is in pain as he uses his hands to cup his testicles and moves slowly with his legs separated in an unnatural way. He looks up at the approaching women with one brow raised and says, tightly lipped, "Hello".

Once Yarjies has moved away from the motorcycle Baetus swings his leg back over the seat and stands erect momentarily before bending over to stretch his hamstrings. As the women greet them Baetus remarks, "You see what age can do to you?" pointing at Yarjies. I know that others have ridden on such bikes as passengers for hundreds of miles." Baetus chuckles as Yarjies stands erect now and moves his hands away from his groin. Everyone gathers their bags again and walk to the terminal where their ride is waiting.

Baetus talks loudly to be heard over the rail yard noises. "We will first go to the center that is being abandoned in order to meet with everyone there and get our bearings before going on to our new location."

Norsha, "How much of a presence do we maintain in Speyer?"

Baetus, "I do not know currently. That is one of the reasons for our visit. Activities, personnel movements and other logistics are fluid now and the pace is increasing. This visit will tell us what the coming days will be like."

Everyone gets into the small van and becomes quiet as they pull away. The road noise fills the van and everyone looks out their window at the passing landscape. After a ten minute ride away from the rail yard, east, to a lightly populated area near the Rhine River everyone is a bit invigorated by the brief rest and stillness.

The van drives into the small complex, a shipping company for local hot shotdeliveries and a small network in the area. Everyone unloads from the van and walks to the office of the warehouse building. There were only light operations in the yard and no foot traffic. A staging tractor is moving trailers to and from the loading dock, all normal activities. Entering the building becomes troublesome immediately. Identification is required because they are not known and an insignia or emblem of some sort is expected to be displayed by each person.

Fripree, "Are we not prepared? Baetus, were you given these items to distribute? Norsha, who do we speak with? Yarjies, are you recovered from your injuries? Get involved, this is unacceptable and embarrassing."

Megan, "Here we go! It is time to move into the flow of the present. Fripree is giving us direction so we need to find an entry attendant to set us up to enter. Everyone will know us soon!"

Once through the initial security the group makes their way to the office of The Affairs and Assignments Oversight Director.

Fripree, "Cool title, have we come at a bad time?"

Director, "Any time can be a bad time. It depends on who you are and why you are here." The Director was not smiling. "Without some answers I don't care about your questions."

Yarjies does not recognize the Director or the name on his lapel pin name tag. Over recent years Yarjies has spent many days as a member of the leadership and management hierarchy who practiced the deliberate avoidance of titles, commissions, committees, protocols, and bureaucracies of perpetual processes and priorities that take on a life of their own by supporting the approach of addressing issues without a matrix for progress or a realization of success. The attitude and approach being exhibited before him now brings him back to those beginnings to relight a fire that has been smoldering but lacking the fuel he finds in this inexperienced, arrogant, smart ass. "You, young man, are out of line! I must speak to your supervisor now!"

Turning back as to look at Baetus, Yarjies reaches into his pants pocket to remove a ring he has concealed until now. He places the ring on his middle finger. As the Director hangs up the phone to tell Yarjies that the visiting commander of the facility will be with him momentarily Yarjies exhibits the ring by presenting his left hand in front of himself at chest level with all fingers pointing up except for the middle finger which displays the ring with the remainder of his finger bent at the knuckle. The message is clear and the Director immediately knows he is disrespecting someone of importance. He offers Yarjies a seat and then seats himself behind his desk. Yarjies remains standing for the short time it took for the Commander to enter the room.

Unknown to the director, the Commander is someone that Yarjies has known for a long time. The Commander addresses the director, "What is going on Captain? Is this honorable gentleman waiting for you to be able to grab both ears at the same time?"

Captain, "Yes? Sir? I have not intentionally stressed the 'gentleman' but I do not know who he is."

Commander, "I understand. When in doubt calling first rather than last should be doable. If I were to need more privacy I would tell you."

Captain Tom, "I understand and I apologize."

The Commander, "All is forgiven. I know you are learning from any mistakes and I appreciate that. I need for you to verify the transportation for this group which will be leaving when we finish here." The Director bowed his head slightly before leaving the room.

The Commander and Yarjies look at each other and smile. Yarjies, "Good to see you Yeshi."

Yeshi, "I cannot go anywhere without solving somebody's problem. It can be stressful being popular." Yeshi laughs.

Yarjies, "I don't feel your pain. I am okay with being a background guy."

Yeshi, "Every time you say something like that you get into trouble. You are you and I will be cool about it!"

Yarjies, "Being unpredictable is being 'me'."

Yeshi, "As a background you should be stable and consistent even in change."

Yarjies, "Break it down! If my back is on the ground I am as stable and consistent as I can be." Yarjies chuckles.

Yeshi, "Enough, how has it been so long since seeing you?"

Yarjies, "Be careful there you are bordering on dishonesty. You know that you cannot go there."

Yeshi, "Got it, I was checking you."

Yarjies, "Since you are where I am and you know what I know, you see me before I see a new day has been offered to me, your question must be rhetorical. I cannot say thanks for it all quick enough and I love you for it." Yarjies realizes that the other members of his group are witnessing the exchange and he is slightly embarrassed that he has not introduced them sooner.

Yeshi responds, "Now it is you who is bordering on mistake. You and most others are a bit self-serving with your attention, most of the time. But, of course, it is all circumstantial." Yeshi smiles and walks to Yarjies and the two embrace. With a mutual pat on the shoulder they walk to the inner office which is located behind the Director's desk. At the doorway Yarjies pauses then gestures toward his company and requests of Yeshi, "May my companions join us?"

Yeshi, "In a few minutes." He then enters the small office and Yarjies follows knowing the others heard the response and will be waiting. The door swings closed.

First Field Trip

First on Rand's agenda after everyone is gone is to call for a pizza to be delivered. After making the call he turns on the television and plants himself in front of it to try and catch up on world events and maybe some entertainment. He flips through the channels looking for news and finds World Net 1. He then reclines on the couch and falls into a deep sleep as the vortex of a nightmare presents the scene of a courtyard at night and then pulls him in.

The area is enclosed by large buildings which are very grand with a lot of marble both very white and very dark. The courtyard is paved with tiles. The only other structure is a large, ornate fountain with figures of mermaids and angels. The water spouts rise almost out of sight into the night and come crashing down onto the figures that are arranged around the center of the fountain. Lights from within the fountain partially illuminate a crowd of spectators who are to one side and looking at something behind the fountain.

Within the dream Rand is captured by a darkness beginning to come over him as he is numbed by the images. The scene changes and so does his awareness of what is before him. A wooden pole has been erected and a naked, severely beaten and bleeding man is hanging by one forearm which has a spike driven through and his other arm is hanging limp at his side. The flesh of the victims forearm is tearing from the weight of the body pulling downward and only the wrist joint is holding the body in position.

A ladder is then rested against the vertical pole and a grotesquely disfigured person or a feral humanoid creature ascends the ladder, raises the limp arm and finished the work by binding the arm with wire. The creature then howls, slides down the ladder and runs away into the darkness with the crowd of onlookers chasing after him.

Suddenly a television commercial for toothpaste blares loudly and brightly and Rand awakens with a start and hears a nervous rapping on the door. Sitting up he knocks off his eyeglasses which fall to the floor. He is too overwhelmed by the experiences of the dream to respond. It took a minute for him to figure out that he has experienced a dream and then he begins to cry uncontrollably. After a few seconds more the door is pushed open and little Michael runs in, nervously asking for somewhere to hide. Michael darts into the bathroom and closes the door.

Forced back into his present situation by Michael's entrance Rand begins to hear what sounds like a struggle taking place behind the closed door. Rand can hear two voices even though only Michael has run in. The voice of a man and of a child with the two screaming at each other as Rand cautiously walks toward the door to open it and intervene to help his friend. Having never been a brawling sort of man he overcomes his fear at the sound of breaking glass. He forces open the door to find no-one inside.

The room is a disaster from the violent struggle. There is a small pool of blood on the floor beside the commode and a smeared, bloody hand print on the window sill. Rand assumes Michael has crawled out the window or has been dragged out of the window. Rand finds himself wondering which is stranger, his dream or his reality. As he looks out at the ground under the window he sees only one set of foot prints in the dirt and another small stain of blood a few feet from the house. Rand guesses that Michael, or whoever it is, to be wounded and on foot.

Rand cannot place the second voice heard during the struggle. He could clearly make out Michael's voice but the other voice was very deep and threatening. He wanted to help his friend so he went back inside to review the events and look for any clues to help him understand. He finds the door key on the dinette table, whisks it up, opens the door and steps out to the patio. He looks right and then left before beginning to track the foot prints from outside the bathroom window.

The foot prints are too large for a child and their deep imprint on the dirt were made by someone of weight or by someone carrying something of weight. After studying the immediate area closely Rand follows the foot prints and occasional blood drop stains toward the street in front of his bungalow where they stop. He finds one right footprint about one foot into the roadway and then a crossing set of tire tracks. He cannot remember hearing a vehicle at the time of the incident but his conclusion at this point was that the person was picked up at the road. He cannot tell which direction the vehicle was traveling so he stopped his search there for the moment.

Returning to the patio Rand sits at the table and tries to figure out what might be next. Finding himself perplexed again he goes back inside. It is now 3:30 p.m. He walks to the television and turns it off. He then realizes that his pizza was never delivered. It didn't really matter anymore so he doesn't bother to call them again.

Looking out at the landscape beyond the residence across the street he decides to go for a walk. All of his experiences since arriving here have been so bizarre and overwhelming. The peace of nature may help his frazzled psyche. The more he thinks about it the greater his desire to escape into the forest. He quickly goes inside, throws a few cans of food into a bag, grabs his jacket, puts on his hiking boots and is out the door before anything can change his momentum. He is as anxious as a kid going on his first field trip. He hopes that no-one saw him as he jumped the small ditch running along the other side of the road and then briskly walk across the small field to the edge of the trees. There he stops and looks back to see if anyone is following. Childhood memories of adventurous days playing in the countryside on Saturdays when his family would visit friends who lived away from town now entertained his imagination.

Rand can hear a woman's voice singing as he walks into the woods. He thinks it might be a breeze blowing through the trees or a bird's song. The more intently he listens the clearer the sound becomes. A woman is singing a beautiful song of love to someone. Rand begins walking in the direction of the singing and after passing through a growth of bushes he can see a very large willow tree about seventy or eighty yards away. There is a woman sitting on a blanket close to the tree as she sings the melody which is leading him. Rand thinks there must be someone else there just out of sight at the moment that she is singing to. He squats down where he is and listens until the end of her song. He finds himself drawn to her. He feels a sense of peace and joy in the song. He wants to know this woman and thank her for this moment of reprieve from his troubles that her song has given him.

As he stands the woman also stands, turns toward him and waves. Because of the distance he can faintly hear her call to him. In his heart he can hear her as though she were standing next to him. Rand returns the wave and begins to walk toward her, expecting to see her companion appear and stand between them. No-one else revealed them-selves so Rand absorbs himself in her presence.

She smiles warmly and asks him to rest awhile. "Maggie is my name." she says with a smile as she extends her hand in greeting.

"I am Rand. I do not want to impose on your privacy. I heard you singing and could not resist finding the source of such beautiful music. I must be intruding. I'll not bother you any longer."

"No." she replies, "You are not intruding at all. I knew you were coming, I just didn't know when."

"How did you know I was coming?" Rand asks.

"To be more precise, I knew someone was coming. This is my place of meditation and prayer. The song you heard is a part of my worship. The one I worship told me that someone would be here today that I could be a help to."

Rand feels his heart warm to the friendliness of her smile and the soothing tone of her voice. He does not desire her in a sexual way although he has not excluded the possibility. Her genuine warmth and compassionate outreach to him is irresistible. "Are you here alone?" he asks.

"No, I am never alone." She answers, "there is no-one here to disturb us but I have friends that are never far away."

"I understand." Rand responds without really understanding.

"Are you just out for a walk in the forest?" she asks.

"Well kind of. Really though I am kind of trying to create enough space to be able to figure some things out." Rand answers with uncertainty.

"Have you been here for more than a couple of days?" Maggie asks.

"About three days I think. It is hard to tell actually. Everything has been so confusing since I arrived. I started my trip as a vacation and hoped for an opportunity to discover some truths but my experiences here have been too intense to work through." Rand speaks slowly and carefully.

Maggie continues, "Are you confronting feelings that have not been a part of your life before now?" Rand nods his head, "Are you making decisions that have not been a part of your thinking before now?" Rand nods his head, "Are there fearful events taking place around you that you cannot explain?" Rand nods his head. "I don't mean to pepper you with so many questions but I do want to hone in on your feelings at this time so that I may offer my constructive perspective as one who has been through the same type of psychological convulsions upon arriving here."

Rand exclaims, "Yes! I don't know why or what to do!"

"I cannot answer all of your questions but I can take you to someone who can," she comforted Rand.

"I have heard that before", he says. "All they wanted was my money and my influence."

"Let me guess", she queries, "Was it a religious leader?"

"Yea, some guy who is part of some sort of committee that barged into my place. He told me basically that I had three days to choose his way or there would be no way to leave here." Rand recalls.

"Well", Maggie responds, "let me tell you the truth now. There is another way. You have actually taken the first step by separating yourself and coming into the wilderness. I was once in a similar position. I was rescued by someone who has also been through this but he did not make any mistakes or fail in any way. Because of his intervention I am here today."

"I still don't understand. How can I fail when I don't know what the goal is or the rules of engagement?'

Maggie, "I can only tell you what I know. If I can't answer your questions then I will take you to my brother who is the only one to encounter the third day and overcome it."

Rand, "Your brother is here too?"

He is as my big brother because that is what I liken him to. Actually he is much more than that. I was adopted into his family. He lives over there in the foothills." Maggie pointed toward the distant mountains. "His father adopted me but I have never seen him. He lives in the mountains."

Rand presses, "Why haven't you seen him? Is he a recluse or just think he is too good to come out of his comfort zone?"

Maggie responds defensively, "No, he has allowed his son to manage the estate property under him so that he can attend to his other interests."

"You know," suggests Rand, "I would like to just relax and forget about all of this. I want to just spend a quiet evening with you to talk and enjoy your company."

Maggie replies, "I would like that too but first we must gather up all of these things so that we can walk to my brother's house. We should hurry to get there before the darkness settles."

Rand is eager to get inside somewhere safe, "I can probably carry most of these things so that you can lead the way."

Maggie replies, "Okay but if you need help just let me know and I will carry some of the load."

They begin to walk rather briskly. Rand is following as closely as he can. He cannot see any pathway that is marked or even visible from use as most paths are. Maggie seems to know where to turn and when to go straight because she had traveled this unseen path many times. The trees become dense and entangled with vines and thorns. There are low hanging branches that Maggie would hold for Rand to pass under then she would trot past him and continue unhindered. Rand realizes that without her knowledge of the way and her care for his condition along the way he would be completely turned around and groping hopelessly for his way.

The route becomes markedly hilly as the darkness begins to settle in on them. Maggie comforts Rand with the news that they are close to their destination. Rand is breathing heavily as they come to a stop by a big rock that split the path they are on. Rand drops the blanket and back pack to the ground, straightens up and wipes his forehead with his right arm sleeve to get the sweat out of his eyes. He looks up at the huge rock that rose above them some twenty feet.

It is so massive, dense and heavy in appearance that he has the thought that it may be able to support anything. The face of the giant edifice is smooth and sheer as though a master craftsman has formed it. Each side is rounded toward its peak with grass, ferns and rich green moss growing on the sides and near the top. The thought also occurs to Rand that it could have once been the corner stone of some mighty ancient structure that has deteriorated through the ages except for this indestructible piece.

Rand is surprised back to reality by a rustle in the trees just to his right which put him between Maggie and whatever made the sound. Rand quickly thinks to himself, 'I may get to save a damsel yet!' Before the thought completely leaves his mind out jumps a man who lands just out of Rand's reach.

"Caught you by surprise, did I?" The man says with a humorous look on his face. His shoulder length brown hair frames his oval face and his olive skin highlights his clear, greenish blue eyes.

"Jake!" exclaims Maggie, "What are you doing sneaking up on us like this?"

"I have a way of doing that even without trying!" Jake chuckles as he steps forward and slaps Rand on the shoulder.

"Hello Randal" continues Jake, "As you have already heard I am Jake and this is my territory you are wandering in with my lovely sister no less."

Rand responds apologetically, "Hey, don't get the wrong idea we are coming to see you. Hey how do you know my name?"

"It is my vocation in life to know who you are and what is going on in your life at all times. That is how I met Maggie here. I know that she has already told you that she and I are brother and sister by adoption." Jake's smile never leaves his face. Jake is the essence of pure energy, very animated, charismatic and joyful. Rand instantly likes him although he does not understand how Jake could know about him. Rand did feel comfortable in his presence and that was a major improvement in his life of late. Rand surmises that Jake will fill in the blanks soon enough.

Rand asks Jake, "How did the two of you meet?" As Rand was asking the question Jake put his hand on Rand's shoulder, turned and directed him toward the path to the right side of the large stone. Maggie ran ahead of them as the two men walk side by side along the path. As Jake begins to speak his arms and hands and shoulders move as expressions of every word.

Jake, "From the top of this large rock I can see the entire area, including the streets of the city that you have come out of. I watch for the ones who are called out by my father. That is, the ones who hear the call and respond. Maggie was one of them just as you are. Of course all that are called are not chosen because some choose for themselves to return to whatever they have fled from. Some are sent back because they only came out thinking they could cause trouble or could escape their choices for shallow reasons. Those who remain work under my leadership to care for the estate and eventually will be sent out as ambassadors to represent our interests to those whom they are designated to encounter. One of my duties as master of this area is to decide who will stay."

"So, anyway, I will never forget one rainy day I walked to the lookout point and saw Maggie running as hard as she could across the fields from the city toward me. There was a group of five or six men chasing her and it was obvious that she was in danger. I had heard her cries before in my dreams as she walked among many men in the night, many nights. Her cries rose to my ears with such despair and longing for relief that I took her situation to my father and asked for his blessing on bringing her out and saving her from her pursuers. With his approval I sent my guardsmen to bring her here. She is one of the first to become part of our ever growing family."

Rand, "There are others? Where do they live?"

Jake, "Yes there are others but we will not talk about them now, Okay?"

They came to a place where the pathway joined a very wide road. Though it was dark now Rand could see that they were entering a clearing in the woods and that the darkness stops at the edge of the clearing. The air feels lighter; the hue of the night appears to brighten to be similar to the light of dawn. The roadway has the luminescence of pearls as though it glows with its own light. The three walk together silently for a short distance before Rand can see the large mansion that is mostly secluded in the forest just off the road. Only slim sections are visible through the trees. Every room is lit and Rand can see people passing by the windows. He gets the sense that there is a big party or celebration of some sort going on. He can also hear many peoples' voices, laughter and shouts. There is music with cymbals, flutes, drums and horns. All of the sounds combine to make one great crescendo after another.

As they walk toward the mansion Rand feels an excitement coming over him. He compares it to the excitement he experiences whenever he was going to a sporting event or a concert. To hear the sounds of the event and the involvement of the crowd already inside generates an urgency to get there because he is missing something. Rand continues to analyze his excitement and anticipate what he will experience inside the mansion. He isn't aware of his companions who have stopped walking until he runs into them and almost knocks Maggie down.

Rand apologizes as he catches Maggie. Jake also reaches for her in more of a protective gesture and as they all stand he separates Rand's grasp on Maggie.

"Thanks Randal," Jake says, "Boy you are ready to party!"

"No, not really, but I can feel the excitement and I guess I assumed we were going to join the festivities. Is that not why we are here?"

"Not exactly", Jake answers, "Maggie you go on in and I will see you a little later. Tell everyone I will be there soon, okay?"

"Everyone will be waiting as always." Maggie responds as she smiles. She then looks at Rand and smiles, saying "Hope to see you again Rand. Take care." She then turns and walks to the entrance of the mansion. Rand looks to Jake for an explanation and hears his voice become a bit subdued.

Jake explains, "I am sorry you won't be able to fully join us in our celebration tonight. There is a certain protocol in place here, established by my father long ago. We must follow his direction as I am committed to do. Now is a time for you to refresh yourself and rest. Tomorrow we will talk and get you fitted for your new clothes if you decide to stay and join us tomorrow."

"Well okay." Rand replies a bit puzzled but happy for what he expects to be his first good night's sleep in some time.

Jake escorts Rand to the guest house which is to the left of the main house and outside of the wall which encloses the residence. Rand begins to observe Jake the man. He is not a big man physically, being about five feet eight inches tall with dark, curly hair which is thinning in the front to give him a slightly receding hair line. His eyes are piercing always even when he was smiling. Rand guesses that he is older than he looks. Rand did notice lines on the sides and back of his neck that may be old scars. He has strong hands like someone who works with hand tools and performs physical tasks. He is muscular in build with a deliberate, determined gate to his stride.

As they approach the guest house door Jake turns to Rand and as he looks at him squarely he speaks in a comforting voice, "I want you to be at ease tonight. You are safe here. You are here because you have been called by my father. I know you are confused about what you have experienced these past few days. Let me assure you that I have subdued the forces that are pursuing you. They will not reach you here. Relax tonight we have much to discuss when you awake. Maggie will see you tomorrow."

Rand responds, "I feel at ease here and I trust you. I look forward to tomorrow knowing I will see you and my new friend Maggie. Thanks." Rand goes inside and closes the door. He then turns from the door to find himself in a large foyer with a chandelier suspended from the high ceiling. There is a staircase rising along the wall to his right leading to a second floor where he assumes the bedrooms are. Rand feels the exhaustion of the day's hike settle on his body as he climbs the stairs. Near the top of the staircase the thought occurs to him that the rear of the mansion may be visible from a window. He hopes for a glimpse of the festivities which he can only hear.

At the top of the stairs Rand goes to his right and down a short hallway to the last door on the left. He rushes into the room looking for the window which offers the best view. He finds that there are several very tall trees blocking most of the view until the wind might move a branch to one side or the other. He can hear the music, the chorus rising and falling in a regular rhythm. From what he can see there is a procession beginning to take place. The crowd begins to separate into two groups with an impromptu walkway across the expansive courtyard from the rear of the house to a stage at the center of the courtyard. The orchestra is arranged at the back wall and facing the rear of the house.

A hush falls over the people in anticipation of someone's entrance. Rand strains to see who is emerging into the walkway as a tree straightens up from the cessation of the wind and his view is again almost completely blocked. As Rand begins to mutter his frustration the orchestra's trumpets and cymbals begin a very ornate and exhilarating piece that sounds, to Rand, like a marching song for an emperor or similar, triumphant, celebratory procession. Once again the trees move enough to give him a glimpse of the procession. He now recognizes Jake seated on the shoulders of some men and being carried into the crowd.

Everyone on either side of the aisle begin cheering and waving, some bowing, some throwing flower petals and waving small, leaved tree branches as he passes. Rand gets the impression that the people are worshiping Jake as though he is their master. This level of adulation surprises Rand. He already thinks that Jake is a rich land owner and overseer of a vast estate but this seems a bit much for Rand to correlate with anything he has experienced or his initial sense of who Jake is.

Again the tree moves back to block his view. Rand steps back from the window to evaluate what he has seen as he turns to find the bed so that he can sleep away the weariness. Rand removes his shoes, lies back on the bed and quickly falls asleep.

In The Midst of Shadows

As Rand sleeps he begins to dream. In his dream he is standing on a sea shore looking out at the approaching waves. He begins to hear a thunderous sound which he first thinks is breaking waves. He turns to his right to look along the coast and sees a herd of buffalo galloping toward him and approaching quickly which frightens him. He turns to run but finds nowhere to escape to because there is nothing but an open beach. As he begins to run he can feel the sand loosen under his feet. He is beginning to sink further into the sand with each step. Soon he will be past his knees and unable to move. With the herd of buffalo almost upon him Rand sees a lone rock sticking out of the sand a few feet ahead of him. He takes two more difficult steps and makes a desperate lunge for the rock with both hands outstretched.

As soon as his hands grasp the rock he is lifted from the sand and can stand upon the rock. The buffalo rush toward him so he turns his back to the oncoming herd knowing that his life is about to end. Rand can hear the individual hooves and the snorting of the beasts just before they are to gore and trample him. Rather than trample him all of the buffalo go around him as though he is a part of the rock. He is now in the midst of a powerful current until it passes him by in search of another. As he turns back to face the direction from which he has run the rock recedes to leave him standing on sand that is firm and his steps supported.

The dream ends with Rand walking into the sea until submerged then walking out again and sitting cross legged on the beach facing the land from which the wind blows into his face. He takes a breath and as he exhales he begins speaking in a foreign language which awakens him from the dream.

Rand opens his eyes to see the flat, white ceiling above him. He raises his head, looks toward the window and sees daylight. He slowly sits up and swings his legs around to sit on the edge of the bed as he contemplates his dream. He realizes that there must be an allegory to the rock of his dream, the huge rock that divides the path in the forest that is Jake's lookout point and his personal stability. He thinks back to the beginning of the procession he had observed the night before. Rand cannot immediately identify the connection between all of these facets. He is beginning to have some suspicions but he will not let himself fully consider any possibilities without more information. For the moment he replaces the issue with the expectation of his time with Jake later in the day. With hope he heads for the shower with a smile on his face.

As is her custom Maggie rose before the light of day and walked into the forest to pray and prepare. This day is a little more special to her because she will be sharing her story with Rand. Maggie's past experiences of sharing have resulted in both rejection at times and a warm acceptance at times. So, her feelings before an encounter of opportunity range from nervous to excited expectation. She enters each opportunity with confidence knowing it is her commission in life to help others by sharing her story. She rises and leaves her place of meditation with an inspired spring in her step and a hope for the day to come.

She returns to the estate and stops at the guest house. Maggie rings the doorbell. After a few minutes of no-one answering she rings again hoping that Rand has not decided to return to the city. After another wait of a few minutes Maggie walks away with sadness beginning to creep into her day. She quickly realizes what is happening and takes authority over her feelings to reject all negativity trying to enter her day.

Maggie steps off the porch as the front door opens. She turns to look over her shoulder and sees Rand standing there holding the door open while propped against the door frame. His hair is wet and messy, his shirt buttoned only at the bottom. He is smiling so she returns the smile and turns back to walk into the house as Rand steps aside to let her in.

"Good morning, Glory!" Rand offers.

"Good morning to you," Maggie replies. "It is good to see that you are still here."

"And where will I go?" he asks. "I was led here in the darkness and I do not know my way back. Nor do I wish to return to what I have left behind."

"I hoped you would have a practical reply.Maggie responds, "I knew you must be one of the chosen when I first saw you."

"Chosen for?" Rand questions.

"Oh, I am getting ahead of myself," Maggie says with a blush of embarrassment and insecurity. She realizes how many times she has done this and still is having trouble getting started. Maggie rebounds, "Why don't you finish refreshing yourself while I wait. We can have breakfast and talk."

"Okay," he answers. "Make yourself at home and I won't be long."

Maggie busies herself in the kitchen making breakfast. As she finishes preparing the last dish Rand enters and stands near the small butcher block table by the window which Maggie has set for the meal. Maggie invites him to sit as she lays a flower from the forest on the window sill. They both pause for a moment, their feelings for one another warm. Maggie lowers her head and begins a prayer of thanks. Rand is a little embarrassed as he looks only at her. He begins to acquiesce and look down at the table as she ends her prayer. They both looked back to each other. Maggie grins as Rand kind of stares with his mouth slightly open. He has the thought that she is so gentle and sincere.

"Thanks for preparing all of this Maggie." Rand speaks softly.

"Not at all," she replies. "It is my pleasure. I hope you will enjoy it."

Rand continues, "I must say that this is all so different from what I have experienced since arriving in the area. What you have here is like paradise compared with the hell I walked away from yesterday. How can these two totally different life style realities exist so close to each other and remain separate? How did you come to be here Maggie?"

Maggie, "I should first tell you that the person I am today is not at all the person I was before meeting Jake and then coming here. I was born in a time and place when many girls were born into a life style that was very abusive, very degrading and one which did not offer a very long life. I found out at a very young age what it was to be touched and used by a man. By the time I was thirteen I had been sexually active with many men and I was considered the scum of the streets who would hope to die before the next night fell. I was born into prostitution because my mother was a prostitute and the offspring of a whore is the property of her master."

Rand can see the coldness pass over Maggie's face as she speaks and his heart aches for her. Soon she is past that time in her mind and a smile returns to her.

She continues, "But you know I did continue to live each day. I did not know what kept me alive but I survived. I learned the ways of a man, what he wanted and how he wanted it. I also learned how to exact a price that would be more than some could bear. In a way I became the hunter rather than to remain the hunted. Of course, to me, at the time I was engaging in the act of survival. I did not have anything to compare my life to. I could not see that I was becoming more of an animal each day. I became vicious and cunning in my reprisals against some. I would let a man have his way with me and then I would find a way to reveal the nature of our encounter to his wife or family. I became less sought after which meant I had less to live on but if a man was going to have me he would pay dearly for it."

This time Rand can see the darkness of Maggie's soul as she speaks. Rand becomes very unsettled by the emotion she exudes. As he begins to speak she looks up into his face and says, "I am sorry, I have spoken out of anger unnecessarily and it has upset you. Each time I speak of my past I get caught up in the terrible memories of that time in my life. Thank God that all changed."

Rand, "I was about to comment myself on how very different you are from the person you have described just now. You must have undergone a dramatic change. What brought it about?"

Maggie, "Well, my vindictiveness eventually caught up with me. You know, that is always the way of it in the world. It doesn't matter how much I may have been able to justify my actions. I was just as wrong in my behavior as were the ones that I was judging for their actions. Some people's ways are evident to everyone and nothing passes unnoticed. You know, they cannot get away with any kind of mistake. Others get away with so much and for so long before their ways come back on them. Anyway I had met a particular man whom I liked for some reason. Perhaps I thought of him as needy, I don't know. Perhaps it was his gentleness and fairness. He was not an overbearing brute like most of the men I knew. We kind of began to have a real relationship. We would meet in typical places, in public and spent time together without just having some form of sex and then going our separate ways. I didn't even ask if he was married."

Maggie continued, "Well, one day we were together, across town from where I usually stayed. We were walking through a neighborhood bazaar when a woman, along with a small gang of people burst upon us. She was obviously after me, saying that the man was her husband, he was always faithful and that she would have my body drug through the streets when she was done with me. All kinds of insults and I tore right back into her but some of the men in the group overpowered me and began pulling at me and dragging me to the middle of the street. Merchant's goods were being strewn everywhere because I was fighting against them. My clothes were being ripped from me and my hair was in my face so I could not see my attackers!"

Rand watches her react to her own narrative with anger and fear as she clutches the table's edge. He reaches out to calm her and she flinches at his touch on her shoulder.

Maggie, "Oh, there I go again. I was swinging wildly when these brutes threw me to the ground. I looked up to see that I was at the feet of someone who happened to walk up on the scene. I figured he was some self-appointed, pompous fool who was going to pronounce another hypocritical sentence on me for my adultery. I almost laughed but I didn't want to be beaten any more. I raised my head from the ground and looked through my hair to see only his feet. I had heard rumors about someone who was real controversial because he was helping people and also really bold in his criticism of the social leaders and even the religious leaders of the people because they were taking advantage of them and misleading them. Anyway, I didn't know if this was the guy or not. I just did not want to be hurt anymore."

Rand interrupted, "You know, this is starting to sound a little familiar. I can't quite place it but I feel like I have heard this before. I don't mean to take away from the legitimacy of what you are telling me but . . ."

Maggie cuts him off, "Maybe you have. I've always been told that humanity is destined to repeat its mistakes from generation to generation until the cycle is broken. Perhaps you have heard of someone like me."

"That may be it", Rand mused. "I am not sure but I would like to hear about how everything worked out. I mean, obviously it did work out or you wouldn't be here, right?"

"Yes it did work out in a most profound way." Maggie replied, "This man stooped down and parted my hair back to see my face. I looked up expecting to see a scowl or a look of condemnation. I didn't see either. In fact I didn't see his face at first. I only saw his eyes. He didn't see my face either. He saw my heart, my soul, my being. He looked right into me, not at me. He took my hand, put one arm around me and lifted me to my feet. I saw that we were standing in the midst of a crowd of accusers and some other men, maybe religious leaders that had been listening after everything started. I became the focus of their discussion and I was so embarrassed that I would not look at anyone. The young man gave me one of his garments to cover myself. I heard someone ask him if I should be found guilty of adultery and punished accordingly. I was so disconnected mentally from what was happening that I did not hear his response or if he even gave one. After a few minutes everyone was gone except for the crowd that had gathered to watch. Each of my accusers had left with nothing to say. It was quiet and peaceful. He put his hands on my shoulders, looked squarely at me and said, 'Your accusers have gone. Now go your way, understand what you have learned and make some changes.'"

Maggie continues, "I didn't want to leave his side. My heart was in his hands, my mind was waiting for his next word and my being recognized that he was a source of goodness, love and peace. I walked away a different person as if my life started over on that day."

"Wow!" Rand exclaimed, "Who was this person? I get the feeling you are talking in past tense as though he isn't around anymore. Is he?"

Maggie, "Yes, this was a long time ago, in another part of the world. He is still around. You met him yesterday."

Rand, "Jake? You are talking about Jake? I knew there was something different about him."

Maggie, "Yes, he is a unique person. There is none other like him. Needless to say, I didn't get very far from him after that day. I was not involved in his daily life but I stayed close in my own way. I know, Rand, that you must have a lot of questions. I hope that sharing with you what Jake has done for me will help you realize that he can also help you.

Rand, "I am not the dependent type. I am not usually interested in discussing my feelings or my insecurities. I am a man and I think it smarter to protect myself from intrusions set up by revealing too much unnecessarily."

Maggie, "I know that you have already met some people in the city who said they could help you. I can tell you that their only intentions are to distract you and lead you away from the truth. They can only offer the same confusion that they are living in. I also know that I cannot answer all of your questions adequately. Jake can and will when you ask him."

Rand replies, "I definitely do want to know more. I hope to see him today."

Maggie, "I should go now. I have much to do today. I hope to see you tonight. You will know more about that after talking to Jake."

"Well then I hope to see you tonight." Rand answers as Maggie walks to the door.

"I will see myself out." Maggie says as she opens the door to leave.

Rand is excited and intrigued as well as a little sad. He begins to realize that his stay at the guest house is more conditional than he thought. He hopes to see Jake soon. He walks to the rear of the house, into the kitchen and looks out at the forest beyond the patio. He decides to go for a walk and get some fresh air so he steps outside and takes a deep breath. There is such a peacefulness and calm in this place that he cannot think of leaving voluntarily. He begins walking through the grassy yard toward the woods and sees the beginning of a foot path which he decides to explore.

The sun is now high in the sky. He feels the patches of warm sunlight move across his arms and shoulders when he passes under the varied patterns formed by the branches and leaves above him. The air is cool and moist. He can slightly see his breath in the shade of a large evergreen tree. He begins to detect faint sounds of someone chopping wood. The sounds become more distinct as he walks deeper into the forest. At first the sounds mingled with the sounds of the birds singing, water dripping and his footsteps on the leaves and twigs.

He continues to seek out the source of the chopping and as he walks along the path he begins to notice that his ascent is bringing him close to the top of a hill. As Rand starts down the far side of the hill the path becomes overgrown with vines and branches that are difficult to get through. As someone who does not give up easily he continues until he finds himself entrapped in a web of vines and briars with leaves smacking him in the face and his clothes being snagged on the thorns. He has to stop fighting the entanglement and think before he can extricate himself.

Finally free from his trap he finds a way around the thicket and back onto the path. Around a small bend in the path Rand surprises a squirrel that scampers to a nearby tree and up its trunk. When the squirrel stops it drops a nut from its mouth. Rand amuses himself with the thought of perhaps having just saved the kernel from being eaten and a tree may now grow to join the forest.

Rand marvels at his own emerging philosophy which is so foreign to his usual scope of reasoning. He considers the possibility of enlightenment from a higher source for the first time with a real faith in that possibility. Again he can hear the sounds of an axe against wood. Rand guesses that he is near because he can see a clearing just ahead. The sunlight is illuminating the area within the otherwise dimly lit forest. The area has taken on a golden glow from a combination of the yellow, red and orange hues of the turning leaves mixed with the sunlight streaming through an opening in the canopy. 'A sanctuary of light in the midst of shadows' he muses. As he approaches the clearing with more of a 'big picture' view the scene takes on a more panoramic perspective. The pathway becomes an aisle with the trees offset on either side with one tree close to the path and the next farther away so that they look like pillars with their branches forming the beams of an open ceiling.

At the center of the clearing is a lone figure wielding an axe against the sacrificial heartwood of a felled oak tree. Rand begins to see a transfiguration of harmony and rhythm into pulses of life and light sustaining the universe. Rand pauses in the shadows of the forest to watch and absorb the vision. The man hard at work is wearing shorts and sandals only. His bare back and arms are wet with sweat, his dark hair now stringy from the perspiration. His back is covered with crossing stripes that are obviously scars. Rand considers retreating further into the cover of the forest. As the thought crosses his mind the man stops his motion as he finishes the strike and brings the axe to his side with the axe head now resting on the ground with the butt of the handle under his right hand.

Rand changes his mind and takes a step into the sunlight. "Hello Rand I am glad you decided to stay." As the man turns to face him Rand sees that it is Jake.

Yeshi

Yarjies sits down and waits for Yeshi to take a seat. Yarjies knows that crunch time is at hand and this conversation will set the tone for the anticipated push to eradicate the Rochukas and to accomplish the secondary initiatives of establishing the community leadership and societal safeguards. This will be critical for a self-sustaining future. Success will be assured when the metaphysical rift has been corrected, closed and healed. Yarjies rehearses these points in his head during the few moments he waits. 'The operation will be multifaceted and multidimensional. We will strike like a thunderstorm and the resistance will shatter like an old mirror that is brittle and fragile.'

Yeshi, "Okay Yarjies we now have our resources staged in this area for this operation. On the ground we will have engagements to complete while behind the physical activities we have spiritual distortions to correct. When both are accomplished we then will have a tribal coalition to empower and safeguard. The greater challenge will be safeguarding the exercise of personal responsibility and the liberty to uphold a rule of law and secure an autonomous identity without seceding from the greater union of the region."

Yarjies, "yes, I agree."

Yeshi, "Before we go any further I must remind you that humans are very capable of complicating the simple. We have ten days to train and be prepared. There are some untested strategies and tactics for movement coordination which we will explore during training. Correct?"

Yarjies, "Correct."

Yeshi, "I know you have a separate role as the Discree and I also want you working with Lana. Her goal of identifying the true Stroy is going to be critical. Your activities will coincide with hers."

Yarjies, "I will deal with the Rochukas we isolate when the opportunities arise. Lana and I work well together."

Yeshi, "You are first responsible for the assignments of personnel and the scheduling of training." Pointing to the canisters of rolled up documents standing in the corner Yeshi continues, "Here you will find topographical maps and some layouts of trails, water ways and roads. We will avoid rail. It is to slow and cumbersome. We must be quick and precise. The training and preparation of resources and a clear understanding of our strategy will enable our tactics to succeed. Are you ready?"

Yarjies, "The ones I know that are here are very capable, very dedicated and very anxious to get it done."

Yeshi, "Very good,I have other places to be for now so I will leave this task in your capable hands."

Yarjies, "I hope you will check in occasionally."

Yeshi, "You know me, never far away."

Yarjies, "Before you go will you spend a few minutes with my comrades in the other room?"

Yeshi, "Oh yes, I certainly will. This is your core group. Please bring them in."

Yarjies steps away and as he opens the door and looks into the outer office for everyone to invite in he finds everyone seated and asleep. Yarjies claps his hands together loudly and awakens everyone with, "Good morning kids! It is time to move!"

Each member of the group snaps awake and stands except for Baetus. Norsha kicks his leg and he opens his eyes widely to see everyone looking at him. "I am awake! Hey, let's go! What are we doing?"

Everyone laughs until Yeshi enters the room. He is smiling so everyone quickly relaxes.

Yarjies, "Everyone please introduce yourselves to Yeshi." Before anyone can speak Yeshi takes over the moment. "I see that we have Fripree, Megan, Norsha and Baetus. It is great to see you all and I look forward to following your successes. Norsha I am pleased to see that you managed your challenges well."

Norsha, "Thank you I am excited to be here."

Yeshi, "Let us all be clear in our understanding and if you have questions ask. If you allow pride or fear to distract or control your performance then you have become a weak link. I have every confidence that each of you is capable and willing to put it all out there to get us where we intend to be. You will be learning new procedures and new tactics. You will be fully informed as to our primary and any secondary goals. Dig in and be determined. Working together we will succeed."

Yarjies, "We begin today when this briefing concludes. Everyone is stoked about putting plans on the ground."

Yeshi, "As I leave you I do so knowing that we are at the threshold of an epic time. Yarjies, this is your team. This assembly of companions, the warriors destined to achieve more than they can know exists. These are special times."

Everyone present bows their head slightly, deferring to Yeshi and Yarjies as his right hand and his touch point of interaction. Yeshi turns again to Yarjies with his hand extended. As Yarjies reaches for the hand shake Yeshi pulls him in for a hug. Yeshi speaks softly to Yarjies, "I am never too far away. Be nimble and stay connected to your good senses."

Yarjies knows better than to respond. The two men part and Yeshi walks to the door to leave as Yarjies faces the group and says, "Let us begin."

Yeshi steps through the outer doorway and immediately transitions to the forest chopping block and blends into the person of Jake completing the last swing of the axe before pausing for Rand.

Rand changed his mind and took a step into the sunlight. "Hello Rand I am glad you decided to stay." As the man turns to face him Rand sees that it is Jake.

Rand, "Hello Jake I am glad to see you." Rand walks closer and extends his hand in greeting. Jake grasps his hand with a strong grip and pulls Rand to him. Rand is at least six inches taller than Jake but he feels overpowered by him. As they hug Rand feels one of the scars on Jake's back and as they part he asks, "Man, what happened to you that you have so many scars?"

Jake, "Well, this may be a bit abstract for you right now but when I was a young man, at a time that my father had set, I went into the city. So, I went to share a new way of life by living my way as an example. I saw how they treated each other. The most distressing thing was to hear them malign my father without knowledge or understanding.

Some did listen and did accept my offer of freedom from the oppression of the city's task masters. But the leaders, the very ones entrusted with everyone's guidance, rejected everything I was trying to tell them. They rejected the truth in order to maintain their facts. So, for my rebellion I was beaten and whipped until my flesh shredded. They could not even acknowledge the truth that was contained in the result of their actions. I gave myself willingly that day to accomplish my father's resolution."

Rand, "How are you here now?"

Jake, "Because my father intervened and preserved my soul in order to prove that they have no power at all unless it is first given to them. So, you can call the scars my right of passage and the proof that I do overcome all obstacles by the power of my father through me as an ambassador. It is a price I chose to pay in order to accomplish my destiny which was ordained before time began."

Rand, "I don't understand why your father would allow you to be treated that way. What was the purpose of that?"

"My father is very just." Jake said seriously, he smiled slightly and continued. "He just told me to go and I went." Jake cracked a big smile and laughed. Rand didn't get the humor right away. "Seriously though," Jake continues, "Being a part of him and having come from him I understand the need for complete obedience even during times when I do not fully understand in context."

Rand, "I actually do have a lot of questions, Jake, but I don't really know where to start."

"Truthfully, Rand, if I answered everything for you now you wouldn't understand the answers. The time will come when you will understand if you stay true to your commitments. I have much to tell you. Let us spend this time together as two new friends and get to know one another."

Rand agrees, "I get the feeling you already know everything about me. In fact, you seem to know about everything before it happens. Just like a few minutes ago. I was being extra careful to avoid making any noise yet you knew that I was there in the shadows. I suspect that you also knew my thought to withdraw when you ceased from your work and called me into this wonderfully warm and soothing sunlight. So, how can I tell you anything about myself?"

"You are right," Jake answers, "I do have a special sensitivity to time and motion. I have known you longer than you have known me. The things that are hard to understand now will become clearer. If not today then as your knowledge and understanding grow and you gain wisdom through your experiences. I think it is good for a person to verbalize thoughts and contemplations so that one's rationale and the challenges from others can buffet one's notions and either establish or dissolve the perceived essence. You can believe something in your heart, whether truth or a lie, as long as it is hidden there and unchallenged. This form of deception carries away many. To speak thoughts or beliefs into life is to expose them to the forces contained in reason as well as inspiration."

Rand interjects, "You are coming at me on a level that I have not challenged since I was in college. I am speaking of everything about my life, my mind, my heart and my concepts of purpose and fulfillment."

Jake continues, "Besides, I want you to tell me what is important to you. You know, we all have a free will and we each have a sense of self-worth. I would like to know you as you perceive yourself. Do you feel comfortable with that?"

Rand, "Well, I am not sure I know what you are asking but I will tell you about myself as best I can." Rand replies. "I grew up under parents who controlled every aspect of my life although I doubt they would agree. I always wanted more from life than they were offering. I saw such possibility for excitement, adventure and fun that I was being denied.

I couldn't have a car, I didn't have money. When I did earn some money from a job in the summer or on a weekend I would have to save it or follow their discretion when I spent any of it. I wanted to do anything but what they wanted. In short, I was rebellious and selfish. I know now that they were trying to teach me but I wasn't mature enough to appreciate it.

At the first opportunity I was out of the house and on my own. I found out pretty quickly that the world can be very harsh and uncaring. Friends were friends when I had something to give. If I got into trouble, which I did, they were gone. I would be in a jam and they would be carrying on with their lives as before.

I was really naive. I thought everyone would be like my family. Even though my parents were controlling they were loving and caring. I could go to them no matter what I had done, or hadn't done. Man, when you leave that cocoon of your parents' home everything changes.

The world really is a cold place. I learned to adapt and eventually realized that I wasn't as smart as I thought but I was too proud to go home. So, I learned to subdue my feelings and concentrate on doing a good job and providing security for myself and my interests. In the long run, though, I find myself becoming more like my parents."

Jake, "Amazing."

Rand, "Yeah, I have heard that each generation has the opportunity to break from the past and set their individual family history on a new course. I want to be the one to break the cycle. I want to, somehow, get past the recurring mistakes and flaws in me and my family's tree."

Rand realizes that Jake is listening to a story he has heard countless times. Rand becomes a little disappointed because of his perception that Jake isn't sincerely interested in his rationalizations of himself. It is odd enough to be sitting in the woods talking to someone that he didn't really know about his life as though he owed him some sort of explanation and now the guy isn't even paying proper attention to him.

By his body language, smile and a kind of look through you gaze Rand just knows that Jake is probably off somewhere in his mind fishing or playing or solving the world's problems and not giving precise attention to what he is saying. So, Rand decides to change what he is saying and begins a ridiculous story about pigs and chickens.

As soon as he puts his plan into action Jake immediately laughs and says, "So, you don't think I am listening? Rest assured I am. I have the ability to do many things at one time. What I was also hearing is another cry from the city. Someone is being nailed."

"Is 'being nailed' what I think it is?" Rand asks.

"Yes, you have witnessed someone being nailed when you witnessed the murder of the girl in the courtyard."

Rand asks, "Why?"

Jake, "A fact is that horrible, frightening things happen. I want to explain what you have been experiencing here. I know that you took this time so that you could explore other experiences and find deeper answers about yourself and your purpose in life. Your time here has been waiting for you to step into it. Does that make any sense?"

Rand, "Yes, it does, but I am not accustomed to such bazaar and abstract experiences."

Jake, "Let me bring together a couple of loose ends. Remember the woman and child that you encountered on the train? The look in her eyes is the look of fear. She is one of several women who are randomly singled out by the Rochukas for breeding. When a selected woman rejects the Rochukas they become a victim of cruel, vindictive abuse and eventually death such as the receptionist, Amber. The woman on the train has repeatedly eluded them because she is one of us. Another targeted group is the offspring of the Rochukas who have rejected their past and are forming an opposing force to end the cycle of their elders. In some situations they are working with us."

The Whole Package

Yarjies asks everyone to sit down as he rests on the edge of the desk. "I know everyone needs rest. We will cover a few things now and then relax for the night. This will likely be the last of our meaningful rest times for the coming weeks. We will have two more trainers join our group tomorrow early. Their names are Pilo (the fairgen) and Kania. Megan, Pilo will report to you. Baetus, Kania will report to you."

Baetus, "Report what?"

Yarjies "Let that wait for now. I want to briefly review each of our primary responsibilities. Let me remind everyone that Yeshi made these assignments. We will fill in the blanks and make adjustments very quickly. Okay here we go. Fripree you have a specific field role and a leadership responsibility to work through. You are the facilitator of logistics and a member of the rapid response team for post sightings' identification and extraction. You will be reporting to Norsha. Note: Kania will also be arriving tomorrow."

Norsha slowly looks over at Baetus and raises a brow to tweak him. Yarjies, "Okay, Norsha you will have to keep these knuckleheads all heading in the right direction. You are operations security and subgroups' oversight. You will report to me."

Everyone in the group takes a moment to make eye contact with each other and offer a slight bow of acknowledgement.

Yarjies, "I am tasked with general oversight and planning. I will be leaning on each of you as need be for constructive feedback and support. Of course we all must perform our tasks effectively. Agreed?"

Everyone simultaneously shouts, "Got it!"

Yarjies continues, "Our team interaction will be essential. Once we begin to track and locate the targets we must respond with precision. We have ten days to prepare. There are bunks upstairs and there are showers on the other side of the warehouse. We will be in close quarters going forward. Everyone will have to be respectful and flexible." The group disburses with Megan and Norsha going to inspect the showers and the others going upstairs. Yarjies is the last to come in.

Norsha, "Megan, you know, as I, how this goes. Once in the field the choices go away."

Megan, "You got it. I will take a shower over food right now."

Norsha, "Yup."

Once upstairs, Fripree and Baetus become distracted by the thought of food.With their noses leading the hunt, Fripree, "I guess the showers are next for us so, I say food first!"

Baetus heads downstairs and is pleased to find a working kitchen. "Down here!" he shouts up to Fripree. "Got it!" she shouts back and finds the stairs. During a search of the cabinets Baetus finds dry pasta and beans. The refrigerated work tables held cheese and butter on the left side with ground meat patties and sliced ham on the right side. "Daaamiiit" Baetus growls, "We are going to eat tonight!"

Fripree, "What a great time for some REAL food! Man, a little fire and something to burn some of this together in and I am working it."

Baetus, with a view of the warehouse, sees Megan and Norsha reach the outer staircase to get to the bunks where their gear should be for clothes, etc. for showering. Fripree has memories bubble up of her time with Yarjies and their food hunting excursions. Now with a different man, a different personality, she begins to relive the experiences verbally to Baetus. He offers a polite level of attention because his goal is to get food. Megan reaches the stairs a few steps before Norsha.

Megan, "You run well. I thought I would have more advantage but I guess that is what I get for thinking!"

Norsha, "Because you are not accustomed to it? Really though, I invest more in training to be equipped and capable when real life happens."

As Megan reaches the top step she quips, "Distraction can be useful, don't you think?"

Norsha looks up, having several steps yet to go and offers a sarcastic smile then shoots back, "It takes the whole package, whatever that is at any given time."

Together they are through the door and down the short hall to an open room with half a dozen cots and gear sitting on each. Norsha and Megan head for their respective areas to gather what each needs for the exotic shower that each anticipates. Of course, it is a stone cold trucker's shower of white tile with curtains missing from the small individual dressing areas. This shower will be an exotic experience because it is the first in three days and it will likely be the last for the near term.

Returning with clean clothes both showers are turned on and beginning to steam up the area. After the invigorating showers the two women emerge from the dressing area and walk together slowly across the warehouse to the lower level door. Baetus finishes off his grilled ham and cheese sandwich and looks up to greet Megan and Norsha. Megan walks to him for a hug and a quick kiss. They both have been anxious about having time together that is not immersed in their assignments. Norsha understands the dynamics of the moment and continues on to the kitchen to inventory her options.

Fripree is seated at the island counter to enjoy her salad before having some form of protein that is cooked in some way. She has always been more adept at cooking on an open flame whether of wood or gas. A fried meat patty doesn't sound good but Fripree convinces herself that it can be burned slightly to mimic charbroiling.

Megan and Baetus walk together toward the warehouse door. Megan to the others, "I will be right back."

Norsha, "You two had better not get lost. I will send Fripree to find you and you won't like her attitude."

Through the door they went as Fripree and Norsha laughed. Fripree, "I found that there is plenty here to eat so help your-self. I will wait fifteen minutes before embarrassing them, although I doubt they are at the showers anyway."

Norsha smiles again, "You are likely right. I will remind Baetus that you are in the shower so that he won't embarrass you!"

Fripree smiles, "Maybe, maybe not."

Megan and Baetus, once through the doorway, turn right and walk past the stairway, along the wall and find an unlocked receiving office door. They know that they have but a short time together so the intimacy they crave can only be a tease. They embrace, kiss deeply and fondle each other briefly. Baetus, "I want you but I don't want our desires to weaken or distract our focus but I need you."

Megan, "That made no sense but I agree with you. Hold me right now." The two embraced tightly for several minutes, feeling each other's heartbeat, listening to one another's breathing. Baetus's long, curly hair in Megan's face begins to tickle her nose. Megan pulls away slightly and sneezes, ending the silence, the moment and their secrecy. Megan, "It is great to be so close to you right now, Baetus."

Baetus, "What?"

Megan, "You need a shower!"

Baetus, "Oh, you are so sensitive! I will take care of the details and be looking for you after."

Megan, "Cool!"

Yarjies enters the kitchen area as Fripree is clearing the counter.

Fripree, "There he is. Help yourself there is plenty here. Are you done for the day?"

Yarjies, "I am done for the evening and ready for some food, a shower and sleep. You okay?"

Fripree, "Yep, I just had a shower and food. So, yea, I am winding down to sleep soon."

Yarjies, "Where is Baetus?"

Fripree, "Shower. If you want to shower first your gear is upstairs. Tell me what you want to eat and I will put it together for you."

Yarjies, "Okay, thanks. How about a ham and cheese burger?"

Fripree, "There is no bread so it will be just that on a plate. Okay?"

Yarjies, "Sure. I will be back soon." He starts up the stairs as Baetus enters from the warehouse. Yarjies, "Hey Baetus, how was it?"

Baetus, "Great!"

Norsha, "Okay, everyone, we will need to clean up after ourselves and get some sleep. I have an alarm set and each of you should also for 0600. For the next two days we have this facility to ourselves. Starting Monday we will be getting out of here before 0600 which means getting up at 0400. Fripree, will you wait up for Yarjies to return, please?"

Fripree "Got it. See everyone in the a.m."

Yarjies heads out the door into the chilly warehouse. Three hundred feet can be a long way with nothing filling the space. The shower area converts the atmosphere instantly into a clinging, humid sauna with the warmth to relax one's shoulders as the cold, wet floor invigorates ones toes. "Okay." Yarjies speaks to the room and hears the faint echo from the open, tiled area, "this is right and I am back in gear." He returns from the showers soon after the three had gone upstairs to their bunks. Fripree, "Here you go, medium well okay?"

Yarjies, "I go more for rare but I am not complaining."

As Fripree begins to turn from the counter Yarjies reaches over and touches her hand, "Fripree can you stay for a few minutes?" Fripree pauses and turns back to Yarjies. He continues, "I know that you and I have similar, interdependent goals. We will be coordinating many of our activities and I want you to feel comfortable working together and confident to raise questions and challenge what you disagree with. We will have one shot at this and we must succeed."

Fripree, "I agree. I get the sense that my role or my objectives are not what I understood them to be which is not a problem as long as I do know, with clarity, what I and we are doing. I expect tomorrow to be the beginning of defining our objectives and strategy."

Yarjies, "You are right and by this time tomorrow the picture will be clearer as will be the case each day following."

Fripree, "You and I have worked together through some tense and challenging situations just to get here. Tomorrow should be the beginning of the last phase, correct?"

Yarjies, "Indeed it will be. Sleep well and I will see you in the morning."

Fripree repeats, "In the morning" As she walks to the stairway.

Yarjies finishes cleaning up after himself, sets the security alarm and joins the others upstairs. Seeing everyone asleep but Fripree, Yarjies finds his bunk.

A 0600 revile pops eyes open as daylight first distinguishes the tops of trees against the sky. This first mornings resemblance of uniformity and coordination can be seen as a choreographed movement of five with two having sat up to look around, two with raised heads from the cot and one with an arm hanging from the side of the cot motionless. The movement continues until all are standing and the alarms are silenced.

Norsha shouts, "Food, farts and freshen up!" Everyone scatters with differing schemes for pursuing the basics. "We have forty minutes before our first inspection. Anyone who eats cleans up after themselves and everyone should eat."

Megan's first essential is coffee. With a thirty cup brewer she is thinking that she can have several cups without depriving anyone. Baetus is also waiting to pour as the aroma of the brew fills the air. By 0730 everyone is ready but not sure about an inspection? Yarjies comes out of the office and announces, "We have two group members at the gate. I would like for us all to walk out and greet them. I am opening the gate now."

Everyone gathers at the entrance door and look out to see Pilo and Kania waiting outside of the gate. Both are distantly related to the survivors from the war that started their community in the forest. Each is around twenty years old but they have significant years working and exploring in a wilderness environment. Yarjies leads the group out of the building as Baetus coaxes the group into a trot toward the gate. He knows both well as does Megan and Yarjies. Megan runs past him and the others catch up as the gate opens. Megan almost collides with Pilo as she puts an arm around her neck and squeezes her tightly. "Welcome, welcome!"

The group forms a circle around Kania and Pilo and start an impromptu jig that is led by Baetus. They are jumping up and down while taking one step forward then one step back, one step to the left then one step to the right. After a couple of repetitions of the movements the jig stops and Yarjies steps into the center of the circle with the two.

Yarjies, "As you can see we are excited to have you both here and we hope you are as pleased to be here."

Pilo, "Speaking for myself I am pleased yes and ready for this assignment."

Kania, "Same here. Someone I trust once taught me, 'though you are a part of a team, the team is made up of individuals. As an individual you work to be the best you can be so that the team is enhanced by your involvement. We will all be expected to learn our roles and allow the team to form us.'"

Yarjies laughs, puts both arms around Kania and picks her up. Yarjies has a big smile of acknowledgment, knowing that she was referring to him. Norsha has been standing silently and observing the group after the dancing stopped. She feels a little disconnected from the group. No special reason, she is naturally more of an introvert unless provoked or after having a few adult beverages. Fripree walks to her and reaches up to put a hand on her shoulder. Norsha looks down and smiles. She then picks Fripree up and squeezes her so tightly that Fripree can't breathe. Fripree takes it as a sign of appreciation for providing the touch point for a release of pent up anxiety but she quickly wants to be released so she can catch her breath.

With everyone on their feet and the energy winding down slightly Yarjies addresses everyone. "Let's get these two inside and their gear unloaded. Have you ladies eaten? If not check the kitchen and be fairly quick about it. We will get behind quickly if we are not mindful of the time. Norsha, we will all meet back here in thirty minutes. I think we will forgo the inspection this morning. I don't know what I was thinking anyway!"

Norsha "Got it. I need to begin stepping in now to maintain our schedule and the momentum of our progress. Agreed?"

Yarjies, "Agreed. I have maps and some beginning strategy outlines to share with you. So, when we all meet again I will give you copies."

Norsha, "I will take them now if that is all right. I will use the thirty minutes to give everything a first look."

Yarjies, "You are all business now? That is Awesome!"

They walk together to the office. Norsha receives the documents and retreats to the warehouse shipping office to study the maps without interruption. Yarjies remains in the office to finish one of his outlines and have a minute of meditation to center his self. Unlike some forms of meditation which involve a focusing on the absence of anything and attempting to enter the emptiness, Yarjies focuses on a specific principle or truth to understand, to engage, to adjust to. For him meditation is communication. It is expression and reception for assimilation.

Yarjies begins to hear some of the group moving around in the outer office. He opens his eyes and stands just before someone knocks on the door. After a brief delay the door opens and Norsha looks in to get Yarjies' attention. "We are gathered and ready to get started."

Yarjies, "Thanks, I will be right there."

Norsha withdraws, leaving the door partially opened. "Okay everyone take a seat and prepare to take notes as you may need for review. All notes taken must be turned over to me when they are no longer needed. This is very important. Everyone understand?"

Everyone acknowledges the directive as they scramble for their notebooks. Yarjies enters the room and reclines against the desk, "We will begin with general discussions before breaking up into groups to work on specifics for each sub group. I have tried to provide a framework with these outlines which we will use to construct a body of information and plans as well as any challenges, obstacles, strategies and tactics we will use."

Yarjies continues, "In general then we will be in pursuit to destroy the Rochukas; however this is more complicated than just ending their physical lives. We are here geographically because the dimensional, spiritual breech that we are also to resolve exists here. Although we are present in Germany this is not a struggle against the German people."

Kania offers a question with an overly polite raise of her hand, "I have gathered from local reports that the targets are migrating as they track their prey. They are becoming more belligerent in their disregard for established locations. They are escalating their attacks. I raise this question because we are maneuvering and occupying lands not our own and we are planning as though the land is ours. Simply put, we must be in and out before we are known to be in." After a pause Kania concludes, "I know that I am not well known in this area but I know what it takes to get things done. Giving one's all and to do the best that one can do does not always translate into success. Doing what it takes gets it done." Kania realizes that her question has become a speech. She lowers her head and retreats to her chair.

Yarjies, slightly annoyed, "Well, now that we have gotten that out of the way."

Norsha intervenes, "If I may, I am relying on each of you to be personally responsible for our performance as a force in this endeavor. We must find the discipline to remain engaged and focused. We no longer have months for planning. Everything is right now. The preaching has to be on your own time. Kania you raise an important point. The activities of the Rochukas over the past three months have been increasingly threatening to the populated areas. It will be important to lead any confrontations away from these areas.

Their movements have been tracked during the past six months by intelligence gathering from eye witnesses, monitoring of security bandwidths of radio and tracking by our personnel.

So, in general, we will be using a variety of tactics to encourage them to move into an isolated area where we can pin them down."

Yarjies interjects, "I know everyone present, with the exception of Fripree, is familiar with this districts geography. We will be operating in mountainous terrain with heavy pine forest. The sandstone rock is covered by a relatively shallow mixture of clay and sandy soils which should help with tracking the remaining three and the Stroy."

Fripree pins up an aerial photograph of an area that includes the northern portion of the Black Forest with an area highlighted as roughly triangular with Bad Wildbad on the northern boundary, Neuweller to the east and Forbach the south west. "This is our area of activity by all six. We must first establish the boundary as outlined on this map as the outer perimeter."

Megan turns to Baetus and sarcastically responds, "We have some preliminary targets and we have some training to do!" "Let's get our sub groups assembled!"

Baetus, "I have Kania to involve but we have no one to train. You have Pilo but no people."

Megan, "Evidently we will have to trust the network that has brought us here. Even if not by design this could be a good opportunity to get to know each other so as to be more likely to accurately anticipate the actions that will produce results as effectively as possible."

Pilo, "Numbers can be deceiving when it comes to expectations. Fear accomplishes more with timely and proper application. Such tactics will work for both sides in conflict."

Kania, "So, we have likely locations on the targets but what about their prey, if you will?"

Fripree, "We have the same level of preliminary information. Thank you for bringing that point up. The return of an early dispatch from here will be expected to give us more detailed intelligence. These will be comprised of small, quick teams for covering this large area. When our 'individuals' arrive they will be evaluated and assigned to you right away."

The time is nearing for lunch so Norsha speaks up, "Everyone, we will break for lunch now and then we will divide into our subgroups. So, it is now 1130. I will see everyone here and ready to get after it at 1300." Everyone scatters.

At about 1230 the gate intercom delivers a surprise, "Jack Rabbit here, we are loaded and ready to deliver." The van brakes squeal as the vehicle stops. Norsha responds, "Stand by" and walks out to open the gate as a second van and a small box truck arrive. Norsha stands to the side and motions for the vehicles to enter. Once inside the gate the doors of both vans slide open for the passengers to exit. The second van is pulling a trailer loaded with gear and supplies. It is driven past the group to the warehouse to wait for the roll up door to be opened.

With the core group now present and the 'individuals' disembarked the vetting process begins. The count is twenty four with fifteen young men, appearing to be aged eighteen to twenty five, four men in their forties and two possibly in their sixties. The nine women also are mostly of a young age with one older, possibly mid-forties. The vans are moved to the warehouse and everyone gathers in the parking lot.

Norsha, "Hello every one. Welcome to your weekend getaway." Everyone smiles before giving Norsha their attention. "We will get you situated as soon as possible. Food will be first. Everyone will enter through the door just inside the warehouse on this side", Norsha pointing toward the pedestrian door leading to the kitchen area.

Fripree, "I will interview each one of you to start the evaluations and then pass you to your lead for assignment."

Norsha, "You got it. You should be able to start in thirty minutes and I will follow up with you a little later."

Fripree, "I will start now, if I may, so we can transition as quickly as possible. I will collect the background information from each that is for Yarjies and also basic skills information for our use during training."

Norsha, "Right. I see you are ready!"

Baetus helps Megan to pull ham and cheese and condiments to put on the counter. Baetus lets everyone know, "Sandwiches for now so make what you like. We have coffee or water for now. So, help yourself, we have about thirty minutes." The new arrivals begin talking among themselves as they gather around the counter to eat.

With Norsha evolving into her natural role Yarjies begins to take a more enhanced posture as observer. With the pairings of complimentary assets the small task forces should have adequate preparation and opportunity to excel. Yarjies will be floating between groups as they train while monitoring remote field activities with a hair trigger response setting for counter protective measures.

Pilo and Megan are anxious to have individuals to train and equip. The skills needed for the mountainous terrain and the endurance to be fast and aggressive in their maneuvers will be critical. The practice can only vaguely replicate what their reflexes and their level of anticipation will experience but it is a starting point.

Megan, Baetus, Pilo and Kania have been students of the great wars' scouts, messengers and demolition teams that did transition to mountain bikes for quiet and fast transportation when appropriate. The equipment now available to Pilo and Megan's group are surplus folding bikes as used by paratroopers and carried by some on foot for field deployment.

The hope here is that the riders are capable of utilizing the resources exceptionally. Pilo begins thinking out loud, "We need to make individual selections and assign the field training needed for experience".

Megan is thinking about a four day field deployment exercise to quickly remove barriers and bull shit to have the squad solidified. Pilo agrees in principle but suggests three days, "I want us to have a minimum of eight ATCs ready to enter the wilderness for two days with you and me to consecrate our duty."

Megan, "You may have to unpack that for me a little later."

Pilo, "Why later?"

Megan, "Break out for me, 'consecrate our duty', for my understanding, please."

Pilo,"Perhaps a bit over the line metaphorically, how about, 'commitment to our duty.'"

Megan, "I get it, a little edgy myself?"

Norsha interrupts, "You ready for some excitement? I have ten warm bodies for you. It will be up to you to turn them into what you need. You have four women, three experienced in wilderness trekking and familiar with the area and one older woman experienced with the mountain terrain style of riding. You have four men, with little experience but they are strong and teachable. One young man has extensive experience with biking maneuvers in all terrain riding."

Megan, "I need to see the background info."

Pilo, "We need access to the gear and equipment today."

Norsha, "That's what I expect to hear. It is time to move!" As Pilo and Megan give each other a jumping shoulder bump Norsha walks across the room to where Kania and Baetus have their concentration buried in topographical maps. They are evaluating the geography to reduce their strategies for simplicity and to formulate their tactics.

Baetus points to the area just east of Bad Wildbad. There are two parallel valleys with a narrowing ridge running from south to north. Baetus, "Now when we pursue the beasts they will withdraw to this ridge. Then we can continue to maneuver them from three sides to follow the ridge northward past Bad Wildbad."

Kania, "Once our teams locate each one how can we identify and contain the 'Stroy'?"

Baetus, "We are not to arrest or contain at this time. Our goal is to locate the targets and influence their movements in the desired direction. Let us focus on those tasks and leave the other aspects to those assigned to that mission."

Kania "Got it. We need our 'individuals'."

Norsha, "Did I hear the term 'individuals' used for the last time?"

Kania, "Probably so."

Norsha, "Okay, I have for your squads a total of eight to be divided according to your criteria. You will be able to meet each and know their names as soon as you two are ready."

Baetus, "That is awesome, Norsha, we are already set up in another room to assemble and begin our initial briefings. Please show us to them."

Norsha, "Warehouse, six young men and two older will be there together."

Baetus and Kania quickly gather their maps and notes, stuff all into the bag left with the maps and then hurry to the door.

Norsha remains standing with the warehouse door to her right and the desk with the inner office behind it to her left. Yarjies is standing in the doorway of the small office. Both observe quietly the beginning choreography of the teams clicking to different timing routines then, as quickly, finding balance in their motion. With the closing of the warehouse door after the last group Yarjies shouts, "We are on!" Both smile approvingly with the thought. Norsha leaves the room and Yarjies returns to the small office.

Chop Wood

Jake continues, "The Rochukas embody elemental life with indwelling souls of hierarchical beings. The creatures are humanoid physically with the self- awareness and the cognitive thought priorities of a human as each once was. They are in relentless pursuit of their own regeneration and also a way to escape their own fate. This may be hard to explain, Rand, but I know that you can handle it. It is the spiritual or metaphysical, as some refer to the third aspect of life that is both mingled with the flesh and transcends the physical realities of life.

The Rochukas will never be able to redeem them-selves but they relish every opportunity to punish those who reject them and those who are leading others to the same end as they by telling them what they want to hear without correcting what is wrong."

Rand, "Please, please. I am not familiar with the history that you are talking about. What is this perversion really about?"

Jake, "I know that you have not learned much of truth about God or creation or your own spiritual self. I know that you have always had an empty place inside of you that nothing in your life has been able to satisfy. Would you say that is a true statement?"

Rand, "Yes, I would have to agree with that. I have had thoughts of where I come from and why I am here. You know, especially when I was younger. Some nights, with friends, we would talk about things like; how far does outer space go and what is on the other side of the dividing line. We wondered about the idea of God but no one in my circle of friends had any answers. We would try to solve the unanswerable questions with facts but there weren't any facts to work with in a scientific way. We would always come back to considering nature, the stars, people and the things that our five senses could tell us about. That always led to dead ends. Now you are telling me that there are answers to those questions?"

Jake answers "Let me first tell you that there is a difference between truth and fact. Truth is eternal, unchanging and not always understandable. Fact is a deduction of the mind. Depending on the basis of the reasoning used a fact may not always be the truth, whereas, the truth will always be a fact."

"And?" coaxed Rand.

Jake, "After you return home from here you will experience a day when the obvious will be obscure and your purpose clear."

Rand responds with a little resistance and rebellion in his voice, "You are saying there is a way to have a relationship with God that will fulfill my life? I am not even looking for such a relationship. I think our conversation is getting into the weeds, as the saying goes."

Jake answers with a calm, compassionate tone "Let me ask you a question. Can a worm who lives in the earth direct the planet's orbit?"

Rand, "Of course not."

Jake, "Can a bird, by flying through the air, change the wind's course?"

Rand, "No, no, I see what you are getting at."

Jake, "No you don't. Answer another question for me. Can a mighty ship, by striking a wave, halt its motion?"

Rand answers with a bit of resignation, "No."

Jake pursues the point, "Can a man, although ruling over others, determine a future that he cannot see?"

Rand, exasperated, answers, "Again no. So, what is your point?"

Jake, "It is this. The creation does not say to the creator, 'Why did you make me so?' and get an answer. If a raindrop were to say to the cloud, 'Why did you put me here?' The cloud would say, 'I created you and you are a part of me. I released you to nourish the earth and bring forth life.' If the raindrop asks, 'Why am I here?' The cloud will say, 'You are where you are needed. Fulfill your destiny there.' The purpose for your time here is to strip away much of what your life has consisted of for many years. The process can be difficult and fruitless if you reject it out of fear and selfishness or it can be a potentially painful healing transformation as you have said you are seeking. When you turn from the fear and embrace the transformation you will gain the clarity to understand your destiny."

Rand, "Wow. I feel like I have fallen from a cliff and I don't know what to expect next."

Jake, "I am revealing to you an offer from the very source and sustainer of all that is. Not a demand, not a deal of some sort that is merely expedient. It is a loving, merciful offer of hope. You are as free to reject it as you are free to accept it. Will you allow yourself to know the truth?"

Rand, "What truth?"

Jake, "God is the creator and the sustainer of all and that all includes you. God is perfect and His nature is unchanging. The creation has the potential to be perfect but it is not because it also has the potential to be flawed as a result of natural processes. Human beings are the only creatures with physical existence that can choose to pursue either potential as the result of free will. The first humans have already established the inclination to pursue the selfishness and self-centeredness of imperfection."

Rand, "So, I am living out the results of what someone did thousands of years ago? Is that right?"

Jake, "Yes, as an extension of those original people."

Rand notices the intensity of sunlight is fading. He turns back to Jake and realizes that he is intentionally silent and looking into the sky. They look at one other until Jake smiles and asks, "You want to chop some wood?"

Rand laughs aloud with his hands extended at shoulder level, "About the time I am relaxing with your concepts you break everything up with levity. I love the mental dexterity. Chop wood?"

Jake, "Yes! It is a good exercise for clearing the mind and challenging the conscience. I grew up doing this sort of work, with my father, building with wood and stone."

Rand falls back into the discussion, "How so?"

Jake, "We are architects of a sort. We design great works for others to accomplish. We cut and set the corner stone and then find faithful men and women to work with. "

Rand answers with hope and conviction, "This I will do, with your help".

Jake returns to the center of the clearing and begins to dance. As the cloud passes overhead the shadows begin to withdraw. Jake dances harder and harder so that a cloud of dust begins to rise from the crumbled leaves under foot. Rand begins to see movement in the cloud of dust as the sunlight filters through onto the forest floor. As the density of the cloud increases, forms become visible. Forms of winged creatures, possibly angels Rand thought are dancing around Jake.

Rand finds himself a spectator at a joyous celebration. In a complete release of inhibitions Rand jumps up, runs into the cloud and begins dancing. He dances deliriously until he collapses into the leaves below him. The cloud of dust slowly settles over him as the area becomes quiet and still. Rand lay there breathing heavily. The peacefulness has absorbed every movement, every sound and every thought. The day has played out its story of communion for the salvation of a man. The heartbeat of nature brings the question, a touch of God the answer. A generation may rise that has never known either. Sorrow can be a grave burden.

Rand rises from his healing rest, brushes himself off and leaves by another path which leads to the guest house. In the bedroom he finds a note pinned to clothing intended for him to wear to the celebration. 'The festivities begin at 7:00 this evening. Come early if you like.'

Rand lifts the jacket from the bed and looks at it closely. Its material is unfamiliar to him. It is very light weight and its color has a mixture of silver and gold which sparkles and shines in the light. As he put the jacket on it clung to him as though it was now a part of him. It felt good to have it on. With a bit of reluctance he removes it and places it on the bed. He hurriedly showers and dresses for his visit to the mansion for the first time.

As he put on each piece of clothing it wraps itself around his body snugly. The material, to the touch, feels metallic. Rand likens it to a light weight male such as knights of ancient times wore. Once on he actually felt as though he was wearing nothing because the clothing was so light weight. After a studied view in a mirror Rand's inhibitions are calmed. He is clothed and covered. There is a pair of sandals as well. Once dressed, Rand leaves the guest house quickly with the excitement of a teenager going on a first date.

He walks to the front door of the splendid mansion and lifts the door knocker with his right hand. As he does so Rand sees the letters, J., A., K., E., above the knocker in brass letters. He realizes that Jake is not a name but rather an acronym. He thinks for a moment before allowing the heavy metal arm of the knocker to fall against the door. 'I must not shrink back now, I could never forgive myself.' Rand challenges himself. A deep, resonant sound emanates from the wooden door when struck. As the door begins to open Rand takes a step back from the threshold. There is no one to greet him. With the door fully opened the foyer is brightly lit and the atmosphere is soothed with a soft melody from a piano somewhere inside the mansion.

Rand steps inside, with the door standing open behind him. He could hear a distant, agonizing scream coming from the city as he pushes the door to close.

There, Then

Megan introduces Pilo and herself to their group before releasing Pilo to go to the warehouse and begin an inventory of their gear and equipment. Pilo rushes to the warehouse and digs into the gear on the trailer. The driver and passenger, both unidentified, approach her and ask what she is looking for and then offer to help as a way of stopping her from recklessly pulling things from the trailer.

The driver, "Excuse me, I am responsible for this trailer and its contents. You need to stop dismantling the contents and tell me what you need."

Pilo, "Uh, o.k., I am Pilo. You are?"

Driver, "Claus, my name is Claus."

From the truck cab a shout, "I am Rega. I have the bill of lading. I can tell you that we have what you are looking for without pulling everything apart!"

Claus responds, "Get out of the truck and change your attitude!" Then to Pilo, "Sorry, this has been a long week and a good sleep will do wonders."

Pilo, "I understand. With this being crunch time for everyone it is going to be tense. Please remind your passenger as well that it is a learned skill to find flexibility of attitude because no one wants to be distracted unnecessarily."

Claus "Got it."

Pilo, "I will need backpacks with water bladders, the bikes and gear for riders such as helmets, gloves and possibly lights, for now."

Claus, pointing to the front corner of the trailer, "Everything you will need is on this pallet." Pilo moves around the trailer and loosens the tie down straps that are over the pallets. She then looks across the warehouse and sees a fork lift to use. With the fork lift she removes the pallet from the trailer to locate it near the roll up door at the far end of the warehouse.

Claus, "O.K., Pilo, if you need anything else please let me know.

Pilo, "Will do, thanks."

Megan pulls her group together and leads everyone away from the distractions of the others' mingling. Her impatience with chatter has usually been misunderstood as anti-social. She just doesn't like wasting time when there are more important priorities. "Okay, everyone, we will begin right away with conditioning and training maneuvers. Everyone in this group will be using a bicycle for transportation and as a tool for both offense and defense in the field. If anyone cannot adapt they will be reassigned with no regrets and no judgment. We have a role for you so keep your edge. Reassignment is totally acceptable when it is appropriate because we want to have the right person in the right place. I want everyone to be aggressive, positive attitude, relentless. Anyone have questions?" No one raises a hand.

Pilo gains access to the materials and begins removing items and placing similar items together on the floor. Soon she has several piles of gear and equipment spread out on the warehouse floor. With everything separated she waits for Megan and their squad.

Megan, "First up I want you all to return to the vans, collect your things and put them on a cot upstairs. Take fifteen minutes to get that done and meet over by the rollup door where Pilo and I will be waiting. Got it? Go!"

Baetus and Kania also gather their squad and have them collecting gear to put on a cot before meeting in the shipping office Baetus has set up for briefings. While everyone is busy Baetus and Kania walk to the supply trailer to see what is available. As they near Claus steps toward them, "Hello, my name is Claus and I will locate what you need."

Kania, "Do you have a manifest we can look at? We will likely need to adapt what is available so I don't have a list. Let us see what you have that we can make useful."

Claus, "I understand your approach. Let me get that for you." Claus returns to the cab of the van and Rega hands him the inventory.

Kania, "Baetus are you thinking anchors, rope, tranquilizer rounds for a shotgun and gear for repelling and climbing?"

Baetus, "Kania, we are thinking together already. Awesome."

Claus, "Let me pull the remaining pallets off the trailer so you can find what you need."

The two back away as Claus restarts the fork lift. Once settled on the floor and the bands removed both pallets yield enough materials for their anticipated activities once in the field and coordinating with the trackers. Baetus, "We will have a small number of bikes to work with. We may be able to up our game and reduce the time of our direct involvements with the pairs because of the speed and lowered sound profile on the bikes. Cool!"

Kania has similarly separated materials by groups for subdividing, per individual, once training has begun. With everyone returning from upstairs the two groups separate and each begins their routines. Baetus and Kania, with their first group briefing, while Megan and Pilo have their squads assembling outside to begin physical fitness routines.

After thirty minutes of stationary routines Pilo calls a break and has everyone reconvene after quick hydration to pick up individual gear and equipment from the warehouse. Now mid-afternoon the sun is warming everything and a sweaty day of exhausting field maneuvers with gear and an introduction to the bikes will have everyone sleeping well.

Baetus has everyone in his group focused on a map while he leads a narration and presents a big picture representation of the area on the wall. Pilo begins footnoting with short burst statements to highlight or stress points and specifics of detail. The two have already recognized their individual tendencies to overload the informational aspects of training without proper attention given to the practical and tactical planning for the execution of strategies in the field with the flexibility to anticipate out of the box possibilities. The trainees are getting confused and overloaded mentally. Baetus and Kania agree that getting everyone into the field will bring everything together and give the maps a better context.

With darkness falling earlier due to the time of year the trackers' group returns after sundown having ridden for five miles, the last one in the dark because no one had lights. The cloudless night did help them see well enough to be able to stay out of the ditches. The binders' group ends their day's strategy reviews with coordinates outlined and perimeters identified. Everyone is hungry and tired. The showers will be in high demand as well.

Norsha and Yarjies, having anticipated the crush in the kitchen and bath were just finishing their own evening routines and clearing from the areas. Yarjies calls both Baetus and Megan over, "Good to see you wrapping up this first day well. Is everyone working with you and working together?"

Megan, "All is good with some real effort out there for a first day. Skills checks tomorrow early so tonight is food and sleep, soon."

Baetus, "Yup, looking alert, tomorrow will be fun."

Norsha has, at the same time, corralled Pilo and Kania. "So, give me a quick word."

Pilo, "I need a shower before the herd gets there but, in a word, allot to learn fast."

Kania, "Today was a bit one dimensional. Tomorrow will bring a change of pace and evaluations."

Norsha asks Kania, "You in for food first?"

Kania, "Definitely. I will be getting some work in tomorrow. I can't wait to get outside. Do you know the weather for tomorrow?"

Norsha, "It should be like today mostly with possible late afternoon thunderstorms. The two continue together to the kitchen area.

Three hours later, a little after 9:00 p.m., everyone is cleaned up, full and insmall groups talking about the day. With everyone in the sleeping area Norsha walks from the stairway to the center of the room and gets everyone's attention. With a growling yell that could be mistaken for that of a bear Norsha begins, "Tonight will likely be the best night's sleep until our assignments are successfully completed. I am just giving you a heads up. Some aspects are always unpredictable. Bottom line, rest well and center your selves by morning. A 0500 breakfast is served. See you then, there."

Everyone repeats, "Then, there!"

Norsha leaves the room with a smile of hope and appreciation. It has been several years since her last field action in real time and she is beginning to realize that her own level of mental acuity, physical stamina and reflexive balance under pressure are no longer sharp and she may not be reliable. Norsha becomes instinctual and releases the tension with a low level growl. No one is around to hear it but the moment became a point of change in Norsha's psyche that put her on a fast track to engage in the squad level activities as though a cadet. She intends to gain their perspective and be in a position to maneuver the groups emotionally while sharpening her personal edge. While walking toward the office Norsha notices Fripree hanging out alone in the kitchen area. Her wave does not illicit a response. Fripree is sitting at the counter, in the shadows, very quietly as though meditating or sleeping. As Norsha turns to engage her Fripree opens her eyes and raises a hand to say hello. "Hey Norsha, how is everyone responding?"

Norsha, "Everyone is coming together well so far. How about you? Are you isolating or just resting?"

Fripree, "A little of both. I know this time of preparation is beginning to coalesce but I am beginning to struggle with my own preparedness. I need more activity and interaction to be better coordinated with the overall strategy. Perhaps I am getting ahead of the time line. What do you think?"

Norsha, "This evening you, me and Yarjies will spend some time together and get more specifics ironed out. I realize that everyone has been focused on organization, materials and the beginning of training. Everyone is on a compressed schedule so you must stay engaged and we will get you there, beginning tonight."

Fripree, "O.K., sounds good. Question, do you expect Jake to visit us before we leave Speyer?

Norsha, "One thing I have learned is that I cannot predict his movements at all. I or no-one really knows his activities. I do know that he always shows up when needed and he leaves when he is not. I would like to say yes but I plan as though he will not."

Fripree, "I think I understand. I gain a lot of confidence when he is present and my perspective is clearer when he speaks."

Norsha, "We will see him when we need to and won't when we don't."

Yarjies walks up as the two hug. "Hello ladies, everyone is settled for the night but you two. What's up?"

Fripree, "We were just discussing a need for the three of us to go over some aspects of our organizational progress and for me an orientation of my involvement and the specifics that I can focus on when I am not otherwise engaged."

Yarjies, "Okay, in fifteen minutes. I need a cup of coffee and to make a jog across the warehouse to the bathroom. See you both in the office soon?"

Norsha, "There, then."

Fripree, "There, then!"

With the three now at the office and everyone else asleep upstairs they enter the office and close the door. They form a small circle, sitting close enough together to avoid speaking loudly so as to prevent being overheard unnecessarily.

Yarjies, "For starters, Fripree, you are currently in a status of hurry up and wait. Most of your preparation for your primary role will be to study archival records of the Rochukas to know their habits, their motivations, their goals and their appetites. This background knowledge will not be for engaging them but to enhance your ability to detect irregularities and recognize any other entities using them as hosts."

Fripree, "That sounds like a counter-intuitive anticipation of responses. I have heard mention of the Stroy. A puppet master that moves in and out of their existence to avoid detection. Is that correct?"

Norsha, "That is correct. Whenever you can see one of these beasts while motionless there is an opportunity to look for indications of the Stroy's presence. Once we can contain and isolate the Stroy the Royal Guardian will begin to interact with our awareness."

Fripree, "So, the Stroy has power or authority over the Royal Guardian?"

Yarjies, "Not at all, a time has been allowed for the Stroy to be active in our realm. That time is coming to a close and one of our collective goals is to complete the Stroy's time by binding and forcing him into his realm so that we can then close the breach that once allowed him access through the Rochukas."

Fripree, "Then my ability is not a natural one?"

Yarjies, "Your ability is a gift that you were endowed with before birth. Once our mission is completed the endowment will cease."

Norsha, "Here is a rough outline of our strategy. The field groups will disburse from Bad Wildbad to locate the targets and then work to maneuver them toward the ridgeline where we want to isolate them for the Discree to extract their names and tribes. Also the Identifier will then quarantine the Stroy. Once this is accomplished the second field group will destroy the physical bodies of the Rochukas while the Discree will eternally bind their spirits. Once this stage is reached the Royal Guardian will take control of the Stroy's soul and will place the heart of evil that is the Stroy behind the veil and the breach is then sealed."

Fripree, "And then?"

Yarjies, "We all have a beer!"

Norsha gives Yarjies a stern look as scolding for his out of place, dry humor. "Such a time is still ahead and there is much to do for us to get from here to there."

Fripree, "Okay Norsha I can recognize a joke. I am ready for that beer NOW!"

Before everyone separates to salvage as much of the night's sleep as they can, Yarjies has on more suggestion, "So now, to wrap this up for tonight, let us join and connect."

The small group comes together in a close circle with each placing their left hand onto the right shoulder of the one to their left. Each raises their straightened right arm at an angle toward the center with straightened fingers angled uniformly at a forty five degree angle downward, as though forming the container opening of which they are its boundaries. Their empowerment passes through this center point to envelope the group and connect each with a heightened presence of creation. After a few moments the group relaxes and separates with each remaining silent and absorbed by the significance of this moment in time and in each of their lives. The peacefulness allows each to reflect as the day draws to a close and all are now asleep.

The coming morning will sober the thinking and quickly challenge the physical endurance of each. Megan and Pilos' squads of trackers will have less than eighteen hours before relocation to Bad Wildbad for two days of terrain and elevation acclimation before staging for deployment. As well, Baetus and Kanias' squads of strategists and hunters will have the same time to get lost at least once in the terrain and acclimate to the elevation.

The group as a whole needs to have an edge that has not yet been attained. The fear of failure cannot be allowed to control their decisions or performance. Their intelligence must be guided by experience that is being gained now and will be enhanced as everyone is challenged physically and psychologically. Anyone failing to perform during this ramp up to engagement will be reallocated to alternate assignments and continue for twenty four hours as a reserve, even if injured. Realistically the combined group cannot lose more than three individuals. The fires of conflict that have smoldered for years are igniting in the hearts of the combatants as the chant quietly begins.

With everyone fed and the gear assembled Pilo begins at 0630 with an outline of activities for the assembled group. No established course of trails exists in the area except for trail heads of cross country, unmarked possibilities to explore. The first activity for the trackers will be a five mile ride with full gear at an aggressive pace to get everyone's blood flowing and sweat pouring. At the first trail head with a check point all gear except for personal firearms, water and protein packs of nuts and cheese will be dropped for the first round of maneuvers.

Baetus and Kania separate their groups to focus on differing aspects to master or at least become proficient with. Baetus will have the strategists and Kania the hunters.

Fripree and Yarjies begin working together to prepare and pack meals and additional water to deliver to the check points so that the groups can remain in the field until near sundown.

With everyone having now left the facility but Yarjies and Fripree the warehouse is quiet. As Yarjies prepares to leave in the van to deliver the supplies Fripree interrupts him, "Yarjies I will make this trip for you. I am familiar with the map and it is just an out and back route. Okay?"

Yarjies, sensing Fripree's continuing need to be actively involved replies, "Certainly! Just remain aware of what is going on around you, complete the deliveries and I will see you back here in a couple of hours."

With a big smile Fripree climbs into the driver's seat, puts the manual transmission in gear and lurches through the gate and on the way to the first check point. She hasn't driven with a manual transmission before now but she knows that she will figure it out. Yarjies turns back toward the office shaking his head. He knows that she needs the involvement and he hopes the van survives because they will be leaving in two days for Bad Wildbad.

The area of training is just west of the old city of Speyer in a wooded area to the south of HaBloch and east of Neustadt. Although not very hilly the area is surrounded by farming fields and isolated enough to allow the group's activities to be unnoticed.

The riders leave the compound and briskly ride for a quarter mile on the paved roadway to the trail head. There is a wood fence separating the trail from the roadway with an opening for the riders to enter through and start down the trail. The terrain of the area is a mixture of hilly areas with a creek running through the large ditch that borders a pasture on the opposite side that leads into the hills north of their starting point.

As everyone rolls into the parking area Megan addresses the group, "Is everyone here? David? Hang in there you are doing well." Everyone applauds in support and David shakes his head. The question is meant as an encouragement because he has been lagging behind everyone. His fitness level is not on par with the others.

Megan, "Okay now, we are going to spread out along the trail to give everyone space and to avoid running up on one another. This way everyone can work on maximizing their skills and speed. Of course, if you catch up with someone make your presence known by shouting 'rider'. If you have to stop do not stay on the trail. Move to the side so someone does not run upon you. Everybody got it?"

Pilo, "Megan is our lead rider for this first ride and I am the sweep. So, work hard to catch Megan and don't let me catch up with you. Look down the trail and not down at your front wheel. We know this is a first ride for most of you but you will likely be pleased with how quickly you adapt. Now, let's move!"

Everyone quietly swings a leg over their bike as Megan leads off and Pilo counts to ten to space out the other riders. The terrain will be rather flat or rolling slightly until near the hills in the distance. The pace is vigorous and everyone should be able to keep their spacing for the most part.

After the first mile some riders begin to slow and others begin to observe the surroundings. It is a combination that leads to further slowing and a grouping of the riders. Suddenly the trail presents the first challenging feature of a creek crossing. The combination of about a one foot drop into the creek with moving water, a rocky bottom and then a gradually rising bank on the other side becomes an opportunity to teach some technical skills.

Megan shouts out, "Water crossing!" as she maneuvers through the obstacles and rides out the far side. The next rider, Michael, gets about half way through the creek before hitting a stone big enough to stop his momentum and his right foot comes off the pedal and is into the cold water. He lets out a curse word or two, mostly from embarrassment.

The riders behind him stop so Megan circles back and laughingly kids Michael, "Did our big, strong guy get his foot wet?" Everyone smiles but no one says anything because each knows that they are just as vulnerable.

Pilo, "Okay everyone, we will stop here and work through some technical strategies for riding through obstacles." Everyone dismounts, lays their bike down and gathers around Megan and Pilo.

Megan, "This is our first little obstacle. As we move into the more hilly areas the terrain will be much more challenging with climbing, downhill drops, rocky areas and tree roots. Everyone must learn to navigate the varying terrain at speed. If you are going to walk then you don't need the bike and you are useless out here without one."

Pilo, "Once we begin to encounter rough riding conditions your butt should be off the saddle more than on it."

Megan, "Elle, grab your bike and come up here, please." Elle walks to her bike as Megan speaks to the group, "Elle has experience riding in mountainous terrain so she is going to demonstrate for us the correct way to ride through this type of obstacle. The technical principles will apply with or without the water."

Elle, "For what it's worth, I haven't been on a bike for a couple of years so, I may be a little rough in my riding but here goes."

Bjorn, also experienced in mountain biking, stays back so the others can observe and ask questions. Pilo recognizes what he is doing and allows it because, even though he is not aware of it, he will be demonstrating techniques at the next training session.

Elle starts a short distance back from the creek in order to have some momentum. As she nears the bank of the crossing she is off the saddle with her knees flexed and her center of gravity shifted by having her butt slightly behind the saddle. Reaching the bank she pivots the front wheel up and off the ground slightly to be above the rear wheel so that she is balancing on the rear wheel slightly to enter the creek bed and prevent any obstacles from catching the front tire enough to slow her momentum. The water is but two to three inches deep so it is not a factor. Elle uses her legs to power through and across the rough creek bed, exiting up the far bank smoothly.

Megan, "There you go! Everybody ready? Let's all get across now and move onto the trail ahead of us. Elle lead us out." The other riders are contemplating their own attempt. Megan, "Okay now it is just water so, let's go! As I call your name head out, Michael, Nahan, Lexa, Drew, David, Claus, Livvi and Bjorn."

Each struggles with different aspects of the crossing and of all the riders Bjorn's front tire slips on the far bank and he falls, landing on his right side in the water. Megan, after a few minutes of Bjorn laying in the water, asks simply, "You okay?"

Bjorn, "Yep, nothing hurt but my pride."

Megan, "Alright then everyone is waiting so, let's go!"

Bjorn hops up, grabs his bike and walks out of the creek. He takes off without a response and he soon catches up with the others. Megan is the sweep so she is the last to join the group. As she nears the stopped line of riders she can hear Michael, "Hey Bjorn were you expecting to get a bath so early today?"

Claus adds, "We will all get to 'kiss he earth' before it is over. You might be next Michael!"

Bjorn, "The hills and the trees are waiting."

Lexa, "I have been called a tree hugger but this may be a little rough."

Pilo, "Here we go now through the fields for a couple of miles so enjoy the easy ride while you can." Pilo moves to the lead position and Elle drops back to the middle of the group.

Megan, "Same as the first part of the ride, you gotta catch Pilo and stay ahead of me."

Pilo, "We are not stopping unless mechanics give us trouble. If you have a flat move to the side of the trail and fix it or replace the tube." Everyone raises a hand as saying yes. Pilo makes eye contact with each as their hand remains raised. She then takes off quickly and accelerates until she has shifted to the bike's highest gear. The group in in pursuit but they are not gaining any ground.

Bjorn is near the back of the line and is becoming impatient with the slower riders in front of him because he is being enveloped by the dust that is kicked up on the dry trail. He leaves the path running along the edge of the field to pass but the maneuver puts him into the rows at a right angle which will slow his progress if he can't overcome the rough surface and power through the resistance.

The bikes are military grade which doesn't mean they are highly sophisticated, only that they are rugged and reliable. It is up to the rider to get the most performance he or she is capable of. Bjorn works his way past Livvi and Claus before moving back onto the path. The group has gained some ground on Pilo as Megan is on the back wheel of Livvi. She is shouting encouragements to everyone who can hear her. Pilo can tell that everyone is lagging a bit but she is encouraged by Lexa and Drew who are hollering like they are on a carnival ride.

With two miles behind them now the terrain begins to change as the plowed fields transition to brief but higher inclines. After a rise of approximately one hundred feet over the next quarter of a mile most riders are struggling. As she reaches the crest Pilo stops to turn and see the group still somewhat separated and in line but moving slowly. She can see Megan signal for a circling of the group.

Once everyone is together they lay down the bikes and gather in a circle with their arms over one another's shoulders. Megan speaks up, "Nice little ride, huh? Overall everyone did well. At least we stayed on top of the bike, right?"

Everyone laughs and looks at one another. Pilo, "We are going to learn some foot work that will help you to keep your feet on the pedals whether riding up hill, downhill or if rolling over rough obstacles. It is obvious that we don't have much rough terrain or elevation to work with here. Keep in mind that when we are in Bad Wildbad everything will be extreme compared to here. That being said, we can work on fundamentals here so that the movements you will develop there will be somewhat less challenging."

Bjorn raises his hand, "If I may, I can demonstrate the techniques everyone will need."

Megan, "You are on point, Bjorn, and we will be using you to lead this training segment."

The others clap their hands in support as they break up and return to their bikes while mentally preparing for the challenges and wondering when lunch will be happening. Bjorn's segment is conducted on the crest of the hill with everyone in a line for him to ride before them and demonstrate tactics for the foot to pedal angle to use along with the terrain to one's advantage. After two passes the line breaks up and each rider uses the available space to explore the methods Bjorn has demonstrated.

Megan begins calling out names as the order of the riders through the downhill section. The trail leads through a level, rocky area for about fifty yards then descends slightly through a slight curve to the right before descending approximately fifteen feet quickly into a ravine that is about twenty feet across. The momentum helps each rider to ride up the other side near a large tree which has roots that are crossing the trail on the incline.

With Megan positioned across the ravine, near the exit point, Bjorn leads the riders through the exercise. The biggest challenge for most of the riders is to gain enough momentum to clear the obstacles. The tree roots in particular are slippery when they are crossed linearly which is normal in this type of scenario. Pilo shouts to Megan, "We get this down and everyone will be well on their way to understanding the technique.!" As she finishes her sentence Bjorn emerges on the far side, approaching the tree with momentum to quickly hurdle the rim. As he powers up the climb his front wheel catches a surface root and begins to slide along its surface, peeling bark and slowly leaning the bike, with Bjorn, until he slams shoulder first onto the compacted, dry trail with a thud.

Megan leans down, looking down at him blankly and asking, "You okay?"

"Yep" answers Bjorn, "I am getting used to it."

"Well, everyone is waiting on you, graceful." Megan pointing to the group of riders he started with.

"Yep", again answers Bjorn. "I hope everyone learns from my mistakes. He quickly collects his bike and with his right leg slung over the bike his down stroke is quickly into the next turn.

Megan signals each to follow after a five count. With the last rider in the chase she falls back with Pilo to strategize and review as Bjorn leads the ride. Pilo shouts to the riders as they quickly ride away, "At the road take a right to come back to here." She shrugs her shoulders and smirks, "I doubt they heard me."

Megan, "What do you think about staying out here tonight?"

Pilo, "We have nothing to work with."

Megan, "I asked Fripree, before we left, to bring supplies and gear o the drop off. She is going to be there later today."

Pilo, "Well, we will need to know soon."

Megan, "Yep, I have a radio for emergencies so I will check in with her before it gets too late."

Pilo, "We can do it. It is your choice to make."

Megan already has the radio in hand and keys the mic, "This is Megan calling base." Then to Pilo, "Let's start getting a layout in our heads for this area. Water source, high point, a sense of the weather."

Pilo, "I think we will be okay with the farmers and the locals but we should keep fires at a minimum and use low light practices."

Megan, "I know, it is like hiding in plain sight although we are not doing anything wrong.."

Pilo, "We are assuming a lot when we cross others' private land unannounced. We must be strong with that word."

Megan, "Okay preacher lets relax and put that plan together."

A call back on the radio crackles, "Base here, go ahead." It is Fripree answering?"

"Megan here checking your time line for your first stage stops and what you will be delivering."

Fripree, "Hey guys! I did what I could to provide for your request. I think I am in the 1500 hour time frame for this drop. I have enough food but not a lot else. I have small tarps for each and some rope. Will that get you through?"

Megan, "See you there, then." She turns to Pilo, "How are you at sleeping out with no cover regardless of the weather?"

Pilo, "The only way I haven't slept outside is naked so I am okay. I am not sure about our crew. The skies are fairly clear and the temps have been in the forties at night. We have sleeping bags so we should be fine."

The two hear someone shouting and turn to see Elle riding toward them and pedaling as hard as she can. The trail dust is kicking up behind her as she slides to a stop and points down trail. "It is David! He has had an accident and is hurt pretty bad."

Megan, "Let's go! Is it only David?"

Elle, "Yes, Bjorn is tending to him, maybe his ribs or shoulder? I was sent for you."

The three, with Elle leading, ride to the area where the ravine drops down from the trail. They find David at the bottom of the ravine, standing now with Bjorn who is checking his physical condition while talking to him to calm him and get information.

Bjorn, "Man, David, you took a nasty fall."

David, "Yep, I feel pretty banged up but I don't think that I broke anything."

Bjorn, "Let me help you check a few things, okay?"

David, "Sure, I was doing pretty well I thought until I rode into the silt. The bike stopped but I didn't until I landed in that bush!"

Bjorn, "Now, take a deep breath for me."

David, "It hurts but I don't feel any restriction."

Bjorn, "That is great. Now, raise both arms from your sides to over your head."

David, "I am just beat up. This hurts but my shoulders feel normal."

Bjorn, "That is great! You just stand still for me now so I can remove your helmet." As he lifts the helmet from David's head he sees a branch of the bush that is approximately one inch in diameter and four to five inches long impaled into the top of the helmet and a crack in the helmet interior cushioning along the temple and behind the ear areas of the right side.

David, "I may have been disoriented for a brief time but I don't think I lost consciousness."

Bjorn, "I think you took a hard enough knock that you should not ride for at least a day."

They both look up to see the trio of Elle, Megan and Pilo observing their discussion and the other riders waiting nearby for a word on David's condition. Bjorn announces. "Nothing broken just bent." Everyone laughs and bounces the front wheel of their bike on the ground.

Pilo, "Now let's everyone make a couple of more rounds of the circuit we have been riding and then we will have a break. David will not ride again before tomorrow so he will assume a fall back role to establish a camp and manage the gear for now."

Everyone looks at each other at the mention of a camp. Each assumes they would find out soon enough.

Michael speaks up, "I am ready for the creek bank trail. Is anyone with me?"

Drew, Lexa and Claus respond, "Let's do it!" The four head out for that area.

Nahan then speaks up, "I need more work on the trail leading through the ravine and before the creek. Do the rest of you want to hit that area again? Then we will follow into the creek bank."

Livvi and Elle join Nahan and they return to the beginning of the trail on the incline side of the hill. Bjorn stays back to talk to Pilo about David's temporary role and what was the mention of a camp about. Megan, Pilo and Bjorn circle up and David slowly separates from them, a little unsure what to do but wait on one of them to fill him in.

Megan, "Let me first address what I know must be on your mind, Bjorn, and everyone else as well. We will be staying out here tonight to get everyone into the flow of our activities and lifestyle in the field. This will be a coming together for our group and, hopefully, a breakdown of any barriers that still exist."

Pilo, "I think the area between the ravine and the creek may be the best for shielding our presence. We can have a small fire and also be somewhat shielded from the wind. I will work with David on that project while you, Bjorn, work with the riders. You are doing a good job, Bjorn."

Bjorn, "Alright, it sounds like the beginning of a plan."

Megan, "I am leaving when we finish our discussion to ride to our supply drop and update our schedule with Fripree. It is now 1300 hours. If the training runs until 1430 and you break then for snacks at 1530 have everyone ride to the drop off location and pick up what we will have there to bring it here before it starts getting dark."

Pilo, "Okay, we've got it. Let's everybody get busy." She looks away and calls David, "Hey, David, it's you and me on this little project." David walks to her, anxious for something to do that is useful.

David, "As my Dad would say, "Do something even if it is wrong. Do we have any tools?"

Pilo, "For?"

David, "Uh, cutting wood, driving stakes, digging holes, for example?" With a big smile to turn the awkward question into a joke, he hopes.

Pilo, "We have what is needed for tonight. That being said I need for you to walk the area near the creek and under the trees to pick up firewood and small diameter branches or pieces we can use for starter. If you find enough to need help getting it moved to the camp area make a pile and let me know, alright?"

David, "You got it." He gets busy and notices that he can hear the others yelling at each other and whooping it up as they ride. He is determined to return to riding so, he focuses on stretching his arms, shoulders and legs as he gathers the wood.

After leaving David Pilo walks to the area to be used for their overnight stay. She too hears the riders and is reminded of her own enthusiasm and excitement during her first experiences on the trails as a rider. She smiles as she reaches the top of the hill and feels a breeze rustle her hair. She knows that this might well be a time of bonding and she looks forward to the camaraderie that will evolve within the group.

Pilo looks up from assembling a circle of rocks she had gathered for a fire ring. David is jogging toward her with an arm full of small, broken branches to begin a wood stack near the fire ring.

Pilo, "Is that all you have found?"

David, "Uh, no, another trip with your help and we will have plenty. I have plenty collected and I have broken up as much as I can without an axe or a saw."

Pilo, "I will help you in a little while."

David starts back to get another load. Pilo stands up and as she looks around the area she notices that the area has been a camp before. The stones she has collected are from a previous fire ring and she can see the layout with log seating and the location of her fire ring having been used before now. Her realizations bring to mind part of a poem. The verse is, 'picking up stones and stepping on bones, hearing the sighs of memories gone. The moment brings her a sense of connection with the spirit of the past in this place.

David gives a shout, "Pilo I need help!"

She looks toward the wooded area for David and sees him struggling to roll a log of about twelve inches in diameter and about four feet long up the hill. She laughs and shouts back, "Stop until I get there!"

David stops his efforts and stands to stretch again for relief of the pain. He is feeling much better but some movements are still difficult. Pilo jogs to him as he is now sitting on the log.

Pilo, "We are not building a bon fire David. We need much smaller pieces, like four inches in diameter max. You have done a great job but this one is a bit much."

David, "I see but since you are here how about helping me with the rest." He points to enough gathered wood for them each to have a load to carry back.

Pilo, "Yep, let's get it done." The two finish stacking the wood as the riders roll into the camp. Everyone is muddy and sweaty, hungry and thirsty.

Pilo, "Everyone, we will break at the creek. You can clean up a bit and eat what you have brought. Get some water inside you too and then I will give you our new plans."

The riders roll down to the creek slowly and some into the creek. The water is cold and refreshing. The shade and an occasional breeze cool everyone as they eat. Some are chattering about their riding and what they have learned.

After thirty minutes of the bantering Pilo stands to get everyone's attention. "Okay everyone here is what we are doing. We will be spending the night here tonight."

Everyone looks at one another then all look back at Pilo as she continues, "The gear and supplies we will need are at the supply drop which is where Megan is now. David will be staying here to continue making and we are all riding to the drop off to pick up what is there and return here. We have about two hours before dusk so we don't have any time to waste. Let's clean up here and be ready to roll in fifteen minutes. Bjorn, you will be the sweep. Don't let anyone stop unless they are injured or the bike has problems. Now let's break and clean up. We leave in fifteen. If you need to find a tree or dig a hole be quick about it."

Everyone begins to scramble. Drew bumps Elle's shoulder as they stand. Having her attention Drew comments, "Should be a starry night."

Elle, "Yep, that is great but it also means it's going to be cold. No wind and we will be alright."

Lexa, "Hey Livvi, wanna set up together?"

Livvi, "By together you mean near each other?"

Lexa, "No, but that is good enough."

Livvi, "I am not being judgie but it is better to be open."

Lexa, "Yes, I agree."

Michael, "I guess that leaves me out?"

Livvi, "Probably."

Lexa, "Definitely." She walks close to Michael and whispers to him, "I'm playing with her. I am straight and for you it's a maybe."

Michael, "Got it."

Nahan is quietly surveying the area and choosing a place to set up his sleeping bag. David catches his attention and walks toward him, "You ready for this gear trip?"

Nahan, "Sure, I am just trying to picture our layout and be prepared to set up for the night. It is my way to avoid surprises. I think I can be flexible when I have a strategy in mind."

David, "Cool."

Pilo shouts to everyone, "Let's get out of here. The day is moving quickly."

When everyone has their gear secured and bikes ready Pilo leads off with everyone in the same order as given before. The pace is brisk and everyone is enthusiastic in their ride to get there.

David can be heard as the group pulls away, "Be safe! See you here soon!" Everyone raises a hand to acknowledge him. The ride time for the group is forty five minutes to the drop location. They are greeted by Megan who has been anxious to see them. Bjorn pulls in last and shouts, "clear back!" Everyone understands that he is saying 'no one left behind'.

Megan has the gear and supplies divided into ten piles with each containing an eight foot square tarp, a sleeping bag from the 1960s era military surplus and dried foods with some fruit. This, combined with the necessities each already carries such as personal hygiene materials and first aid supplies will be enough until they return to the Speyer compound.

Megan, "I have what you see here. Everyone load your back pack and get a tight roll on your tarp and sleeping bag so that you are as balanced as possible."

Pilo, "We have twenty minutes. As before, if anyone needs a latrine break, make it happen with the surroundings we have and be as discreet and respectful as possible, please."

Megan looks at Pilo and jokingly asks, "Please?"

Pilo, "Sorry that little bit of civility escaped. I will do better."

Both laugh then Pilo realizes she needs to make a deposit at the nearest bush. "Where is my little digger?"

With everyone relieved, packed and ready they find themselves waiting for Pilo. They straddle their bikes and look toward Megan who is distracting herself with tightening her helmet chin strap. After a long moment of silence Pilo pushes through the bushes and shouts, "What are you waiting for? Let's go!"

The group smiles at one another and follow Megam's lead to roll out, heading back to the camp. Pilo finishes putting her pack together and straps it on. She soon catches Claus who is the last rider of the group. The trip is slightly longer in time due to the extra gear because the group did slow down with the extra effort.

With the daylight beginning to dim David prepares to start a small fire. He thinks he can hear the riders in the distance. He notices the noise, the energy, the excitement of the day beginning to transition into the night. This time of twilight when the darkness of the sky and the darkness of the earth approach with a narrowing sliver of light that separates the two beginning to compress until the two are joined. It is always a magical time for him. He thinks of this time as a renewing revelation of the consuming darkness that cannot overcome the light unless the light allows it.

Suddenly his thoughts are scrambled by the group of riders pouring in from around the curve with sparse lighting and only two head lamps, Megan's and Pilo's.

With the lit fire for light everyone works to unpack the gear and spread out. David smiles as he listens to the sounds of the camp alive with the activities of everyone setting up for the night. He stretches his shoulders and lower back. He feels ready to rejoin the group as a rider. He says to himself, "After tonight so I will."

Megan breaks out some spare flashlights for everyone to be able to see well enough to open food packs and find a seat near the fire. She speaks up, "Once you have eaten and gotten settled with your tarp and sleeping gear then come and sit around the fire."

With everyone somewhat, but sufficiently, satisfied with the food they had brought and everything squared away for sleep the group has gathered around the fire. No one is sure what comes next.

Megan begins the discussion, "I made the call for us to be out here tonight so that everyone will begin to settle into the lifestyle we will have when we are on location in Bad Wildbad. I know that most of you are accustom to the wilderness and are comfortable. I want those who are new to living out like this to rely on your buddies out here and to ask questions to acclimate as best you can. I believe that when this is all over you will look back on these days as an epic adventure."

Pilo, "What we want everyone to do here tonight is to share a little about yourself with the group, such as, your background, your understanding of our purpose, any fears and any personal intentions or goals for this mission."

Nightfall is complete now with the air cooling and everyone seated but quiet and in thought. The only sound is the crackling and occasional hissing of the fire. Most of the riders are captured by the fire in the common stare when fatigue from the day's activities, a satisfied hunger and the uncertainty of the coming days filter into everyone's consciousness. With everyone's focus coalescing, a kinetic crackle of tension gives the group atmosphere an excitement. Megan allows the moments to extend until restlessness begins to creep in.

Megan, "Michael, will you lead off?"

Michael, "No, I don't know what you are asking for."

Drew speaks up, "I am familiar with what you are asking. I will lead off." Megan nods her agreement. "Anyway, I grew up in Frankfurt. I am the youngest of three daughters. I had everything I needed and parents who love me. Unfortunately, as I grew out of childhood they didn't know me as well as they thought and I didn't know how to bridge the gap. So, here I am at twenty seven, ready to do what I can to find and herd these creatures to the mountain. I am not sure why but I am ready to bust it with the rest of you."

Megan, "Thanks Drew, I will be filling in some of those blanks for everyone soon. Okay, now let's go to your left and Claus go."

Claus, "My name is Claus and I am twenty six. I am from the Cologne area. I went to university in Cologne as well. After two years I felt like I was being indoctrinated more than being taught meaningful information. Rather than learning to think critically everyone was accepting what they were told without any questioning. I left school and I have been pursuing a self-directed form of investigative journalism which led me to involvement with this group. This is my purpose, to be personally responsible for doing what it takes to put an end to these beasts."

David, "I am here for the adventure. I have been doing a lot of wilderness trekking since high school. I am nineteen. I grew up around Offenburg so I am familiar with this area although I am not familiar with the story of these Rochukas."

Elle, "I am thirty five and I grew up near the German and Austrian border in Bregenz. Early on I liked the rough terrain, the trees, the vistas when looking toward the harbor. I am not much of a water person for recreation and such. I have trained for years on my bike in the mountains and low land, cross country trails without knowing why. Just something internal for me that I have been doing because I could. It has always been a way to calm my mind too when stressed. Now I know that this project is my purpose. I am also ready to help some of you 'kids' learn to ride correctly." With a round of hoots and whistles everyone cheers

Lexa, "I too am from the Bregenz area. I spent a lot of time on the slopes skiing and I worked at the lodge and lift several winters during high school and since then. I am twenty two. I know that this task is going to be difficult with the terrain we are going into. If we can avoid the snow it will be much better."

Livvi, "Well, I am twenty and I am from Heidelberg with no accomplishments and no cute stories. I have been on my own since I was thirteen. I am hoping to find some meaning, some purpose through my experiences with you guys. I do adapt well and I am accustomed to getting by without much. I want to kill one of these bastards."

Pilo, "Wow, you have got some edge to you, Livvi. You will get your chances and I hope you will be ready."

Megan, "Alright let's complete this. Bjorn, you are up."

Bjorn, "I am twenty five and I am from Denmark. My father wanted me to be a soldier. I chose sports like soccer, downhill skiing and competitive mountain biking. Once this is over I will return to those things. I hear that the mountain biking is becoming a popular sport in the U.S. and I hope to compete there. Until then we are warriors on the hunt for the Rochukas!"

Michael doesn't wait to be called on. "I am twenty one, from Munich and ready to ride. I have a lot to learn correctly so that I won't have to think so much about what to do. I will be better when I can respond with the correct technique. Before here I have been a druggie. I am ready to ride hard and pursue our enemy with a relentless hunger for their destruction. "Michael looks up from the fire, surveys the group and with a big smile raises his hands overhead and shouts, "How about you!"

Everyone cheers and whistles as they stand. Megan and Pilo are quick to get everyone's attention. Pilo, "Everyone calm down. We don't want to get run off from here." Everyone quiets down somewhat but continue talking.

Megan looks to Pilo and winks, "We have got what we need in this group."

Pilo, "Yep"

Megan, "Okay everyone we have an early start tomorrow. Let's get some sleep. We will clean up, load up and head back to the compound for breakfast. Everybody sleep! Got it? No horseplay!"

The whole group applauds and some whistle at a low level before everyone says, in unison, "Huh?"

Pilo, "Alright and good night."

The night temperature was forecast to be in the low forties but when everyone woke up in the morning they found frost on top of their sleeping bags and some containers of water partially frozen. After an hour of cleaning up the area in order to leave no trace and packing the gear everyone is ready to ride. David is also with his bike and has his pack on. As they leave the area he rides in the middle of the line with everyone glad to see him working to keep up.

Back at the compound with full stomachs everyone wants to shower. Yarjies walks from the office and greets everyone. "Welcome back! You can clean up and use the showers in pairs of same gender only, please. Make it quick because we have a full day planned."

Yarjies makes eye contact with both Megan and Pilo then signals for them to see him in the offices area. Both women drop their back packs in the cafeteria and proceed to the offices.

Yarjies, "Just a moment of your time to let you know that I have new intel and perhaps an escalation of our time line. When you are done with showers join me, Baetus and Kania back here. Make sure your crews have something to focus on until we are done, maybe twenty minutes."

Both women respond, "Got it."

A short time later the leadership group is together with Yarjies and Fripree. Baetus and Kania have also been in the field with their group having returned earlier the same day. Yarjies, "I want just a quick review of the field work progress from each of you. Baetus, you want to go first?"

Baetus, "Sure, I first want to say it is great to see everyone again. Our group has done as much as we can, I think, o prepare without being in the area where we will be in Bad Wildbad. Here there is no real comparison with the terrain we will be working in there. We were able to work out our differences internally so that everyone is on the same page and using the same approach to communication and logistic tracking. I am a bit concerned about the time lag because of the decision to limit use of radios. Riders will be a critical link to get our communications to the field on an effective time line in order to be useful. Kania, do you have anything to add?"

Kania, "Only to emphasize the need for radios between groups so that the riders are as a backup rather than the reverse."

Fripree, "We will check resources but I think there are other reasons for limiting radio use. Yarjies, will you address this for us?"

Yarjies, "We have enough radios to equip group's leaders only. The risk in relying on radios for broad communication between individuals in the field is that the Rochukas can manipulate most frequencies' wave lengths and actually distort voices to change what is being transmitted. The threat is that our communications can be used to confuse and misdirect our efforts which will endanger our safety and the effectiveness of our strategies. So, we will have to limit the duration of any transmissions and also restrict the time of day to early morning."

All of the group leaders in the room become angered by this new information. Megan, "Why are we just now hearing this?"

Baetus, "Why, Yarjies, are you withholding such information from us?"

Pilo, "We are the ones, in the field, putting our lives on the line and you are treating us like idiots!"

Kania, the calmest of the group for a change speaks directly to Yarjies, "You are screwing this whole thing up!"

Fripree, "Please, please everyone calm down. Let us remember our place here."

The four begin yelling and standing as if to attack Yarjies and begin shoving one another. Fripree recognizes that, as she had experienced during her travels, the behavior is the result of a spiritual attack that has everyone losing control of their faculties. She separates from the group, stands with her back against the door and raises her hands as she begins to pray, "God Almighty be our shield against our enemy I ask through Your kindness."

After a moment the edge in the room softens as the threats become statements of fear and concern for one another. Soon the group is quiet and looking at one another as though they are uncertain about what has happened. Fripree walks back to the group, "Alright now let's finish this meeting on a positive note with the updates and outlook for the coming days."

Yarjies stands before the small group assembled and begins to provide the application of a principle transitioning from Fripree's prayer as an athlete rides the culmination of the hydraulic sequence we all know as surfing. He quotes a memorial for the matriarch of an ancient ruling family who learned sacrifice through her commitment to a cause greater than herself and took up arms during the great wars.

"She is,
In the trenches of accomplishment,
To cross the bridge saved.
In the harbor submerged,
To rise above the waves.
Overhead convoy,
Downwind formations,
Close the escape to satisfy revenge."

Everyone remains silent because the interpretation of such a tome can be so that any response will be inadequate. Megan breaks the silence, "We have much to be thankful for, much to look forward to and much to accomplish in order to bring both intention and accomplishment together."

Fripree, "We carry the mantle of our generation because we know the need to preserve our people. This is a time to embrace our destiny. If anyone is wavering, say so now! We have no judgment of anyone who cannot die for this. We have absolute judgment for anyone who does not live out a commitment made. Now is the time for decision. This group will use their wit, their emotional strength, their ability to inspire and direct the combatants through their challenge ahead."

Yarjies, "Alright, here is our update. The weather patterns are beginning to become a factor in our time line. Increasing cold will possibly change the beasts' willingness to retreat to higher ground. Of course, it will be an influence on our performance. There may be snow so we need to get ahead of this. Every day we can reduce our time line will be a plus for us."

Baetus speaks up, "Do we have current locations on our targets?"

Yarjies, "Somewhat, yes, they are loosely tracking toward the valley east of Bad Wildbad."

Baetus, "Then we need to influence their direction toward the ridge before they can enter the valley."

Kania, "At the lowland area leading to the mouth of the valley we have coordinates set for an eighteen mile outer perimeter to keep them within. We will begin to shrink that perimeter once we have them within the area. The direction will then be north to north-west, toward the western ridge."

Megan, "I think we will need to travel to Bad Wildbad tomorrow and then use the next day to ride toward this perimeter. We will do some training along the way. This is going to be more of a learn as the situation develops scenario."

Fripree, "This is going to be more reactionary than any of us want but I have confidence in our team's ability. The courage is there, the desire is there, the hope is there and I know our purpose aligns with this situation whether we can see it or not."

Pilo, "We have a group of believers in this cause which will carry us through the challenges."

Kania, "We are giving our ass when or lose!"

Yarjies, in a slightly subdued response, "We use our head and we won't lose our ass."

Fripree, "Having backed out of the rapid fire exchanges, again takes control. "Your ass is mine if you do lose! Then, jokingly, she shifts language and mood, "Ride the trails and we will see who finds who."

Megan, "You are making me tired and I need sleep."

Baetus responds to Megan, "We have been back a little longer that your group. Food is ready in the kitchen and the nourishment will be good for your body and mind." With a grin he adds, "You get the dishes!"

Megan, "You can be so childish at the worst times."

The next morning finds everyone surprisingly up on time and beginning to work together to assemble breakfast and gather gear in preparation for the day. Only the leadership group knows about the changes and they have decided that after breakfast will be the time to explain the changes and layout the strategy for moving forward.

As group members begin sitting to eat Norsha enters the room. Everyone gives her their attention without her need to roar. As she moves to the front of the room everyone continues eating slowly and quietly. She approaches the leadership team, "Good morning everyone I am here to begin the briefing and I will call on you, Yarjies, Megan and Baetus so we can give everyone as much of a comprehensive view of our situation and our strategies going into this engagement. Fripree I need for you to be available for keeping everyone focused and engaged, please. My comments will be brief. You guys are in charge of these groups in the field. So, grab your food and I will begin in fifteen minutes."

Baetus and Megan meet up in front of one of the refrigerators. The supplies are sparse now that their stay here is winding down. Megan, "Are you ready for this?"

Baetus, "Well, as ready as I am going to get, I guess. You?"

Megan, "About the same. We are still going to be thrown into the fire to get this done. Planning is great but our natural abilities, reflexes and intuition will be what we live by."

Baetus, "That is true and that is why we will succeed. I think that we really are as ready as we can be."

Megan, "Looks like we are down to leftover scrambled eggs, a little ham and some bread. Let's make it count." As the two stand together at the counter Baetus puts his arm around Megan's shoulders and ells he softly, "I know that we must carry through on this endeavor even though we both are risking our lives. I firmly believe that we will succeed and that, together, our teams will succeed. Above all, my sweet Megan, you and I will forever be together as you become a shield for me and I for you. We will fight our enemies together and we will love one another in the struggle."

Megan lays her head on his shoulder and pauses before saying, "I love you and I will fight for you as I will fight with you to provide a future for our family both now and in the future. I believe in you and I believe in us."

After a quiet moment looking into one another's eyes both return to their leftovers and their teammates sitting nearby begin to clap their hands and say, "aw". Both Baetus and Megan look up at their audience. Megan throws a fork full of eggs while Baetus throws a piece of bread. All laugh and clean up their mess.

Yarjies stands to get everyone's attention. "Alright listen up. Norsha, you have the floor."

Norsha, "I want to give you all kudos for working hard to learn and be prepared. In general we are changing our time line again and your leadership will give you more details. I am here to tell you that everyone behind the scenes have been working hard as well to support your efforts, especially in the coming days. That being said we all know that you men and women are the front lines. You will be tasked with the dirty work of herding the Rochukas, corralling them and once stripped of their power and perceived value you will destroy them physically.

You have the trust and respect of those you may see as distant or disconnected because they are in the background but nothing could be further from the truth. It is you who will look each creature in the eye, it is you who will have to out maneuver each one and it is you who will have the final say!"

Everyone jumps to their feet shouting and pumping their fists in the air. "Kill the beast, free the name! Kill the beast, end their reign! We set us free by God's decree! Forever damned by justice be!"

Norsha remains standing to absorb the energy of their chants. A warrior resurrected to fulfill her purpose by leading this onslaught of righteous power soon to be unleashed against humanity's foe. Her heart is pounding, her strength pulsating through every muscle, her breath hot from the life she breathes.

The leadership group who are all standing at the back of the room begin to feel like they must keep the control of the group from exploding. After about twenty minutes of chants and a raucous atmosphere Yarjies and Fripree ask the others to spread out and be at every door to keep everyone inside. Fripree then gets Norsha's attention so that she will begin to calm her involvement. As she does others also calm and the room is reduced to a normal level of chatter. Norsha walks from the room with a huge smile and confident stride.

Kania and Pilo remain at the back of the room while the primary leaders;;; Yarjies, Fripree, Megan and Baetus stand in a line in front of the assembly. Yarjies, "Okay everyone, here is the bottom line. We have changes confronting us, namely, changes in the weather forecast and in the activity of our targets. We will be moving out from here early this afternoon and we will begin our preparations in the field near Bad Wildbad early the next morning. We will be sending out locators from the tracker group and coordinators from the logistics group at daybreak the following day. We will be live with this engagement beginning tomorrow morning."

Baetus, "Everyone remind one another and work yourself to be aware, flexible, relentless and powerful in your mind, your heart and your body. Remember that we are doing the work of a power greater than all."

Fripree, "It is time to fulfill our destiny and conclude our task."

Megan, "Let us finish what we have come here to do. No big words needed, just courage, strength and trust in one another as we trust the one who has brought us here. Honestly, I am tired of talking and I am ready to get this done."

Pilo and Kania have moved into the group and begin giving out partner assignments for in the field and in camp. Everyone now has someone to check in with regularly and to be accountable to. Everyone knows each other so there should not be any surprises."

Soon after the group briefing Yarjies, Megan and Baetus return to the outer office to find Yarjies and Jake standing at the doorway of the back office. "Hello everyone!" Jake shouts out as he gives each a hug and motions for all to enter the small room. He continues, "Okay everyone the time is at hand for us to act. The fluid elements such as the Rochukas activities and movements are developing rapidly. I know that you all may feel that you are just getting started with training. I understand any reservations you may have about going into the field unprepared. Once in Bad Wildbad this afternoon you will have the remainder of today, Monday and Tuesday. Your operations will begin on Wednesday as it stands now.

I want this time with you, as the team leaders, to reassure you that you have the best people and adequate resources needed. It will be up to each of you to bring the best out of everyone and to utilize your resources efficiently. I know that you each have what it takes and I expect you each to do what it takes to accomplish your goals.

There are resources in the background that will support you as well. So, the time for pep talks and subjective calculations is over. As you all have been saying, 'It is time to move'! That time is now. I have some loose ends to tie up elsewhere and when appropriate I will see you all again. Before I go I need to see you, Fripree, for a few minutes."

Fripree, "Okay, what's up?"

Jake, "I want to share something with you."

Fripree walks to him and the two remain in the back office while the others disburse to manage their groups.

Jake, "I met someone who asked about you. I acknowledged that I knew you and that I would tell you we met."

Fripree, "Okay?"

Jake, "Do you know a man named Randal?"

Fripree begins to respond, pauses with a wince of pain, "I do. I had to leave him abruptly to be here. I can't believe, how did you meet him?"

Jake, "The meeting was intentional on my part. It was providential for him. All is good with him. He has become a part of the big picture aspect of our activities here without knowing more than his role as a personal commitment to his vocation. For now just know that you will see him again."

Fripree, "My intention has been to return there assuming I survive what we are about to do."

Jake, "You will see him again."

Fripree, "That is Awesome!" After a quiet pause, "I have tasks to attend to. Thank you for everything, Jake."

Jake, "You got it, Fripree." Jake walks from the room and is gone even though the door didn't open or close.

Time to Move

Rand walks past the staircase to find someone and make his presence known. From this vantage point he can see through to the back porch area and the yard beyond. He hears no one and has not seen anyone. Rand does not want to be found in the house alone so he walks through the dining room to the double French door leading to the patio. From there he can see the grounds keepers working along the wall and the gate areas with hand tools. As he begins to walk onto the grass he hears Jake call to him from his left, possibly from the yard near the corner of the house. Rand walks around the shrubbery to get to the side yard and sees Jake seated at a table with Maggie. He walks to them, a smile on his face, pleased to see both. He speaks first to Maggie, "I thought you were gone already."

Maggie, "Not yet. How about you? Are you staying?"

Rand, "I don't know after tonight. I am sure I will be leaving as soon as I am ready."

Jake, "Have a seat and join us won't you?"

Rand, "It is good to see you both. I have been expecting Jake to tell me what I can do now that I am involved."

Maggie, "Excuse me, guys, before any confidential discussions get started between you two let me say good bye to you both. I have a time line to keep."

Jake, "Maggie you are a special woman. I know you are prepared to return and complete your purpose. Be thankful to the one who has established you and for the resources you will have in that time. I love you!"

Maggie smiles as she approaches Jake and hugs him tightly. "I love you, Jake."

Rand, "Well, Maggie, I barely know you but I will miss you. I have learned that we each have a purpose established before we are born. So, good luck on fulfilling your potential. I hope to hear of your success. Take care."

Maggie hugs Rand briefly and withdraws from the area with a wave to leave the two men alone. Jake motions for Rand to sit with him, "I want to give you a perspective that will help you to understand the activities we are engaged in."

Rand, "I do need that. I feel that I am still free falling and I need some tangibles to grab onto and slow my experiences down to my level of understanding."

Jake, "Of course, although I will first have to expand the scope of your intake in order to have room to reduce the various aspects to the level you need. Even though the steps you must take can sound simple the underlying reality of your decisions are not simple and will take a lifetime to accomplish."

Rand, "Okay, I think."

Jake, "Let me start with a gift." Jake hands him a small display stand as might be used for the viewing of jewelry or gem stones. It is made of gold and silver and it sits on a mirrored base which reflects light into the displayed item.

Rand, "This is for me? I don't understand."

Jake, "Do you have anything that you would consider displaying on this unique stand?"

Rand's memory is jolted about the gem which Lana left on his pillow. He blinked then quickly rebounded and attempted to cover by rubbing his face with open hands. Rand looked up and saw Jake's big smile, "Now why do I feel like you are setting me up again?"

Jake, "When have I set you up a first time? I am just a little quicker than you. After all, I do know what is coming before you do. This is all good, Rand, all good!"

Rand, "I know. Yes, I have a gift, a treasured memory of someone that is currently out of my life except for a gem that just may fit nicely and be displayed beautifully on this stand."

Jake, "Her name is Lana. You will see her again."

Rand, "You know her? You know where she is? You have talked to her?"

Jake, "I will tell you that I know her, yes. I also assure you that you will see her again."

Rand, "My God, I don't believe it. One of my hopes for this trip was to find her. She left so abruptly and with no explanation. I don't know what to think!"

Jake, "Some things cannot be understood without first placing trust in someone or something which you cannot control. I am telling you that it will make sense at a time in the future. I am giving you this and I want you to place it on your desk at work with the gem and know, from me, that Lana will return to you. This will be the reminder each day of my promise."

Rand, "Okay, well I trust you, so I will look forward to that day. You are also saying that I will be returning home?"

Jake, "That is correct, as Maggie has just left to return to her time to work out the fulfillment of her purpose so will you return to begin a new phase in your life that is aligned with your true purpose. First, though, you have a choice to make. Do you recognize that your self-centered choices expose your imperfection?

Rand, "Yes."

Jake, "Are you ready to reverse course in your life and ask forgiveness?"

Rand, "Yes."

Jake, "Do you choose to trust in me when I tell you that your debt has been covered by another?"

Rand, "Yes. Are you telling me that you are the one who has done this for me?"

Jake, "I am."

Rand, "Then are you saying that the one you refer to as your father is something more?"

Jake, "Someone more? Yes. I am of Him as is the Royal Guardian."

Rand, "I turn from my old self. I ask forgiveness as I give my life to you."

Jake, "Now we can move forward. Once other factors, which you are not involved with, are resolved your awareness will recognize the shift and your understanding will be clear."

Rand, "I will be here tonight?"

Jake, "Yes, enjoy tonight because you will be welcomed by all as family.Tomorrow you will be returning to your home. It is going to be important for you to stay in touch. You will begin to shift your priorities and your perspective will change as your relationship grows. There will soon come a time when you will make some significant lifestyle changes. Again I am telling you about future events that you must trust me to enlighten you about going forward. Agreed?"

Rand "Agreed. I have chosen to trust you."

The following morning Rand awoke on one of the couches. He knew that he had not been drinking any alcohol the night before but he couldn't remember how he ended up on the couch. The house was quiet and no one else was in the room. Rand gathered his jacket, put on his sandals and started for the door.

Jake shouted out, "Hey, where are you going? Want breakfast?"

Rand, "Yeah man I am hungry." As they ate at the same table on the patio Rand realized that this would likely be his last meal before starting his return home. "What is next Jake?"

Jake, "Next is a reality check. Theory and thoughts can inspire and teach but they cannot accomplish anything. I have some friends who have a little saying that is appropriate for you. When one of them says it, the others repeat it with a shout. It is simply, 'It is time to move!' Now, for you, it is time to move. You don't know it all but as you continue to learn through study, life experiences and our times together you will be prepared for each day. For now, focus on returning home and living your life with honor, with integrity and with honesty. Seek clarity and understanding."

Rand, "How can I contact you?"

Jake, "Take this journal and use it daily. As you do you will begin to have thoughts and realizations formulate in your writing. Then, in a quiet place, close your eyes and call out to me."

Rand, "Sounds like you are telling me to pray."

Jake, "Some would call it prayer. I call it simply communication. I am not a nothing or a void. I am someone. Talk to me, be specific and listen through your writing, as you study and contemplate within your soul."

Rand, "I am just going to change? What if I don't like the new reality? How will I know if an imposter is at work?'

Jake, "There are other individuals and groups that are part of our big picture, as you are, who are involved in other aspects of our overall objectives. There are spiritual or metaphysical corrections taking place very soon that will remove barriers for a time to allow for some revelations to be fulfilled. The enemy will be put in his place, the door will be locked and many, like yourself, will be empowered to shift the paradigm of influence to the good.

Rand, "So, why doesn't your Father just punch the turd and put him in his place? After all, humans are better at doing the wrong thing and not what is right. Correct?"

Jake, "'You gotta have some skin in the game,' as the saying goes."

Rand "Got it."

Jake, "Has your time here given you a different perspective on your lifestyle and priorities?

Rand, "Well, yes, although I have not had an opportunity to think through everything. I do see that I have a responsibility to be proactive about changes to be made. I am not a victim. I am responsible for my choices and the consequences whether intended or not."

Jake, "You are correct. Keep this perspective and it will serve as a baseline for your awareness and your decisions going forward. Now for your understanding I want to review with you the building blocks of what you are, who you are and why you are. Of course, this is true of every human."

Rand grabs his notebook for Jake to use, "Please use this so I will be able to keep it."

Jake accepts it, turns to a blank page of his notebook and draws three concentric circles with each having openings or doorways. "Here Rand you see three concentric circles with openings in each. The outer circle represents your body as you experience it through your five senses. The middle circle represents your soul which is made up of your mind, your will and your emotions. The inner most circle represents your spirit. In total this comprises what you are – a human being."

Rand, "The doors?"

Jake, "The doors represent the ability and the reality that the three aspects can align either partially or completely and such alignments either empower or restrict your functionality. Let's not get ahead of ourselves."

Rand "Got it."

Jake, "Who you are is determined by your soul's animation of life's memory after the body."

Rand, "And spirit?"

Jake, "Spirit animates soul as the reason why you are. Your spirit is the one element of your being that is of God or you might say is the one element that is not of a physical being naturally except for humans. It is the spirit that asserts a quality of existence to every human which no other created being can have."

Rand, "Are you talking about self-awareness? Now I want to back up. You are speaking of details that make up the building blocks I need to work with. Can we go down another level?"

Jake, "I think you are stalling."

Rand, "I think I am trying to be honest with you."

Jake, "Then you are asking for an application of experience with tangible touch points of life that illustrate principle?"

Rand, "Yep, that's it! As you said earlier, I need more than theories and thoughts. To be able to use intelligence guided by experience I need experience. I can follow what you are saying but I do not know how to apply the knowledge to life experiences."

Jake, "Okay, thank you for your honesty. The experience you gain by putting principles into practice becomes a circle of progression. However outlets are needed for application and renewal. I am not asking you to join me for a leisurely stroll through the park. I am enlisting your talents, your personality, your strengths and your weaknesses to be a part of defeating laziness, selfishness, dishonesty and fear on a grand scale."

Rand, "Yep, thanks for bringing me back. I was headed down a rabbit hole there."

Jake, "Remember that to reduce our focus we must first expand our vision. Each individual is a trinity of body, soul and spirit. Each person represents one point of the trinity of father, mother and child. Each child is the fruit of a trinity of God, mother and father. God is a trinity of Father, Son and Royal Guardian-the triune God."

Rand, "I see the patterns of a design. And you, Jake, are a point of the triune God?"

With no immediate answer given the implication remains suspended and the two men remained silent for a few moments before Jake stands and walks to the grassy yard. Rand begins to anticipate his time to leave and softly says, "I have learned a lot and I have a lot to learn."

Jake turns toward Rand and responds, "Be your-self. As you learn, gain experience and grow. Your personality will guide your manner as you simply do the next right thing and remember, 'UYB&DTRT'! You will have to walk through each day trusting the strength and courage you have gained here. Without being challenged your experience is not transitional. There will be diversions but as long as you have a relationship with the one who has created you and who is now partnering with you the path will be well marked."

Rand "Got it."

Jake, "I will be in touch."

Bad Wildbad

The last preparations for battle have been taking place at Bad Wildbad. The leadership group gathers early this Sunday morning, the fifth day of intense training. Everyone has engaged in extensive maneuvers that incorporate logistics, tactical adjustments, intelligence, teamwork and physical endurance with the pressure of subjective situational compromises dictated by the force of the trainers.

The trackers now have defensive and offensive tactics for using the bikes as weapons. They also have developed rudimentary but effective technical riding skills to be able to traverse varying terrains with speed and the ability to climb efficiently while maintaining their strength level. Also they have practiced hand to hand techniques once off of the bike.

The binders have learned roping techniques for capturing the beasts and confining them. They also have gained some basic familiarity with the bike and the maneuvers for defensive use. Their primary ability will be to direct the Rochukas or otherwise engage the beasts as a way of generating a reaction that results in the Rochukas withdrawal toward the designed trap at the summit.

During this same time frame Fripree has been immersed in gaining an understanding of her role by researching the creatures she must observe and interact with. The Rochukas have an ancient lineage that pre-dates civilization. The Stroy's existence pre-dates humanity.

The current generations of the Rochukas contain and represent the collective mutations of the spiritual or metaphysical perversions that are to be ended by the binding and sequestering of the Stroy and the sealing of the breach between the physical and spiritual realms.

Her information concerning the Stroy is purposefully limited to the indicators of location and the commands to control as a metaphysical binding until the Royal Guardian finalizes the expulsion from the physical realm and then seals the breach. Fripree's most difficult task will be the accurate locating of the elusive Stroy and the forceful commands with the correct intonations that will bind emotionally and psychologically. The binding of the Stroy will also confuse and disorient the Rochukas.

Fripree has realized through her studies that her knowledge of the Rochukas backgrounds or motivations is not constructive. She will be engaging the beasts for specific reasons, through specific processes with a small window of time to work in. She doesn't care why they are evil. Her intent is to stop them. Her focus has become her movements, timing, correct delivery and accomplished results.

Everyone involved with the operation is energized and motivated to do their part. The week of training has passed quickly. The next week in the field may grind to a slow pace because of the unknown. The projection of the leadership is seven to ten days.

The Bad Wildbad area is fairly rugged with a median elevation of 3,000 feet. The mountain trails provide both lateral and vertical access to the terrain. During the training some of the trackers joked about how awesome the area would be for a competitive complex and a recreational biking network.

From the camp the trackers will dispatch first to the area beyond where the targets are located. The binders will be positioned between the targets and the entry to the ridge line area. The whole movement will progress from south to north and will pass the current camp to reach the peak where maneuvers will bring the Rochukas to a state of confrontation. Fripree and Yarjies will be preparing for their arrival.

Megan and Pilo know that the training has been limited by time but the effort has been exceptional from everyone. Their group is up to the tasks at hand. Megan is now moving fully into her element with the exercises transitioning to maneuvers in the field. She can now employ all of her abilities which may be greater than even she knows. This campaign has no restrictions other than the area of operations and the goals to be achieved. She is ready.

Pilo, as well, is excited. She is anticipating a fulfillment of her potential for the first time. Though younger that Megan she has trained for years and she has both the commitment and confidence that she needs.

The two have challenged each other at times over tactics but the resulting understanding each has gained forms a bond they will rely on as they go into the conflict. They have also encouraged their group members to know each other in the same way by challenging the training and planning when it is appropriate to do so. The result is that the trackers are able to move independently over distances and remain coordinated without frequent verbal communication.

Baetus and Kania have been struggling with the communications aspect of their duties because of distance and terrain causing interference of the radio signal. Baetus knows that the trackers will, or should, keep the momentum of their strategy flowing past any dysfunctional binder groups and that all will work together to push the Rochukas to the killing zone.

Norsha meets with the group leaders at the center of the small courtyard to begin the deployment. The once abandoned, small, family farm on the outskirts of Bad Wildbad opens to the river valley they will cross to enter the forest and begin their pursuits. The trackers need to cover approximately twelve miles using hiking trails and unmarked mountain trails. The group should be in position by early afternoon. This day is clear but the weather is always a factor because the early winter patterns can be unpredictable at elevations that experience colder temperatures and precipitation unexpectedly. Rain and snow are somewhat manageable but ice can be dangerous.

With everyone assembled and the order of dispatch understood Norsha dismisses the group leaders to join their groups. Norsha remains at the center and commands everyone's attention as she addresses the assembly, "We are not here for ceremony or stirring speeches. We are here to take the next step which you have all trained for diligently and I commend you. Today is the day and now is the time to move!"

Everyone gives a low level 'whoop!' and applause which is muffled because everyone is wearing gloves. Some of the riders bounce the front wheel of their bikes on the ground.

Norsha, "Megan, lead us out."

From the background Fripree and Yarjies have been observing as excited and confident coaches would when sending their teams onto the field for the first game of the season. They both know that there is no backing down and they know that their plans are dependent on the skills of the individuals they have entrusted with the task.

Baetus looks over his shoulder toward Yarjies and nods his head as acknowledgement of the time that is at hand. As he turns back to Kania she signals their riders to proceed after the trackers have left the area. She walks toward the vehicle that will transport the mappers and coordinators who are already at work. Baetus then rides away to catch up with the small contingent of riders he will begin with.

Fripree steps to Yarjies' side and puts a hand on his shoulder, "Here we go."

"Where are you going?" she hears someone from behind them where the van is waiting. Yarjies and Fripree turn to see Jake with his usual smile walking toward them.

"Well, what are you doing here?" Yarjies responds, "We thought you might be off solving the world's problems or something."

"I was and I am." Jake answers, "I hear that you have started the program."

"Yes Sir", Fripree responds. "We are the last to head out."

Jake, "Okay, the timing is correct. Again, I tell you. Be strong and be courageous. Be wise and be sly. Fripree, I will see you again when your time is at hand. Be sensitive to distractions and cut through the fog with your intuition. You will be fine." Jake directs Fripree.

Yarjies, "Hey, Jake, can I talk to you?"

Jake, "Sure, I will be right there." He walks to the rear of the van as Fripree gets into the front passenger seat.

Yarjies, "We are on schedule and should be in theater late today."

Jake, "Got it. Are you and Fripree synced with the procedure to make this happen?"

Yarjies, "Yes, although some actions and reactions at the point of contact will be fluid and organic. I cannot anticipate every factor."

Jake, "I understand. Is there something you need to tell me?"

Yarjies, "I am honestly scared and unsure. I may not have the command I will need to extract the names."

Jake, "You must be flexible, within the framework of options, and avoid any distractions."

Yarjies, "I understand."

Jake, "I may not see you again before the absolute last moment before revelation. The success of this endeavor will be impactful on many levels instantaneously and in that moment of the Royal Guardian's revelation your purpose will be complete."

Yarjies, "Meaning?"

Jake, "Meaning I will step into your existence to absorb the encounter so that you will not be destroyed."

Yarjies, "And you?"

Jake, "I will see you again."

Yarjies, "I think Fripree and I need to leave now. I look forward to our next meeting."

Jake, "Yep, I will close things up here. Be safe in your travels."

Yarjies climbs into the driver's seat and starts the van, "Fripree you are navigator."

As they travel from the mountain community Fripree takes in the beauty of the day. The sky is a bright blue and the green of the forest intensifies the contrast to make the area just above the tree line appear to pulsate. The river can be heard coursing through the rapids as the wind moves the grasses along the roadway. It is a normal day of tourists driving too slowly and the locals driving too fast. The small caravan sets out to alter time and heal the universe quietly and unnoticed as it should be.

Fripree's thoughts become abstract for the present moment because she is remembering her home and life in the U.S. She then quickly realizes that the thoughts are a distraction of the sort she was warned to avoid. Her life is here and now. She reminds herself to stay focused. Looking at her map she gives Yarjies the directions.

This small group of dedicated individuals is now in motion to accomplish a feat that has been attempted before without success. The nature of man has always been suspect when the spiritual forces they are confronting are most threatened. They are relying on the forces they represent to work through them and not to use them as any excuse for failure. There is no justification for such thoughts but such is the nature of man. It is Yarjies that is subconsciously setting up an excuse to fall back on. His weakness and doubt will be exploited by the enemy if discovered. This conflict will be between the ancient and the timeless, between hope and the desecration of truth. Throughout time there has been one promise, one fate and no escape for the Stroy. Healing the pierced heart of divinity requires a final stroke of judgment which exacts due punishment irreversibly.

A Little Vulnerable

During his return trip from Europe to the United States Rand is purposefully engaged with everyone he comes in contact with. His interest is in individual experiences and ideas. He is intentionally shedding his sub-conscience circle of protection to be more vulnerable in his conversations and his interaction with others, especially children which, before, would have only annoyed him. He can tell that he is more comfortable with people because the world has expanded in his awareness and rather than focus on his presence in the crowd he now thinks more about the crowd as individuals with varying levels of awareness within life's realities.

Rand makes some new friends while in the Munich airport with a small group of families with young kids who are working off their energy while waiting for their flight. Rand isn't sure why they chose to befriend him. Maybe he reminds them of someone. He went back and forth with the young kids but noticed a young man who is a part of the group that is trying to position his self far enough away from both the adults and the kids to have his own space. Rand has a brief conversation with Keath who is an impressive thirteen year old with a keen intellect and a lot of energy that he is learning to coordinate with his emerging, highly athletic body.

Rand has the realization, 'life is so diverse, challenging and so rewarding if one will engage and is willing to be a little vulnerable.' The thought put a big smile on his face. As his flight is called he picks up his bag and waves good bye to the kids, shakes Keath's hand and acknowledges the parents, "Thanks for letting me meet the kids." The parents wave good bye.

Once in the air Rand retrieves his journal and begins his first entry, 'on this Friday, November 16, I take the reins of a life I never knew before now to bring it into the life I had before. I suspect that changes will bring me closer to what will become the normal I will embrace as I leave the past where it belongs.' He has a following thought, 'Many there are who bounce between the rails of life while the trained explorer steps quietly along a narrow trail with vision and confidence.' After transcribing the thought Rand becomes drowsy. He puts away the journal and pushes back his seat slightly to rest.

As he relaxes the scent of perfume fires his senses and he opens his eyes to watch a form of beauty glide by in a tight skirt that moves with the toned hips and tight butt of a woman who knows she is being appreciated. Rand's imagination dances in his head as he closes his eyes with the thought, 'I will always enjoy the pleasures of a loving woman.'

Rand awakens to the Captain asking everyone to prepare for possible turbulence and to check their seat belts. Rand sits up and repositions his seat. Opening the window shade he looks out through the light cloud cover to see the ocean stretching to the horizon. This part of the trip home will be a grind for him because he has always preferred standing to sitting for long periods of time. He will be up as soon as the all clear is given to move about the cabin.

Rand begins to ponder the coming days back at his familiar places, routines and people. The one bright spot is Rachel whom he will be so pleased to see again. He has a sense of the changes he will be making but he has a lot of uncertainty nagging him. He is relying on Jake's advice to just be himself. There in may be the biggest challenge. He knows 'himself' and he knows that old habits cannot just be dropped and forgotten. He will need to develop replacement thought patterns, guiding principles, strength of character and re-apply his determination to remain motivated.

His next line of thought is of Lana's return, her presence, her love, their reconciliation and renewal. Rand's journaling is interrupted by the same perfume. He looks to the aisle to see the muscular thighs, tummy, firm breasts, bare shoulders and, "God!" Rand says to his self, "I cannot fall back into this old way so quickly!" As the woman looks at him and smiles he returns the smile and then quickly looks back to the window nervous and unsure of how to change his long practiced approach to such encounters. He stares out the window, embarrassed by his insecurity in the moment.

The long flight over the Atlantic nears its destination and the announcement is made for everyone to be seated and seat belts put on for the thirty minute approach. The temperature at La Guardia Airport is forty degrees Fahrenheit with light winds and no precipitation. With a layover in New York, Rand will use the time to begin his reorientation to the pace of activities in the U.S. He has been away long enough to be anxious about his itinerary as though he were visiting a foreign country.

The airport quickly becomes too confining for Rand. Once at his gate waiting area he takes the first available seat, places his bag on his lap, lowers his head and closes his eyes. He spends some quiet time 'communicating' with Jake. He doesn't have a pattern or form to follow so he just begins a mental conversation as though he were beside him. "Hello friend I am reaching out because I suddenly feel alone here in the midst of thousands of people. This is just a trial run so let me know if I need to change something." He feels awkward even though to anyone observing he is just a guy sitting in the airport, resting as he waits for his flight to be called.

About twenty minutes later he is boarded onto his flight to Chicago. Three hours later he is in a taxi to travel from O'Hare Airport to his townhouse. He walks through the lobby of his building unnoticed and rides the elevator alone. Taking a deep breath during the ascent the interiors smell of cigarette smoke is mingled with the automatically dispensed air freshener. A new layer is puffed out as the elevator doors open. As Rand steps across the hallway threshold from the elevator he has a feeling of being out of place. His emotions slowly build as he walks to his door and inserts the key. He whispers, "Here we go."

Inside his home the time speeds up again and he follows his usual routine when returning from regular travels. The exception of course is that Lana is not there. His loneliness consumes him when he looks from the kitchen into the living room area where the fireplace and the large chair bring back his memories of the last hours the two spent together, intertwined as though they were a part of the chair. He thought of himself as an alien peering in from another world to understand. After a few long, quiet moments Rand again whispered, "I miss you, Lana. Come back soon."

The early days of winter this year have been cold, dry and windy. The temperature of Rand's first night back is expected to be twenty eight degrees with a wind chill temperature of fifteen degrees. For this part of the country the conditions are better than most years. With a bottle of wine opened and a glass half full he lights a small fire to quickly warm the living room area and also turns on the central heat which is always slow to come on.

Rand avoids sitting in their chair and instead sits on the couch that is in front of the television and positions him with his back to the fireplace. He turns on the television as a distraction and after watching a couple of thirty minute situational comedies he has finished his portion of the wine and turns off the set. He moves now to the big chair to stare into the fire until the wine nudges him and softens his resistance to his feelings of sadness. After allowing his self to enter the darkness for a short time an impulse from deep within him rushes into his mind. "Randal Wayne!" he hears his conscience shout from within, "Get a grip and get out of the hole you are in!" He straightens up saying aloud to himself, "This pity party is over!"

Being a Friday evening Rand knows there are plenty of distracting activities just outside of his front door. It is time for a shower, change of clothes and a short hike to the eatery around the corner for starters. Once inside the warm café and seated at the counter Rand shivers off the cold. As the attendant approaches he requests a cappuccino. Rand removes his gloves and lays them on the counter. With the steamed aroma of his coffee mingling with the aromas of baked goods and fresh fruits he is reminded of some mornings in Germany.

Rand picks up the cup to sample his drink and as he does he looks into the mirror that is behind the counter which reflects the scene of the café behind him. As he begins to sip his coffee he sees Jake looking back at him. Before he can put his drink down Jake is seated beside him at the counter. "Well hello stranger." Rand responds, "It is good to see you again so soon."

Jake, "Hello, I am just dropping in briefly to give you some feedback on your outreach communication."

Rand, "I see, do you want to go somewhere else or is this environment okay?"

Jake, "This is fine. That is one point for you to understand. Ninety nine point nine, nine percent of anywhere is okay. Maybe every place, all of the time is not optimal but you drive that consideration. You will always have 'skin in the game', as the saying goes.

That being said, there will be situations when you may not receive what is needed because you simply don't ask. There will be situations when you ask but do not receive because you ask for the wrong reason or you ask with alternative motives that you do or possibly do not recognize. The keys are honesty, clarity and understanding in our relationship. Remember that you must fool yourself before you can attempt to fool someone else."

Rand, "How am I to know these things?"

Jake, "Developing your relationship with me on a personal level is critical because it is always true that you must be honest with yourself before you can truly be honest with others."

Rand, "That will take time."

Jake, "There will be reading materials to learn from and there are people you will meet who will help you. I will not leave you alone but I will expect you to do your part."

Rand, "I have the sense that I don't have a lot of time to position myself because I have a lot of changes to make in my arrangements here."

Jake, "This is a journey and a process. As you remain focused on the process the journey will take care of itself. Live one day at a time with all you've got."

Rand, "Sorry but I think you are being too vague. Are you covering something up?"

Jake, "Yes, perhaps a bit vague. Covering something up? No. I want you to begin the work of finding, through your understanding, the base line truths upon which all is built. To be clear, it is time for you to locate home base mentally, emotionally, spiritually and literally. I will give you part of a great, ancient manuscript when I visit you at your place tomorrow, a little before sun down. Okay?"

Rand, "Okay, tomorrow is Saturday so call and remind me. I will be prepping for my return to work next week."

Jake, "You got it. I will see you there, then."

Skin in the Game

During the day's travels Fripree has been monitoring the radio chatter as the different groups navigate to their staging coordinates. As each group calls in to confirm their position Yarjies and Fripree are becoming anxious as their mental picture is correlated with the activities on the ground. The map which Fripree has spread across her legs is overlaid with a grid for orienting the fluid logistics of the group movements and soon the targets' movements as well.

The van they are driving is not equipped for any aggressive off road maneuvers. Their primary location is accessible by gravel roads after leaving the highway. They are headed away from the others because she and Yarjies will be positioned at the capture and kill zone on the steep grade leading to the peak.

The communications coming in confirm the trackers are at their center position. This will be their last transmission on the shared channel unless there is a catastrophic failure. They will fan out, keeping the center positions as the reference point for determining the general direction as the outer positions make adjustments to cover the area. With a total of ten bikes and each position maintained at a fifty yard separation a lot of area can be covered fairly quickly. Once a target is located everyone becomes fluid and the roundup begins.

Megan wants to personalize her group's individuals as she dispatches each knowing that any one may be lost during the next few days. First out to the East is Drew, Lexa, Therun and Nahan. As each is recognized she or he will ride out toward their position. The second group of Bjorn, Elle, Claus and Livvi will be moving out to the west flank ready to redirect any beasts that are located. Michael will take the center position and be the pivot while Jacob will shadow him and be a courier if communications without using the radio is required. Everyone is a little nervous and wanting the encounters to begin. Too much kinetic energy pent up for too long allows stupid ideas to make a mess of things.

Fripree is able to hear the assignments through an open radio microphone so that she can track initial movements and beginning locations until the radio is reset. Yarjies is working hard to get their operations in place and set up.

The trackers have already begun with their surveys to hopefully complete the first mile at a minimum before darkness stops them. Each rider is carrying supplies for two full days with crude locator maps of known water sources. Each night in the field will be the highest risk because everyone will be sleeping where they are at sundown. It is known that the Rochukas do hunt at night. The tracker's best chance of avoiding them will be to climb a tree, find a branch to support them and sleep as much as possible. The beasts are not known to be climbers although much of what is known is sketchy.

Everyone will be looking for indications such as broken tree limbs, foot prints, or uncovered waste. With every one anxious for progress the risk of missing indicators this first day are likely. When a beast is located their location will be unquestionable because their inclination is to avoid humans and their frantic attempts to elude them can be attention getting enough unless the days of darkness are occurring.

The Rochukas are humanoid physically so they do vary in size and strength. When excited or alerted to threats the spiritual entity that inhabits each can enhance the individual's speed, strength, situational awareness and other factors that normally exceed the abilities of their pursuers. The tendency to react unpredictably combined with the ability to blend with objects and surroundings creates the most difficult situations to maneuver for the trackers because they appear to vanish. When one is surprised a momentary fear triggers the response to be absorbed into a tree, a rock, a wall or anything the Rochukas considers safe. The Stroy uses this tactic to avoid detection by entering a Rochukas and has the ability to stay transient for a longer period of time so that detection is normally impossible.

The responsibility of Yarjies and Fripree is to reduce the options for the Stroy's movement and to eventually isolate it for extraction and neutralization. The entire exercise of this group effort is to produce the one opportunity to end the Stroy's threat and to end the days of darkness by removing the Rochukas and the Stroy who works through them. Other secondary goals are not so critical.

Radio reports that Fripree and Yarjies are monitoring indicate that all of the targets have been located and maneuvers are in progress to drive them toward the summit. Yarjies has been working to erect and cover a series of mirrors which will be used to intimidate and confuse the creatures as well as to help flush out the Stroy while preventing a transfer into any part of the surroundings by any of them.

The strategy is to drive the Rochukas into an area where the incline is steep and which leads to a clearing where the mirrors are set up in a circular pattern with each attached to a tree around the perimeter of the clearing. The mirrors will deny the Rochukas an escape except for the ground or the air. Neither of which is possible because the earth will not release them and the air will not sustain them. The mirrors are camouflaged until the time of extraction. Both Yarjies and Fripree will be the only ones within the area with the Rochukas. Everyone else, after the drive to push them into the area will remain behind the mirrors to uncover them at the appropriate time. Megan will be coordinating the activities outside of the area and Norsha will secure the outer perimeter with Baetus's group. In the event one was to escape the outer perimeter must contain them. Two of the logistics individuals are marksmen. Kania has each positioned on the perimeter where they can see both the killing zone and the outer area so they can eliminate the Rochukas when the time comes and also stop any runners that try to escape.

The death of each creature will reduce the options of the Stroy to transfer. Once their number is reduced two quick actions without doubt or fear will be essential. Fripree will begin the commands to the Rochukas that will allow her to identify which is concealing the Stroy.

With everything now in place Yarjies joins Fripree to monitor the radio transmissions and then to be in place as they approach. Fripree, "The time to get things done will soon be upon us, Yarjies."

Yarjies, "Yes. Yes. I know that you are ready and that I am equally sold out to this mission but I do have doubts. You do know that both of us may not survive this operation."

Fripree, "Uh, yes, I have had these thoughts. When I do I revisit the expectation of backup from Jake and the presence of the Royal Guardian that will accomplish our goals. We do have 'skin in the game' but I focus on the reality that God is God and we are not. I think that any possibility of one of us failing has been the one weak link all along. It is humans who create messes and it will be God working through humans to make changes. The Stroy is on His level and the Rochukas are on our level, more or less."

Yarjies, "I understand. I know that Jake will step in at the appropriate time. My real fear is that I cannot complete the steps necessary to reach that point. I have a level of doubt."

Fripree, "I suggest you check in with Jake before it is too late."

Yarjies, "I don't think that is necessary. I will just cover up my doubts, be brave and everything should go well."

Fripree, "I thought you were wise enough to recognize your pride when it became a barrier for you. It is just such an attitude that will give an advantage to the Stroy."

Reacting to the sounds of activity below them Yarjies redirects, "Here they come. We must get into position now."

Fripree sees what is happening to Yarjies and for the first time she realizes that she must fulfill her personal responsibilities without him. With everything collapsing at this critical time she closes off her internal debate and takes her position near one of the trees and behind the camouflage inside of the enclosed area. In her spirit she reaches out in prayer, "Grant us your favor and your help."

Yarjies stands on the other side of the opening as well behind the camouflage of one of the mirrors. He reasons with himself that isolating the Stroy quickly, before he allows any doubt or fear to enter his mind, will eliminate the possibility of the Stroy detecting his weakness.

The Rochukas struggle to maintain any momentum because of the steep grade. They all enter the area and fall to the ground exhausted. As they are distracted by each-others' complaining and yelling and screaming the gate is moved into place with someone staged by each mirror to remove the covers.

Fripree takes a deep breath, exhales completely then walks from her cover and speaks the commands to draw the Stroy out. The beasts become silent and fix their gaze on Fripree who is walking slowly toward them. Yarjies observes the beasts to look for indications of the Stroy's presence.

The Rochukas are all now on their feet and are beginning to make gestures to intimidate Fripree. The screeching and the movements begin to influence Yarjies rather than Fripree. The tension continues to build as Fripree continues her commands. Two of the creatures become immobile and silent. The four remaining are continuing to escalate and appear likely to challenge Fripree. Yarjies reveals his presence even though he is unprepared to extract the names. He timidly demands the common names and is struck by one of the beasts. He is hurled to the perimeter like a rag and lies motionless as the smaller of the Rochukas becomes emboldened and gestures for the others to be calm. With his gaze fixed on Fripree he begins to slowly dance as he moves toward her. With his hands extended above his head he starts to hum the rhythm of a festive jig. As its movements quicken the creature becomes ecstatic and looks up as though a contact is being completed.

Fripree has become entranced and cannot move. Yarjies slowly stands and screams the first name as a Rochukas collapses. Then, with more courage Yarjies repeats a second and a third name with a Rochukas falling with each name. As the creatures fall the marksmen end their lives.

Just before the climax of the confrontation erupts shots are fired from outside of the area and the two docile beasts are hit. Neither moves again and both are lying limp on the ground, dead. The remaining two first look at one another before looking back at Fripree. In that moment their movement exposes, to Fripree, which is the Stroy. Fripree yells as loud as she can, "Now! Yarjies Now!" As she does she removes a pistol like device from her back belt area and fires a tranquilizing and tagging round at the Stroy.

Everyone that has been waiting for her command, together, remove all of the covers from the mirrors. The resulting combination of light being reflected within the area induces the vision of each Rochukas to be contorted to see only themselves and the illusion that there were many more of them and that they have nothing beyond their number that they could be absorbed into.

Fripree retreats to be concealed by the camouflage she had used by the entrance. As she does, the remaining Rochukas are running into each other and fighting with one another. Yarjies signals for the binders to drop in and isolate the Stroy. With the tag visible to the snipers that are staged at the perimeter shots ring out and the remaining beast is taken down. All of these actions are occurring almost simultaneously. As each beast is killed their flesh releases a stench and the rot is accelerated. To look at one the humanity is recognizable even though the features have been distorted by the evil that inhabits them.

The binders enter the area from the trees above and corner the Stroy. Ropes are cast by each. The first around the upper body, a second around the neck and a third catches one foot as the beast is attempting to run. With the binding completed Yarjies must approach the Story, complete the separation of the Stroy from the Rochukas and then touch the Rochukas to signify completion of the separation.

Yarjies knows deep down that this is his critical moment. Should he fail to complete this step he may lose his life and the entire effort may be thwarted, allowing the Stroy to escape. With the Stroy having been dragged to near the center of the area and Yarjies now approaching slowly the Rochukas host is squirming because the light level being concentrated by the reflection of each mirror toward the center is absorbed by its body. Yarjies stops about ten feet from the Rochukas and turns around so that the beast is behind him. He then falls to his knees, raises his hands straight up over head and looks up as though to receive something.

After a moment of silence the sound of a wind can be heard. Yarjies remains kneeling, separates his hands and lowers his arms to be parallel to the ground on either side as he looks straight ahead now. The wind increases and the trees begin to sway severely. Fripree looks up to see a tornado like formation directly above Yarjies and descending with him at the center point if the formation were to lower to the ground.

The spiraling wind stops its descent just above Yarjies who has remained motionless with his eyes closed. Slowly he begins speaking in a language unknown to Fripree. As he continues to speak his voice becomes more audible and commanding. The sound of the winds increases and carries his words to the point of an echo coming back from the forest. The remaining Rochukas begins to uncontrollably speak their individual names in an attempt to avoid their fate. As the creature's voice echoes as well the torturous pronunciation that is extracted is difficult to understand. "Heeeeerschhhhheeeeel-Herschel, Daviiiiidooooviiiich-Davidovich, Ahhh-Ahhhntipaaaaasssss-Antipas, Voloooodyaaaa-Volodya, Schhhhhhwarrrrrtz-Schwartz, Hueeeeettler-Huettler."

The strength and speed of the winds begin to lift Yarjies from the ground and turn him slowly clockwise until he is facing the Rochukas. As he descends he now stands with his feet close together, his arms still extended to his sides he now straightens his fingers and bends his wrists forward for his fingers to be toward the beast. The Rochukas body continues to contort in an effort to break loose but the eyes are fixed on Yarjies. The Stroy speaks, "You have no authority over me."

Yarjies does not respond. He continues his chant and begins his movements. He pushes himself to complete the extraction. He raises his voice as he brings his hands together in front of his chest, his arms fully extended. He then pulls his hands, still together, toward his heart with his arms bending at the elbow.

The Rochukas begins to howl uncontrollably and a second entity becomes visible as a reflection or a shadow which is the Stroy beginning to shed the host Rochukas. Yarjies makes a sudden, forceful lunge forward with his right foot landing as he thrusts his hands forward as if he were holding a sword or a lance. He bows his head and then returns to his previous position. He performs this movement two more times and then the Stroy separates from the Rochukas who is thrown to the ground as the Stroy stands before Yarjies.

Although the Rochukas was six feet tall the Stroy is a large being of about eight feet tall. He locks eyes with Yarjies and begins to move slowly toward him. Yarjies remains transfixed by the Stroy as he has the realization that he is being controlled. Yarjies begins the last element of his command but he cannot speak as though he is mute. The Stroy is beginning to overpower Yarjies.

With his doubt re-emerging Yarjies calls out in his spirit, "Forgive me I am failing!" As the last word leaves his thought the swirling winds dissipate and Jake appears between Yarjies and the Stroy. Yarjies collapses to the ground and the Stroy vanishes into the control of the Royal Guardian at Jake's command. The host Rochukas dies from the trauma. Jake walks to the carcass and touches its forehead to signify completion. He then looks to Fripree who is at Yarjies' side, "See to Yarjies and I will return soon."

Everyone there gives a shout and walks into the area from the surrounding forest. After a sustained celebration Norsha gets every one's attention with her growling yell, "Okay, let's dig some holes and get rid of this mess as soon as possible. We need to leave no trace. Got it?"

Every one responds, "Got it!"

As Fripree begins to attend to Yarjies he inhales deeply, opens his eyes and says, "Am I going to get that kiss now?"

Fripree smiles and puts her hand over his mouth. Yarjies licks her hand and she withdraws it, wipes the spit on his shirt, "Never!" Fripree smiles again. Everyone walks up to surround them and begin the same dance routine as was danced when the groups were first together. Fripree and Yarjies stand up and take their places in the circle to be a part of the celebration. Again Norsha gets everyone's attention and points to the decaying, stinking carcasses to be buried. Without saying a word the celebration is suspended until the work is done. Yarjies questions in his heart if the goal of having the Royal Guardian come forward was fulfilled.

Fripree, "I don't know if you have any memory of what took place just now. Jake intervened as you collapsed and he took control of the Stroy to drive him from us. He then left immediately but told us that he would be back soon."

Yarjies, "I know that my doubt and my fear were being exploited and had become anchors for the Stroy to latch onto. I did call out to Jake but it was too late."

A large hole for the remains was dug and covered over after being filled with the bones and hair that was left being all that was left because of the rapid decay of the Rochukas bodies. Yarjies was overseeing the dis-assembly of the mirrors and coverings to be loaded into the van. Fripree opened the van doors.

With everyone engaged in the cleanup Jake emerged from the forest unnoticed and joined the activities. As he approached Fripree she tapped Yarjies on the shoulder. He turned to see Jake walking toward him with arms open wide to embrace the two of them. The three engage in a group hug. Yarjies begins to cry because of his perceived failure. The group hug continues as Jake responds, "Why are you crying Yarjies?"

Yarjies attempts to answer, "I, I, uh I failed because of my fear."

Jake, "Look, you are still human. You were confronting the principle manifestation of the enemy."

Yarjies, "I know that but I have prepared for years. My basest of emotions became a barrier."

Jake, "I told you that I would step in to preserve your life. It is your pride that is the barrier. "

Yarjies, "I am too emotional even now to work through this."

The group hug ends but the three remain together to use the time to bring this conflict of mind, for Yarjies, to a constructive, understandable resolution for Yarjies and Fripree to build on as they move forward.

Jake, "The one question I have for you, Yarjies, is 'what could you have done differently to avoid your crisis at a most critical time'?"

Yarjies, "I should have admitted my growing fear and doubt to myself and to you much sooner."

Jake, "What would you like to say about it now?"

Yarjies, "I acknowledge my failure to be honest, to do the right thing and to ask forgiveness and help."

Jake, "Will any change occur because of your prayer alone?"

Yarjies, "No, I must do the work necessary to grow, to understand, to prepare and be aware of my soul."

Jake, "Explain what you mean by 'be aware of my soul'."

Yarjies, "My soul is my mind, my will and my emotions. To be aware is to be in a right relationship with each aspect so that the spirit will be active both in and through my life."

Jake, "Fripree is there anything you could have done differently?"

Fripree, "I don't know. Everything happened very quickly once events converged here. I think that I fulfilled my responsibility. Do you have something in mind?"

Jake, "No but I want you engaged in this conversation. Do you have anything for Yarjies?"

Fripree, "Yarjies, I commend you for giving all that you had and doing what it took even though you knew that you were becoming weak. You may have been afraid but your courage supported your determination."

Jake leans toward Fripree's ear and whispers, "you would make a good politician." Then to both, "Okay now, is everyone ready to wrap this up?"

Yarjies and Fripree both affirm their agreement and understanding, "All is good."

Jake, "Before we separate I want to be clear about the outcome of our efforts. The threat of the Rochukas is now ended. The Stroy is in its place until the end of days when judgment will be rendered. The Royal Guardian has begun to reveal the work of the spirit through the lives of our greater family."

Fripree, "I thought the Royal Guardian would be appearing here as a result of the accomplishments today."

Jake, "You were expecting lightning bolts and voices from the heavens or something? No, those times have long passed. The empowerment and the equipping of every aspect of our family's work with love, honesty and accountability will be the primary revelation of the Royal Guardian's presence. This is not going to be a play time now as though another great war has ended. The significance is that individuals will be empowered as they are enlightened through their studies and emboldened to be a reflection of the reality that God works through men and women to bring His kingdom to Earth."

Yarjies, "That is awesome."

Fripree, "Thank you for this opportunity to be a part of what is happening."

Norsha walks up, "Okay, are you all going to stand here all day? We have work to do. Let's get it done and get out of here, please?"

Jake, "Yep, the boss has spoken. We will have time for broader discussions with everyone back at camp." Jake smiles and pats each on the back as they separate to help with the cleanup.

The Cornerstone Is Set

After drinking his first cup of coffee Rand picks up the telephone receiver to call his brother then pauses to orient his thinking. It has been an extreme, insane time away. For now he thinks it best to pick up where he left off with his brother to avoid giving any impression that he has a changed perspective. He will be honest with his brother but he doesn't want to unload everything after being out of touch for almost two months. On the flip side Rand wants to know if there has been any new developments concerning Lana. Rand knows what Jake promised but the vagueness of his assurance was not concrete enough for Rand yet he holds onto his hope of seeing her again.

The phone rings several times before it is answered by George's youngest son Caleb, "Hello?" Caleb has just turned five and he is a rowdy, high energy, inquisitive and fearless boy.

Rand, "Well, hello. Is this uh. . ."

Caleb jumps in, "Caleb! It's me, Uncle Rand. Where you been?"

Rand, "I have been on an adventure. When I see you again I will tell you all about it."

Caleb, "Okay, sounds fun. Was it fun?"

Rand chuckles as he answers. "Yes, a lot of fun." Rand knows that he will have to make up a grand tale before he sees Caleb because it will now be Caleb's quest to hear the whole story.

Caleb, "Do you want to talk to dad?"

Rand, "Yes please."

Caleb, "Sorry, he is not here. I think he is mowing the grass."

Rand, "Is your brother there?"

Caleb, "I think so. Wait, okay?"

Rand "Okay, tell him to hurry."

The only answer was the sound of the receiver landing on the table. After a few minutes George answers, "Hello? Rand?"

Rand, "Hey George I made it back!" How are you?"

George, "I am prepping the house for the cold weather that's heading our way in a couple of days."

Rand, "Well that's good. Caleb thought you might be cutting the grass."

George laughs, "Yea Caleb is a trip that's for sure. I wish I could keep up with him but I love to see him bouncing around. It drives his mom crazy when she has him but such is life!"

Rand, "Have you been falling down any more stair ways?"

George, "Well I take the elevator more often now." They both laugh.

Rand, "I just got back yesterday so I wanted to touch base with you and to also ask if you had any more contact with Lana or her phone or whatever?"

George, "Not a thing, so, I hope she is safe wherever she is and whatever she is doing. I don't know what else to say."

Rand, "Okay, I guess time will tell. I sure would like to know what happened. Listen even though I just got back I have to prepare to return to the office next week. How about, I will call you during the week and let's all of us get together next week."

George, "That sounds great. Don't forget about us. I look forward to talking to you soon."

Rand, "Yep, bye for now."

George, "Bye."

Rand goes to the kitchen and finds nothing. He has some instant oatmeal so he can eat enough of that to hold him over.

His quick mental review of what he can do to prepare for work is that nothing is available because he had left everything at the office. His thought, 'more time to get resettled and be ready for Jake's visit. He knows that he wants to get past the generalities and the uncertainties to delve into the realities and the practical applications he must learn. Rand knows that he needs to understand the foundation upon which he now stands. He knows that his purpose must grow from that foundation and lead to results.

Rand lives in the somewhat upscale area of the South Loop near Grant Park and Monroe Harbor. The wind, when coming off the water, drops the temperature an additional ten or fifteen degrees. After five years he has learned how to manage it. It is good that he is close to his office down town when it comes to navigating the cold and snow.

With the morning having slipped away Rand decides to spend some time burning off his restlessness and slight anxiety about returning to the office totally unprepared. 'After all,' he muses, 'I can't chop wood!' The gym down stairs will do this time.

After twenty minutes on the tread mill and forty minutes with the weights Rand decides to break for a shower and then lunch. Jake should be calling soon and Rand does not want to miss the call.

With the shower and lunch complete Rand lies on the couch and turns on the television. After what seemed like minutes to Rand he is awakened by a shake of his shoulders. He flinches and looks up to see Jake standing over him.

"Wake up lazy man!" Jake says with his always present smile, "You have been on vacation for over a month and you are tired?"

Rand, "Yea, such a relaxing, refreshing tour of Europe. I remember that now."

Jake, "I guessed it would be okay to let myself in."

Rand, "Sure. What's mine is yours, I guess. I can't relax anymore. I know that I have no reason to be stressed about returning to work but I have the sense that I will not fit in. It's weird. I do look forward to seeing Rachel."

Jake, "You have a couple of days before returning, right? Try to get out and be around people, even strangers, but don't isolate yourself here."

Rand, "Okay I get what you are saying. Anyway that will be tomorrow. What we have is today, right? Do you want something to eat or drink?"

Jake, "Not now thanks. Let's get down to it because I may have to leave unexpectedly as is common for me."

Rand "Got it. Make yourself comfortable and begin."

Jake drops his jacket over the back of the couch and moves around the couch to sit on the floor, facing the television and resting his back against the couch with his arms stretched across the cushions. "Rand, can we turn the T.V. off?"

Rand, "Sure," And turns it off. "If I may, let me repeat the concerns I raised when this conversation began. I know that I need to understand the foundation under me because I know that my purpose must grow from that foundation to produce results. My point is that my understanding must surpass generalities and I need to delve into the practical applications."

Jake, "I understand your concerns and misgivings. Every foundation develops a history after the cornerstone is set. I have a portion of a manuscript for you to explore, as I promised earlier, then we can move forward." He hands the book to Rand, "This is the writings of a wise man known by many as a prophet or as one who becomes God's voice to man. His name is Isaiah. His writings predate the fulfillments by a thousand years or more. So, please focus on chapter fifty three to understand his description of one who was to come. When we see one another again we will discuss it."

Rand, "Well, again, that sounds open ended to me. 'When we'? Am I asking too much? I guess I am to assume that you will know when that time should occur?"

Jake, "As I have said in the past, I see things coming before you do, so yes I will know and as we develop our relationship you will have a better idea of things as well. Remember, you are among a limited group of individuals whom I have interacted with in the physical realm in order to accomplish goals that will benefit the greater family we have. I must ask you to be flexible and patient as we walk through this current valley of learning, so to speak, so that you will be prepared for the purpose which will become more evident each day."

Jake, "Some have called this time of preparation a form of kinetic waiting. Even though you do not have specific activities to pursue or organized programs to follow you do have your personal need to know your foundation and be prepared to give an answer from your personal experiences and your understanding. Honestly such opportunities will not come from organized programs as much as from personal encounters when you may not be expecting anything."

Rand, "So, using the available time, whenever it occurs. To review past experiences, to learn and prepare will be the difference maker?"

Jake, "That's right, consider this scenario. You are leaving work and walking to your car in the parking garage. You get to the car and open the passenger door to put your computer and brief case on the seat as usual. As you close the door and turn to walk around the front of your car when seemingly out of nowhere a young man walks up to you and asks for help and money because of some problem. What would you do?"

Rand, "I would most likely tell the guy I can't help him and that I have no cash. I would push past him and get in the car to leave thinking that he was just pan handling."

Jake, "That is all very understandable but what could you do differently to be of service?"

Rand, "I don't know exactly but I get your point. I need to prepare for such encounters."

Jake, "Look at all that you have received, Rand, the awareness of your spiritual condition and the resulting understanding of the need for a reversal of direction in your life. Like your choice of a relationship with me which others do choose to reject. From your vantage you will have a story to tell although the telling will be through your living as my influence saturates your life to the point of being your norm rather than the result of conscious thoughts to be, to do, to say as a method. That is why I have told you to live your life daily and work to do the next right thing."

Rand, "There are people who do this type of thing through community initiatives and psychology group therapies and even religious programs that have nothing to do with you."

Jake, "Oh, I know. People can do impressive things through self-discipline and organizational directives and even religious rituals and practices. If the spirit is not genuine there will be a sorrow that mocks hope to block the path to a relationship with the Father and the Royal Guardian as one's guide. It is I who guards the door but it is the individual who holds the key.

Rand, "I guess this is a portion of what you are referring to when you say that people are good at complicating the simple."

Jake, "Unfortunately yes, but to be fair all people share the same enemy and there is one failing that is common to all. The one seed that has borne all of the bad fruit in this world is from the enemy's first thought of dominance. The pride which brought him down exists in each human heart. This is an understanding to be gained through the study of the manuscripts."

Rand, "Rather than offer a pair of slightly dissimilar alternatives you are explaining two starkly opposed alternatives.

So I, or anyone, will choose and will be responsible for our fate. Correct?"

Jake, "Yes sir! By choosing to join me, your path will be rewarding even though there will be challenges and at times the way will be lonely and unpopular. You must remain aware of the enemy's ability to misdirect and to imitate what he opposes as a tactic to draw you out. His challenges will come in pairs. They may be the beasts of your dreams, the thoughts of your mind, your principles of conscience, even tenets of a religion and so on. Learn to recognize both and dissect them by choosing the way that defeats both. The discernment you will gain equips you to thwart the enemy because he struggles when confronted with the wisdom of truth and the transparency of humility."

Rand, "I understand but I must ask you to bring this discussion a little closer to earth. I know, at least in my mind, that I have been walking around the standard for right and wrong."

Jake, "Okay, I ….."

Rand interrupts, "I'm sorry but there is one question I have wanted to ask for a long time. Can we cover this first?"

Jake, "I suppose. What is it?"

Rand, "When we first met you invited me to your home and when I arrived and looked at the engraving on the door I realized that 'JAKE' is not a name. It is an acronym. So, what is the meaning of the acronym?"

Jake, "You have asked an important question at an appropriate juncture in our discussion. We will start with the common secular definitions. So, the J represents justice, the A represents atonement, the K represents kindness and the E represents Emanuel. This, again, must first be expanded so that it can be simplified for memory and application in everyday life."

Rand, "Can we first review the interconnectivity of these four elements?"

Jake, "No, because we must first unpack the meaning of each on a rudimentary level before the interconnectivity can be understood. Now let us review each element in order. Justice is the use of authority and power to impartially, fairly and consistently uphold what is right, just or lawful by administering reward or penalty as deserved."

Rand, "Who determines what is the right, just or lawful standard?"

Jake, "We will get to that. Next, atonement generally means satisfaction given for wrong doing or injury."

Rand, "Can anyone adequately complete the act of atoning for murder?"

Jake, "We will get to that. Next, kindness implies the possession of an ability to project one's own personality into the personality of another in order to understand the person better by sharing in another's emotions, thoughts or feelings."

Rand, "Kind of like a fortune teller?"

Jake, "Uh, no. But we will get back to that. Now, lastly and most importantly, Emanuel encompasses and fulfills all by demonstrating the utmost application of the three. Unlike the three Emanuel is a name. The literal meaning of the name is, 'God with us'. The name also refers to the one known as the Messiah."

After a minute without Rand responding Jake continues, "The standard is perfection of thought, intention, action and purpose. The atonement to fulfill the absolute standard of justice must be perfect. Only a perfect substitute can complete the bridging of communion between the perfect and all else. It is a covering such as a new suit. A new soul emerges that is made perfect by the kindness of God who is with us, in us and about us in a perfect state which we enter through the door once recognized by the individual with the understanding that we each carry the key."

Rand, "Where is my brother when I need him? He can reduce the complex to the simple in a way that I can understand. I love you man but I need this as it applies to me so that I can know what the next right thing is for me. I think you are doing this intentionally. I probably need to just figure this out myself. Forgive me for being so 'hard headed', as my mom would say."

Jake, "You go it. After spending time with Isaiah go to the writings of John. He is like a brother of long ago. You will find the understanding you need. Start with honestly loving yourself so that you can love others honestly. I have to go for now."

Rand, "I am not trying to make you mad. I hope you understand."

Jake, "I do understand and I do know that you will get it figured out before too long. Remember to live your life daily and work with me to keep our dialogue open and our relationship growing. I am on your side."

Rand, "Thanks, Jake."

Jake was on his feet with jacket in hand. At the door he turned back to Rand, extended his hand. As Rand responded he drew him into a strong hug. "See you later Rand. Hang in there."

The yearend holidays passed without anything extraordinary happening. The time also passed without Lana. Rand found himself missing her every day and looking forward to the day, as promised by Jake that would return her to his life.

Rand is spending his spare time delving into the writings he was referred to by Jake and he is forming a mental framework to place the principles, the practices and the consequences into a perspective that he can work with. He has also asked his brother to help him apply what he is learning.

There is no interaction with Jake in the physical realm but their relationship is growing and maturing. Although Rand is still working with the same company he knows in his heart that he will be making changes soon. He has discussed some of his plans with Rachel who repeatedly tells him to first be sure of his intent and then to jump in whole heartedly.

Rand is developing a growing desire to open a community center that is independent with no reliance on government funds or on local grants. The funds needed to operate and provide the services to be offered must come from individual donors and from those who are being served by the center. He has enough in savings to buy a property and open the doors for the first year.

The property that he favors is on the south side of Chicago, on Halsted. The area is currently depressed so the real estate is undervalued by maybe thirty percent. With a street front that is presentable the building has a large room and an office that may double as a bedroom for him and there is a bathroom. The back is all glass pained windows from about the waist up to almost the ceiling. There is a parking area at the back that will double as a basketball court when not in use for parking.

If everything goes well with the sellers Rand will be able to take possession soon after signing. So, his next big move is to speak with his supervisor and give him notice of his leaving. That meeting is set for two days after purchase of the property which should be this week.

Rand knows that he is a different man. He has surprised himself by the pro-active approach he is applying to the move forward with his plans to radically change his life's purpose in practical ways. He feels as though he is positioned to be of service in effective, constructive ways for the community he now knows to be his home base.

Now on this first Saturday in February Rand is in his office at the center. He has an appointment with someone who he wants to interview him for an upcoming book and he has the father of one of the young men who frequents the center coming in for counseling. There are a couple of guys also playing basketball out back although the temperature is around twenty five degrees.

It is just another cold day in Chicago with the wind gusting, the icy air is blowing discarded paper and dust about the court. The cold is always on the prowl for any exposed flesh to consume. A breath takes the form of a thick vapor following, in this case, the bouncing heads of the basketball players as though trying to catch up and reenter the warmth to escape the merciless cold. The basketball is hard as a stone as it clangs against the steel back board and forces its way through the stiff chain net.

I stand inside the warm building, looking through the large windows which face the activity yard. Though large, the windows are divided into many one foot square panes which give the motion of the players outside a broken movement when passing across the expanse of the large windows. Some of the panes are cracked and two have been replaced with sheet metal squares.

I am at the office to interview Mr. Wayne at 9:00 a.m. When I arrived he informed me that an emergency situation has postponed our meeting. I decided to wait as Mr. Wayne returned to his office and closed the door. I could gather from the broken sentences that escaped the office the man he is with is distraught over his son. The son frequented the center and is well known for his abilities on the basketball court as well as his likeable personality. Unfortunately, like many of his peers, the son had become part of a circle of friends who looked for diversions from their troubles in drugs, sex and rebellious activities. As I took a step closer to better hear the muffled conversation I realized that the son had committed suicide. I could hear the pain and disbelief in the father's voice.

This is Mr. Wayne's reason for being here. Each time he spoke I could feel a love and a peace in his voice as though God was speaking through him. After about thirty minutes stillness settled over the inner office, the area where I was waiting and even the activity yard. I realized that Mr. Wayne was praying with the man and his words were subconsciously heard by everyone and each ceased from their activity in order to agree and acknowledge the plea for this man and his son. The air became still. I could feel my heart beat and I could sense the presence of a soothing, loving peace that enveloped the area.

As I stared into my cup of coffee I thought about my own children and the times that I may have been too selfish to care for their needs adequately. I thought of their training when they were young and the importance of knowing each well enough to recognize a problem and to care enough to intervene if necessary. I asked God to forgive me for my mistakes as a man, as a husband and as a father.

I had come here to find out how this man named Randal Wayne was able to establish this center and why. I discovered the answer without speaking to him. It is not the man who is accomplishing anything in his own strength. It is his God working through him, the willing servant, to call all those who will hear.

The office door opens and the game outside resumes as I look up from my coffee. It is as though everything had stopped for those brief moments as my thoughts had filled my consciousness and then everything restarted at once.

I look up at the man as he leaves the office. Sadness still marks his face but his eyes are clear and hope is shining through. He quickly put on his red flannel scarf and cap as he left the building. The cold air quickly enveloped him and pulled the door shut after him.

A shiver went through me as I sat my cup down and stood to extend my hand to Mr. Wayne when he emerged from the office. I have not yet asked but he appears to be in his mid-forties. His hand is warm, his smile comforting and obviously genuine. The coldness left me as I walked into his office and sat down.

Mr. Wayne told me of his incredible adventure, his personal renewal and the regeneration of his spirit. I could not determine if it was true or not. It was obviously true for him and for those who sought his help. His life has been radically different since returning to Chicago more than a year earlier. Before his experience he was a perfectionist that was always critical of others and demeaning to him-self. The past year has been devoted to changing his surroundings to be better than he had found them. He is always reaching out to anyone who needs help in any way.

He takes pride in fulfilling his responsibilities as everything from founder to janitor of an urban outreach center which is located in this once powerful business district. Many external forces have changed the face of this area. It is the people who have been left behind. What the growing decay is attracting now is more dangerous than anything he has seen. The new breed of 'urban terrorists' as they are becoming known are ruthless. Life means nothing to them. Allegiance to their particular clan is the only meaning of commitment they know. These new clans are the new family.

Randal knows that these people have needs but their bravado will rarely allow those needs to be seen. He knows now, from experience, that every person has a moment of silence which is always waiting to be experienced. That moment when the ever present question of, 'why?' is asked. Randal's task until that time occurs for each of them is to be here and to be ready to give them the answer he has the privilege to share.

I can affirm as he tells me of his purpose here that his compassion is sincere. The mission house never closes. No one is ever turned away, no one is ever forsaken. Randal has seen some give up on themselves which leaves him at a loss to explain. Some have past oaths or promises catch up with them as they prepare to consider a change and are dragged off kicking and screaming. The reality he acknowledges is that, "Just as it was given to me the offer is an offer. It is not a demand or a command. Many are called but few embrace even the possibility. It is a choice."

I completed my notes and looked up to find Rand, as he asked me to address him, looking back at me with a big smile. We both stood and I thanked him for his time and for his commitment and extended my hand. He clasped my hand and pulled me toward him. I moved toward him a bit uncertain until he hugs me and says, "Thank you for your interest and your commitment to write the story. I would like an autographed copy please." As he winks to confirm our agreement I nod my head slightly and respond, "My name is Gus. Here is my card. You will receive the first copy. I will call before I come by."

Rand, "Very good, if I can be of any help let me know."

I responded, "You got it." Admittedly I am a bit cynical. Mr. Wayne has hired me to record the experiences of several comrades which rest lightly on obscure historical facts and his personal transformational events whether real or imagined. Perhaps I will learn something.

With the interview concluded I open the office door to leave as the front door opens. I leave Mr. Wayne's office as a woman enters the building. She is naturally beautiful with no apparent makeup, maybe late forties. Her reddish blonde hair is pulled back into a braid. Her physique is strong and slim. Her blue eyes look past me. As she walks toward the office its door closes. She reaches for the office door as I open the front door to leave. Walking out I hear the lady, with a confident, calm, loving voice say, "Hello Rand."

CPSIA information can be obtained
at www.ICGtesting.com
Printed in the USA
BVHW070411161221
624023BV00011B/1017